Maya Blake's dreams of becoming a writer were born when she picked up her first romance at thirteen. Little did she know her dream would come true! Does she still pinch herself every now and then to make sure it's not a dream? Yes, she does! Feel free to pinch her, too, via Twitter, Facebook or Goodreads! Happy reading!

Joss Wood loves books, coffee and travelling—especially to the remote places of Southern Africa and… Well, anywhere. She's a wife, mom to two young adults, and is bossed around by two cats and a dog the size of a small cow. After a career in local economic development and business, Joss writes full-time from her home in KwaZulu-Natal, South Africa.

Also by Maya Blake

The Greek's Forgotten Marriage
Pregnant and Stolen by the Tycoon
Snowbound with the Irresistible Sicilian

Brothers of the Desert miniseries

Their Desert Night of Scandal
His Pregnant Desert Queen

Also by Joss Wood

Hired for the Billionaire's Secret Son
A Nine-Month Deal with Her Husband

Cape Town Tycoons miniseries

The Nights She Spent with the CEO
The Baby Behind Their Marriage Merger

Discover more at millsandboon.co.uk.

ACCIDENTALLY WEARING THE ARGENTINIAN'S RING

MAYA BLAKE

THE TYCOON'S DIAMOND DEMAND

JOSS WOOD

MILLS & BOON

First published in Great Britain 2024
by Mills & Boon, an imprint of HarperCollins*Publishers* Ltd,
1 London Bridge Street, London, SE1 9GF

www.harpercollins.co.uk

HarperCollins*Publishers*, Macken House, 39/40 Mayor Street Upper, Dublin 1, D01 C9W8, Ireland

Accidentally Wearing the Argentinian's Ring © 2024 Maya Blake

The Tycoon's Diamond Demand © 2024 Joss Wood

ISBN: 978-0-263-32003-9

04/24

MIX
Paper | Supporting
responsible forestry
FSC
www.fsc.org
FSC™ C007454

This book contains FSC™ certified paper
and other controlled sources to ensure responsible forest management.

For more information visit www.harpercollins.co.uk/green.

Printed and Bound in the UK using 100% Renewable Electricity
at CPI Group (UK) Ltd, Croydon, CR0 4YY

ACCIDENTALLY WEARING THE ARGENTINIAN'S RING

MAYA BLAKE

MILLS & BOON

CHAPTER ONE

THERE WAS A reason Mareka Dixon's life was series of challenges centred around proving herself, whether it was beating the alarm clock and waking up before it went off, or getting off the bus two stops early to prove she could walk off that extra helping of ice-cream she'd had with dessert last night. Or proving she could kick herself six ways to Sunday when she thought about *him*.

She didn't need to be a psychologist to work out where it came from.

No—not now. There was an allotted time pocketed within her 'all work, zero play' life to contemplate her excess emotional baggage—Sunday nights between six and eight p.m., when she returned home after a visit to her parents.

Right now, she needed to concentrate on where she was going: Smythe Square, Knightsbridge.

Specifically, an establishment called Smythe's. Another one of those eye-wateringly chic and stratospherically expensive places where simply looking lost drew suspicious, disdainful glances, even from staff. Where her unfashionable corkscrew curls and curvy figure drew second and third looks, each one incrementally judgemental and condescending. Where sleek super-cars were as common as chips and prettily coiffed poodles wore accessories more expensive than her whole year's salary.

Today, she'd dressed for the fact that, as far as she was aware, her ultra-demanding, ultra-suave and astute billionaire boss was safely on the other side of the Atlantic. She hadn't bothered to spend a painstaking fifteen minutes to tame her wild hair, nor had she been as meticulous with her make-up as she usually was when he was in town. She'd made it in for seven-fifteen, however, and worked through her lunch as per usual, the demands from her two counterparts in New York and Argentina seemingly relentless.

But Mareka thrived on the challenge, because each week she remained Cayetano Figueroa's European PA was a notch on her CV that would be worth gold when it was time to move on.

And there would come a time because…

Nope, not thinking about that.

Mareka ignored the heat gathering in her belly and glanced at her phone. The blue map-dot said she was nearing her destination. She fingered the black card in her pocket for the dozenth time to make sure it was there. It had been the only thing nestled in the black box delivered to her office this afternoon by the sharply dressed courier, for the attention of Mr Figueroa.

As Cayetano's PA on this side of the Atlantic, Mareka was used to organising extravagant events and purchasing lavish gifts, the scale of which she'd only ever seen in over-the-top movies and TV shows. It had been a humbling and jaw-dropping experience to comprehend that, for men like her boss, spending like this was a run-of-the-mill activity.

Still, the cryptic delivery of the box and its contents were evidence that Mareka was operating on a whole new level. Which had made her doubly nervous when Cayetano had called an hour ago to inform her he was actually in London, at a meeting in Canary Wharf which had overrun.

Mareka hadn't wanted to examine why she felt disconcerted and hurt that her boss hadn't bothered to inform her he was in London. And, yes, it had been even more disquieting when the thought had triggered old feelings of inadequacy.

I don't need this...

She'd buried that feeling because, firstly, she needed to hang onto the best paid job she'd had in her life; and, secondly, because Cayetano Figueroa had been speaking at his usual fast clip, expecting her to follow and execute his every sexily accented word.

So, in her best crisp voice she'd answered. Yes, a box had arrived for him. Yes, it contained a black card with an address on the front, a phone number and what looked like a code on the back. Yes, she could most definitely visit the address in Knightsbridge and hold his place until he arrived.

Who cared that it was nearly seven p.m. and her only highlight on a Friday night was with her streaming service and a tub of her favourite ice-cream? So what if it was over twelve hours since she'd shoved her feet into three-inch heels, and the tight belt that cinched her Figueroa Industries-expensed designer suit was strangling her?

As of three months ago, she'd outlasted Cayetano's last four PAs. And, while her over-achieving parents would sneer at her, she would take that as a success, a vital steppingstone to achieving what *she* most desired. It was the reason she was risking exposing herself to feelings she shouldn't entertain towards her boss...

You have arrived at your destination.

Mareka jumped at the chirpy prompt from her phone, then froze on the pavement. Peering in through the glass frontage of the four-storey building, all she could see were striking paintings and pieces of art skilfully backlit to exhibition standards.

It was the sort of art her parents could spot and name at a thousand paces. The sort of art they'd expect her to utilise as fodder for 'skilful discord' on the rare occasions she was invited to one of their academia soirees. And it was the sort of painting that—when she inevitably failed their test and they snippily corrected her that, no, it was a Haydon, not a Margaux—she secretly vowed *never* to buy should she triumph over near-impossible odds and win the lottery.

'Excuse me, miss, are you lost?'

Mareka snapped into focus and blinked at the military-lean man watching her with naked suspicion from a dozen paces away.

'No, I'm exactly where I need to be, thanks,' she returned smartly.

Perhaps a little too smartly because, casting a quick glance around, Mareka could spot neither the name she sought nor an entrance to the art gallery.

Was *this* why she'd had to give up her evening in front of her TV—to pick up art for her boss?

Disgruntled, and a little terrified to make eye contact with the man whose crisp suit didn't disguise the tell-tale bulge of a weapon beneath his jacket, she reversed direction by several paces, only to be confronted with a carbon-copy guard.

'And where is that, exactly, miss?' the new guard demanded.

Despite the rush of traffic a few streets away, the square was ominously hushed, the growing scrutiny sweat-inducing.

'Because, if you have no business here, I suggest you leave before I'm forced to call the authorities,' Guard Number One snapped.

You're Cayetano Figueroa's representative—act like it.

Reaching into her pocket, she extracted the black card and held the small rectangle in front of her like a suit of armour. 'I have an appointment...' Mareka's words froze as both guards reacted, their transformation almost comical.

'Of course, madam. Apologies for the misunderstanding.' One arm swept out, deferentially ushering her up the short steps towards his colleague, who pivoted towards the wall next to him and swiftly tapped on a discreet panel. 'Please, this way.'

Mareka watched, goggle-eyed, as a twelve-foot door with no visible handle swung inward to reveal a wide, stunning hallway. The second guard stood to attention as she entered.

The click of her heels and the deeper footfalls of her escort echoed on the gold-veined cream marble. Several steps in and she realised that the magnificent foyer was in fact part of the art gallery, the artwork on display leading to a lift tucked in at the end of the space. A wide *chaise longue* sat beneath one giant painting she knew she recognised but couldn't quite place.

Mareka bit the inside of her lip as she looked around. Did she wait? Take a seat and pretend to admire the art until Cayetano Figueroa arrived?

'The lift will take you to the floor you require, madam,' Guard Number Two said, his attitude much more cordial. 'You simply enter the code at the back of the card to activate it.'

Her nod was pure 'fake it till you make it', her insides knotting in bewilderment. Mareka willed her hands not to shake as she carefully inputted the numbers and watched the doors slide smoothly apart. The moment she stepped inside, the guard reached in, pressed the button for the second floor and promptly stepped back out.

'Have a good evening, madam.'

Since she wasn't sure she could speak, Mareka simply nodded, then sagged against the wall once the doors slid shut again.

As the lift surged up, so did her nerves.

If Cayetano hadn't sent her here to acquire a painting on his behalf, then why was she here?

The lift arrived far too quickly for her fraying nerves. Swallowing, she brushed her damp palms down her skirt and stepped out into a windowless space lit only with three exquisite and expensive-looking chandeliers. The walls were decked out in floor-to-ceiling rich, cream silk curtains with the same colours echoed in the plush grouping of sofas and luxurious carpet underneath her feet.

As with downstairs, there wasn't a single person in sight, but as Mareka approached the long banquet-like glass cabinet set out in the middle of the room, she got the faintest inkling why she was here. Because displayed beneath the spotless sheets of glass was row upon row of the most magnificent pieces of jewellery she'd ever seen in her life.

The first cabinet housed brooches in animal themes: a jet-black panther with eyes and curling tail made of diamonds; a hummingbird with feathers of sapphires, emeralds and rubies; a serpent formed entirely of yellow gold with scales of yellow diamonds.

The second cabinet held headdresses, crowns she'd only ever seen nestled on the heads of royalty in the pages of glossy magazines.

She was drifting, slack-jawed, towards the third cabinet displaying breath-taking necklaces and bracelets when a discreet, feminine cough sounded behind her. Mareka spun round to see a slim, tastefully dressed woman standing several feet away.

Dressed in a black boat-necked dress that cinched in at her narrow waist and flared to her knee, she was arresting in a way Mareka couldn't quite put her finger on. Perhaps it was the boxy glasses she wore, or the severely chopped sable-black hair Mareka was certain was a wig, that puzzled her. Or the bright-blue eyes instinct told her were contact lenses. She didn't have time to dwell as the woman stepped forward, her hand held out at a precise angle.

'Miss Smythe,' she stated in a voice completely devoid of inflection, as if she wanted to be forgettable.

As if...

Mareka took her hand, noting that the handshake was also entirely neutral, neither firm nor soft. 'Mareka Dixon.'

She glanced pointedly at the card Mareka held. 'I was expecting Mr Figueroa.'

'I…yes, I'm his PA. He's running a little late. He didn't want to miss his appointment and sent me in his place.'

A hint of displeasure flashed across her face but she remained eerily composed. 'And will you be choosing the piece for him?'

Mareka's gaze darted back to the cabinet, her heart jumping into her throat. Deep down she knew the safest thing to do was to tell this mysterious woman that she preferred to wait for Cayetano. But…hadn't she'd lasted this long as the latest Figueroa PA because she listened to her instinct?

Feigning bravado, she nodded. 'Yes, I will.'

So what if her voice trembled a little when she glanced at the priceless pieces, and grew terrified at the thought of picking a piece for some unknown recipient without Cayetano Figueroa's express permission?

Faint amusement crossed the woman's face before it settled into staid neutrality once more. 'Very well. Come with me, please.' Skirting the cabinets, she aimed a device that looked like a miniature remote at the right wall.

As Mareka thanked her stars that she wouldn't be handling a diamond-festooned crown just yet, a pair of heavy silk curtains slid back to reveal another, smaller glass cabinet. Peculiar dread tickling her senses, Mareka was confronted with dozens of…engagement rings.

While shock unravelled through her like a waterfall, that wasn't the reason every cell in her body was reacting so negatively to the task she needed to perform. That could be attributed to a specific reason. The same reason every man who featured in her dreams sported moss-green eyes, wavy brown bronze-tinted hair and towered over six-foot-three. The same reason why they were sleekly built like the most streamlined of athletes, with mile-wide shoulders and lean hips.

Why they spoke with a distinct, pelvis-melting, Argentinian accent.

At some distinct, unforgettable point in the past year, while on a trip to the G7 Summit with her boss in Italy, she'd committed her most foolhardy act yet—an act that would probably damn her for ever in the eyes of her parents, if they found out. Not that she planned to divulge it to a single soul. She'd accepted a dinner invitation from her boss and finished dessert with a colossal crush on one of the most magnetic, intensely handsome and, according to the tabloids, most ruthless man on earth.

Did it matter that she'd immediately recognised the futility of her predicament and buried it deep? Judging by the distress churning within her as she stared at the white, velvet ring trays, not very much.

'Miss Dixon?'

Sucking in a breath, she raised her gaze from the display to the woman whose name suggested she was the proprietor of this ultra-exclusive establishment.

Even as the fierce urge to ask her *who* Cayetano was getting engaged to assailed Mareka, she dismissed it. She didn't need to add joblessness to her plight, and being in-

discreet enough to demand to know who Cayetano intended
to wed would most definitely risk just that. Snatching every
crumb of composure she could find, she moved to the sofa
and coffee table, which held a sterling-silver tray contain-
ing a bottle of vintage champagne set in an ice-bucket, two
glasses and what looked like chocolate truffles.

Mareka had parcelled off enough of the same vintage to
her boss's executive staff to know its worth. This wasn't a
run-of-the-mill errand for her boss.

This was a life-altering event. A 'Cayetano Figueroa is
getting off the 'world's most eligible bachelors list' type
of event.

She cursed her knees for weakening as she sank onto
the sofa, her dazed gaze fixed on the tray of rings. Which
one would Cayetano grace his fiancée with? The rare blue
diamond, perhaps? The pear-shaped pink diamond with the
baguette side-stones?

Miss Smythe stepped forward, lifted the bottle and
filled a glass with a quiet elegance that spoke of breeding.
Whether it was cultivated or ingrained, Mareka was too
distracted to tell as she accepted the chilled glass.

When the other woman murmured, 'I'll leave you to it,'
all Mareka could manage was a nod, barely noticing her
retreat.

She took a first sip of champagne, more to quiet the roiling within than anything else. If she was going to drown
out the clamour of her foolish crush, what better way than
with vintage champagne? She shook her head as hysteri-
cal laughter threatened, then jumped again as her phone
buzzed. Setting down the glass, she hurriedly answered it.

'Miss Dixon, have you arrived?' Deep, unflappable, intensely masculine and utterly sexy in a way no other could
sound; Mareka's belly flipped over at the sound of Cayetano Figueroa's voice.

Her shaking fingers tightened around her phone. 'Yes, I'm here.'

'*Muy bien.* I'll be there in half an hour. I'd prefer not to have to wade through a hundred samples. Have a small selection ready for me to inspect.'

'So…this is for you? You're getting engaged?' she blurted before she could hold her tongue.

Thick silence. '*Sí.* I am.' The words were uttered in the same deep, unwavering timbre, which gave little indication as to his true feelings.

Something shrivelled up and died inside Mareka, and she hated it even more because it didn't set her free. Instead, the reflex that rose to her defence whenever her parents denigrated her surged to the fore. Holding on tight to it, she answered, 'Congratulations are in order, then, I guess.'

Another bout of silence dragged out—designed to make her squirm, or because of another facet to his character? Because why would Cayetano care about her feelings at all? Finally he responded with a rasped, '*Gracias.*'

'Would you like me to put together a press release? I could—'

'That will not be necessary. Everything is taken care of.'

That far too familiar pang of inadequacy lanced her. She breathed through it. 'Oh. Okay. I'll see you when you get here.'

'Indeed.' He rang off abruptly.

This is a good thing, she reassured herself as she reached for the champagne and gulped down another mouthful. If Cayetano was off the market, then she needn't expend any more of her day-dreaming on him! She needn't dwell on that 'moment' they'd shared at that dinner in Abruzzo, when she'd been one hundred percent sure her boss had wanted to kiss her.

She could devote her evenings and weekends to more

productive endeavours. Such as taking the first step towards her lifelong dream of creating a charity to help younger women advocate for themselves. She'd saved enough to get a small foundation going, hadn't she?

She attempted to close her mind to the voice that whispered that it wasn't enough. That *she* would never be enough…

And what if she failed?

Heart squeezing, she pushed the line of doubts aside and forced herself to look at the sparkling gems. With another sip of champagne to bolster her, she plucked the first ring from its setting, gasping as the light caught and danced off the exquisite oval diamond.

Setting it to one side, she picked up another, then another. On the sixth, she paused, her breath catching at the flawless, cushion-cut diamond surrounded by pink micro-pave stones. It was beautiful, feminine and so utterly gorgeous.

She wasn't going to try it on. *No. No way.* That way lay madness. Setting it down, reluctantly, she grabbed the bottle and refilled her glass. Fifteen minutes later, she'd selected eight rings, each stone perfect enough to make any woman swoon. Especially with a man like Cayetano Figueroa going down on one knee, his heart-throbbing, chiselled face tilted up as he…

No—enough. That way most definitely lies madness.

Her gaze returned to the dazzling rings—specifically, the cushion-cut diamond. *It was so beautiful.* Surely it wouldn't do any harm if she slipped it on for one moment?

The giddiness in her belly screamed *yes*. She would most likely never return to a place like this: this moment in time was a fluke. Why not see how the other half lived?

Before she could talk herself out of it, she set down the glass with an unsteady click, a shocked, impish giggle escaping her as she reached for the ring… A fantasy of one

Argentinian man sliding it onto her finger and completing the beautiful illusion with that kiss they'd never shared swelled like the best forbidden fairy tale.

Mareka's mouth gaped in wonder. Turning her hand this way and that under the chandelier, she gasped as the stones caught fire and shone. 'Oh! How utterly gorgeous you are!' Conscious that she was talking to an inanimate object while being slightly tipsy, she giggled again, lifting her hand for a closer look. 'I don't care,' she murmured. 'You're worth every moment of temporary madness.'

She yelped at the deep throat-clearing, rushing to her feet in panic. She knew who it belonged to; she didn't want to face it, even though the force of his presence rushed at her, taking hold and commanding the attention he believed was his due.

It took a moment of Mareka cringing in dismay before she lowered her hand and faced the statue-still form of Cayetano Figueroa standing not more than three feet away. She met those intense moss-green eyes boring into her like industrial-sized drills. His hands might have been shoved into his pockets, his bespoke jacket open and his tie loosened the way he tended to wear it after a crushingly long day, but Mareka wasn't fooled for a moment by his easy stance.

She stumbled back because everything Cayetano felt was displayed in his eyes: irritation; disbelief; thick cynicism. Maybe a hint of pity...?

It was that last emotion that stayed and seared. It reflected what she'd seen far too frequently in her parents' eyes. But it was a hundred times more potent in this man's eyes—enough to make her take another desperate step back, gasping in alarm as she caught her heel in the carpet. Her arms windmilled and she knew without a shadow of a doubt that she was about to pitch over like a sack of potatoes.

As shame filled her bloodstream and air rushed into her

ears, she closed her eyes, unable to watch another demeaning expression flit across his face. So she didn't actually see him lunge forward, hands whipping out to catch her, one arm banding her waist, the other cupping her shoulder.

But, oh, did she feel him as he pulled her close, his powerful athletic body plastering hers from chest to thigh.

'Are you all right?' he murmured in her ear, his breath brushing her earlobe and sending a delicious shiver cascading over her.

She opened her eyes. Perhaps it was a combination of where they were, the rarefied air of the jewellery establishment, the idealistic fantasy she'd indulged in minutes ago or just the sheer magnetic, animal attraction she'd felt toward her boss for so long that made her reach for him too, her hand curling over his shoulder and brushing the hair at his nape.

'Yes.' She breathed. 'I... I'm fine.'

He continued to hold her, to stare down at her, as if doubting her response. Her blood thickened, her breath fluttering wildly as she waited and watched his gaze drop to her mouth, his own breathing sharpening. Sweet heaven, was he about to...?

The ear-piercing shriek that ripped through the room sent her jumping a mile high, her already racing heart thundering harder as she attempted to find the source.

Cayetano jerked them both upright, his eyebrows clamping in a frown as his gaze sharpened from volcanic heat to edgy wariness.

'Is that what I think it is?' he demanded, barely needing to raise his voice to be heard.

The mysterious owner nodded, magically reappearing. 'I'm afraid so. We must evacuate the building. Please come with me.' Without waiting for them, she turned on her heel.

Cayetano glanced down at Mareka, a pinched look setting his features as he released her and stepped back. 'After you, Miss Dixon.'

Mareka took a step, then felt her foot give way. She cringed. Oh God, she *really* shouldn't have had that second glass of champagne, especially on an empty stomach.

Hyper-aware of Cayetano's presence behind her, she tried to quicken her steps, following Miss Smythe's swaying figure to a landing and steps that led down. Reaching for the handrail, Mareka took one step down, then stumbled again.

Behind her, Cayetano uttered a muted curse, then strong hands were sweeping her off her feet. 'W-what are you doing?' she stammered as she was tucked against a hardpacked chest.

'Preventing us both from being burnt to a crisp, ideally.'

Mareka squeezed her eyes shut for a moment, growing intensely aware of his arm beneath her thighs and around her back, of the rippling muscle of flesh beneath the hand she braced against his torso. 'I can walk, you know,' she protested feebly.

'Evidently not efficiently enough in those heels. And most definitely not in an emergency,' he rasped, the rumble of his voice seductively moving through her.

Mareka's face heated and she admonished herself for the trailing pang that reminded her yet again that she was useless. That her inadequacies were always lurking, ready to shame her. 'Well, if you'd waited one more second instead of swooping in like a caped superhero, you'd have seen me take off my heels so I could take the stairs a little quicker.'

In the dim stairwell, his eyes glinted at her even as he took the stairs with an assuredness that bordered on arrogant. 'I'm a little short on time today, Miss Dixon. Feel free to get your next saviour to enact that scene for you,' he stated dryly.

Her fingers dug into his shirt as he sped up, his feet making light of the stairs. Mareka couldn't quite curb the snort that erupted from her throat. 'Yeah, right. As if I'm ever going to be in this position again.'

The words emerged way more mournfully than she'd intended. Her face heated further, her gaze locked on his hooded expression as her words bounced between them. Scrambling for something that would dissipate the atmosphere, and finding nothing but turbulent thoughts better kept to herself, Mareka let out a stupid little whimper. Because now her boss was staring at her as if she were a specimen beneath his microscope, all her emotions on display for him to explore.

Abstractedly, she registered that they'd cleared the building and were out in the square with a handful of people milling around them. But she couldn't break the traction of Cayetano's stare. His heavenly masculine scent was in her nose. The powerful thud of his heartbeat danced beneath her fingers, his breathing a touch erratic after his gaze dropped to linger on her mouth, his own lips parted to reveal a hint of even white teeth.

And, just like that, she was once again thrown back to that night in Abruzzo when this foolish crush had taken a deeper hold. When the only thing she'd yearned for was to kiss Cayetano Figueroa and find out if the flashes of hot, Latin magnificence she'd imagined lived up to her fantasies. Who cared that she'd sworn to be rid of this madness a mere…half hour ago?

Half an hour ago…while she'd been choosing the engagement ring he intended to give to another woman.

Her eyes started to widen. He sucked in a sharp breath. A camera flash went off, dancing off the diamond ring she'd forgotten to take off and illuminating their expressions for a nano-second before immortalising them in life-altering pixels.

CHAPTER TWO

OF COURSE THINGS would happen this way.

Hadn't he been lurching from one crisis to another for the last three months? His mother had checked herself into a secret rehab, probably another ploy to torture his father and to bring unwanted attention to Cayetano.

His latest deal hovered on a knife's edge.

His fake fiancée was refusing to sign the pre-nup she'd agreed to a month ago.

Now his tipsy London PA—deep down, the reason he knew he chose to conduct his European business remotely as often as possible; the reason he'd *almost* crossed a strict professional line one night in Italy—had just landed them on the front page of the tabloids, her with a ring on her finger.

Cayetano swung towards where the flash had come from, despite knowing it was futile to confront the culprit. By now the picture would be in a greedy tabloid hack's inbox or splashed across social media. He bit back the growl that threatened to explode from his throat. The hand braced against his chest curled, fisting his shirt as she wriggled in his arms.

He redirected his focus back to Mareka, his senses sparking with what he wanted to think was irritation. *Dios mio*, he'd almost kissed her back there. If she hadn't distracted him with that absurd conversation about superheroes in capes, he would've been more alert. He wouldn't have relished her delicious weight in his arms, marvelled at how soft and firm her skin was or wondered how her lips would taste beneath his.

This was her fault.

She gasped, then those delectable lips pursed in outrage. 'Excuse me?'

He realised he'd spoken his accusation out loud as footsteps approached. His bodyguards arrived at the same time as he set her down, unable to take his eyes off her face as she glared up at him.

'What do you mean, it was my fault?'

He glanced pointedly at the hand still braced on his chest, the diamond ring on full display for all to see. At least she had the grace to redden at his speaking look.

'I employ you for your discretion, Miss Dixon. This is far from discreet.' He breathed, mindful of their growing audience.

She opened her mouth to speak, but his bodyguard interjected, '*Perdón*, Señor Figueroa. We came as fast as we could.'

Cayetano was irritated by how hard it was to drag his eyes from Mareka to give a brisk nod. He could hardly blame them for the fire alarm going off. What he could do was direct his ire towards the woman who stared at him with a mixture of nervousness and defiance, then lowered her hand from his chest and curled it into a fist to hide the evidence of the ring.

His lips pursed. 'It's far too late for that now.'

'It's not my fault. The fire alarm went off. I tried to say something, but you were too busy sweeping me off my feet.'

Her blush deepened as she spoke, and for an absurd reason Cayetano found himself staring at her mouth again. Her very lush, very pink mouth.

He cursed the heat weaving through him. This was *not* the time for this. And most definitely not with this woman.

His jaw clenched tighter as he remembered the other woman who was contributing to the other crisis in his life. There was a reason he kept his life free of emotional entanglements.

'Bring the car around. We're leaving,' he instructed his bodyguards. 'And you're coming with me, Miss Dixon.'

'But I thought…'

He raised his eyebrow. 'You thought?'

Her delicate, pointed chin rose. 'I have plans this evening.'

He told himself the reason he objected was because he didn't want to be inconvenienced. His day had been hellish from the start. 'Cancel them.'

Rebellion blazed in her eyes. 'Why should I?'

He allowed himself a tight smile. 'Because, according to a document lodged on a hard drive in my HR department, when I'm in town you will be available to me twenty-four hours a day. In return, you get to keep your own hours when I'm not. A contract you signed of your own free will. Am I mistaken?'

His voice was cool…reasonable, even, Cayetano assessed. And yet he felt almost volatile, staring down at her. Had he ever noticed this strain of defiance before? Was it a product of something else, like that almost-kiss? She wouldn't be the first PA who had committed the grave misfortune of developing feelings for him. Hell, it was why he'd got rid of her three predecessors.

But Mareka, that aberrant night in Abruzzo notwithstanding, had surprised him in the last eighteen months by being efficient without being intrusive.

Had he been wrong? Did he have another crisis on his hands?

'Well, you're not wrong, but I wasn't expecting you—'

'I wasn't aware I had to send you my diary to get you to fit me in, Miss Dixon.'

Her face tightened a fraction, drawing his attention to the smoothness of her jaw, the slender line of her neck. 'You don't need to put it like that, sir.'

Aware of the sparks still fizzing inside him, he took a step closer. 'I'd rather you not compound your gross error of judgement with insubordination. Would you?'

She glanced from his face to the car that was pulling up beside them. Then she shook her head. 'No.'

'That is the first sensible answer you've provided this evening.' He nudged her towards the vehicle. 'Get in.'

She took one step towards his car and wobbled on her feet again. A different sort of sensation churned in his stomach. He'd seen the half-finished bottle of champagne on the table upstairs. Now, peering down at her, he wondered whether it was just a blush that stained her cheek, or an alcohol-induced flush. Cayetano wasn't sure exactly why he felt so strongly about it.

Yes, you are.

He suppressed the emotion and forced himself to relax. But when she took another step, and immediately twisted on her heel, he couldn't quite bite back the growl. 'You are testing my patience, Miss Dixon.'

'I'm sorry to hear that, but the fire alarm has stopped. Are you sure you don't want to return upstairs?'

His lips formed one small, tight smile. 'Considering our very public exit, and the fact that we've already been photographed, I sincerely doubt we would be allowed back.'

Her eyes widened. 'Really? Why not?'

'Because Miss Smythe values extreme discretion above all else. Gaining re-entry might be permitted, but I'm certain it won't happen tonight.'

She looked over her shoulder, as if to make sure he was telling the truth. His nostrils flared as he tried to gather his patience. But as he inhaled his PA's unique scent assailed him, as it had done on the way down the stairs. A mixture of crushed flowers, it lingered far too alluringly.

'Get in,' he ordered again.

Perhaps she sensed his fraying temper because she obeyed without further argument. But the moment she secured her seatbelt, the action dissecting her ample breasts, she began to tug off the diamond ring as if it offended her—the same ring she'd so longingly admired upstairs.

'Here, I believe this is yours.'

He held up his hand. 'It stays on your finger for now.'

Her jaw sagged and her eyes clouded with confusion. 'What? But don't you need to return it? Or give it to your fiancée, whoever she is?'

Fastening his own seatbelt, his mood soured at the thought of Octavia and the drama she was creating back in Argentina. And as they drove away from the square he stared at the ring, now lying in Mareka's outstretched palm, begrudgingly accepting that it was the same one he would've chosen. But it wasn't Octavia's style. It wasn't ostentatious enough.

'Mr. Figueroa?' Her voice was firm but a little hesitant.

'How much champagne did you have to drink?' he asked abruptly, the issue bothering him more than he was willing to examine.

'What?'

'You heard me.'

She reared back in offence, but her long lashes swept down, her lips firming a little. 'It wasn't much. And I haven't eaten since breakfast. Maybe the second glass wasn't entirely advisable but it's not fair to blame me for any of the chaos back there.'

Perhaps he wasn't being fair, but his hellish few weeks didn't make him feel charitable. 'You don't think so? I can come up with at least half a dozen ways it could've gone.'

'Do you want me to apologise? Fine—I'm sorry.'

The sliver of intent that sparked through him surprised him at first, but as it thickened and grew Cayetano relaxed against his seat.

'You'll have a chance to redeem yourself yet. As soon as we get an idea of just how bad things are.'

Cayetano found out much too soon.

The buzzing in his pocket as he entered his hotel signalled that yet another crisis awaited him. From the looks directed his way as he strode across the open space, he knew the picture had already found several homes on the Internet.

Stifling a curse, he shortened his footsteps, aware that the woman who'd caused all of it was scurrying along behind him. He turned towards his harried looking PA. Beneath the chandelier of the five-star hotel that was his home when he stayed in England, the light glinted off her dark-golden locks, sparking another uncharacteristic thought.

'Your hair is different.'

Her eyes flared again, her hand darting up to the shoulder length. 'Yes, I wear it naturally sometimes.'

'You mean it's not usually straight?' He wondered why the question drew another flare of heat as she shook her head.

'No, it's not.'

He bit back the urge to instruct her never to straighten it again. What the hell was wrong with him? Was it a side effect of the relentless upheavals he'd faced in the last three months? His parents' marriage was forever on the brink of collapse, cynically held together only by financial incentives, and he was caught perpetually between the two.

He'd thought himself immune to his role but lately, with his mother's alcohol-fuelled emotions becoming increasingly erratic, Cayetano had found himself more on edge in his already strained relationship with his parents. *That* was yet another drama waiting for him back in Buenos Aires.

He stabbed a finger at the lift button. Entering his code, he held the doors for his PA, who hesitated, watching him with a wariness that set his teeth on edge. The moment they were alone, he addressed the issue chafing at him. 'Let's get a few things straight, shall we? How much do you drink on a daily basis?'

'How dare you? You have no right to ask me that.'

He took a deep breath and shoved his hands in his pockets. It was either that or frame that far too delicate jaw and run his hands over her heated cheek. A move that would most likely earn him a ticket to an employment tribunal.

'Since you were operating under my instructions, I think I'm well within my rights, don't you?'

'I told you already—I don't normally drink, and I had the champagne on an empty stomach.'

He stared down at her, attempting to see beneath her bluster. Her fire was pure enough for Cayetano to give her the benefit of the doubt. 'Very well. I believe you.'

Her shoulders sagged a little and she swallowed. 'Thanks,' she said, a touch snippily, and perhaps what he deserved.

He wasn't sure why that sent a flicker of amusement through him. The situation was far from humorous. He'd seen far too often what alcohol did to his mother.

As if on cue, his phone buzzed again as he entered his penthouse. Ignoring it, he crossed the living room to the phone sitting on the coffee table. Lifting it, he placed an order and hung up. Then he poured a tall glass of water from a crystal carafe. Approaching Mareka, where she lingered by the arch between the hallway and the living room, he held it out.

'Drink this. Dinner will be delivered in fifteen minutes. I have a few phone calls to make. Then we need to talk.'

She tried to hide the flare of alarm in her eyes. 'Talk about what?'

He paused on his way to his study. 'I suspect the next fifteen minutes will be crucial, Miss Dixon. Just pray that the outcome is more congenial for you than I expect it will be.'

Mareka opened her mouth to ask him what he was talking about, but Cayetano was walking away, his purposeful strides expressing firmly that he didn't intend to explain himself.

Her hand shook, sloshing water all over her wrist and onto the marble floor. Grimacing, she gulped down a few mouthfuls. If she'd refused the champagne earlier, she wouldn't be here.

But she hadn't done anything wrong! Had she? She hadn't even asked to be saved from a potentially dangerous situation. She bit her lip, hating the spike of guilt declaring her ingratitude.

Striding into the lavish living room of the penthouse in the Hainesborough Hotel, she hesitantly unfurled the tight fist she'd wrapped around the diamond ring.

After seeing the other jaw-dropping pieces on display, Mareka knew without a doubt that the ring in her hand was worth a substantial fortune. And yet Cayetano had treated it like it was a cheap trinket. Hell, both he and the mysterious Miss Smythe hadn't even bothered to secure it when the alarm had gone off. Mareka wanted to think it was because her boss trusted her, or that the jeweller had an agreement with her rich clients, enough not to bat an eyelid when they swanned off with a ring worth a king's ransom.

But Mareka couldn't help the bitterness that surged through her belly. The kind of money people like Cayetano played with and discarded could change lives. The kind of change that could either mean a life led with dignity or burdened by self-doubt and drudgery. The kind of change *she* had sworn to use her charity to bring about. The more she stared at the ring, the more she wanted to be rid of it.

Whirling away from the window, she wandered down the same hallway Cayetano had taken. As she neared the open doorway, his thick curse, muttered in his mother tongue, slowed her feet.

'How foolish of me to think I had even ten minutes to get this under control.' The words were set with such heavy sardonicism that Mareka flinched. 'So, what does she want now?'

She held her breath, knowing she shouldn't be eavesdropping, but unable to move. A handful of seconds later, Cayetano burst into laughter. Except there was nothing amusing about the sound ricocheting around the space.

'Are you serious?' Whatever response he received drew another curse. Then, 'No. You will do no such thing. I'll speak to her myself.'

The digital beep of the call ending drew another wince from Mareka.

Move.

Her feet refused to obey. She stood there, the priceless ring clutched tight in her fist, as Cayetano placed another call.

'Octavia…' He breathed.

Mareka's heart jumped into her throat. Octavia Moreno was Cayetano's Argentinian PA. The pictures she'd seen of the stunning woman was enough to ruffle any woman's confidence. Even from this side of the door, Mareka could hear the heated, sultry tones of the PA who'd worked for Cayetano for over six years.

'I hear you're still refusing to sign the pre-nup,' Cayetano drawled, an edge of irritation in his tone. Whatever answer she gave made him exhale. 'That is not what we agreed before I left Buenos Aires.' A pause. 'Of course I value you. But I also need to be able to take you at your word when—' He stopped as a torrent of Spanish spilled out of the phone.

Mareka's eyes widened at the borderline-shrewish outburst.

Before today, Mareka would've sworn that no one would dare to speak to her formidable boss that way, and yet the evidence was unquestionable. From her own strict, albeit occasionally charged, relationship with Cayetano Figueroa, she would've sworn that he would never dally with an employee—that the rumours he'd once dated Octavia Morena were simply malicious lies.

Listening to the heated exchange now, Mareka reversed that assumption. Was this a quarrel between lovers?

Her stomach churned, threatening mild nausea at the thought. Her hand rose to her mouth as if she could stop the bile rising into her throat just by willing it away.

She *really* shouldn't have drunk that champagne. And, with the mood her boss was in, she doubted she was doing herself any favours by eavesdropping. Forget lasting six years—she might not make it another six *minutes*!

And what had he meant by 'the next fifteen minutes'? The question scythed through her hazy brain, sending her scrambling to retrieve her phone from her bag.

Cayetano could only have meant one thing—*the picture of them outside, in Smythe Square.*

'We're getting nowhere with this, Octavia, and you should know better than to threaten me with a deadline.'

He inhaled sharply at the muffled response Mareka couldn't hear over her thundering heartbeat.

'*Basta*. I have another call coming through. I'll call you back shortly. I suggest you take the time to think things through properly.'

The doorbell rang.

Hurrying to the door before she was caught eavesdropping, Mareka opened it to the executive chef, who introduced himself as Manzano and wheeled in his silver trolley with a familiarity that said he'd done this many times. Feeling a little unnerved by the whole evening, Mareka followed him into another jaw-dropping space that boasted floor-to-ceiling views of London.

She kept out of the way as the chef unpacked the heavenly smelling dishes onto the smoked-glass dining table, set out the cutlery and, with a courteous nod, took his leave.

Silence interspersed with bursts of furious Spanish kept her rooted in place for several minutes. Then the combination of the incredible aromas and her belly's increasingly growling demands sent her to the table. Grilled lobster and roasted vegetable on the first platter made her groan. Plates of what were discreetly labelled on the silver dish as 'Argentinian steak with buttered asparagus' made her mouth shamelessly water. Another six dishes she was sure could easily feature in a high-end gourmet's magazine severely weakened her resistance.

Quickly sliding the diamond ring back onto her finger before—*horror of horrors*—she misplaced it, she pulled out a chair and sat down, reminding herself that Cayetano had told her to eat…because they needed to talk when dinner was over.

She considered serving a plate for him. The volley of ferocious chastisement echoing down the hall suggested she was better off staying put.

Mareka had just finished sampling a tiny portion of every dish—ignoring the expensive bottle of wine breathing in the middle of the table, and opting for more water until she was sure her light intoxication had passed—when Cayetano strolled in.

She most definitely wasn't going to watch him walk towards her with that prowling gait that made her think of graceful predators, of kings of the jungle. She wasn't going to stare at that breath-taking face evocative of stunning works of art that graced museums. She most definitely wasn't going to glance at those mouth-watering lips and wonder what would've happened in that jewellery house, had she given into the madness and kissed him when he'd stared at her lips.

No. No. No.

Not looking didn't mean she couldn't *feel* the volts of energy vibrating off him or couldn't sense that something had him positively seething.

Something, she suspected strongly as he drew closer, that involved *her.*

The next fifteen minutes...

Four words that made her discard the vital need to avoid him, her gaze scrambling to meet his and see pinched lips and pure displeasure bouncing off his mile-wide shoulder.

A combination that made her clear her throat while scrambling to stand. 'Is...is everything okay?'

'No, Miss Dixon. Everything is most definitely not okay,' he replied in a voice coated in fire and ice as he rounded the table towards her.

Livid green eyes pierced hers. Then he set his phone down, face-up, and shoved it towards her.

She held his gaze a few more seconds, primarily because she couldn't drag her eyes from the hypnotic power and vortex of his, but also, because she was a little terrified to glance at his phone.

Curiosity won out. Her gaze dropped. A gasp flew unbidden from deep inside her. His low, animalistic growl echoed the turbulent sensation spinning around them.

'I see you concur—that this is much worse than I thought.'

'I… It's… How could…?' She stopped, judging it was wise to shut up than attempt in any way to ascribe an explanation to the vivid picture on his screen.

But, really, what could be worse than this? What could land her in further disaster than seeing the way her hand was pressed deep into Cayetano Figueroa's shirt, her face tilted up to his, his angled down at hers? And, worst of all, the priceless diamond blatantly blazing on her finger…

The headline screamed: *Figueroa's Secret Love Revealed!*

As she stared in cringing stupefaction, he calmly flicked to another, even worse, headline.

Figueroa Proves Office Romances Are Still Alive and Kicking!

Out of the Boardroom… Headed Down the Aisle!

'Okay, that's enough.' Her plea was hoarse, barely intelligible.

He swiped his phone off the table, his precise movements belying the flames alive in his eyes.

She scrambled to quench the fire. 'Look, before you go blaming me again, I've already told you I didn't mean for any of this to—'

'The way you keep protesting makes me think the opposite.'

'What? No, you're wrong!'

'Am I?' he challenged silkily. 'There's no shame in admitting it. You wouldn't be the first to spot an opportunity and capitalise on—'

'I would take great care before you finish that sentence if I were you!' she protested hotly.

'Oh yes? And why is that?'

'Because you couldn't be more wrong if you tried,' she shot back, aware her breathing was erratic and her palms tingled. Dear God, it was almost as if she wanted to slap his drop-dead gorgeous face. She, who'd never entertained bodily harming another person in her life!

Perhaps he sensed the volatility that infected the room. For an age he simply stared, his gaze delving deeper with each passing second. Then a muscle rippled through his jaw. 'We are where we are, Miss Dixon. I'm more interested in where we go from here,' he said with chilling finality.

Her heart ricocheted behind her ribs. 'Well, the obvious response is to tell the truth. I can have a press release drafted in five minutes that this was all a huge misunderstanding.' Nervous laughter spilled out as she shook her head. 'I don't even know why the tabloids are in such a frenzy. Surely they know that you…and I…? That this will never be a possibility…?'

Her voice trailed off, her mouth drying as something untamed flared in his eyes. He was so at variance with the boss she knew that she wondered if he was suffering from some unknown condition.

Scratch that—maybe she needed to worry about her own condition. Because, when that scorching gaze left her face to chart a path over her body, lingering with that same penetrative demand, she feared she would never again be able to take a full breath.

'Enlighten me why you think not, Miss Dixon,' he invited with a voice so soft and deadly, it sent seismic tremors charging over her.

'B-because I'm your employee, for starters,' she blurted a little desperately. A totally disingenuous protest, because the thoughts she'd had about this man for the better part of a year had crossed the professionalism line a long time ago. Her face heating at the reminder, she ploughed on, boldly doubling down on the excuses she'd told herself in the dark. 'And because you…you're not my type either.'

She didn't dwell on what his response might be to her declaration, but the last thing Mareka had expected was for him to blink those silky eyelashes that were unfairly wasted on a man, before his shoulders shook in distinct amusement.

Her mouth dropped open in wonder. In all her time working for him, she'd never seen Cayetano Figueroa smile, never mind laugh. That it was entirely at her expense didn't even seem significant in that moment. Not when she couldn't drag her gaze from the sensual curve of those lips as they twitched. Nor stop herself from yearning to see what true mirth, full and unfettered, would look like on him. If this was a hint, he would be simply breath-taking.

'Are you sure? I recall an after-summit dinner a year ago when you all but *melted* in my arms,' he drawled wickedly.

No.

By mutual unspoken agreement, they'd never mentioned that incident. It had been her first and only G7 Summit with her new boss, the invitation to attend alone having ramped up Mareka's excitement. Hell, it had been one of the very few occasions she'd caught a glimpse of something approaching respect in their eyes when she'd told her parents.

High on a shocking number of successful deals for his company, Cayetano had taken her to a Michelin-starred restaurant—another first. And somewhere between dinner and the walk back to their hotel she'd found herself in Cayetano's arms under a starlit night sky. His lips had hovered dangerously, *roguishly* close, his strong, muscled arms holding her, drawing a lustful sigh from her. She'd felt the magnificent power between his legs, her own secret place responding with shockingly wanton arousal. His thick groan and incoherent Spanish words had drawn delicious shivers, the anticipation of his kiss *finally*, after months of secret yearning, making them strain closer.

In her lowest moments, Mareka cursed the police siren that made Cayetano stiffen, his eyes flaring in alarm before, cursing, he'd quickly released her. He hadn't explained or apologised. Neither had she. They'd swept the incident under the carpet.

But it had never gone away. Definitely not for her, since she'd revisited it with shameful regularity for months after it had happened.

'I suppose you're about to blame me for that too?' she asked shakily, the power of recollection, of awakening arousal, hammering through her.

A look passed through his eyes.

'Not for that, no. We were trapped in a…moment.' His voice was pure, sinful silk. 'But it proved my point then, as it does now—that I'm yours and *every* heterosexual woman's type.'

Mareka wanted to weep with how utterly right he was. She was battling with the injustice of all it all, scrambling for a rapier-sharp retort to the arrogance-soaked works, which was why she almost…almost missed the conclusion to his conceited statement.

'Which is why not a single person will dare to question us when we capitalise on this unfortunate but possibly significant opportunity.'

It was her turn to blink, although she doubted she looked half as sexy doing so. Time to try and force her brain to connect the vital dots. And, when she couldn't, to inhale and ask, 'I'm sorry, opportunity for what, exactly?'

'For you to fix what you've broken. Because, you see, with those images now splashed across every digital medium, I find myself regretfully minus a fiancée.' Another ripple went through his jaw. 'So I have no option but to pivot to the alternative. And that alternative, Miss Dixon, is you.'

Pivot… Alternative… Surplus… *Dispensable*…

Mareka ignored the hurtful bruising occurring inside her and reached for the anger triggered by his repugnant words. 'Excuse me? Where the hell do you get off thinking you…?'

'Let's cut to the chase; you can reach for the outrage later in your own time. For now, I'll present the advantages. You will accept my proposal to become Mrs Cayetano Figueroa with all the advantages that involves. In return, we will marry in two weeks.'

CHAPTER THREE

BENEATH THE CHANDELIER lights of his dining room, Cayetano watched the parade of emotions race across his PA's face, with emotion that should've been a lot more detached than it was. As for the anticipatory breath currently locked in his solar plexus...

That, he told himself, was merely the urgency to lock down at least one thing—one important thing. Without it, everything he'd worked for, since he'd been old enough to assume even the most menial responsibility within the company his grandfather had built from nothing, would be worthless.

It didn't escape him that it was the old man who'd put him in this position in the first place. After an exhaustive twelve months without finding a loophole, Cayetano had begrudgingly accepted that this was his only path. So, yes, he was interested in her every reaction to his proposal.

What he hadn't expected was what it turned out to be: bafflement; disbelief; panicked amusement; cynicism. Then...*outrage*?

That, he accepted with a punch of surprise, was unexpected. He could claim without an ounce of conceit that no woman had ever expressed outrage at anything he'd demanded, through word or deed. The unprecedented reaction held his tongue hostage as she sucked in a sharp breath.

'Mr Figueroa—'

'If we're going to be man and wife, you need to adjust yourself to calling me Cayetano. Or Caye if it pleases you,' he tacked on after a moment's thought. Why, exactly, he wasn't entirely sure. Very few people addressed him that informally, and most of those were blood relatives.

'*Mr Figueroa,*' she insisted, her hazel eyes now sparking with irritation, while still reflecting several layers of shock. 'If this is some sort of practical joke, then okay, you got me. Ha-ha!'

'It is not. I can guarantee that.'

Why was it that he didn't mind that flash of fire at his interruption? *Dios mio*, didn't he have enough on his plate? Hadn't he, just ten short minutes ago, divested himself of another spirited candidate? And one he hadn't had the insane inclination to touch or kiss or *savour* the way he did this one.

Hell, the faintest twinge of regret about getting rid of Octavia as his fiancée had already vanished. Despite her melodramatic and demanding tendencies, she was a hell of a PA, her ability to navigate the sometimes delicate avenues of the corporate world when his patience was frayed quite exemplary—not to mention her very useful pedigree.

But…

'Then I'm afraid I'll have to decline this…interesting offer.'

Insane—she meant insane. The word had all but screamed from her quivering voice when she'd uttered the word 'interesting'. And, from the bewildered look in her eyes as she examined him, she thought he'd taken leave of his senses.

Perhaps he had.

But she hadn't taken the exquisite diamond ring off her finger…yet. Nor had she stopped tracing the edges with her thumb every few seconds.

Did she even know she was doing that? Did she know she wore her every emotion on her face? That, when she'd announced she wasn't his type, the pulse had been leaping at her throat and her alluring eyes had all but *devoured* his mouth?

With every fibre of his being, he yearned to demonstrate to her how utterly useless her protests were. But he'd *never* taken what wasn't freely given. Until she gave him the answer he sought, he had to maintain strict professional barriers. Hell, even then, whatever interactions came after would be strictly for appearances' sake.

The reminder that this was far from an emotional match, the kind he had no intention of indulging in any time soon—perhaps ever—cauterised his wandering thoughts. She'd said no...while she caressed his ring. Perhaps he could incentivise her.

Money and wealth were powerful influencers. As the controller of his parents' purse strings, he knew that bitter truth all too well. He could catalogue on the fingers of one hand the times either of his parents had contacted him *without* financial scrounging having motivated them.

'If it sways you, you can keep that ring. You seemed very enamoured of it earlier this evening, if I recall.'

Cayetano watched her dazed glance drop to the ring, then back again, anger morphing into awe. 'What? Did you just say...?'

'*Si*, you heard right.'

'But...it's priceless.'

His lips twisted. 'Hardly. It's unique and quite magnificent—you should commend yourself for choosing it—but it's far from priceless. I'm yet to receive the exact figure but I believe, since Miss Smythe's pieces start from a million at least, the ring on your finger is worth at least three million.'

Her gasp was sweet and sultry, sexy but strangely innocent in a way that made Caye yearn to hear it again. *And again*. Hell, if it wasn't as contrived as he suspected, she would be eaten alive in the shark-infested, corporate waters of Buenos Aires.

Tightening his gut against the resurgence of the libidinous heat he'd experienced at Smythe's, he watched her alarmed gaze dart back to the ring.

'No way!'

'Oh, yes.'

'And she just let you walk out with a ring worth that much?'

'Perhaps because she knew I value integrity more than most characteristics and won't attempt anything underhanded. Which is why you should reconsider my proposal, Miss Dixon.'

As much as the circumstances infuriated him, it was the time for the 'honey not vinegar' approach. Although, that sage internal counselling fractured when she shook her head again.

'Even if I wanted to consider this…this *proposal*…' She spat the word as if it was offensive, and Cayetano made a mental note to pay her back for that at some point in the future. 'I feel like you've skipped several vital steps.'

Her hands waved expressively as she spoke—another first he noted. Seriously, at this point he was wondering if he was dealing with a split personality—the spirited siren versus the level-headed PA. And, *Dios*, his body knew which it preferred.

But her observation sobered him. Glancing at the table, he saw her half-finished meal.

'Sit down, Mareka.'

Her blatant suspicion ratcheted up his irritation.

'You claim you haven't eaten since breakfast. I interrupted your meal and I want you clear-headed for this next bit.'

Her lips pursed, instantly drawing his attention to their

plump curves. To his eternal relief, she took the seat but, though she reached for her cutlery, she didn't eat, instead sending him furtive glances from beneath her lush eye-lashes. Glances that held flashes of innocence he wanted to explore far more than was wise. He suppressed the absurd need and served himself a cut of the prime Argentinian steak that usually improved his mood.

He took a bite and chewed, although the satisfaction in this instance was marginal. Cayetano suspected nothing would elevate his mood short of a stone-carved assurance that his birthright was intact. 'To summarise—I have to marry before my thirty-fifth birthday to secure the company I've spent almost twenty years devoting myself to.'

'You mean Figueroa Industries?'

'Si,' he responded, the very act of confirming this ridiculous situation threatening to blacken his mood once more.

'Why? You're already the CEO.'

The meat congealed in his mouth, the very idea of having to say this out loud sticking in his craw. 'My grandfather created a stipulation in his will that demanded that every CEO, male or female, needed to be married by their thirty-fifth birthday to keep the position. It's a clause that has withstood vigorous opposition—including mine.'

While he'd loved his grandfather, he'd contested the constraining clause on principle. That it was one of the very few battles Cayetano had lost was a failure that wasn't easy to swallow.

'Why would he do that?'

Cayetano resisted the urge to grind his teeth. It would earn him a trip to the dentist and not much else. 'Because my grandfather believed that a married CEO would make a better leader than a single one,' he supplied with a bite of bitterness he couldn't avoid.

Wide hazel eyes regarded him with practised aloofness. 'You don't share that view, obviously.'

There was no point denying it. 'No, I do not.' The words were cold, detached—exactly how he felt about tying himself to another person in the name of some lofty emotion that rarely lasted a week, never mind a lifetime.

His grandparents might have beaten the odds to sustain a union that had lasted decades, but Cayetano suspected it hadn't been without its challenges, no matter how the old man had loved to boast. That he'd passed within a month of Cayetano's grandmother's death, supposedly from a broken heart, was a mournful but wistful tale some family members liked to regale to suit their own blinkered outlook.

He knew better... Hell, he'd *lived* the truth. He'd seen his parents drop even the pretence of a united front and collapse into all-out war long before he'd shed his baby teeth. And still his grandfather had insisted on some farcical 'one true love' myth. So Cayetano had been practical and put it to the test. To say he'd come up shockingly short was the understatement of the century.

What he'd discovered instead—through a series of relationships in his twenties his grandfather had laughingly dismissed as him sowing his wild oats—were the many tools available to dismantle even the staunchest of unions: infidelity; apathy; cruelty; mistrust.

And the recurring theme of good, old-fashioned greed. He'd been scrupulous about laying all his cards on the table since then. No woman who'd graced his arm or his bed since he'd hit the milestone age of thirty could have accused him of misleading them or misrepresenting his intentions.

And he intended to deal with his PA in the same vein. He refocused on her, to glimpse something shadowed and surprisingly bleak pass through her eyes.

'With respect to everything you've said, and appreciating the dilemma you're in...' she paused, swiped her tongue over her lower lip before continuing '...what makes you think I'll accept a ring you chose for another woman?'

And there it was—one of those obstacles created by unnecessary emotional attachment. He suppressed a sigh. 'But I didn't choose it, did I, Mareka?'

The noise she made when he uttered her name sent another lance of heat straight to his groin. *Maldita sea!* He really needed to find time to blow off steam if simple things like his hitherto unflappable PA's reaction to his uttering her name made him think of sweaty sheets and the sublime sensation of a woman's nails scoring down his back.

He needed a few rounds in the boxing ring with his personal trainer. Maybe a skydiving trip in his beloved Andes. Or even a good old-fashioned sex marathon with a woman who knew and accepted the 'sex only' score. *After* he'd done away with this rose-coloured glasses nonsense and secured Mareka's agreement to his proposal.

'*You* chose it. Out of the selection you created for me, this was the one you favoured above all else. True or false?'

She wanted to protest, but she knew he spoke the truth. Her lips firmed and she remained silent. He pressed on, wanting this over as quickly as possible.

'I watched you at Smythe's for a few minutes before you noticed me.'

And he'd learned a few surprising things about the PA whose efficiency impressed him but whose unobtrusive presence had made her almost forgettable.

Until that night in Italy...and tonight.

'You're a hopeless romantic,' he declared without inflexion or judgement. He didn't care either way. All he cared about was her cooperation with his plans.

Heat and outrage surged into her face. 'I...' She paused, then her chin lifted. 'So what if I am? The way I feel about...

certain things…hasn't affected my job, so I'm not even sure why you're bringing it up.'

'I'm bringing it up because it will expedite you accepting that ring you're reluctant to take off your finger. So can we cut through the bull and get on with it?'

'Why are we still even discussing this when I've already given my answer?'

He allowed himself a smug but resigned little smile and pulled out the big guns. 'Did I mention the one million pounds that will be deposited in your bank account if you accept my proposal?' he slid in smoothly.

And watched her eyes turn into wide saucers.

She'd misheard him. 'I… What?'

'Marry me and, on our wedding day, you'll receive one million pounds free and clear,' he enunciated slowly, clearly, as if he doubted her hearing.

Mareka glanced around the room, wondering if she'd slid down some rabbit hole without realising it. Nope, she was still in his penthouse. The view in the distance still showed the glittering lights of London. 'I heard you the first time, Mr Figueroa. What I meant was…'

She snatched in a breath, much like she'd been doing ever since he'd walked into the room and announced his absurd proposal. When she couldn't quite catch her breath, she shook her head. 'It doesn't even matter *why*. I don't want or need your money.'

Not entirely true. Think of how that could accelerate your goals.

One eyebrow arched; dear God, why did every motion make him even more breath-taking? 'Nonsense. Everyone wants money,' he delivered with bone-dry cynicism. 'On very rare occasions, not for themselves, but for someone else they care about. Not even saints turn down money.'

'And you're familiar with saints, are you?' she snapped before she could stop herself, then lowered her gaze as his glinted with the beginning of a blaze she was a little terrified to watch directly.

'Not from personal experience, but I'm sure there are reams written about them seeking patrons for practical causes on behalf of lost souls. And guess who made that happen?'

Her gaze flicked up and was immediately captured by his. 'Men like you?'

'Indeed. So, you see, even saints need men like me.' His gaze left hers and conducted a lazy survey of her body while his luscious mouth twisted. 'And you'll have a hell of a time convincing me you're a saint,' he murmured, his sexy drawl making her belly clench and heat pool in between her legs.

This shouldn't be happening. Not when she'd so efficiently talked herself out of her foolish crush on her boss. Not when she'd vowed to maintain the utmost professionalism the next time Cayetano Figueroa graced his London headquarters with his presence. 'I can't. I work for you. This is—'

'Another role that will earn you a salary.' His gaze dropped to the ring. 'And benefits you'd probably never see in this lifetime.'

'I'm sure you think your offer should impress me, but don't you think you're being presumptuous by assuming I won't earn that kind of money on my own *in this lifetime*?'

A hard smile played at his lips. Then he strolled towards her. 'I started working in my grandfather's company as an errand boy in the staff kitchen. He refused to allow me to use my real name because he didn't want me getting preferential treatment. Do you know what that taught me, Mareka?'

'That, regardless of whatever lesson he taught you, you would still inherit the throne one day?'

His face hardened. 'No. It taught me not to be too proud to accept opportunities when they came my way. In whatever form they arrived in.' He leaned in closer, looking her in the eye. 'Are you really going to walk away from potential millions?' he taunted with a near-whisper.

A near-whisper that screamed in her head in the silence that ensued. Because, now she'd heard the offer for the third…or was it the fourth?…time, the shock was clearing and paving way for the dream she'd yearned for and dismissed as impossible. A dream that would require a miracle to turn into reality.

He's offering that miracle.

But at what cost? Not to mention…what would her parents think?

Mareka shied away from that thought for the simple fact that it didn't bear thinking about. They would condemn her whatever decision she made. Not that she was considering it…was she?

She shook her head, desperate for a clear path through her rumbled thoughts. 'I should go.'

Cayetano's eyes narrowed. 'Go where, exactly?'

'Home. Where else?'

'Do you think that's wise?' he enquired.

She frowned. 'Why wouldn't it be?'

Moss-green eyes regarded her steadily. 'You've been photographed in my arms, wearing my ring. Do you really think the luxury of privacy is still yours?'

'They don't know where I live,' she protested, alarm leeching through her voice.

That eyebrow arched again. 'You want to bet?'

The silky question made panic surge through her. Glancing round, Mareka dashed across the room to where she'd left her handbag. Grabbing her phone, she activated her video doorbell, eager to prove to him that she'd been a no-body this morning, and she still was.

A gasp leapt free of her throat when she saw the live feed of her front door. A dozen strangers—at least—wielding cameras prowled just beyond the small patch of lawn that fronted her ground-floor flat. As she watched, one bolshie character pranced down the stone path and leaned on the bell. The jangle echoed through her phone, making her jump.

'I suggest you turn that off and leave it off for the time being.' Cayetano's breath rushing over her earlobe caused shivers all over again. 'And that's an order from your boss. Because, in case you've forgotten, you were supposed to make yourself available to me this evening anyway, were you not?'

'To assist you with Figueroa Industries matters, not...'

'Being presented with an opportunity you're still too prideful to grasp? And, before you spew further inane protests, look me in the eye and tell me you have no use for what I'm offering.'

She...couldn't. Now the seed had taken root, she couldn't shake it. She knew deep in her soul that rejecting it out of hand without further thought would haunt her for ever. She could help *so many people* with that money.

But at what cost?

The question returned, stronger.

'I need to think about—'

'No. I don't have time to waste. My New York lawyers are on standby. If your name isn't going on the contract, I'd like to know tonight.'

'You already have a contract drawn up?' She frowned, then answered her own question. 'Of course you do. Could this be more clinical if you tried?'

'You disadvantage yourself and me by believing this is

anything but a business transaction. I'm purchasing your services for a finite amount of time, Mareka. Imagining anything else is ill-advised.'

Something hard and rough twisted in her chest. She pushed it away, just as she'd pushed away every impossible thought surrounding Cayetano Figueroa. As much as it burned to hear it, he was right. Hadn't she admonished herself for that very same notion minutes ago?

A business transaction. That was all this was. All it could ever be. And, when it was done, when she'd fulfilled her end of the bargain, she could fulfil her lifelong dream. Prove to her parents that she wasn't a hopeless cause after all. And if they continued to believe that...

She shrugged. She would live her life for herself. She would hold her head high and revel in her achievements.

'You should know by now that I'm not a man who likes to be kept waiting,' Cayetano bit out.

She focused on him—on this man who intended to pluck her off his corporate shelf and put a ring on her finger. This man who'd looked at her and seen her as nothing but a replacement for another woman.

She would do well to take a leaf out of his book. Be cold and detached and seize an opportunity for the sake of every young person who needed a helping hand, be it financial or psychological.

Wasn't it ironic that, despite his warning to keep emotion out of this, that was what would grant her emotional satisfaction somewhere in her near future?

Yes. It was.

Welcoming the layer of balm that thought provided, she raised her head and looked him in the eye. And, despite the wild drumming of her heart and churning in the region of her heart, she shrugged and said, 'Congratulations, Mr Figueroa. You've just earned yourself a business partner.'

CHAPTER FOUR

YOU'VE JUST EARNED yourself a business partner.

Her words didn't sit well with him—not when she uttered them, or in the hours that followed. Her mercurial transformation from shock, being almost nonplussed and showing outright rejection to cool, professional acquiescence rubbed something raw and uncomfortable inside him. Something that would be diffused with sleep, he concluded at two a.m., when a ping on his phone signalled yet another helpful 'suggestion' from his lawyer on how best to further constrain the woefully scant demands of his PA.

He passed a hand over his gritty eyes and frowned.

Cayetano hadn't expected her to drive negotiations as hard as Octavia had, but neither had he expected her to have so few demands, especially considering the matter-of-fact way she'd accepted his proposal. Her main stipulation had been to reduce the length of their convenience marriage from four years to three. Which should have suited him just fine.

Except… He rubbed his chest, the chafing digging in deeper, eluding his attempts to eradicate it.

'Are we done?'

His gaze snapped up from where her feet rested on the sofa.

At some point she'd taken off her shoes and got more

comfortable as she read the contract. Cayetano hadn't drawn her attention to it. He had been far too captivated by her smoothly arched feet and her slim, delicate, perfectly grab-bable ankles. It wasn't a stretch at all to imagine himself between them, gripping tight as he thrust hard and...

'Mr... Cayetano? What are you doing?'

He jerked, looked down and realised his finger was strok-ing the arch of her foot. *Dios*. Had he lost every crumb of sanity?

He clenched his traitorous hand into a fist and started to withdraw. But then the sometimes-innocent, sometimes-si-ren who'd confounded him since he'd walked into the secret diamond boutique in Knightsbridge floored him. She moved her foot *into* his hold, a soft moan escaping her plump lips as their skin brushed.

His snatched-in breath stalled in his lung as he watched the pen tumble from her fingers to the floor, their marriage contract slithering after it. He watched her chest rise and fall in seductive, arousing agitation. His fingers unfurled. He gripped the enticing ankle and tugged it until her legs parted. Until that maddening little pencil skirt inched up her smooth thighs.

He stopped then, trying to regain some semblance of control. But she moved again. *Moaned* again. A pulse flut-tered at her throat.

And Cayetano... Dear God, he was *enthralled*.

He parted her legs, made space for himself and, as her alluring eyes locked on his, he pressed her back against the sofa, his lower body fusing with hers as he gave into the craving and tasted that maddening pulse at her neck.

Santo cielo! Her skin tasted like sin and heaven. He wanted to gorge on both! He found her perfect breasts and toyed with her nipple until her back arched. Then he moved lower, the centre of her a siren's call he was too weak to refuse. A hoarse groan tore from him as he yanked up her skirt, his fingers delving beneath her panties to discover…

'*Dios mio*…how wet you are for me.' He grunted against her lips, drawing back to watch her as he caressed the heart of her.

A deep flush suffused her cheeks, a soft mewl falling from her as he plunged one finger inside her.

'Oh, God, please. I'm… I'm…'

He surged forward, still high on madness, ready to give them both what they craved.

Another ping sounded from his phone. Mareka's fingers froze on his shoulders, her eyes widening in alarm. Then she shoved at his shoulders.

Cayetano jerked backwards, shock duelling with thwarted need as he stared down at her. Sweet heaven, what had he done?

He had truly lost his mind.

Even accepting that, he couldn't stop looking at her. Couldn't stop his gaze from dropping to the heart of her— the *damp* heart of her.

He surged and whirled away from pure temptation, his erection straining painfully. Dragging his fingers through his hair, he placed vital distance between them and cleared his throat.

'That was—'

'Something I want to forget ever happened,' she whispered, her voice husky and shaky, affronted.

His jaw tightened. He wanted to tell her he wouldn't forget it any time soon. That even now he could barely restrain himself from finishing what he…*they*…had started. But Cayetano knew when retreat was better in battle. So he wrested back his control and nodded briskly. 'Agreed.'

He turned round just as she wrestled her own bewilderment, her eyes sweeping away from his as she scooped up the document and pen.

'You have a list of our UK legal counsel, I'm sure. Arrange for one of them to come here first thing in the morning to witness the signing.'

She nodded and Caye just about managed to keep his gaze from shifting to the rich, dark-gold curls bouncing over her shoulders. To the gap in her shirt granting him a tantalising view of her breasts.

He most definitely wasn't going to think about how it would feel to shove his fingers into that glorious mass, feel its silky weight on his skin and grip it tightly to tilt her head so he could read her every expression. So they could both savour what came next.

'Okay.' She sucked her lips between her teeth for a fraction of a second, during which heat flashed through his groin. 'What happens after that?'

His disgruntlement at his body's relentless reaction to her bled through his brusque reply. 'Then you get to sit back and reap the rewards of your bargain. Who knows? You might even thank me for the honour of becoming Mrs Cayetano Figueroa.'

He strode away, ignoring the flash of hurt on her face and the stinging sensation that all of this was getting to him far too much. That he would love nothing better than to wipe the last twenty-four hours out of existence.

In his bedroom, he stopped in the middle of the room, teeth gritted. It was a waste of energy to curse his dead grandfather or to feel guilty that, had the old man been alive, he would've been disappointed by Cayetano's vigorous opposition of his demand.

But how could he not have done so when he'd lived with the very brazen evidence of marriage failure in his childhood? When even now he witnessed his mother's bitterness far too frequently, expressed in acerbic outbursts every time they were within speaking distance?

Basta. Enough.

He'd found himself a convenient wife to secure his birthright. So what if he couldn't shake the notion that this decision would trigger challenges down the line? That what seemed like an easier outcome than he'd anticipated might turn out too good to be true?

Whatever. He wouldn't be where he was today if he shied away in the face of challenges, big and small. Whatever came next, he would deal with it, just like he'd dealt with everything in his life—with cold, strategic, emotionless thinking that ultimately got him what he wanted.

Mareka held her phone to her ear, listening to the ring with growing dread. She'd stumbled into bed after that incident on the sofa, her needy body raging war with her stunned mind, despair nipping hard at her heels.

She couldn't believe what she'd allowed to happen, and how easily she'd fallen into temptation the second Cayetano had touched her. Maybe she was as rudderless as her parents accused her of.

No. She killed the thought, but her stomach continued to churn.

They'd stopped before they crossed a line.

Even though he had his fingers inside you?

Heat storming her body, threatening to rile up that need once more, she willed the phone to be answered. She'd risen bleary-eyed after a restless night, to the alarmed horror that she'd forgotten one vital thing—informing her parents of the decision she'd made last night.

Her father had his one and only cup of coffee while catching up on current affairs at six a.m. so he could discourse with her mother when she woke at seven. It was now six-fifteen. And her parents weren't answering her call.

Dread charted a slow, taunting trajectory through her chest. It was foolish to hope her parents hadn't seen the picture from yesterday. They were far too regimented to deviate from their morning routine without just cause, and this morning Mareka suspected that cause was her. Even across the miles, their disappointment weighed heavily.

'Yes?'

She jack-knifed in bed at her father's crisp greeting. 'Hi, Dad, it's me.'

'Yes, I'm aware,' he said. The extra-chilled tone confirmed her worst fears.

'I… I have some news. Is Mum around?' She'd rather get this over with in one go.

'She's here. You're on speaker.'

Mareka opened her mouth, but every word that formed in her brain seemed nonsensical, trite. It was a rash middle-of-the-night decision made entirely from believing she could go toe-to-toe with an enigmatic billionaire whose charisma and intelligence often left her slack-jawed.

Concentrate on the end goal—how much you'll be helping those who need it most.

'I'm…getting married. To the man I work… To my boss, Cayetano Figueroa,' she eventually blurted, sticking to the bare facts. They appreciated that more often than not.

Except the arctic silence that ensued made her wonder if she should've tried for a little embellishment. Such as, she'd once had a secret crush on the same boss she'd agreed to marry so he could secure his company? Or that her first emotion when he'd proposed had been a nanosecond of un-adulterated joy before reality had killed it dead?

She could say none of that, of course. For starters, she'd agreed to keep every aspect bar the news that they were marrying strictly confidential. Plus, she wasn't about to hand her parents another reason to label her a disappointment.

The silence stretched, as did Mareka's nerves. 'I know it seems rash and rushed...' She trailed off, cringing at handing them the perfect rod with which to whip her. Her father's response didn't disappoint.

'What else is new?' Lately, they didn't even bother to curtail their disdain.

'Have you got yourself pregnant?' That bald, coldly snapped question came from her mother, disappointment already staining her voice.

'What? Of course not!' But, despite her protest, she was stingingly reminded of why her mother would reach for that supposition. After all, it had been a similar *unplanned* dilemma that had produced Mareka.

An impatient huff burst from the phone. 'Your outrage is misplaced, young lady, considering you've been photographed with him in a compromised position and are calling the next morning with this...highly questionable news.'

She fought off a cringe that her parents had already seen the pictures.

Brush off the hurt. Don't take the bait. Don't take the...

'Why is it questionable? Because you think a girl like me can't land a man like Cayetano Figueroa?' Even as the words left her mouth, Mareka regretted them.

Sure enough, another canyon of silence stretched between them, one her parents didn't hurry to break.

'I'm sorry,' Mareka offered, even as bitterness filled the stretch. She'd been apologising for one thing or another for as long as she could remember. When would she learn that engaging only led to hurt?

Because they're my parents. It's not normal to be made to feel like this.

Futile tears building at the back of her throat—because, no matter how hard she tried, the hurt never went away—she cleared it quickly.

'It's early days, so no firm plans have been made,' she said, swiftly straightening the fingers beginning to cross on the silky duvet. 'I'll let you know when that changes, if you want?' She hated herself for the hope that tinged her voice.

One beat passed, then two.

'That would be welcome. We wouldn't want to be any more embarrassed if we're found not to know the details of our own daughter's nuptials, would we?' her father enquired coolly. 'Now, we must get on with our day before our schedule is further disrupted. Goodbye, Mareka.'

Her murmured response bounced off the dead line. Dejection attempted to creep into her chest. Tossing the phone away, she forcefully ejected herself from bed, as if doing so would disperse the fog shrouding ever closer.

Brisk strides took her to the spotless, luxurious bathroom. She wrenched the shower tap with more vigour than was necessary. But stepping beneath the hot spray and angling her face up to the wet needles didn't dispel the fact that tears were spilling. That, once again, the parents who should love her, or at the very least *care* for her, had made her feel inconsequential and hopeless. An inconvenience they couldn't wait to be rid of.

Her parents had been careless with birth control and had regretfully reaped the consequences on their honeymoon—a caustic fact meticulously recorded by her mother in her diary and discovered by Mareka when she'd been the tender age of nine.

Robert and I agree that nothing will change. This is simply another task to be managed.

Her mother's words were seared on Mareka's psyche for ever. Did she wish she'd never given in to curiosity and peeked in the diary her mother wrote in every night before dinner? *Yes.* But at least she'd finally understood why her parents were so cold and indifferent towards her.

Mareka scrubbed at her eyes, impatient with herself for picking at old wounds. She'd done her duty and told them, just as she would do her duty and honour the agreement with Cayetano. All she needed to do was remind herself of the rewards she would be reaping.

In a matter of weeks, she could be on her way to setting up her charity, helping displaced young people find their place in the world. For now, though, she needed to face Cayetano, the man who'd reawakened so many forbidden cravings in her last night.

Mareka wrenched the tap to cold when her body started to heat up once more. Ten minutes later, confident she was once more under control, she grimaced at the thought of wearing yesterday's clothes, then got on with it.

She entered the living room at the stroke of seven. Only to stop short at the sight of Cayetano sitting at the dining table, fully dressed, a tablet at his elbow as he enjoyed a poached egg and the specially cured Argentinian ham she took pains to ensure was on hand whenever he visited England.

His gaze flicked up in a searing once-over before returning to the screen. *'Buenos días.'*

'Good morning,' she murmured, a little thrown that he was addressing her in his mother tongue when he never had before.

'You should learn rudimentary Spanish if we're to go ahead with this.'

Something snagged in her midriff, then triggered a dreadful little tremor through her frame. 'If?' The question emerged tight and hoarse, not at all showing the composure she desperately sought. She took a breath, then blurted entirely against her will, 'Are you having second thoughts?'

His eyebrows rose, as if she'd surprised him. A second later, he set down his fork and sat back. 'On the contrary, that *if* was directed at you. I've been reminded very recently that women are prone to changing their minds faster than a speeding bullet,' he stated drily, with the edge that seemed never far away.

Hard on the heels of having her parents call her character into question, Cayetano's veiled vilification landed like a slap. Her fists bunched at her sides before she could will them not to. Another step closer to the table, and she was near enough to smell his aftershave, close enough to see the tiny flecks in his eyes. She hated herself for noticing these things about him, just as she hated herself for the emotions she couldn't keep bottled down.

'I'd thank you not to tar me with the same brush as your other women. Surely you're experienced enough to know no woman likes to be compared to another, especially one her future husband had a connection with? How would you react if I compared you to a boyfriend?'

His eyes flared, then his face tightened. 'Not favourably. And most definitely if it was a present one.'

She heard the clear question in his response but refused to give him the satisfaction of an answer. Instead, she arched her brows, her fists remaining tight despite the composure she willed into her being.

For an age, they stared each other down, then his gaze travelled down to her clenched fists, the tiniest twitch lifting the corners of his mouth. 'I don't recall you displaying such fierceness before,' he mused. 'But you have my apologies for causing offence.'

A little mollified, Mareka breathed out, ignoring the tiny

voice wondering if she'd overreacted a touch. 'Apology accepted,' she muttered.

His gaze remained on her for another stretch, then he rose fluidly to his feet. Her breath caught in her throat as he took a single step towards her, swallowing the gap between then. Feeling her pulse skitter wildly, Mareka was about to ask what he was doing when he reached around and pulled out her chair.

'Oh, I...thanks,' she said, further cringing at how he so easily left her tongue-tied. How, for a moment, she'd thought there was to be a version of last night played out.

'De nada,' he said, his voice low, deep and sending shivers down her spine.

She was lamenting just how dismayingly clichéd it was for her to find his Argentinian accent so sexy when a butler glided in, thankfully saving her from doing something stupid.

Mareka grabbed the chance to clear her mind of everything that had happened in the last few minutes and to distance herself from the searing jealousy she'd experienced when Cayetano had compared her to the woman he'd intended to marry only a few short hours ago.

It was merely an aberration, a remnant of emotions she'd had no business feeling in the first place. But a few sips of coffee and a couple of mouthfuls of delicious muesli and she was once again hot and bothered, Cayetano's gaze having returned to examine her.

'W-what?' she stuttered.

'You're yet to answer me.'

She flailed around for several seconds before she remembered. 'Oh. Well, I haven't changed my mind. I tend to keep my promises.' Such as the one she'd made to herself a handful of years after reading that diary entry—that she wouldn't spend her life feeling like a spare part. More importantly, she'd ensure she helped other women feel the same as she wanted to.

Last night, despite his left-field proposal, Cayetano Figueroa had propelled her towards keeping that promise.

'Is that so?' came the silky reply.

'I haven't let you down so far, have I?'

He shrugged. 'Professionally, no. Your work is exemplary. But this assignment requires exceptional attention to detail.'

'Such as?'

'Such as knowing each other to a level that will ensure we pass muster where it matters.'

She stiffened. Was that what the sofa incident last night had been about—a test of her mettle? 'What does that mean, exactly? Who do we have to prove our relationship to—the papers?'

'What the tabloids report of me is of very little relevance,' he answered in a clipped tone. Before she could remind him that it had seemed quite the opposite last night, he continued. 'My inner circle back in Argentina and several key people need to believe that our marriage is real, not a paper-only contract.'

She frowned, a part of her feeling that tremor again. 'You didn't say any of this last night.'

He gave another shrug. 'I didn't see the point in overwhelming you with too much detail.'

Pique ruffled her nape. 'I'm not a hothouse flower you need to coddle, you know?'

'Good, then you won't clutch your pearls or protest when I touch you or kiss you in public.'

Her next swallow of coffee went down the wrong way, triggering a fit of coughing. 'Did you wait until after I agreed to marry you to spell out those...*addendums*?' she demanded when she'd caught her breath.

'Does it matter?'

'Of course it matters! We'll be... You're asking me for... intimacy. Was last night...?'

'Last night was, as we both agreed, a late-night aberration.' Something dark and secret passed through his eyes, gone before she could plant an accurate label on it. Still, she grew hotter when his gaze dropped to linger on her mouth. 'Considering how much I'm paying you, a small show for appearances isn't much to ask.'

A small show that would involve them touching. That risked her betraying her indecent craving. 'To you, maybe. Not to me. You're paying me to act as your wife. You're not buying my body or my...my...' She floundered, the reminder of his hands on her, *inside her*, stirring her temperature, all while he sat in his chair, the picture of composure. 'You should have told me this last night.'

'Hmm. It seems we're either at an impasse or this is a deal-breaker for you. Which is it, Mareka?'

The way he said her name, with an emphasis on the 'r', sent another wavelet of heat through her belly. She suppressed the sensation while struggling to look away from the lips that uttered it, the sensual curve of it, the way it was now slightly pursed as he watched her with narrow-eyed intent. The thought of kissing those lips in public, even for the benefit of their ruse, made her heart hammer and her pulse spike even harder.

That was out of the question, of course. But...maybe it didn't have to be his way or the highway. 'I propose a compromise.'

'*Si?*'

God, she really needed to get over this belly-flip every time he spoke Spanish. 'I agree to...um...a small degree of touching, but no kissing...on the lips. That's my final word on it.' Considering what they'd done last night, it was probably a ridiculous request to him; but she'd fantasised about kissing this man for so long, she knew deep in her bones she would be lost if that became a reality. Especially a reality that was only a means to an end for him.

His eyes glinted, wicked, earthy and, oh, so cynical. His fingers reached out, plucked his coffee cup from its saucer and downed the remaining contents. He set it back down, all without taking his eyes off her. She was fighting the urge to squirm beneath that raw gaze when he said, 'I'm beginning to wonder at your level of experience, Mareka.'

'What do you mean?'

His amusement intensified, sardonic humour lighting his eyes. 'I mean, I wonder if you've known the true touch of a man if you think kissing on the lips is the height of intimacy you can achieve with your clothes on.'

Heat surged up her face so fiercely, her skin tingled with the force of it. 'I don't—'

'It's okay, you don't need to defend your stance. I accept your offer.'

He held out his hand to her.

And in that moment, torn between taking back words she suspected had just landed her into an unforeseen quagmire and congratulating herself for not blowing her chance, she felt the earth shake and tilt beneath her feet.

But…what was the worst that could happen?

She got her first taster when she sucked in a breath, placed her hand in his and watched him tug it firmly but gently towards him before brushing those lips over it, lips she'd daydreamed about only a minute ago. Panic made her stomach dip, roll and drop like a rollercoaster before surging back up to drive the breath out of her lungs.

Cayetano released her almost immediately.

But the impression he'd left—that he could set her body alight with just a simple touch—lingered long after the law-

yers arrived and she signed the documents committing her
to three years as Mrs Cayetano Figueroa.

Some time later, he officially slipped the engagement
ring onto her finger and had a car drive her home to pack
her bags so they could leave for Buenos Aires early that
evening.

CHAPTER FIVE

THE WEDDING TOOK place two weeks and one day later at Cayetano's private estate just outside Buenos Aires. Mareka barely caught her breath in all that time. Every time she'd thought she had five minutes to herself, some sleekly dressed assistant, event co-ordinator or haute couture designer *simply had to have* her input on one thing or another.

She'd accepted a mere three days after their whirlwind arrival that perhaps she would've been better off not trying to compete with the other staggering parts of Caye's empire—especially the Argentinians.

The London and European offices easily employed a thousand people. While she'd known Argentina was where Figueroa Industries had been started by Caye's grandfather, Mareka hadn't quite grasped that Figueroa Industries employed close to twenty-five thousand in South America alone, with only a fraction less in the States. And that the inner circle and key people Cayetano had spoken of numbered several dozen, all clamouring to meet their CEO's new wife.

She'd attended more dinners, garden and cocktail parties and galas in the last two weeks than in her entire life so far.

Which brought her to why her heart continued to twist even now, the night before her wedding, when she'd finally been left alone by the co-ordinator. The older woman had stated plainly that she didn't want a tired bride ruining the wedding photos and risking the spotlight being taken off the wedding dress. Mareka had been too shocked by the blunt statement to do more than smile and escape to her private suite.

But, while she could console herself with knowing she wouldn't have to see a large proportion of the organisers after tomorrow, the people she would have to see again were her parents.

Mareka had thought of their arrival two nights ago, and the quietly icy disapproval they'd displayed all through the private pre-dinner drinks she'd hosted with Cayetano in his Buenos Aires penthouse, would be the height of her anxiety.

She'd been wrong.

Somehow, Cayetano had withstood her parents' near-monosyllabic non-engagement for all of ten minutes before he'd launched into a charm offensive, systematically dismantling their icy demeanours with a focus that had been disarming and spellbinding to watch.

Her jaw had almost dropped when she'd discovered Caye knew the ins and outs of her parents' careers, engaging them and drawing them out with astute and challenging conversation they'd latched onto, easily extending the two hours she'd intended for the ordeal into three and a half.

Watching her parents fall under her future husband's spell had filled her with a feeling she couldn't quite describe—something like pride, but not quite, since that would be misplaced; Cayetano Figueroa wasn't *hers* to be proud of. The darts of jealousy seemed petty, considering Caye had singlehandedly turned a much-dreaded ordeal into a passably pleasant evening. She'd settled on gratitude as her parents had bid them goodnight. Her mother's gaze had lingered on Mareka with a look that had skated the very outer rim of approval before the cold indifference had slotted back into place.

Fortunately, or unfortunately, that sliver of approval had lowered her guard, enough that she'd been disarmed and dismayed when her mother's text had arrived just before she'd gone to bed last night.

I require five minutes of your time before the wedding.
Mother.

No matter how many times she told herself her parents would be gone this time tomorrow, she couldn't shake the renewed anxiety swirling through her.

Or the fact that it had only exacerbated the dismay at the new facet of Cayetano's treatment. Since their arrival, he'd stuck to their strict agreement that any physical contact between them be minimal. While Mareka was glad of it—*she needed to be*—the last thing she'd expected was the coldly neutral dismissal that came with it.

At first, she'd been sure it was her imagination, that her hang-ups from her parents were spilling over into her thoughts about Cayetano's interaction with her. But two weeks of standing next to him and smiling for the cameras, after which he'd treated her with stiff formality bordering on apathy, had opened a vein of despair she couldn't seem to suppress.

On top of that was Mareka's other problem. The insanely breathtaking PA and *almost* fiancée whose place Mareka had taken. She had assumed—wrongly, it turned out—that Caye's Argentinian PA would interact with her boss only during business hours, perhaps even choosing to stay out of sight altogether. But the statuesque beauty had made an appearance at every notable occasion so far.

Rational deduction suggested it was to have been expected, since a quick Internet search had revealed that Octavia Morena and her family were powerful and influential, highly regarded in Buenos Aires. That, even before she'd taken the role as Caye's assistant, she'd been part of his inner circle, their association going back to adolescence.

If Mareka had expected the other woman to be upset about ending her agreement to marry her boss, she'd been wrong. She'd showed no such emotion. Mareka had watched as her low, seductive laugh had turned the heads of men and women alike.

Including Cayetano. From the way Octavia had nodded and smiled at friends and business acquaintances, as if she didn't have a care in the world, it was almost as if she hadn't vigorously rowed with Cayetano and been discarded a mere two weeks ago.

And it was also clear that the other woman was taking her cue from Cayetano. Mareka had suffered enough of those looks from her parents to recognise Octavia's a mile away—the blank look that said that, while she found Mareka inconsequential, she was still an object of intense dislike.

A combination of all her worries added to the butterflies already swarming her belly as Mareka stood frozen in front of her mirror on her wedding day, clad in a jaw-dropping lace-and-silk wedding gown.

Telling herself that things would all change once she was married didn't matter. Hell, it sounded borderline desperate, because she'd spent far too much time wondering if Cayetano *would* change his mind. Whether his coldness stemmed from cold feet. She hated herself for dwelling on it, and hated that she couldn't dismiss the cold churning in her belly.

That jitteriness made her jump at the knock on her door. Her head snapped up as her Tahitian mother entered. She'd chosen a sleeveless, saffron-coloured gown with an arched collar that highlighted her dark-gold skin to perfection, the faint grey hairs at her temples swept up into the mass of corkscrew curls Mareka had inherited. A matching saffron-coloured clutch bag, satin heels and the small but tasteful teardrop diamonds her husband had given her for her fiftieth birthday five years ago completed the look.

Their eyes met in the mirror. She wanted to tell her mother she looked beautiful but the thought of inviting the disdain she'd just been lamenting stopped her.

'This isn't a sentimental mother-daughter talk, if that's what you're afraid of,' her mother said coolly once the make-up artists and couturiers had made themselves scarce.

Mareka wondered if that was what her mother feared. But she had enough butterflies swarming her belly; she didn't need any more by asking. 'Then what it is?'

'That…fiancé of yours is quite charismatic.'

'Is he?'

Her mother sent her a droll look, then brushed invisible lint from her dress. 'Your father and I merely wanted to say, if you feel out of her depth, it's not too late to pull out.'

Alarm knotted in Mareka's throat. 'Thank you for your concern, Mother. But I'm going to marry him.'

The firmness in her voice was new to both of them. Her mother's eyes flared the tiniest bit, then faint colour flared across her cheeks. 'Well, if you insist on going ahead, don't say we didn't warn you.'

The knot melted to acid, threatening to choke her. It took several swallows for Mareka to speak clearly. 'Is that what you're really worried about? Or are you more worried that I'll embarrass you somehow?'

Another flash of surprise, then the customary disdain. But Mareka felt the faintest triumph for standing up for herself. For not being lessened on such a crucial day. Before her mother could confirm anything, she hurried to end it. 'I really need to finish getting ready. Thank you, Mother.'

Still she lingered, as if she wanted to say more.

It was a relief when a brisk knock interrupted her. 'Come in,' Mareka called out, desperate for a saviour.

When that saviour turned out to be the man she'd promised to wed, she couldn't halt her gasp.

'Caye... Cayetano.' She wasn't quite used to calling her boss and soon-to-be husband by his first name, at least not out loud, and especially not when he'd reverted to being a remote stranger these past two weeks. Every time she did, she felt a little jolt in her midriff. Telling herself she had a right now, that he'd all but commanded her to use his first name, didn't stop the waves of shock from travelling through her system as he prowled into the room.

Or was it because, simply put, he looked criminally breath-taking in his morning suit? It really should be a chargeable offence—on top of all his other lofty accomplishments—to look this magnificent.

His hair was slicked back, the sunlight slanting through her French windows catching on his angled cheekbones and jaw, outlining the thick, sensual curve of his lower lip.

'Everything all right, Mrs Dixon?' The question was aimed at her mother but Caye's assessing eyes were pinned on Mareka.

'Of course. I was just leaving.' She hesitated, her gaze darting between Caye and Mareka.

Mareka barely registered when her mother left the room, her focus so absorbed in Cayetano.

'Traditionally, I'm guessing this is where I gasp and protest that you're not supposed to see me until I walk up the aisle?' Her attempt at humour emerged with cringing doses of nerves and breathlessness.

Had he come to tell her he'd changed his mind, finally?

That, like her mother had suggested, he found her unsuitable after all?

He shrugged thick shoulders that would have drawn envy from a rugby player and kept coming, not stopping until he was within arm's reach. 'You could, but it'll just waste time. We both know what this marriage is.'

A clinical and emotionally devoid vacuum. 'So, was there something you wanted?' The question was low, tremulous, far too reflective of her inner agitation. But she supposed, if he was going to tell her the wedding was off, it was better done here, in private, rather than out there where the eyes of nine hundred guests would gleefully judge her for her inadequacies.

'I saw your mother entering your suite. I noticed at our dinner the other night that you two don't seem to have the... warmest of relationships.'

Mareka was highly disturbed by the relief that swarmed her. Just as she was both ashamed that he'd noticed the frostiness between her parents and her and astonished that he'd been moved to check on her—pleasingly so, she alarmingly admitted to herself. 'So this is a... You just came to see if I was okay?' she pressed, despite her relief. For some urgent reason, she needed to be sure.

One brow rose. 'Just?' His gaze lingered on her face, then conducted a slow, thorough survey over her body. 'A wellness check on my future bride minutes before we're married isn't a trivial thing,' he delivered, sending peculiar sensations on a whirlwind tour through her belly.

When those incisive eyes rose to rest on the pulse hammering at her throat, she swallowed. 'So you haven't changed your mind?' she blurted before she could rethink the wisdom of it.

If he hadn't been as close as he was just then, she wouldn't have seen the tiniest jolt move through him. Narrowed eyes drilled into her. 'Is there any reason why you would think I'd change my mind?' he asked, his voice low, charged...*suspicious*

'Mareka...' His voice held something heavy—a warning, maybe.

Peering closer at him, she was stunned to see the expression in his eyes. Not quite panic—men like Cayetano Figueroa didn't panic about anything—but it was a faint facsimile of it, heavily overlaid with warning.

For some reason, Mareka wanted to laugh, because it was a relief to see that tiniest chink in his formidable armour. That he wasn't completely as conceited and indifferent enough to believe he only needed to click his fingers for everyone to fall into line. Maybe she'd overblown his chilliness these past two weeks.

It lent her much-needed strength to lift her chin and look him straight in the eye. 'No. I haven't changed my mind. It'll take more than a five-minute conversation with my mother to do that.'

The flicker disappeared, replaced now by curiosity. Something she wasn't about to satisfy since she'd given away way more than she'd intended. 'And, now that's settled, shall we get on with it? I'm sure your guests don't want to wait for ever.'

'They'll wait as long as I want them to,' he said dismissively, his eyes still boring into hers. Then, just when she thought he'd leave, he did the opposite and stepped closer.

Her breath hitched. 'What...what are you doing?'

'Something else I think we need to get out of the way,' he murmured. She knew exactly what he meant because her pulse was leaping, the blood thundering through her veins. And those incredible eyes were now on her lips.

'Caye...'

'Hmm, that's exactly how I want you to respond, that's

exactly how I want you to look when we repeat this out there in front of everyone. *Si?*'

Before she could answer, he cupped her cheeks, propelling her body into the heated column of his.

She was too shocked to move, possibly too *afraid* to move, just in case he stopped whatever it was he planned to do. Because the blood rushing through her veins, the faint roaring in her ears and the racing of her heartbeat screamed that she wanted to find out.

Perhaps it was because of the dispiriting encounter with her mother, or even the detached front he'd displayed in the past two weeks that had battered her, that made her pliable. She willingly curved into his warm body as he pulled her closer. As foolish as it was, she wanted a new experience to dispel this constant feeling of inadequacy that cloaked her.

It made her move into his body, arms rising to circle his neck almost of their own accord, welcoming his tight, masculine moan as his lips sealed hers for the first time.

She knew she shouldn't be doing this but, even as the argument rose, it died away, the sweep of his tongue wreaking magic, making her moan in turn.

Their first kiss should have been at the altar. A formal brush of lips, held long enough to fool everyone present. *This* was far more than that. This was the kind of magic that could make a mockery of everything she needed to hold at bay. And yet she couldn't have stopped it if she'd tried.

Because she had fantasised about this; had wondered what he would taste like, whether it would compare to anything she had experienced before. To her mild dismay, it didn't—not even close. It was heaven and, a few desperate seconds later, it was hell—because, now she knew, she feared that nothing else would compare. This kiss would stay with her for ever, canonised as the ultimate example of what a kiss should be.

It was this disturbing little thought that made her take a hasty step back far too late, trying to pull herself out of the wreckage before she was completely annihilated.

'W-what was that for?'

One eyebrow rose even as his tongue slid over his bottom lip, as if still wanting to taste her. And, of course, that sent another surge of heat through her. She wanted to tell him to stop doing that, to stop delivering mixed signals that assaulted her emotions, but her heart wouldn't communicate the plea to her lips.

He gave a slow, lazy shrug. 'I needed to be sure.'

'About what?'

'You think I haven't noticed that every time I've touched you, you either jolted or startled like a frightened little bird? I couldn't have that at the altar.'

She lifted her hand, again the movement outside of her will, and touched her lips.

So, this had all been a test.

Mareka wasn't sure whether she hated him or envied the clinical, strategic focus of his every deed. But she hated that he could be rational in moments like these when her senses were flailing all over the place.

She turned away, hoping to hide her dismay. 'I suppose you now have your answer.'

He shrugged. 'Perhaps a deeper moan will work better, and if you feel inclined to cling to me for a little longer we might just pass muster.'

Despair grew colder, engulfing her whole body. Still, she managed to nod. 'I'll bear that in mind. Now, if you're quite finished, should we get on with this?'

Her brisk tone drew narrowed eyes, a flash of irritation passing over his face before he nodded. 'Indeed. I will see you at the altar.'

His sharp gaze lingered a few more seconds, as if gauging the veracity of her response. Again, she saw that flash of vulnerability cross his face. It shouldn't have melted the knot of desolation, or even loosened it a little, but by the time his imposing form disappeared through the doorway her emotions had turned a full one hundred and eighty degrees.

And, for good or ill, her emotions were shrouded by the memory of that kiss. As the designers and co-ordinators returned to the room and bustled around her with the last-minute touches, she dwelled within that bubble, all the way outside to where her father waited, his face a neutral mask, hiding his disdain as he held out his arm.

As the minutes passed, she welcomed that little haze. It kept her from freaking out when she walked downstairs, stepped out onto the lawn and saw the sea of faces staring back at her. Besides her mother and father, not a single relative was present. She'd wanted it that way, unable to face adding the scrutiny of curious family members of this marriage of convenience.

Inside that little bubble, she held her head high, dismissing whispered conversations and lingering gazes on her dress and diamonds.

Not that she would have been able to concentrate on them for long. Because, at the head of the aisle, his eyes fixed squarely on her, waited Cayetano. His gaze propelled her forward, her father forgotten beside her. It was only when his eyes darted sideways, with a brisk nod to her father, that she summoned a smile before her gaze was recaptured by Cayetano.

Everyone else ceased to exist the moment he held out his hand to her. She knew what this was—she accepted deep down in her bones it could be nothing else. They'd made an agreement and she was here to fulfil it.

Yet somewhere in her heart lurked the excited little illusion that just wouldn't quieten down. The chirpy little voice that dismissed the nature of this endeavour and simply revelled in the fact that she was wearing a gorgeous wedding gown, holding on to the man who'd taken hold of her secret little fantasies for far too many months.

And when she faced him, their audience now significantly quieter and more attentive, she couldn't help but look into his eyes. Did she care that he looked as solemn and grounded now as the first night he'd put this in motion? Her heart didn't. She followed the celebrant's direction, locked eyes with the man whose ring she would wear for the next three years and repeated vows that should've been clinical and emotionless, but instead resonated deep within her until they touched a special place that should've been secret. Even so, she couldn't dismiss the little nugget that, for good or ill, she was living out a secret yearning.

Giving a little mental shrug, she allowed the bubble to linger, to swell just that smallest bit. After Caye's deep, even tones repeated his own vows, they were pronounced husband and wife.

A dart of alarm struck her when he pulled her close, his warm hands wrapping around her shoulders, eyes steady on hers. She knew what was coming. They'd already had a practice run, after all, so she didn't flinch or gasp when Cayetano's lips lowered to hers.

What she did feel was that resurgence of electricity, right from the bottom of her toes to her hairline, from the base of her spine to the pulse racing at her throat. And, because she was growing shamefully addicted to that feeling, she slid her arms up his chest, resting them on his shoulders as he kissed her, murmuring growing around them as he lingered, and lingered, drawing whispers and coughs from their audience.

When he released her, he held her for a moment longer, for which she was thankful. Because her senses were swimming, her eyes blinking in the sunlight as her pulse frantically raced away.

As a ruse, it was perfect, the blushing bride dizzy from her new husband's kiss. From the smug look in his eyes before he turned them both to face their guests, she knew she'd come through with flying colours.

Mareka couldn't help herself. She basked in that approval for the next few hours, accepting congratulations and air kisses from people she didn't know and would probably never meet again.

Even her parents, enjoying glasses of vintage champagne served in eye-wateringly expensive crystal glasses, were just a touch less severe and disapproving, the esteemed guest list seeming to impress them.

As speeches were given—including one by Cayetano in absurdly magnificent tones, drawing equal parts humour and the kind of swoony indulgence that made romantics sigh—she continued to exist in that bubble, ignoring the older couple who'd been abruptly introduced at a gala a few days ago by Caye as his parents.

She told herself it didn't matter that they stared at her with heavy censure and deep scepticism. Her laughter came easily from within the bubble, their first dance a flight across a dance floor that could've been made of clouds.

So, yes, it was entirely bone-jarring when she was brought back down to earth hard, the bubble bursting with soul-shrivelling devastation.

CHAPTER SIX

THE RECEPTION WAS in full swing, guests spilling out all over the estate blissed out on good food, vintage champagne and excellent company. There was nowhere Mareka looked where she didn't see a contented cluster of guests.

Cayetano had opened his home completely to his guests and, boy, were they taking advantage of it. So, the search for her new husband, the man who had slipped the exquisite platinum wedding band onto her finger—a ring, she'd discovered, commissioned from Smythe's as part of an extensive collection—took a little longer than she'd expected.

Mareka went from group to group, pausing to laugh and allow herself to be teased that she'd lost her husband so soon after her nuptials. Slowly, though, the teasing stopped being amusing, the ominous tingling at her nape rising to mock her.

She noticed the hand clutching her barely touched glass of champagne was shaking, due to her stretched nerves, and gave a half-hearted snort under her breath. Her thought screeched to a halt, along with her feet, when she heard the loud voices coming from Cayetano's study. The room was in shadow except for the beam of late-afternoon sunlight slanting down onto father, mother and son.

Their body language spoke volumes.

She should know. From the age she'd begun to be able

to read body language, she'd deciphered her parents' with unerring accuracy. She knew when a simple glance from her mother, or the way her father angled his body, meant Mareka shouldn't speak or approach but remain seated or supply a specific answer to a specific question posed by a dinner guest.

Right now, Cayetano stood opposite his parents, his shoulders frozen in formidable challenge. And, while rage bristled from him, Mareka spotted that same faint fracture she'd caught earlier.

'You choose today to confront me with this?' he demanded.

His father shrugged. 'You hardly take our calls any more. This was an opportunity we couldn't pass up.'

Caye's jaw clenched. 'I don't take your calls because, just like everyone else, you only contact me when you need something—namely money.'

Mareka's heart squeezed, despite the acid in his voice, then she flinched as his father laughed. It was an echo of a sound she'd heard from Cayetano before.

'Surely you're not still hung up on the sentimentality of your youth? You're your own man now, as you're so eager to laud over us. And you should be thankful—we were responsible for your single-mindedness. It's time to show some gratitude.'

Cayetano's fists bunched, even as a bleak shadow darkened his face. 'Or what? Let me guess, you think you have some leverage over me?'

His parents exchanged a smug look that curdled Mareka's blood.

'We know this marriage of yours is a sham. And, yes, we want a place on the board in return for not causing ripples in the company. Or are you going to claim you've fallen in love with the gold-digging little nobody?'

For a tense moment, Cayetano remained silent. Mareka feared the blood rushing through her ears would prevent her hearing his response but it did not. She heard it loud and clear.

'No, I don't love her, and I may barely even know her. But unlike you, Father, I don't plan on letting capricious emotions stand in the way of securing my birthright. And you forget, if you do anything to jeopardise this company, you will suffer the repercussions too.'

She should've walked away then and somehow found a quiet place to stitch the torn emotions his words had caused back together. But that bleakness wouldn't let her. She knew too well the anguish of having uncaring parents. And that tiny link of affinity propelled her through the doors.

To confront three sets of eyes that held varying expressions. But it was Cayetano's she sought.

'Are… Is everything okay?' she asked, then her breath caught when she saw the cold rejection on Cayetano's face.

His father's glinted with mockery and malice. 'Ah, the fake bride come to rescue her beloved, *si*? Save your outrage, girl. We know all this is one big façade.'

'You will address my wife with respect,' Cayetano warned icily.

His father's brow arched but he didn't reply. Perhaps sensing he was treading on dangerous ground, he remained silent.

It was his mother who spoke. 'Call us next week. We expect a place on the board by the end of the month. And don't even think about slithering away from this, son. We can make claiming your precious birthright harder than you think.'

Cayetano's nostrils pinched white, his mouth settling into a thin, formidable line. But he kept silent. And, after another mocking glance at Mareka, his parents left.

Mareka's insides continued to shake like a leaf. She

sensed Cayetano coming closer but she couldn't bring herself to look at him, chiefly because she feared exposing her pain to him.

'Mareka, are you…?'

'You want them to speak to me with respect? Where is yours?' she spat out.

His eyes narrowed to slits. 'Excuse me?'

Shut up. Don't say it!

But her lips were already moving, her anguish demanding an outlet. 'You told them you don't love me, that you don't even know me.'

That I'm a little nobody.

His face clenched tight. 'And which part of that was untrue?'

Her insides shrivelled, because of course he was right. The only thing wrong with this situation was that she'd fooled herself into existing in that bubble for too long.

'I thought it didn't need to be spelled out, Mareka, but perhaps it does. So, before this goes further, you should know that it'll be a mistake to develop feelings for me.'

That shrivelling intensified. Still, she managed to raise her chin. 'You really think incredibly highly of yourself, don't you?'

His chin went up sharply, then he exhaled. 'As long as we understand each other.'

'Don't worry. I know exactly where I stand.' She turned away, desperate to find that quiet place now. Desperate to address that tightness in her chest.

'Oh, and Mareka?'

Her feet stalled, dread stiffening her limbs. 'Yes?'

'In future, don't feel the need to rush in to defend me. I've been dealing with characters like my parents my whole life. I'm quite adept at it. Perhaps you should try dealing with your own parents,' he delivered with a dark, distinct edge.

That final spear of hard truth killed the last of her fantasy. The hard diamond cutting into her flesh told her she'd closed her thumb over it. But, as much as it hurt, it grounded her. 'You don't need my help. Got it.'

She fled to the nearest bathroom. Shutting the door behind her, Mareka blinked hard and fast, desperate not to the let the building tears overflow. When she failed and a few drops fell, she swiped at them, a half-exasperated sob leaving her throat.

She would *absolutely* not cry over this. Because she didn't care what Cayetano thought of her. *Right?* She was in this solely because she'd felt a tiny bit responsible for his plans falling apart. That stupid crush was well and truly behind her, and she could finally stop believing there was any affinity between them. *Right?*

When the affirmations failed to rush forward to her defence, she gritted her teeth, a terrible little eddy of panic making her insides dip and dive before she clenched her belly. She swiped at her cheeks again, thankful when no further tears fell.

Dragging in a breath, Mareka checked her reflection in the mirror. Mercifully, the damage wasn't too awful. A quick tissue repair and she looked almost good as new. Lifting her chin, she turned away from the wisps of desolation in her eyes and strode to the door.

The past fifteen minutes had been more than enlightening. Cayetano's past had hardened him against all feeling. Against anything that would hold him back from achieving the only thing that mattered to him—his precious Figueroa Industries.

He'd married a woman he felt little regard for to achieve his aims. Mareka needed to emblazon that fact on her heart and mind, even if it left a cold, hollow ache inside her.

* * *

She thanked her stars when the reception started winding down less than an hour after the unfortunate incident in the study.

But, even in that short time, it was hard to avoid Cayetano's piercing scrutiny. She managed it, barely, by making sure she always talking to someone else when she sensed he was about to address her.

Her grandmother had often commended Mareka on her stoicism, but had then added that she lamented that stoicism was sadly finite.

Mareka felt that finiteness dwindling every time Cayetano slanted his green-eyed gaze at her, his imposing personality attempting to prod her into acknowledging his presence. Perhaps even into simpering, the way she had the past two weeks?

Recalling how accommodating she'd been made her stomach churn, even as her chin lifted higher, the fervent need not to be cowed burning through her until she feared she would alight with it. Until the champagne flute trembled in her hand.

Mareka sensed more than saw Cayetano's gaze on her shaking hand. 'Careful, *querida*,' he murmured. 'Your emotions are showing.' His tone thick was with warning.

She couldn't help the grating laughter that erupted. 'And we can't have that, can we?' she retorted, sharper than she'd intended.

A few guests sent them furtive glances, sensing a delicious plot twist in the air. Mareka wasn't at all surprised when a strong arm circled her waist, the hand resting on her hip delivering a warning all on its own.

'It's time to whisk my beloved wife away, I believe,' he said to the nearest guests. 'I think I've shared her with you all for long enough.'

Good-humoured ribbing and laughter followed and within a minute applause heralded their definitive exit.

She allowed him to guide her across the room, his easy smile belying the tension rippling through his body. It wasn't until they were outside on the terrace that she spotted the helicopter at the end of the lavish landscaped garden, its rotors slowly picking up speed.

She remembered then that somewhere on the endless itinerary was an item she'd paid very little attention to: *honeymoon in Cordoba.*

Her feet dragged, her senses spinning as she kicked herself for not paying more attention to it. Her hesitancy drew Cayetano's attention. His own feet slowed, then he stopped altogether. Before she could act, he was drawing her close. Mareka opened her mouth, desperate indignation burning another path through her.

'Before you say something you might regret, remember we still have an audience,' he warned silkily. 'We've come this far, *mi esposa.* Let's not ruin everything now, *si*?' The back of his fingers drifted down her cheeks as he issued the warning.

But she was on the last of her reserves of stoicism. 'What would you care about not ruining anything?'

He leaned in, brushed the tip of his nose over hers and, on the pretext of mimicking a kiss, he breathed, 'I'm moments away from shutting you up as the only way I know how to salvage whatever is causing this riot within you.'

She gasped. 'You have a nerve. If you don't want to concern myself about your feelings, that's fine. But don't you dare demand that I turn mine on and off like a tap. Besides, you've got what you wanted now. I think I've fulfilled my part, don't you?'

His eyes flared just that small fraction, then it narrowed before his gaze dashed to the left. The action drew her own gaze. Her pulse leapt when she saw that their guests had indeed gathered on the terrace high above the garden and were watching them.

And, almost in the same space of awareness, she felt Caye's hands reposition over her body. One hand drifted down her arm and over her waist to hold her still. The fingers caressing her cheek only moments ago slid to her nape, curling warmly and solidly to hold her still.

Without warning, he bent her backwards in a romantic dip that made the terrace erupt with applause. Then he did the thing he'd threatened and sealed her mouth with his. The riot he'd mocked just moments ago erupted inside her but it was created entirely by the feel of his mouth moving over hers, not the righteous anguish blazing in her heart.

And, yes, Mareka hated herself for every second she allowed him to toy with her for the sake of their audience. Every second she secretly relished his touch when she should've pushed him away.

Dizzy when he pulled away, her response was pure self-preservation. 'What next? You're going to get on your knees and remove my garter with your teeth?' she threw out tartly.

'I would if you were wearing one.'

'How do you know I'm not?'

A strange light glinted in his eyes. 'Because I pay attention, *querida*. To everything.'

'Is that supposed to scare me or reassure me? Because, I'll tell you now, it's doing neither.'

'Then I'll have to work harder, won't I?'

'This is funny to you, isn't it?'

'What are we talking about, exactly?'

'Are you serious? Did you hear what I said two minutes ago?'

He grimaced. 'All I see is an overwrought bride.'

'An overwrought bride you don't care one jot about,

isn't that right?' she whispered, those sharp spikes digging deeper.

Another gleam came in those hypnotising eyes. 'Why, dear wife, I don't remember us agreeing to *care* for one another.'

The breath strangled in her lungs and once again her heartbeat thudded in her ears. 'You're right. I'm being a fool. But I didn't think you'd be so surprisingly cruel.'

He stiffened, then his eyes shadowed. And once again she was stunned by the mercurial emotions swirling in the eyes of the man she'd only recently thought was an unbreakable enigma.

Cayetano straightened, still holding her firmly in his arms. Ignoring their audience, he swung her into his arms and strode for the helicopter.

Just before they boarded, he lowered his lips to her ear. 'Perhaps learning that this early is for the best, *querida*. Now neither of us will be disappointed.'

The words ricocheted in her head for the fifty minutes they were transported to another of Cayetano's lavish residences, this one in Cordoba.

Perhaps it was her emotional agitation, or the fact that she'd already become numb by the sheer scale of Cayetano's wealth, that her stunning surroundings failed to move her.

The sun had just set but remnants of fading light shone over the light stone building, casting it in a golden glow. But all Mareka could concentrate on were the fingers wrapped around hers despite their lack of audience as he led her into the villa in which they would be spending the next week.

She'd discarded the train to her dress after the ceremony, the clever design having transformed it from ceremonial dress into an elegant ball gown that enabled her to move freely. So, when she yanked her hand free the moment they stepped into the opulent living room, she could move away unhindered, her glare warning him to stay away as she wrapped her arms around her middle.

Cayetano eyed her for a moment, then sighed. 'This wasn't quite how I envisaged our first evening as man and wife going.'

She scoffed. 'Do me a favour and stop trying to act the beleaguered husband. As you said yourself, outside of an audience you don't really care about my feelings.' She glanced around, the need to put more distance between them growing more imperative by the second. She needed to before any more of those traitorous tears betrayed her again. 'Is there a housekeeper around, or should I just pick the first room with a bed in it?'

He didn't reply, just watched her in that intense way that made her fear he could see deep beneath her skin. Right into the heart of her, in fact.

Unable and unwilling to withstand it, she rushed towards the door. He stepped into her path before she was even halfway across the room.

'I will allow disagreement. What I won't allow is prolonged friction.'

'That's funny, I don't seem to recall that being a specific requirement in our contract.' She threw out a halting hand when he opened his mouth. 'You seem to think you control me, Cayetano. That I'll let you treat me however you want. You may think I'm some low trash, but I won't take insults from you.'

He frowned. 'I don't think lowly of you.'

Anger snapped at the leash holding her temper tightly. 'Really? I didn't exactly hear you leap to my defence when your father called me a little Miss Nobody.'

His jaw tightened. She was sure he wasn't done, but she was.

Weariness sapped at her physically and emotionally. Suddenly, every strenuous second of the past two weeks rushed at her, draining her of energy. 'I've fulfilled my end of the bargain. So just let me be.'

He watched her for an uncomfortable stretch. Then, as if accurately guessing that he wouldn't get anything more from her, Cayetano nodded.

As if summoned by his employer's will alone, the living room doors opened and a short, middle-aged butler walked in. With a few words exchanged between his employer and him, the older man, expression as neutral as a blank canvas, bowed and ushered Mareka out.

She didn't bother to say goodnight to her husband.

He had proved conclusively that she was just a cog in the wheel of his greater plans. Beyond that, she was as inconsequential to Cayetano Figueroa as she was to her parents.

CHAPTER SEVEN

CAYETANO SHUT THE double doors to his private suite behind him, barely suppressing the urge to slam it. Leaning against it, he dragged his hands down his face.

Everything had gone off-kilter, it seemed, from the moment this morning he'd spotted his now mother-in-law lurking in the hallway outside Mareka's room and had felt it imperative to find out what she was up to.

No, scratch that. He knew exactly when the derailment had started—when he'd invited his parents to his wedding. That had been his first mistake. True to form, they'd attempted to manipulate him the first chance they'd got.

He shook his head, despising the swell of bitterness in his gut that they couldn't even pretend to be happy for him, even if that happiness was not really genuine. That they'd mocked him for that brief display of emotion…

And then there'd been Mareka's parents. He'd been stunned that such cold, uncaring creatures could have produced a woman who tried not to but inevitably wore her heart on her sleeve. A woman who'd somehow made being out of her depth in the lofty and cutthroat echelons of Buenos Aires society a fascinating spectacle he'd been increasingly absorbed in observing.

As for the way he'd lashed out at her…

He replayed the conversation in his study, teeth clenched as it unfolded. He could blame his parents and the turbulent emotions they inevitably dragged out of him. *Dios mio*, was this what he'd been reduced to—blaming his flawed parents for his inability to control his own bitterness and disappointment?

He jerked his head back against the door, raising his eyes to the ceiling. 'Thanks for nothing, old man,' he muttered under his breath. 'I hope you're happy, wherever you are.'

He shoved himself off the door, absolutely determined not to be driven insane by this emotional circus he couldn't seem to escape. But, even as he crossed the room to the drinks cabinet, shards of guilt pierced him.

Had he been too harsh with her?

Yes, came the hissed inner voice. He'd gone too far, taken out as frustrations on the wrong person.

But the unwanted well of sympathy in her eyes, as if she knew what he was suffering… *She had no right.*

He snapped open the top button of his suddenly restrictive shirt. But, even after it was loose, shackles of shame knotted his shoulders, Mareka's pained expression flashing in his mind's eye.

He sat down for barely a second before he was upright again, pacing his private living room to disperse feelings he wasn't used to. Feelings that had curiously developed shoots since that night back in London two weeks ago, when the idea of marrying his British PA had first popped into his head.

He could stay on his lofty perch, safe in his conviction that he'd done nothing wrong—that his righteous pique was well-earned. Or he could ensure that this marriage of convenience didn't start off on the wrong foot.

He had enough experience with letting things fester to know that it wasn't a good idea. Hell, hadn't he been apprehensive about her going through with this sham marriage in the first place? The last thing he wanted was to push her into doing something foolish such as triggering the fault clause in their agreement.

Grim-jawed, he headed out of the door again. Urgency gripped him, but that too he tossed on the pile of insane incidents he didn't want to fully acknowledge, never mind dissect.

In under a minute, he was rapping on her door. Seconds felt like hours as he waited, sweat beading the edges of his temple as he waited for her to answer. When she did, she opened the door a mere crack, her dull gaze dragging slowly up from his feet, taking her time, as if she couldn't stand to look at his face.

He wanted to be annoyed with her, but a different tingling took hold of him—as had happened far too often when this woman looked at him with expressive eyes, the effect of which he suspected she had little inkling.

'Come to rub more salt into the wound?' Her voice was stiff, a little shaky, and a whole lot affronted.

Caye opened his mouth, but the words rehearsed on his way over dried up. He shook his head. 'Not quite. Invite me in.'

Raised eyebrows questioned his audacity and promised more fire. And again there was that stirring in his blood. The urge that had driven him to explore her body, to kiss her not only before they'd been married but afterwards, on the lawn, when the compulsion had grown too fierce to resist as she'd stared him down.

'Why would I want to do that?'

He took a half-step closer, glorying in the escalated pulse racing at her throat. 'It's our wedding night,' he replied because, damn it, something about her made him a little crazy. 'Some would say it's practically a crime not to spend at least some of the night together.'

Her eyes widened a fraction, then narrowed, flashing vicious warning. 'I don't know what you're playing at but it's been a long day. I'd like to get to bed, so please just say what you came to say. Then you *will* be leaving,' she insisted.

Leaning against the doorjamb only delivered him a deeper sample of her alluring scent. That off-kilter feeling sharpened. 'I may have been a little harsh earlier,' he confessed.

'May?' she challenged, a beautifully shaped eyebrow arched.

He pressed his lips together. 'I'd really rather not have this conversation with a door between us.' A door she clung to. Examining her closer, Caye got the faint sense that he was missing something. Was she paler than she'd been before?

'Really? This Little Miss Nobody got the impression the conversation was over.'

Damn. As he'd suspected, that slur had pierced the deepest. He debated walking away, but this strain would be there in the morning, and Cayetano didn't want that. Inhaling sharply, he did something he'd never done before—he dipped into his past.

'My father has an unfortunate habit of zeroing in on the things he thinks I care about and…destroying them,' he bit out, jerking upright when she winced and paled further.

'What do you mean?'

'It means that jumping to your defence in that moment would've only made his attacks more vicious.'

'So you let him insult me…to spare me?' Her voice brimmed with scepticism.

'You heard most of our conversation. Do they strike you as people who wouldn't sink to such a level?' he quipped, bitterness searing every word.

Again, something soft and accommodating filled her eyes. He hated himself—and, yes, perhaps her—for the powerful urge to grasp it; wrap it around himself. 'No, I suppose not,' she murmured, then winced.

Cayetano frowned. 'What's wrong?'

She shook her head. 'I… It's noth—'

'It's clearly something,' he cut her off. 'The quicker you tell me, the quicker you'll be able to get rid of me.' The same compulsion had him pushing the door as he spoke, his breath expelling harshly as he saw the state of her hand. '*Dios mio*, what did you do?'

She flinched at his harsh question—something else he'd have to apologise for later. Dropping onto his haunches, he brushed his fingers over hers in silent enquiry. When she flexed her fingers, he examined the two-inch cut slanting across her wrist. Digging his free hand into his pocket, he wrapped the handkerchief over the bleeding cut. 'How did this happen?'

'A series of hilarious mishaps worthy of a comedy skit,' she said, although the visible pain on her face made a mockery of that explanation.

He had to forcibly loosen his clenched jaw. 'I'm not laughing, Mareka. Why the hell would you not mention it when I knocked?' Another question was why he was so unnerved by the sight of her in pain. Since he didn't care for the answer, he rose and, for the second time today, he swept his wife into his arms.

'You're really going to have to stop doing that, you know.'

'Why? Are you going to stop me?' He headed for the bathroom, only to stop in the doorway when he saw the broken glass on the floor. Carefully navigating the minor carnage, he set her down at the wide vanity table. 'Stay.'

As he turned away, he saw her roll her eyes.

Despite the unfamiliar stress turning his gut into mincemeat, his mouth twitched as he went to fetch the first-aid box. On his return, he spotted her wedding dress crumpled in one corner of the bathroom. Until then, Cayetano hadn't fully registered what she was wearing. He looked now and one of the many knots in his gut surged into his throat.

The white lace teddy clung like a second skin beneath the thin layer of her silk robe, the ties of which were loose enough to show her body from neck to thighs. The combination of lace, an abundance of tumbling dark-gold hair and her skin, having gained a deeper glow since her arrival in Buenos Aires, made his fingers tingle with the need to touch. Hunger such as he didn't remember plagued him, urging him to explore.

'Are you just going to stand there with the kit while I bleed to death?'

Dios mio, the way she spoke to him! He tried to recall when he'd been foolish enough to believe her timid or unremarkable.

He bit back a growl when he saw the bloodstains on the sleeve of her gown. Flicking on the tap, he held her hand beneath the cool flow to wash off the worst of the blood, his temperature rising when her pulse jumped beneath his fingers. 'You still haven't told me what happened,' he bit out gruffly. Too many disturbing scenarios darted through his brain and he particularly hated the one taunting him that perhaps he was the reason she was hurt.

Santo cielo. Surely not? He looked up in time to catch the perplexed look on her face. 'What?'

'You looked almost…ill there for a moment. You're not squeamish at the sight of blood, are you?'

Cayetano took her furled hand in his, ignoring the increased tingle in his own. 'I'm not.' Gently coaxing open her hands, he surveyed the damage, then exhaled in minor relief. The cut wasn't deep. Dousing a cotton bud in antiseptic, he warned, 'This is going to sting. Perhaps it'll take your mind off it if you tell me what I want to know.'

She sighed and, when her soft breath brushed his jaw, Cayetano stiffened his body. It was that or lean in and ask her to do it again.

'It's not really a big deal. I was trying to get out of my wedding dress; I underestimated how much effort went into securing me into the thing. I knocked the vase off the vanity and cut myself when I reached for it.' Her hand jerked in his as the astringent liquid touched the wound.

'*Tranquilo... Lo siento...*' he murmured, abstractedly registering that he was gentling her in Spanish and that it worked. Her shoulders relaxed and she released the bottom lip she'd drawn between her teeth. He finished cleaning her hand and reached for the bandage. His hands obeyed his command to move gently, quickly, efficiently. But, everywhere else in his body, Cayetano couldn't control his reaction to her scent in his nostrils or the smoothness of her thighs. To those plump lips she kept gnawing.

Por el amor de Dios, why was his body insisting on behaving as if he were an untried schoolboy? 'You could've called for help.' There was that treacherous bite in his voice gain. He wasn't at all surprised when she responded with a glare.

'From whom? Your butler?'

The taunt was deliberate. She'd had no intention of asking Cayetano for help, and the thought of his middle-aged butler putting his hands on his wife... 'No, most definitely not Manuel.'

'Well, then.' She shrugged, dislodging one sleeve of her gown.

Hunger invaded harder, drawing his gaze to that expanse of silky-smooth skin where her neck and shoulder met. Perhaps he was weak or stressed, or knew when to face the challenge, but he allowed his gaze to roam where it wanted, to devour the way his hands, his mouth and his body wanted to.

And, when her breathing grew erratic, he revelled in it because, *Dios*, it felt good not to writhe through this hell alone. From the corner of his eye, he saw her slick her tongue over her lips once more and he focused there, the action an unwanted reminder that their last kiss had nowhere near satisfied him.

'Stop doing that!' Mareka regretted her outburst the moment it left her lips.

She'd so hoped to stay calm and collected, but he made it so hard. Between the shock of his appearance at her door, the flash of alarm across his face when he'd seen her hand, the gentleness of his tending and the soft, soothing words in Spanish, she was toast.

Hell, he'd even skated close to the outer rim of a reasonable apology for his earlier behaviour—one that had plucked at her disloyal heartstrings. But the sum of it had brought her to this point, the strain of holding back this rampant draw to him driving her out of her mind.

Almost resigned, she watched his eyebrows draw high, the merest hint of amusement twitching his sensual lips. 'I'm dying to know what cardinal sin I'm being accused of this time.'

She huffed out a breath. 'You know what you're doing. The staring at my face and my mouth.' She stopped and inhaled, willing calm. Then she exhaled in exasperation as he did the very thing she'd accused him of. 'It's…it's…'

'Turning you on?' he drawled, his voice low, gruff.

And, heaven help her, there was no point denying it. The evidence was right there, her body betraying her without mercy. She wasn't even sure who moved first, but somehow her thighs had widened and Cayetano had slotted his lean hips between them. All she had to do was lean forward so she could…she could…

She jerked back, not caring that she didn't get very far, the mirror at her back stopping her. 'Yes! Look, it's distracting, okay? We're not in public. You don't need to pretend you find me attractive. I'm... I'm fine now. You can go.'

He did the opposite, closing the gap between them. 'You think I don't find you attractive?' he challenged. His warm breath brushed her earlobe, creating a cascade of shivers over her skin. 'You think I'm not rock-hard right now, imagining the many ways I can get you naked and beneath me on that bed behind me?'

Her breath was snatched clean out of her lungs, his evocative, erotic words skyrocketing her pulse. 'W-what? No...'

His lips quirked but any trace of humour was scorched from the heat in his eyes. 'You seem shocked, *querida*. Why is that?'

Mareka shook her head. 'Because I'm not a fool. Because I'm not your type...'

His finger slid over her mouth, hushing her. She shook her head, halfway between irritated and intrigued, one of the many new states he could fling her into as easily as flicking on a light switch.

'Right here, right now, you're the only woman I see. The only woman I want.'

Words some other woman might have yearned to hear. Except...they were woefully *transient*, the unspoken implication that she was replaceable echoing desolately in her brain. She shook her head again, more for clarity than for anything else.

He sucked in a breath as her movement slid his finger over her lips...her *parted* lips.

Before she could stop herself, or debate the wisdom of her action, her tongue slid out, flicking over his warm flesh.

Another sharp intake of breath and he wrapped his whole hand over her jaw, cupped her nape and brought her close. 'There's the fire I crave.'

'You don't…crave me. You can't.'

He laughed wickedly and low, and so erotically her pelvis melted as heat flooded her. 'Is that a challenge?' he whispered, those mesmerising lips hovering dangerously close. 'Shall I prove to you just how wrong you are, *guapa*?'

The 'yes' her soul wanted to eject thankfully stayed trapped in her chest. Neon signs blazed that this was the height of foolishness, and yet the essential 'no' also remained jammed in her throat. 'This is insane,' she finally managed, even as her fingers twitched towards his lean waist, so tantalising close. It would be so easy to grab and hang onto him.

His face spasmed, then that small, enigmatic smile flashed. 'That we can both agree on.'

'It's been an…interesting few weeks.'

'Indeed, and perhaps we're being handed the tools to deal with it.'

The devilish coaxing in his words caused the melting sensation to intensify. But she strove to hang onto her resolve. Anything else would be catastrophic. 'You don't belong to me.' The fractured words were torn from deep inside, from a place she didn't want to examine. And, just because they made her feel oh, so vulnerable, she tossed in a defiant, 'And I don't belong to you.'

'Also true,' he said. 'But we can lend ourselves to each other just for this night. Just until the insanity passes, no?'

Until the insanity passes…

It was both a highly dangerous but excruciatingly seductive offer. As he'd suggested just now, the moment would be finite, but this time not in a way that would wrench her to pieces, because this would be purely physical…a carnal, mutually satisfying episode….wouldn't it?

What was he even suggesting—a kiss? A make-out session up to a point, then withdrawal? What if she couldn't hold herself back?

Firm fingers speared through her hair, his grip directing her to meet his gaze.

'You're over-thinking this,' he purred, his voice low and thick with need.

Her hands twitched again, then almost of their own volition rose to rest on her thighs, tantalisingly close but not completing the journey to touching him. 'Am I? Because I'm one hundred percent sure this wasn't what we agreed.'

His nostrils flared. 'Maybe not. But we thought we could resist this unstoppable need to have each other two weeks ago. Had I known it was impossible, I would've ensured it was very much in the small print.'

She tried to shake her head, but the formidable man planted in front of her didn't give her a chance, his grip tightening in a way that was deplorably erotic, need arrowing straight between her legs. Her nipples hardened, her blood heating and finally, *finally*, her thighs closed around him, tangling her legs with his.

His grunt was part-need, part-encouragement, all arrogant smugness. His gaze dropped to her heaving chest and the hard points of her arousal, his breath hissing out again, the barely tamed bulge behind his fly flexing with his need.

'You want me,' he declared in that same self-assured tone. Eyes fixed firmly on hers, he added, 'You want this.'

Heaven help her, she did. But one last spurt of rebellion wouldn't allow Mareka to surrender—not just yet. But she could tap into the sensation he'd stoked so effortlessly between them. So with a jagged moan, she surged forward, meeting the sensual lips already bearing down on hers.

Heat, desire and pure sensation flared high, driving them even closer. When Cayetano's tongue swiped over her lips, demanding entry, she freely gave it, starved for this act that felt as imperative as her next breath. He groaned when their tongues clashed, decadently tasting her with bold, hungry licks that drove up her insanity. Wanton, agitated breaths escaped them as they strained for more sensation and devoured what was offered.

He broke the kiss, his breathing harsh as his forehead rested on hers. 'Touch me.'

It was a gruff order, wrapped in savage need. She realised that, through all this, her hands had stayed off his body: perhaps she could take a modicum of satisfaction that a tiny fraction of her was safe. She finally raised her hands and slid them around his waist to pull him even closer.

His groan of encouragement spurred her into exploring the tight, packed muscles of his torso, trailing one hand up and over his chest before her nails dug into his nape, whimpering as her lips searched his for another kiss.

'*Si*. Just like that,' he encouraged.

Was she really doing this—throwing caution to the wind so soon?

It's your wedding night.

It was unconventional, and not at all what she'd envisaged for herself the few times she'd allowed her thoughts to drift into the future, but...

She'd already stepped way out of her comfort zone. What was one more step? The neon sign flashed brighter. But the taste of him, the feel of him... Mareka shuddered as Caye cupped her breast, his thumb torturing the sensitised peak. Heat pooled between her thighs, unfurling fresh need through her.

It was good, unlike anything she'd experienced before, which was why she whimpered again when he broke the kiss and drew back. 'Tell me you want me, *guapa*,' he ordered thickly.

'Yes,' she muttered.

Her greedy, roaming hand wandered below his belt and, in one uncommon move driven by need, she cupped his rigid length, gasping when she felt the power and girth of him.

'*Dios mio!* Not here. I need to see you, feel you properly.'

With that, he plucked her off the vanity table. Her legs tightened around him, bringing her heated centre into direct, searing contact with his steel-hard arousal. Her moan collided with his hiss, and she watched him squeeze his eyes shut for a moment before that molten gaze was directed on her once more.

The crunch of glass beneath his feet as he walked them out of the bathroom sparked a reminder of how they'd ended up there. But it was engulfed by bigger, more demanding flames. So, when her robe slithered off her shoulders in the trip between her bathroom and his bedroom, Mareka let it fall free. And, when Cayetano laid her across his bed, with her clad only in the lace teddy she'd worn for her wedding in a moment of 'why the hell not?', she let those flames move through her, destroying the layers of diffidence and disquiet she'd felt since the study incident.

She allowed her arms to land above her head, heart surging into her body when Cayetano paused as he straightened. He remained braced over her, one hand on the bed and the other on the third button of his shirt, and simply watched her…with fierce focus…with visible arousal…with *hunger*.

For someone who lived in a world where she was either an afterthought or totally forgotten, this was…stirringly *addictive*.

His gaze seared down her body, lingering at the vee of her thighs. 'Knees up.'

She didn't immediately comply. She yearned to see his reaction, to watch that hunger build along with his impatience. The very few occasions she'd seen Cayetano's patience fray had been eye-opening. It was a risky road to take, yes, but she wanted more of it. So she waited until his eyes darkened further, her thighs sliding together as she returned his stare.

'Seems like you're in the mood for dangerous games,' he said.

'Maybe.'

He reared upright and disposed of his shirt. The first sight of Cayetano's bare chest, and the packed muscles overlayed by golden skin, was intoxicating. Powerful enough to make her jerk her knees up, ready to give him what he wanted.

Sensual lips quirked as his hand went to his belt, her reaction fuelling his smugness. She might lose this thrilling little game but not without scoring a point or two. Arching her back, Mareka let her thighs fall open.

Cayetano sucked in a harsh breath, his fingers fumbling with his fly. A moment later, he abandoned undressing altogether to grasp her knees. Nudging them open, he stared at the heart of her covered with the thin layer of lace and muttered thickly in Spanish. The thrill intensified, making her moan, making her restless.

Without warning, Cayetano, the most powerful man she knew, dropped to his knees. But his power was in no way diminished. And he demonstrated it by dragging her body to the edge of the bed, his gaze on fire as he hooked the flimsy material aside, lowered his head and delivered a private kiss that yanked a scream from her throat.

'Oh! Oh, God!' She could barely breathe, her hands dropping down to grip his thick shoulders as her senses dove into free fall.

Green eyes hooked on hers over the undulation of her body, once again delivering that rabid scrutiny that electrified the magic he was delivering. 'Is it good, *guapa*?' he drawled.

Her fingers convulsed on his skin, digging in. 'You know it is.'

He lifted his head a fraction and laughed, low and wickedly. 'Why does that sound like another accusation?'

His mouth continued to wreck her even as he carried on the conversation and, for another deliciously puzzling reaction, it sent her closer to the edge. An edge he pushed her off with the next series of flicks of his tongue that made her scream. She came down from the best high of her life to find him braced over her, she a specimen once again pinned beneath his fierce regard.

'You were saying?'

'D-don't pretend you don't know. You're s-smug and arrogant because you're clever at everything!'

Shadows chased fleetingly across his face. 'At this, perhaps. But not quite everything.'

'Show me, then,' she challenged and, in the tense seconds that followed, wondered why she was pushing this, pushing him, after everything he'd said to her tonight and after she'd discovered just how easily he could wound her. For reasons she couldn't pin down, she didn't repel this man. Hell, she would go as far as to say she had the opposite effect on him. Even now, those eyes were fixed on her as if he couldn't look away. So why not press home her advantage, study him just as he seemed intent on studying her? 'Just one flaw.'

His nostrils flared. 'And why would I do that?'

'Just so I know you're human.' So she knew that the touch of vulnerability she'd glimpsed earlier hadn't been an aberration.

He contemplated her for a long stretch. She held her breath, the need to see beneath the formidable exterior clamouring. The need to learn what made him tick, what made him scared and what made him *happy*.

Mareka realised she wanted to know his *heart*.

Oh, God.

'Does this not feel incredibly human to you?' he enquired, his voice gruff, sexy and far too mind-wrecking.

Her eyes flew open. Before she could voice the question, he breached her heated core, surging into her with a forceful thrust that punched screaming pleasure from her throat.

'Answer me, wife,' he ground out against her ear.

'Yes! Oh, yes.' She lifted her hips as she gasped the words, meeting him halfway as he plunged back inside her.

It made him hiss. 'Ah, *si*. More of that.'

'Only if...if you do that again,' she returned.

Despite the strained control on his face, his teeth flashed in a feral grin. 'Even in this you fight and resist.' He pulled back and thrust deep again. 'Is this what you want?'

'Yes!' She gasped, pleasure tearing through her. 'Please. More!'

'*Si. Mucho más...*' He breathed other hot, sexy words against her heated skin but she was too far gone, too steeped in bliss, to make them out. All she knew was that he more than delivered, each penetration driving her towards a peak she both feared and embraced.

At some point she realised he was doing that thing again—watching her, absorbing her every reaction, perhaps even feeding off it. But this time, far from unnerving her, she revelled in it, tossing her head with feminine abandon, spiking her fingers through his hair until he hissed and groaned. Then she offered up her lips, whispering in a voice she barely recognised as her own, 'Kiss me.'

He did, and she met him lick for lick, stroke for stroke. Fanning the flames of desire so high, she knew she would either be born again on the other side or there'd be nothing left when he was done with her. Either way, she leapt off the peak and into bliss with a scream dragged from her soul. Ecstasy wrung her out but, even as Mareka slipped into the sweet oblivion of sleep, she feared those roots had found fertile ground.

That they were even now digging deeper into her heart.

He needed to get some sleep. To rest and rise with clarity and a fresh perspective on everything that had happened.

But Cayetano wasn't ready to be rid of her—not yet. Even now, his body stirred as he breathed the scent of alluring woman and sex and watched her sleep, wondering yet again just what it was that fascinated him about Mareka Dixon. No—Mareka *Figueroa*.

His gaze shifted from the lush fan of her eyelashes to the pulse thudding steadily at her throat, pausing at her plump, full breasts—shifting restlessly when his body stirred harder to life—before dropping to the rings on her finger.

The primal satisfaction that swelled through him at that very powerful evidence of their union was yet another puzzle he was sure would be resolved with sleep and distance. And he would strive for that distance. Nothing else would be acceptable because he absolutely didn't intend to go down the route his parents had.

He'd effectively distracted Mareka from probing deeper, of course. Revealing what others had dared to call his emotional deficiencies—and he labelled necessary safeguards—hadn't been part of his agenda tonight. Nor would it ever be. He'd already skated too close to losing control during that exchange with his parents.

Already, feelings were beginning to seep into the equation—feelings, disagreements, the need to placate—all of which had led them here, to her bed. At least the outcome hadn't been entirely disagreeable. They'd found mutual satisfaction, perhaps smoothed what had threatened to be a bumpy start to their convenient agreement.

Was he already attempting to justify himself? His disgruntled snort made her stir. For the first time in his life, he found himself holding his breath, not wanting to wake a woman and start the tedious process of disposing of her.

Instead, once she'd settled back against him, one smooth leg sliding over his in a way that made him bite back a groan, he brushed a whispered kiss across her temple.

Two hours later, when he still lay awake, fighting sleep, Cayetano forced himself to admit that the madness hadn't quite worn off yet. That this woman intrigued him far more than he'd been prepared to accept. Her defiance, her fearlessness—hell, even the way she didn't shy away from confronting him when he allowed his strong will and hard-earned ruthlessness to dictate his actions—was provocative. He hadn't been this intrigued in a long time. So maybe he shouldn't be in a rush to put this new...entanglement behind him.

He stared down at her, watched her eyelids flutter, then kissed them, gratified and not even a little bit regretful when she roused, blinking for a few seconds before her gaze flew to his.

'I woke you.'

Her gaze dropped to his mouth, then lower, her breathing growing rushed and beautifully agitated when she saw his erection. 'You did.' She breathed, her voice sexily husky. 'I'm guessing that was deliberate?'

He laughed, zeroing in on the target that commanded his interest—her mouth. '*Si, querida*. And I'm not even a little bit sorry.'

Once more, Cayetano promised himself sternly. Once more, then he would be done.

CHAPTER EIGHT

SHE INTERRUPTED THEIR heated kiss, tried to push him onto his back and failed. Cayetano pulled back to meet wide eyes sparking with fire.

He smiled. 'What is it? You want to be in control?'

A nervous bite of her lip, contradicting that siren-like display she'd tormented him with earlier, was followed by a jerky nod, her lashes dropping for a self-conscious moment before her gaze met his once more.

Heaven above, but even that abashed look made him hard. With brisk efficiency, he rolled them over and settled her over his lap. She moaned at his staff nudging her core, bold in its demand. Jaw tight, he drew his arms up, sliding them beneath the pillow, fully aware of how his flexing body held her mesmerised. Morning would come soon enough and with it the imperative clarity he sought. But he fully intended to enjoy the hours between now and when sanity returned.

'It's your show, *tesoro*. What are you waiting for?'

Mareka flushed at the daring challenge, knowing he was watching her every move. That dual sensation shivered through her again: she'd gone to sleep on a blissful cloud and woken to a dangerous, addictive paradise in the form of the breath-taking specimen of man whose last name she now shared.

The sane course of action would be to draw a line under the heady experience and retreat to her own bed. Instead, she dragged demanding nails down his chest, her insides twisting in delight when his jaw clenched in a visible, intoxicating fight for control.

She rolled her hips, curbing a smile when he hissed and dropped a thick curse. 'You owe me an answer, I think,' she said, unaware the words were coming until they spilled out. She held her breath as his eyes narrowed and his fingers dug into her thighs.

'How very wily you are, to believe you've got me under your mercy.'

'Have I not?' Who was this woman, speaking these words, playing the siren when in her few previous encounters she'd been painfully inhibited, relieved when the experience was over?

'Is this your flaw, then—impatience bordering on desperation?'

A hard smile mocked that observation. 'A little desperation isn't a vice. It reminds us that we're striving for something important—essential, even. I wouldn't call that a flaw but a challenge to reach that goal and satisfy what drives us.'

'I don't think you strike anyone as a man who's ever satisfied.'

'There's a reason sharks don't stop swimming, *querida*.'

The faintest warning in those words chilled her spine. 'So, you plan to live for ever on the edge of desperation, chasing the next goal?'

He gave a rich shrug. 'It's been a success so far, has it not? Why change a winning formula?'

She shook her head and pressed forward. 'In business, maybe. But I'm not interested in that. I'm interested in what feeds your soul—drives Cayetano, the man.'

His jaw clenched. Shadows rolled over his face, reminding her of the exchange she'd witnessed in the study—reminding her that, while he seemed wholly satisfied with his lot, part of him wasn't entirely invulnerable. And, as foolish as it was, that part called to her.

'You'll find there's little distinction between the two. I am what I am, *guapa*. Don't go searching for something that isn't there.'

The warning, like the one he'd issued before, was weighted. It hovered between them, threatening to cool the heat. But even that wasn't enough to dissolve the deep curiosity stirring inside her. She opened her mouth to…push for more? To tell him he should reconsider because…what… there was more to life than wealth and financial excellence?

What did she know? Her dream was still unrealised. What if the fulfilment she envisaged didn't materialise once she'd made it come true? What if in the end she still remained second best, still someone's afterthought? What if…?

The questions and her thoughts careened to a halt when he brushed his thumb over the tight bundle of nerves between her thighs. She gasped, her fingers digging into the tight muscles of his pecs.

'Your window for taking control is fast closing, *mi esposa*. Take it now or lose it,' he warned.

A firmer rotation over her clitoris by him and she was shuddering, no longer cold or distracted. Her head fell back, her skin tightening as pleasure stretched over her.

Clearly, he was done waiting for her. Done indulging her attempts to probe beneath his surface. And, as sensation climbed, it was easier to pretend there wasn't a hollow opening in her chest, that his rebuffing didn't hold echoes of her own past rejections.

It was easier still to rise onto her knees, grasp his rigid length where it throbbed ready and impatient between her thighs and impale herself upon it, her delighted cry drowning out his thick groan as pleasure suffused them.

She might have been on top, but Cayetano mastered her from underneath until she was a screaming mess, her throat raw from the sheer bliss of it.

The smell of coffee woke Mareka, but it was gut-churning panic that jerked her upright in bed. She glanced around, unsure whether to be relieved or disturbed that Cayetano wasn't in bed with her.

Catching sight of the beside clock, she guessed one possible reason why she was alone—it was approaching ten a.m.! Warily edging to the side of the bed, she stood up on wobbly feet, the enormity of last night's events unnerving her.

She'd slept with Cayetano—her boss, her husband, on paper—after having insisted on that very same paper that she wouldn't. Did that mean their agreement was now void?

And the things she'd demanded from him! What on earth had come over her? The sassy siren from last night had faded away in the morning light, leaving her very chagrined at her behaviour. Chagrined, panicked and blushingly sore in a way that left no doubt how sexually enthusiastic she'd been last night.

Sore and without a stitch to wear, because while she'd been in slumber-land the flimsy underwear that would've been a better covering than nothing had disappeared, along with Cayetano's discarded clothes.

She ventured towards the room she hoped was the bathroom. It turned out to be a dressing room larger than her whole London flat, with row upon row of impeccable bespoke suits and shirts lining one side and neatly stacked casual clothes on the other. But it lacked what she needed—a towel or a dressing gown to cover her body with.

Cringing at the thought of parading out naked—totally

out of the question—Mareka grabbed the nearest shirt, white, long-sleeved, in cotton so rich and soft it felt like silk. Knowing it had caressed Cayetano's body at some point heightened the electricity zipping through her body as she emerged from the dressing room.

To find the man in question striding in from his terrace. He froze at the sight of her but his eyes didn't. Despite the slight edge in the green depths, they conducted a thorough examination of her body, lingering on her exposed legs and his shirt before meeting hers. 'You're awake.'

Heat rushed into her face, recalling the last time he'd spoken similar words to her and what had come after—pleasure like she'd never known before. Even now the reminder pulsed between her legs, her heart beginning that wild, anticipatory hammer.

'You should've woken me earlier,' she said, self-consciousness climbing when her voice emerged hoarse and husky, another reminder of how she'd over-used it last night.

'Hmm, perhaps,' he murmured, walking closer, then stopped two arm-lengths away.

Confusion mingled with disappointment inside her. He'd left her in bed and now he was hesitating to come close. She hadn't intended this to go beyond one night, of course, but paradoxically the realisation that he wanted the same thing bruised that vulnerable place inside her.

Enough.

Her handful of experiences had never included morning-after awkwardness, thank goodness. But she would get through this. And, yes, she told herself she was relieved when he took a step back and turned away after another tense scrutiny of her face and body.

'Breakfast is waiting. Come.'

The pressure on her bladder stopped her from following him.

He paused, one eyebrow raised.

'Um…where's the bathroom?'

He nudged his chin forward. 'Through there. Come out to the terrace when you're done.'

She nodded and hurried away.

When she was done, she lingered before the mirror, holding her wrists under the cold tap in the hope that it would calm the roiling inside her. Mareka noticed that she couldn't quite meet her own gaze, couldn't comfortably confront the woman with sex-tousled hair and reddened, swollen lips after the first shocked glance.

But, knowing she couldn't stay in the bathroom, she sighed, turned off the tap and headed back out. Halfway across the vast bedroom, she heard him. The conversation was tense, delivered in brisk Spanish. It shouldn't have made her already knotted stomach tighten even more, but it did, the reminder that she was being quickly relegated to second-best the morning after her wedding striking deep.

Her steps faltered at the terrace doorway as she accepted what was happening to her—she was jealous. Searingly, blisteringly jealous of Cayetano's first love— his company.

It was a low feeling but one she couldn't help any more than as she could stop breathing. Taking a deep, stabilising breath, and vowing to deal with this unwanted feeling, she forced her feet to move.

The sight of Cayetano's tense, bare upper body exposed to the worshipping sun as he cradled the phone next to his ear, his other hand deep in his pocket, made her hesitate. The hard stone that wedged in her chest made it hard to breathe as she watched him turn and heard him bark something into the phone before he hung up. She watched him saunter over to where she stood, that neon sign she'd ignored mocking her with its brilliance.

His eyes narrowed and, once again, he stayed out of arm's reach.

When she couldn't stand that unnerving scrutiny any longer, she raised her chin. 'What? You're staring.'

His face hardened, and his eyes flicked over her shoulder in the direction of the very rumpled bed. 'You woke up in a bed you willingly slept in, *querida*. Therefore, there should be no wrong side to grumble about.'

Heat and irritation twisted inside her. 'Excuse me?'

He didn't answer immediately. He turned and walked towards the corner of the sun-splashed terrace, where a pristinely laid table held a sumptuous breakfast. When he reached it, he pulled out a chair, rested his hand on the back of it then quirked an eyebrow at her. 'Clearly, you're discontented about something. I'm speculating that it's not because you woke up on the wrong side of *my* bed.'

Mareka frowned.

She'd never thought she was a tightly closed book, but she hadn't imagined she was that easy to read either. But evidently one of Caye's many talents included a direct line to her thoughts because, the moment her traitorous gaze darted to the phone in his hand, his own features morphed from edgily neutral to hard, cynical amusement.

'Ah, I see.' He waved her to the seat and, lips pursed, she approached and sat down. Only to exhale sharply when he leaned forward and murmured in her ear, 'And this is where the proverbial claws and ultimatums come out, *si*?'

She tensed. 'I have no idea what you're talking about.'

He tossed the phone on the table, took his seat, reached for a cafetière and poured her coffee as if he didn't have a care in the world. Perhaps he didn't. After all, it was just *her* feelings in the way. And he'd warned her that he didn't deal with feelings, hadn't he? 'I'm assuming that my words are coming back to bite me in the butt,' he commented, nudging milk towards her.

'Cayetano, I don't—'

He held up his hand, and she bit back an unladylike curse. 'I was the one to…encourage a minor alteration in our agreement. And now you feel the door is open to make other demands, yes?' His even tone was in sharp contrast to the cynical disappointment reflected in his eyes.

The gall of him. Forcing herself to meet those incisive eyes, she aimed what she hoped was a carefree smile his way. 'I see why a man who lives and breathes for the next blood-stirring negotiation might feel that way. But you can rest easy that, in my case, you couldn't be more wrong if you tried.'

The flare of surprise was quickly doused by cynicism and narrowed-eyed suspicion. 'I'm extremely well-versed in the act of feinting, Mareka. I think we've established by now that I don't play games.'

'Neither do I. You think I'm about to make lofty demands just because we've slept together.' Praying he wouldn't see how her body eagerly reacted to the recollection, she continued, 'Be reassured that I don't want anything from you beyond what we agreed before we got married. Hell, I'll go as far as to encourage you to forget that last night happened at all. We can carry on as we'd intended to.'

He remained deathly still during her rambling. Now a muscle ticked in his jaw, a forbidding glint turning his eyes hauntingly beautiful…and extremely dangerous.

'You're serious.'

'Why wouldn't I be?' she parried, then let out a light laugh, which thankfully didn't sound as strained as it felt leaving her throat. 'Look, I'm sure you're used to women fawning over you the morning after and pleading with you for repeat performances. Thankfully, for both our sakes, I'm not one of those—'

His ringing phone interrupted her. Mareka clenched her jaw. 'Aren't you going to get that?'

His own jaw tightened. 'No.'

She looked away and took her time serving herself some scrambled eggs, a buttery croissant and a small bowl of fruit, painfully aware he was watching her the whole time. 'Don't stop yourself on my account.'

Displeasure pulsed from him, his lips thinning. Then, in a lightning-fast motion, he stabbed the reject button and tossed the phone away.

'Why did you do that?' she enquired coolly, forking a piece of melon and popping it into her mouth.

'Because I don't wish to speak to my grasping, conniving parents. Especially not today. And also, because we're in the middle of a discussion.'

Oh, yes, the edge was back in his voice. Had they been discussing anything other than last night or the unsettling subject of parental relationships, Mareka would've been amused. As it was, she was playing the role of a lifetime, pretending to be blasé about the most memorable night of her life.

'Are we? Oh. I thought we were done.' She tossed in a moue of irritation and watched his chest rise in a slow inhale.

'No, *mi esposa*. You had just finished expressing how last night was no big deal to you. Except, unfortunately for you, I know different. Your inexperience gives you away.'

She almost choked swallowing the melon. And, *damn him*, his lips quirked just before he poured a glass of water and set it down in front of her. Mareka didn't touch it. And she didn't glare, despite yearning to do so. 'I beg your pardon?'

'Even without the benefit of having you in my bed last

night, I knew beforehand you've only had two notable relationships.'

'How…? You had a report done on me?'

'Are you surprised? Weren't you lauding my business acumen only a short while ago?'

'But that…that was…'

He raised an eyebrow when she stumbled to a halt. 'Yes?'

Her appetite fast withering away, Mareka set down her fork. 'I can be inexperienced and still not care to repeat what happened last night,' she felt compelled to insist.

Her breath shuddered through her lungs, her heart leaping in betrayal at how much it wanted that to happen.

I don't love her… I may barely even know her… I don't plan on letting capricious emotions stand in the way of securing my birthright…

She repeated those harsh words to herself, knowing that, no matter how tempting repeating last night might be, she valued her self-worth more than that.

'You wanted me last night. You still do. It would be no trouble at all to refresh your memory.'

Mareka swallowed, the unshakeable certainty in his voice intensely disarming. She shook her head. 'A refresher won't be necessary.'

'Why not? Because you still feel me inside you, *guapa*?' he enquired so silkily, she felt the intoxicating effect echo through her as if he was touching her.

Her fingers curled around the edge of the table. 'Have you stopped to consider that not letting this…brief entanglement…happen again might be as good for you as it is for me?' His amusement evaporated but she pressed ahead. 'What was it you said—that I shouldn't make the mistake of developing feelings for you?'

She attempted a laugh again, and silently fist-pumped when she pulled it off once more. 'You're totally off-base, of course. But, since you seem to think you're entirely irresistible, why would you want to risk even a mild infatuation when you can chalk this up as the event it was?'

'And what label is it to be slotted under?'

'Wedding night madness? An itch scratched? We're both adults. We don't even need to define it as one thing or another.'

His lips thinned and he glanced off over the terrace for several seconds before refocusing on her. 'Do you really mean that? Or is that a placeholder statement until you're ready to admit your true feelings on the issue?' he taunted.

Recognising that she was nearing the peak of her performance of nonchalance, that she risked her composure crumbling, she rose and set her folded napkin primly on the table, disregarding the fact that she was wearing a shirt...*his* shirt...and nothing else. 'Yes, Cayetano, I really mean that.'

Fortunately, his phone began to ring again. Frustration gleamed aggressively in his eyes.

'You should answer your parents. Or it is business? I guess you didn't send the memo that you're on your honeymoon?'

'As one of my PAs, you know perfectly well that my business doesn't have set hours. My temporary marital status was never going to change that.'

The reminder of the impermanent nature of their pact hit home hard, even as the phone continued to shrill. 'Great, then I'll leave you to discuss your business.'

She headed for the French doors, praying she made it out in one piece. The slight hitch in her step came when he pushed back his chair, ostensibly to attend to his neglected phone.

Mareka told herself she was relieved when he barked out an irritated, *'Si?'* a moment later.

But, long after she'd returned to the sanctuary of her

room, had taken off his shirt and entered a bathroom swept clean of broken glass—long after she'd scrubbed herself clean of last night's debauchery, hoping it would lessen the searing memory of it—that knot remained hard, unsettling and taunting her with its vibrant existence.

From her new, breathtakingly gorgeous wardrobe, she selected a light, halter-neck maxi dress. The sleeveless, backless design left her arms and back cool…and, no, she didn't choose the moss-green colour because it reminded her of Cayetano's eyes. She'd merely learned to dress for the hot climate.

Tying her hair in a loose ponytail, she rubbed sun-protection lotion over her exposed limbs and face, then finished with a slide of colourless lip gloss.

Then, seeing Cayetano's shirt on her bed, she snatched it up. She couldn't exactly wipe her memory clean of what she'd done last night, but the last thing she needed was a visible reminder.

But she hesitated as she neared Caye's suite. Would it be better just to hand it over to one of the maids? God, how hopeless was she if she couldn't stop her face burning over such a simple thing? Clicking her tongue in impatience, she strode to his bedroom door, knocked, waited for a minute and then, when she didn't get a response, turned the knob. He probably wouldn't hear her if he was still out on the terrace.

The room was empty and, curiously, there were no sounds coming from the terrace. Her already unsettled emotions took a lower dive when it struck her that he might already have gone down to his study and started his work day—the day after his wedding.

Had she hoped that after their argument he'd change his mind? Change *who* he was? Shaking her head at her naivety, she headed for the dressing room, only to freeze when she sensed him behind her.

Turning, she felt her jaw sag. 'Oh, I thought…'

He froze when he saw her, his eyes darting all over her before coming to rest on her face. *'Si?'*

She tried desperately to suppress the effect of his mouth-watering body. Last night, she'd been too overwhelmed to take him in fully. Now, confronting a fully naked Cayet-ano, heat suffused her from head to toe. He'd just stepped out of the bathroom, the towel riffling through his hair the only piece of clothing on his body.

When she didn't answer, his gaze dropped to the shirt clutched in her fist. 'What are you doing?' he rasped.

It took every scrap of willpower she had not to drop her gaze below his neck. 'Putting back your shirt,' she replied. Her hand gripped the expensive cotton a little too tightly, almost as if she didn't want to let it go. But she had to. It was entirely too significant a reminder that she was getting used to this. *To him.* And she couldn't afford that.

His gaze darkened, then he shook his head. 'Keep it.'

'Why? I don't need it any more.'

His nostrils flared. 'I have three-dozen more. I'd prefer not to become fixated on just this one because it's been on your body,' he said with a dry edge.

She sensed that, while he hadn't hesitated to reply, he wasn't altogether thrilled about admitting what was tanta-mount to a need—perhaps even a *yearning*. It was such a total, disarming reflection of what she was fighting, justi-fying extreme caution. So why did the thought fizz up her blood, excite her enough to send heat into her face?

The answers to that remained locked inside when he closed the space between them. One finger slotted beneath her chin, tilting her face to his gaze. 'I'm not in the mood

to argue with you, *guapa*. Not when I've taken the day off
just to spend it with you.'

'What?'

His mouth twisted in sardonic amusement. 'Shocking,
I know.'

Her traitorous insides leapt with giddy delight, just before she slammed the lid on the wild joy. 'You didn't need
to do that.'

'It's already done,' he said simply, imperiously. Then
his eyes roved over her dress. 'Although, you will need to
change your delightful dress.'

'Why, what are we doing?'

'I thought we'd start in the stables and see where we end
up. I have a few horses who have been missing my presence
for a while. Have you ridden before?'

Was it insane that the knot shrunk just that little bit? 'I
took lessons one summer a long time ago, when I was a
teenager.' Her parents had made friends with a horse enthu-
siast and academic who'd been well-positioned to offer her
father a tenured professorship. Mareka's sole job that summer had been to befriend the academic's teenage daughter.

'Then you're not a complete novice.' His gaze dropped
to the shirt for several beats before he shook himself out of
whatever thought had gripped him. 'Meet me downstairs
in ten minutes.'

CHAPTER NINE

MAREKA TOLD HERSELF that she was going along because she'd questioned what to do with herself today. Since they were in Argentina, all work fell under Octavia Moreno's remit, and the last thing Mareka felt like doing was clashing with her.

Besides, any outside activity would be a welcome distraction for things she didn't want to think about. And if Cayetano, the consummate workaholic, had taken a day off...

Ignoring the voice teasing her for making wild excuses, she re-entered her suite and crossed to the dressing room. Relieved that her new wardrobe came with five sets of jodhpurs and matching tops, she reached for a green set, once again ignoring the mocking voice. So what if she wanted to wear green today? It was just a colour, for heaven's sake! Done with more than five minutes to spare, she snatched the shirt off the dressing room island, bundled it into a ball and stuffed it in her underwear drawer.

Out of sight and all that...

Downstairs, Mareka drifted towards the living room, returning greetings from curious staff as she went. The living room was even more stunning than she remembered. A grand fireplace over which hung an exquisite painting immediately drew the eye as the focal point. From there, two groupings of contemporary furniture and plush rugs blended comfort with tasteful opulence, the kind she'd come to associate with Cayetano.

She'd just perched on one overstuffed chair when he walked in. For a second, she was glad she was sitting down.

He looked... *magnificent*. The all-white of his riding gear was sharply contrasted by a black belt and polished black boots. The way his polo shirt emphasised the breadth of his shoulders, and the trousers his lean, athletic hips, made Mareka's mouth dry. Finger-combed damp black hair made her fingers tingle with the urge to run though the lustrous waves. She was trying to process the depressingly acute reaction of her body when he stopped in front of her.

'First things first,' he rasped.

Her heart jumped into her throat, but he only reached for her hand. Lifting it, he inspected the bandage that was still mostly in place.

'How does it feel?' he murmured.

'Oh. It's...fine. Just some mild discomfort.'

He nodded, then turned to the newly materialised butler, who held out a first-aid kit. Five minutes later, her cut was redressed with the kind of gentleness and care that left Mareka with the circumspect notion that her husband wasn't the cold, cutthroat individual he wanted projected.

A prospect that weaved deeper within her, leaving her shaky and bewildered as they stepped outside to a waiting electric buggy. Because, in letting that possibility take root, Mareka knew that guarded, vulnerable place within her that wanted someone to...*care* was softening, making way for the impossible.

'Everything okay?'

She startled. 'Of course, why do you ask?'

'Because you vowed to seize the day and yet you look positively pensive.' His gaze dropped to her hand. 'Is it your hand? I didn't hurt you, did I?' he asked sharply.

And there it was again, that increased softening. She shook her head equally sharply to dispel the frightening sensation. 'No. I'm fine.'

His gaze lingered on her for another stretch, then he aimed it at the small hill they were climbing. Cayetano's estate was vast, with groupings of buildings dotted in the distance. After travelling for about ten minutes, they arrived at a long, low wooden building, the equine smell announcing the stables before they pulled up in front of large barn-like doors.

Several stable hands greeted them with respectful smiles, their eyes lingering curiously on Mareka. An older man with salt-and-pepper hair and weathered features stepped forward and shook hands with Caye.

'This is Andrés. He's the head of my stables.'

A small smile cracked the man's face. *'Bienvenida, señora,'* he said in a raspy voice.

Shaking his hand, she returned his smile. *'Gracias.'*

That his eyes twinkled at her attempt to speak Spanish lit up a warm place in her belly. Before she could caution herself for getting too carried away with this soft, warm feeling that might come back to bite her down the road, Caye was guiding her into the stables, his hand splayed on her lower back.

She told herself they were in public, that this was what they'd agreed. Yet, she couldn't help but melt into his touch or stop her body from swaying closer to his. From the heated glance he sent her, he'd caught the betraying movement. And, as they went deeper into the stables, she couldn't help a muted gasp when his hand drifted lower, lightly cupping her backside, before it dropped away.

Her body lit up like the inside of a volcano. Blood roaring in her ears, she didn't make out what Caye said when they stopped in front of a half-door. But she got the gist of it, another gasp leaving her as she saw the creature within.

The stunning horse with a shiny, caramel-gold coat and

chocolate-brown eyes, watched Mareka carefully as she approached, then nudged her the moment she reached touching distance. From somewhere, Caye produced a wedge of apple and held it out to Mareka.

The moment she was fed the treat, the mare nudged her again. 'She's the calmest in my stable. But she can also be quite demanding,' Caye said drily.

'She's beautiful. What's her name?'

'Caramelo. A little obvious, but suitable, *si*?'

It took far too much effort to look away from Caye's indulgent smile as he ran his hand down the beautiful horse's forehead. After murmuring to her for a minute, he turned to Mareka. 'Are you ready?'

She inhaled deeply. 'As I'll ever be.'

At Caye's nod, Andrés opened the door and led the mare out. Caye moved a few doors down. A minute later, he led out a black stallion, whose dark eyes surveyed them before he threw his head back in imperious outrage.

Watching the two formidable creatures was like watching a theatre play of dominance. Cayetano won, of course, mounting the saddle with smooth, masculine grace that sent a pulse of desire straight through Mareka. She strove for even a fraction of that poise when Andrés helped her onto the saddle. A three-minute refresher course—thankfully easy enough, because muscle memory kicked in—and they were heading over another shallow hill. Two more, and the estate was spread out before them.

They rode in companionable silence for fifteen minutes before the vista was broken up by towering cypress trees.

'It's beautiful here,' Mareka murmured.

'*Si,*' he breathed. 'Sometimes I forget.'

She glanced at him, surprised at the touch of bewildered nostalgia on his face. 'Because you rarely take time off to enjoy the fruits of your labour?' And maybe it was the stunning vista, or the air seeping pleasure into her bloodstream, that pushed her to continue, 'We seem to be doing things that are outside of our norms.'

His eyes glinted in that breath-catching way. Then, his face growing taut, he shrugged. 'But I daresay we'll revert to type soon enough.'

He sounded so completely certain that it struck discordantly within her, triggering that absurd need to challenge him—yet again.

Reading her emotions, one corner of his mouth twitched. 'Are those sparks I see, *guapa*?'

She sucked in a breath and resolutely shook her head. 'No. Not at all. I've decided it's too lovely a day to spend it disagreeing with you.'

Was that disappointment dulling the glint in his eyes? His shrug a second later shattered that notion. 'A wise decision.'

He'd taken the day off.

The concept was as foreign to Cayetano as the low rumble of temper simmering beneath his skin, resistant to every attempt to dislodge it. Octavia had been equally as shocked when he'd issued the unheard-of instruction to cancel every appointment in his diary for the next twenty-four hours, leaving his opinionated and increasingly supercilious PA lost for words. He'd gone one better and instructed that Octavia herself should not contact him unless the world itself was on fire.

Knowing that not only were company matters on hold but that his parents couldn't contact him again—couldn't fill his head with harsh but ultimately empty threats that emphasised their avaricious intentions—produced a hollow relief he hadn't expected. And, no, he wasn't about to dwell on the fact that both his mother and father had forgotten what today's date meant. If he didn't talk to them, then he didn't risk betraying that, after all this time, it still seared that they'd forgotten. As they'd forgotten so many milestones in the past.

He'd taken a day off and he'd experienced a peculiar satisfaction in powering off his phone for the first time in... hell...he couldn't remember. When he'd stepped into a cold shower after that, he'd hoped it would restore sense and wash away this ache and need pounding through him, but no. Every breath searched for *her* scent; every rush of the water over his skin had triggered a yearning for *her* touch.

He'd never strayed close to dependence on anything or anyone, and yet, as he'd stepped out of his bathroom this morning, he'd feared that he'd developed a taste for his new wife that couldn't be shrugged off the morning after.

The scent of pine mixed with the smells of smoked meat from the distant *parillas* soothed him a little, but he couldn't take his eyes off the woman as comfortable on his mare as if she'd been born in the saddle. Her initial nerves had evaporated and, from the swing of her ponytail to the delicious curves of her bottom, her ease drew his eye.

Hell, *everything* seemed to draw his attention—including how she'd casually dismissed any prospect of a repeat of last night with a shocking resolve that'd unsettled Cayetano and, if he was brutally honest, bewildered him.

It wasn't because she hadn't found pleasure in his bed. She had—from the way she'd screamed her pleasure, the way her nails had dug into him, her unfettered responses and demand for satisfaction fuelling his desire like never before. *Dios*, he was getting hard just thinking about it and since when had he allowed himself to be led by his body?

He clicked his tongue and his horse increased its speed to match hers. 'Enjoying the ride?'

She blushed, and a strange, rough calm rumbled within him. Misery loving company? Desire fuelling unwise desire?

Her gaze swept down to the mare, and a punch of something absurdly resembling jealousy struck him when she smiled at her and ran a hand down her neck. 'She's a dream.'

He curbed the absurd urge to demand the same touch from her. To tell her he'd given up his day for her and therefore was entitled to satisfaction too. He bit his tongue because he wasn't a needy child. He hadn't been one since he'd recognised that he needed to grow up fast if he didn't want to be trampled on the battlefield of his self-absorbed parents' toxic marriage.

'Does the air always smell like this?' she asked.

He grasped the lifeline to suppress thoughts of his childhood and his parents. 'Like you're in an evergreen forest but with a possibility of discovering barbecue in the middle of a fiesta around every corner?'

Surprised laughter spilled from her. The sound, light and far too delightful, burrowed deep inside him, somewhere he knew he couldn't reach to discard it very quickly.

'Yes. It's fascinating. And also hell if you're hungry.'

He frowned, recalling she'd barely eaten anything before the disagreement had disrupted their breakfast. 'Are you?'

She shrugged. 'I can wait till lunch…'

Her response trailed off to nothing because, seeing a worker tending one of the many posts, Cayetano beckoned him over.

'What did you say to him?' Mareka asked when the young man had hurried off to relay Cayetano's instructions.

'Ensuring my wife doesn't go hungry.'

The colour deepened in her cheeks. 'Oh, you didn't have to do that. I would—'

'We were set to have a picnic in an hour. I'm merely bringing it forward. No big deal.'

No big deal.

For the next half-hour, Mareka wavered between being

touched and fighting to seal up that vulnerable spot inside, torn between being angry and hurt that something
that seemed so simple to him was gaining such significance
to her. Because when had anyone cared *this* much for her
comfort and wellbeing?

'Mareka?'

She jumped, then realised he'd stopped, dismounted and
was staring at her while she grappled with something that
was *no big deal* to him.

'Yes?'

He tossed his reins around the branch of a nearby tree
before he strode towards her, loose-limbed and annoyingly
breath-taking. 'I said we're stopping here.'

'Oh. Okay.'

He watched her for a moment, then raised his arms. Her
heart leapt into her throat. Again. At this rate, the organ
would wear itself out before she completed her first day as
Mrs Cayetano Figueroa. She glanced at the ground, judging whether she could make it down on her own, because
she could really do with her emotions calming down a little around him.

'You've injured yourself once,' he said wryly, accurately
guessing her thoughts. 'Let's not add another injury so soon,
hmm?'

Another wave of heat sweeping up her face, she pursed
her lips and settled her hands on his shoulders. A smooth,
effortless swing and she was on her feet in front of him.

As predicted, his scent immediately attacked her. She
turned her head before she took a deeper breath, then con-
sciously pulled away, striding over to gaze at the vista. Cayetano followed after dealing with the mare, standing far
too close for her roiling senses. To distract herself, Mareka
said the first thing that entered her head. 'This looks like

the sort of place that stays in families for generations. Did you grow up here?'

He stiffened, then shrugged. 'On and off. This was my grandfather's primary residence. I tried to spend as much time here with him as I could when circumstances permitted.'

'Circumstances?' she probed gently. 'Are you talking about your parents?'

His profile grew even more remote. 'My parents aren't a subject I normally discuss if I can help it.' The words were clipped out, his closed-off expression discouraging further interest on the subject.

'Ah, but didn't we agree today was not a normal day?'

The eyes that met her flared with surprise despite the hardness lingering. Then it turned to speculation. It was almost as if he was considering her response, not dismissing her out of hand.

The feeling that came with that notion was…warming. But, when the silence stretched, she started to accept that the feeling had been premature. He wasn't about to open up about what she suspected had been his turbulent childhood just because they were acting out of character.

He opened his mouth, but the gentle whine of an electric engine stopped him. Turning, she saw the young man Cayetano had sent off earlier riding towards them in a buggy. In the bed of the vehicle, a large picnic basket and accompanying accessories were stacked high. Cayetano pointed to the right, giving instructions that the man followed, turning the buggy and driving deeper into the woods.

'Come,' Cayetano said to her. 'Let's get you fed.'

That warmth returned even after she noticed that the stiffness didn't leave his face. Five minutes later, Mareka gasped in delight as they emerged into a circle of trees dissected by a wide, shallow stream. On either side of the stream, the ground was carpeted with soft grass. On the near side, their picnic was laid out on wide, soft blankets, colourful cushions tossed out in a welcoming setting that made a curious lump lodge in her throat.

It was beautiful, serene, thoughtful. And that warmth was expanding, threatening to engulf her whole heart. She jumped a little when Caye grasped her arm and led her to the blanket. She settled down on one end and he took the other. Mareka didn't mind when he chose silence, grabbing a plate and heaping it high with slices of delicious looking grilled meats, warm bread and heavenly smelling chimi-churri that made her mouth water.

They ate, Caye occasionally stiffening and staring off into the distance. Mareka curbed the urge to ask him what he was thinking. It was none of her business. Besides, this had turned out to be the perfect way to spend the Sunday after her wedding, even if that wedding had been for a more clinical purpose than most people thought. She didn't want to ruin it.

'This place was my escape when things got a little too… volatile at home,' he said suddenly, disrupting the calm with the bombshell.

Mareka's heart thudded. 'Volatile? You mean…?'

He shook his head immediately. 'The volatility wasn't directed at me.' His lips twisted with a bleak bitterness that knifed through her. 'My childhood mostly involved my parents being too busy tearing chunks out of each other to be concerned with where I was on their battlefield. My grandfather was a firm believer that every marriage was meant to be, that disagreements worked themselves out eventually.' His jaw clenched once before it relaxed. 'It took him a while to realise that his son's might not be the union made in heaven he'd hoped it would be. That he couldn't even trust him to take over his company after he was gone.'

'And that the adverse effect on his grandson wasn't something he could keep ignoring?'

His head whipped towards her, his expression once again of mild surprise.

She shrugged. 'Don't look so surprised. When you're constantly on the outside of a relationship, whether it's perfect or not, you tend to notice how things should be. When it's great, you slot it into the pros column for what you want for yourself. When it's not, you know what to avoid when you have the chance. Either way, with enough exposure, you learn a few things.'

He absorbed her words for a long stretch, then his mouth tightened. 'I was well past an impressionable age when my grandfather decided that exposing me to his own union might alter my view on things.'

Mareka's heart lurched, an unknown tightness gripping her nape. 'The way you say that… It's as if…'

'He failed?'

Her nod was jerky. 'Did he?'

One corner of his mouth twisted. 'What he failed to realise was that his own marriage to my grandmother wasn't perfect either. They just learned to handle it better than my parents did.'

'That sounds uncannily like you think you know the code to a perfect marriage,' she said, attempting a lightness she didn't feel.

'Absolutely. It's to stay as far away from believing a perfect marriage is possible. Or stay away from marriage altogether.'

An icy-cold sensation froze out the last of the warmth. She was glad she'd managed to eat something before now because, just like this morning, her appetite deserted her with shocking speed. 'So, because you can't have it all, your solution is to have nothing at all?' Her voice was tight with too much emotion, causing her heart to lurch again, because she didn't care for how much his bleak conclusions affected her.

Hell, *she* didn't want to know why it bruised her so deeply. Yet she couldn't stop probing. 'And what about children? Do you plan to leave all of this to your offspring or is all that driven ambition just for self-gratification?'

His eyes blazed green fire. Apparently, she'd hit a nerve. 'I'm lucky enough to live in a time of great scientific innovation. If I ever feel the urge to procreate, there are ingenious ways to do so without trapping myself in a marriage,' he clipped out.

Mareka sprang to her feet, the urge to get away from his emotionless outlook too strong to contain. Tense silence echoed behind her but she felt his gaze on her as she stalked to the edge of the stream.

The sun was highest in the sky, relentless heat beating down on her. On a wild whim, Mareka tugged off her riding boots. The jodhpurs were a little too tight to pull up but they were stretchy enough that she managed to yank them up to her knees. In her bare feet, she waded into the shallow water.

'Mareka, you need to be careful. The bottom can be—'

She yelped, not expecting him to be this close. Turning far too quickly, she lost her footing on slippery stones. Her arms windmilling wildly, she let out another cry as she toppled, landing with a loud splash in the stream. The water closed over her for a handful of seconds before firm, strong hands wrapped around her waist and dragged her out.

Coughing and spluttering, mostly out of embarrassment, Mareka gripped his shoulders as he walked them both to the bank. By the time he set her on her feet, they were both totally drenched. His shirt was plastered to his body, the white turning translucent to reveal the tight six-pack beneath.

Her mouth dried, her fingers convulsively digging into

his shoulders to stop herself from the insane need to explore his body. In turn, his eyes grew heated as they trailed over her body.

Pushing away from him before she succumbed to insanity, Mareka stumbled back to the picnic blanket, grimacing at the discomfort of the sticky cotton. She plucked at her top for a moment then, spotting the extra blanket, she gritted her teeth and tugged it off.

The sharply inhaled breath behind snapped her attention to him. His eyes were glued to her skin, his eyes still dark with latent heat. 'Insisting that what happened last night isn't going to happen again then undressing in front of me seems especially barbaric, no?' he mused, the rough edge back in his voice. Then, with a mocking look, he yanked his own polo shirt off and tossed it away. 'Especially on my birthday.'

She gasped, her eyes going wide. 'It's your birthday?'

There was a mixture of mockery and a flash of bleakness. '*Si,*' he responded simply, his eyes fixed on her.

She examined his face, trying to read him deeper as their earlier conversation tumbled through her mind. 'When you said you didn't want to speak to your parents "especially not today" you meant…?'

'That I didn't want to engage with parents who called to make financial demands without bothering to wish their son *feliz cumpleaños*, most likely because they'd forgotten? Exactly so.'

Her feet carried her to him before she could think better of it. She stopped when she was close enough to feel his body heat, but stopped short of touching him. It was best not to. 'For what it's worth, I'm sorry.'

He stiffened for a moment, then he jerked out a nod.

Her heart dancing erratically in her chest, the melting started again as she added, 'Happy birthday, Caye.'

Green eyes darkened to almost black. *'Gracias,'* he said gruffly.

His chest heaved, reminding her just how undressed he… they *both* were. She slid off her jodhpurs, her face heating when she felt his gaze follow her with an avidness that stole her breath. Part of her almost wished the earlier iciness was back because, as she'd learned to her cost, the warmth was dangerous and misleading to her heart.

But he was walking towards her, reaching for the blanket and unfurling it. And she drunk him in, her arousal snapping over her like a silken net, trapping her within its unbreakable confines. Her gaze lingered on the droplets of water clinging to his vibrant olive skin, her mouth watering with the urge to lick them off. She moaned as he wrapped the blanket around her, then tugged her forward until barely a foot separated them.

His gaze left her face, trailed down to her chest and the scrap of shamrock-green satin and lace covering her breasts, then lowered to the matching panties.

'You have more items to take off,' he rasped, his voice a rough rumble.

The flames engulfing her intensified but she managed to shake her head. 'I don't think…'

'They'll dry quicker if you take them off.'

Glancing down at his sodden boxers, she raised an eyebrow. With a tight, far too distracting smile, he left the blanket draped on her shoulders and whipped off his boxers.

Mareka's eyes widened at the thick, unabashed erection that sprang free. When her gaze flicked up to his, his bold dare taunted her. Lamenting how quickly he dragged her into these dangerous games, she reached behind her and unsnapped her bra clasp. It was oh, so vain to revel in his thick swallow as she tossed the wet fabric away; to thrill in the sweet ache of her beaded nipples and the thick desire unfurling through her as she dragged off her panties.

Between one breath and the other, they were clutching each other, feasting on each other as greedy lips and frantic hands chased pleasure.

When the need to catch their breaths forced them apart, Cayetano's forehead dropped to hers. 'How do you do this to me?' he rasped roughly against her lips.

'Do what?' she gasped.

'Make me forget myself so completely. So damn frequently.'

'I… Are you blaming me for the way you feel?'

His grating laugh tightened her skin. 'That would be as futile as blaming the sun for rising. I'm guessing this is a *me* problem. No, *querida*, I'm blaming myself because I haven't been able to quite work you out.'

She wasn't sure whether to be flattered or disarmed. Giving up on deciphering yet another puzzle, she boldly wrapped her hand around his rigid length, her senses leaping at his thick groan. She threw her head back when he started kissing his way down her neck and chest, gasping when he drew one nipple into his mouth.

Within a minute, she was spread out on the blanket and he was raining hot kisses on her inner thigh. Her fingers spiked into his hair as his mouth found her, but she was too impatient. She needed him in another way that wouldn't be denied.

'Caye…please. Take me.'

His head reared up, eyes smouldering delicious, dangerous fire as he dropped one last kiss on her thigh and prowled his way up her body. She held her breath as he nudged her centre, then moaned in sublime pleasure as he entered her.

It was a soul-searing kind of pleasure. The skin-to-skin sensation earth-shattering…

Wait…

Skin to skin.

She tensed, a layer of pleasure vanishing.

'What is it? What's…?' Cayetano froze mid-speech, the thought careening through her head slamming into his too.

His face morphed into a harsh mask of disbelief as he throbbed inside her. Then he pulled out, rolling away, his pallor increasing as his haunted eyes searched hers. 'Last night. We didn't…'

Mareka snatched up the discarded blanket and wrapped it tightly around herself. 'No, we didn't.'

His expression turned even more haggard. *'Dios mio…'* He breathed in stark disbelief. Then he vaulted upright, his magnificent body, now a pillar of colossal tension, striding away from her. He bit out the two words a couple more times before he whirled towards her.

'I've never done that before.' It wasn't an accusation, but it was a statement of deep disbelief and displeasure.

'I'm glad to hear it, but it doesn't take away the fact that it happened.'

His hands dragged down his face, impossibly making him look even bleaker. 'I'm healthy. You have nothing to worry about there,' he bit out.

The ice crept closer, the realisation that she'd been so careless clawing at her. 'Again, I'm glad to hear it, but that isn't the entire issue, is it?' Her insides flipped over as she said the words, stark reality rushing at her like a runaway freight train.

Agitated fingers spiked through his hair as he pierced her with those incisive eyes. 'The responsibility was more mine than yours, but I have to ask…are you on the pill?' The question was flat, devoid of inflexion. But his eyes gave him away. *Everything* hung on her answer.

Mareka swallowed, her heart thumping with the truth

she had to deliver. 'I was… I am… But I missed a couple of days last week, and this morning,' she whispered.

His face tightened until she was sure he'd turned to stone. *'Dios.'*

'I wasn't expecting what happened,' she felt compelled to say. Then, something sharp and awful drilling through her chest, she added, 'We can discuss the morning-after pill if you—'

'No, I do not.' A feral growl rumbled the ground beneath her, the dark flames in his eyes warning her that subject was off the table.

And, as much as she wanted to call up her feminine outrage and challenge that raw edict, Mareka backed away from that debate because she realised, deep down, she didn't want to go down that route either. Regardless of the consequences, she would allow fate to take its course.

But, despite that visceral response, Cayetano didn't look any less bleak about the prospect that she might be…

Pregnant.

The word ricocheted through her brain, a huff of shock leaving her throat as it sunk in deeper. Beneath the blanket, her fingers brushed over her belly, stroking it before she could stop herself. Then she snatched her fingers away, the spike of growing elation frightening the hell out of her. Until she knew, until they were one hundred percent sure, she was tossing weighty emotion on an already turbulent situation.

'Look, we might be worrying about nothing,' she started, but he shook his head, his movements jerky as his fingers speared his hair once more.

'On the contrary, we can't afford not to think carefully about this. Planned or unplanned, bringing a child into the world requires an essential level of commitment.'

Her heart plummeted to her feet as she recalled their conversation only a short while ago. 'And you're not ready to provide that commitment, of course. Because this is as far from the clinical procedure you outlined for yourself some time in the distant future, right?'

Fury flashed across his face. 'Don't put words in my mouth, Mareka.'

She waited and watched him pace, his expression growing grimmer by the second. She opened her mouth to tell him not to bother finding words, that she could read his body language loud and clear.

'When will we know?' he fired at her.

Her face heated. 'My period is next week. A simple test might work if I miss it, but a blood test in a few weeks will confirm either way.'

A muscle ticked in his jaw, then he resumed pacing.

'Can you…can you put something on, please?' She might have cast aside her inhibitions minutes ago, but she wasn't quite ready to embrace the brazen nudity he so comfortably exhibited.

He sent her a speaking glance before stalking over to snatch up his boxers and shove them back on. Then his hands bunched at his sides, his head shaking in disbelief.

'What?'

A cynical little smile curled lips that wreaked sweet havoc on her less than fifteen minutes ago. 'I think my earlier point is well made.'

'What do you mean?'

There came a clench and release of his jaw. 'I mean we've barely been married for a day and look where we are.'

The sun glinted off her rings just then, as if winking in agreement. A spark of anger lit through the miasma of emotions. 'A fake marriage and a possible pregnancy you don't want with a woman you barely know or care about? Unfortunately for you, the first was your idea and the second, well, that's on both of us. As for the third…' She stopped, breathing at the fresh anguish of the reminder. Then she lifted her chin. 'If it makes you less freaked out, I'll take responsibility for this.'

'I am not *freaked out*,' he delivered through gritted teeth.

She allowed herself a small smile. 'You're making a valiant show of that from where I'm—'

'And, if there is a child, I will most definitely take responsibility.' He ploughed on as if she hadn't spoken, again with the same feral viciousness with which he'd vetoed the morning-after pill.

Somewhere deep inside a knot loosened, but Mareka refused to consider it. Not here. Not now. Because, with his words spoken, Cayetano was snatching up his remaining clothes. Mareka reached for hers too, half-relieved to see that, while they weren't completely dried, they weren't still sodden either. After wrestling herself into them, she retied her hair.

But, when she started towards her horse, Cayetano stepped in front of her. 'Leave her. She'll be collected later. You'll ride back with me.'

She blinked. 'Why?'

His jaw worked as if he didn't want to say the words. 'If you're pregnant, I don't want to risk you falling off.'

'But you said she's the gentlest, and nothing happened on the way over.'

His Adam's apple bobbed but he still shook his head. 'It's not a risk I'm prepared to take,' he stated implacably.

And so Mareka found herself seated in front of Cayetano, his solid torso, arms and thighs braced around her as they made their way back to the villa in charged silence, the journey taking twice as long as before, because it seemed Cayetano Figueroa, whether he'd ever wanted a child or not, was downright primal in protecting the child his wife of convenience might be carrying.

CHAPTER TEN

CAYETANO WAS USED to fearlessly negotiating billion-dollar deals where the wrong word or a delicate ego might mean the difference between winning or losing. He'd never flinched from those challenges and, ten times out of ten, he'd come out on top.

He was flinching now.

Every ripple of horseflesh beneath his thighs ploughed fear through his gut. He wondered why he was putting himself through this. Why hadn't he simply waited for the stable hand to turn up with the buggy to collect their picnic and exchange their horses for a different, safer form of transport?

The answer blazed through his brain. Because the need to put much-needed distance between himself and the bombshell Mareka had delivered had been *paramount*. Because he hadn't been able to contain it there on the spot, where between picnic, cloudless sky and babbling stream the world had looked deceptively idyllic. Where, even in the cold depths of his shock, he had experienced that visceral punch of emotion he'd never have believed himself capable of—*primal possessiveness of his unborn child.*

This was what came of turning off his phone and leaving it two miles away. This was what happened when he recklessly pursued desire.

Dulce cielo.

A shudder went through him as the potential conse-quences of his actions unravelled inside him. Having felt his reaction, Mareka turned and glanced at him, her hazel gaze searching his. He returned the look, probing hers in turn to see how she truly felt. She'd said words that had trig-gered base emotions, but had she meant them? Or had they been as empty as the childhood promises his mother used to make when she'd needed his cooperation to use him to volley shots at his father?

Mareka turned away sharply, her face pinching at what-ever she'd read on his. It didn't matter, Cayetano assured himself. Nothing mattered until they knew the truth.

Then what? What the hell did he know about being a father, never mind a good one? Only this morning, on his birthday, his own father had called to manipulate and ex-tort him. He stared at Mareka, potentially the mother of his child, at the flat belly he'd kissed on his way to experienc-ing a dangerous heaven.

Had he damned himself by voicing his hypothetical fu-ture intentions? An intention he'd expressed in the abstract because he'd never expected to be thrust neck deep into *this*.

His hands tightened on the reins, causing the horse to toss his head. Panic flared once more, and his arm banded Mareka's middle before he took his next breath.

'*Calma. Tranquilo,*' he muttered to the horse, while se-curing her body tighter to his.

She stiffened. 'I'm fine.'

The assurance bounced off him, attempted to settle, but his turbulent emotions wouldn't let it. Thankfully for them both, the villa came into view just then. He was sure she breathed a sigh of relief. But all Cayetano could compute was that there was a real chance he was staring down the bar-rel of fatherhood. And that there were deplorably high odds he would fail at this vital task because *he* had been failed.

* * *

They were barely indoors before Cayetano walked away from her. Mareka had expected it, of course. Yet the ache arrived, sharp and enduring, leaching the last shred of hope from her bones.

Returning to her suite, she looked around blankly, unable to fathom how much her world had turned upside down in the space of a day. This time yesterday, she'd been standing in front of the mirror, wondering what her marriage of convenience would entail.

How quickly she'd found out. With jerky movements, she undressed, tossed her damp clothes in the laundry basket and, for the second time in as many hours, stepped into the shower, washing away the effects of another eventful interaction with Cayetano.

Catching sight of herself in the mirror afterwards, she hurriedly dropped the hand that had somehow found its way back to her belly. At this rate, she'd trigger wild rumours across the tabloids before she'd established for herself whether or not she was carrying Cayetano's child.

The last two weeks had shown her just how well-known her husband was in Argentina. Mareka's own name and image had been splashed alongside his. As much as she wanted to find out one way or another, going out to buy a pregnancy kit from a pharmacy would only invite unwanted speculation.

But…she could order one online.

Grabbing her phone, Mareka paused when she saw the alert from her bank. Activating the app, she inhaled sharply at the sight of her bank balance. Somewhere between last night and this morning, Cayetano had stayed true to his word. She was now officially a millionaire. On any other day, the endless zeros would've drawn more than a little awe. And, yes, when she got over the potential mind-blowing reality she faced, she would start putting the money to the essential use she'd targeted it for.

For now, she couldn't think beyond the plot twist she'd landed herself in by giving into her desires. Groaning, she tossed the phone away, lay back on the bed, tried to slow her runaway heartbeat and to just...*think*.

No matter what happened, she wanted this baby. And not in the way her own parents had taken her arrival—she wanted hers to *love*, to *cherish*. Wanted to imbue it with so much self-esteem it would be coming out of his or her ears. Everything Mareka had been deprived of, she would triple for her child.

If there was a child. Suppressing the deep well of dismay that accompanied the possibility that she might not be pregnant, she reached for her phone. Within minutes, the test was ordered, delivery arranged for the day after she expected her period. She might well be delivering a different message to Cayetano next week. But, deep in her heart, Mareka suspected her life was about to change.

The first change happened at dinner time, when one of the many maids arrived to tell her that the *señor* was tied up so Mareka would be eating on her own. She only forced herself to eat because already her brain was twisting and turning with the need to stay healthy, considering what she could and couldn't consume, what might harm the baby. She knew she drew curious gazes from the butler and rest of the staff when she enquired what ingredients were in the food, but she couldn't be bothered by that. There *could* be a more important element in her life now.

Nevertheless, it was a relief to escape back to her suite. And, when sleep eluded her—when she spent a self-pitying ten minutes lamenting her lack of trusted friends to call or an understanding mother who could've helped her deal with

the rollercoaster of emotions that whizzed through her—
Mareka resolutely grabbed her laptop, propped herself up
on the lounger on her terrace and went to work on the second most important thing in her life.

She worked until the sun peeked over the hills on the
horizon. When a yawn caught her by surprise, she smiled,
the new purpose she'd set in motion warming up a cold,
anxious place in her heart.

Although she managed to sleep the moment her head
touched the pillow, she was up again in four hours. Deciding
she wasn't going to cower in her room, she dressed and went
downstairs to find that Cayetano had left. She was about to
ask the staff the humiliating question of where exactly her
husband had gone when a text pinged on her phone.

Left for an unavoidable appointment. Will be back late. C

The optimistic outlook she'd woken with took a dive. Apparently, the fake honeymoon neither of them had wanted
was already over. She ate then donned a stunning bikini she
would never have picked out for herself in a million years,
but which looked surprisingly good on her. Then, with her
laptop in tow once more, Mareka spent the day by the sparkling half-Olympic-sized pool.

The various emails she'd sent last night about her charity
had already gained responses, some from prominent women
in Buenos Aires eager to meet with her. She didn't kid herself that her new status as Cayetano's wife had nothing to
do with it, but she wasn't going to look this particular gift
horse in the mouth.

After setting up meetings for the coming week, she went
for a swim, grateful for the low burn in her muscles that
made her tired enough to fall asleep beneath the large um-
brella. When the housekeeper shook her gently awake, the

sun was low in the sky. Surprised, she sat up. 'How long have I been asleep?'

The older woman smiled. 'Only a few hours, *señora*. The *señor* asked us not to disturb you but I think you need a drink, no?'

'The *señor*... How did he know I was...? Did he call?' She hated the hope in her voice.

The housekeeper nodded but Mareka saw the way she avoided her gaze. '*Si*, but only to say he would not be home for dinner.'

Was that a hint of disapproval in her voice? What did it matter? Cayetano intended to carry on as normal. The quicker she took a leaf out of his book, the better. She accepted a guava and ginger punch drink, then headed inside.

She was most definitely not going to wait up for Cayetano that night, and she didn't, or on the ten nights that followed.

On the night she heard the rev of his powerful sports car just before midnight, for some reason she fell asleep soon after, her senses absurdly calmer. And, when she went down bright and early the next morning to find Cayetano seated at the table in a smaller but no less gorgeous, sun-drenched room, she was glad of her hard-fought composure.

He was dressed in his impeccable formal attire of light-blue shirt, pinstriped trousers and dark tie, with his jacket draped over the chair next to him. The financial newspaper she usually ensured he had in London was folded next to his plate, and Mareka knew he'd already consumed everything there was to know for today in the business world. One of his many talents was speed-reading with astonishing efficiency.

His gaze snapped up at her entry, then conducted a thorough examination of her body. By the time it returned to hers, heat was rising, engulfing her.

'Are you well?' he rasped, his gaze probing.

Did he mean her or the baby she might be carrying? Despite the bolstering speeches she'd given herself, echoes of past hurts hollowed her out. Sucking in a breath, she attempted to suppress the ache. 'Yes. I'm fine.'

His weighted gaze assessed her for another minute before he rose and pulled out her chair. Murmuring her thanks, she sat and sipped at some orange juice while the butler placed a perfectly made, mouth-watering omelette in front of her. Apparently her appetite had returned in full force because she devoured it in record time, much to the satisfaction of the man watching her with hawk-like focus.

Mareka decided she wasn't going to read anything into it. Cayetano's single-minded focus would remain unsettling for ever, whether she was carrying his child or not. Starting as she meant to go on, she cleared her throat. 'We never clarified my professional role while our marriage is in place.'

He stiffened, his eyes piercing hers. 'As my wife, you have the right to any available position you want within my company. But I'll leave the decision to you.'

She took a breath, hesitated then said the words that left a hollow of loss inside her, despite knowing deep down she was doing the right thing. 'In that case, I'm officially resigning as your PA.'

A flash of surprise was quickly erased by displeasure. 'To do what, exactly? You're not going to work for someone else,' he stated with a steel-edged voice.

'Not that you can stop me, exactly, but no, I wasn't planning on jumping ship. Well, only so far as I intend it to be my own ship.'

His eyes narrowed. 'Explain.'

'I don't intend to sit around twiddling my thumbs while you jet off wherever. I'm… I'm starting a women's empowerment charity.' She held her breath, waiting for signs of mockery. When surprisingly it didn't arrive, she pressed on. 'I'm in the process of setting up preliminary meetings.'

Surprise lit his eyes but again it was overshadowed by deep wariness. 'Kudos to you. But you won't exert yourself and harm the child.'

She breathed through the twin sensations of being touched that he cared but dismayed that the care was mainly for his child.

'First of all, we don't even know if there is a child,' she replied, even though her certainty grew firmer by the second.

Especially since yesterday had come and gone with no sign of her period.

'Even if there is, the *child* is barely even a bundle of cells right now. Women have been known to work right up until birthing a child, you know.'

A healthy fraction of that primal gleam he'd delivered that day by the stream lit his eyes. 'I don't care about other women.'

They both froze at that, their gazes clashing for several seconds before yanking away to redirect elsewhere. She absolutely wasn't going to read anything into that. Hell, hadn't he spelled out that he could never care for her only a week or so ago?

This was all about the child she might be carrying.

Mareka struggled to contain the hurt and busied herself cutting up the fruit on her plate while Cayetano poured himself an espresso. Tossing it back, he immediately poured himself another. This one he nestled in the saucer, his fingers absently caressing the delicate cup. She envied him the ability to ingest so much caffeine, knowing she'd be a hyperactive wreck if she even tried more than one cup. Could she even drink coffee now?

'What are you thinking?' he asked abruptly.

She flicked him a wary glance, then blurted, 'Coffee. I was wondering if I could drink it if I'm...'

His green gaze dropped to her belly for a split second. 'You can, in small amounts. But decaf is best for pregnant women.'

'You've read up on the diet for a good pregnancy?'

He arched his eyebrow. 'You think I would not?'

She wasn't ready to admit how strongly that affected her heart and how it foolishly leapt with something close to joy. 'Like I said, we don't know one way or another yet.'

Another throb of silence echoed between them, then he reached beneath the newspaper. 'This was delivered for you half an hour ago.' He set down a rectangular package next to her plate. 'If my guess is right as to what it contains, then you're as eager to know as I am.'

At her raised brow, he produced a glossy paper bag which had been out of sight near his feet. Peering into it, she saw several pregnancy tests. 'You bought five? I got two.'

His powerful shoulders shrugged. 'Between us we have enough to make sure without a shadow of doubt, no?'

Her fingers shook as she reached for her juice. 'We...?' Of course he planned to be part of this. 'I thought you would be too busy.'

His lips firmed. 'You continue to make assumptions. Be careful, *querida*: I will only indulge you so far. Now, finish your breakfast.'

He passed her a bowl of fruit. She wanted to refuse his order on principle, but the orange and peach segments looked too succulent to resist. Still, she tossed him a glare, which he responded to with a conceited arched brow before he picked up his tablet.

The moment she was done, he rose and pulled back her chair. Every step of the way back upstairs, her heart clamoured in her chest. On the last step, she stumbled.

Strong, firm hands caught her, his sharp inhale echoing in the large space.

'Tranquilo.'

She glanced at him. He'd lost a shade of colour but otherwise he remained as suave and in control as she was flustered.

'Thanks.'

His response was a brisk nod, his gaze fixed on her bedroom door as he led her inside. She felt his tension as he dropped his hands and shoved them into his pockets. She'd thought he'd start pacing but he stopped in the middle of her bedroom, a formidable presence awaiting an outcome he hadn't anticipated.

She learned that outcome five minutes later, three of the seven tests announcing that she was indeed pregnant. And when she opened the door he only needed one look at her face to know.

A shudder went through him, and he lost another layer of colour. But Cayetano Figueroa, the man she was indelibly tied to for the rest of her life, strode forward an instant later, the epitome of power and control. 'My doctor will be in touch with you today. He'll arrange for a blood test and the necessary pre-natal regime. And I presume you'll want to keep this confidential for now?'

'I…yes. But don't you want to discuss…anything else?'

His eyes narrowed with suspicion. 'Anything like what? You're carrying my child. In nine months, you'll deliver it and we will endeavour to be the best parents we can be. There's nothing more to discuss.'

Oh, yes, there was…so much more. But she knew she was in shock, despite having fully braced herself for just this outcome. So, when he closed the gap between her and caught her chin in his hand, Mareka could do nothing but stare at him.

'Mareka…'

'What?'

He exhaled long and slowly. 'I'm leaving now. The house-keeper and the rest of the staff will be on hand if you need anything.'

He seemed to be waiting for something as he continued to stare down at her. At her jerky nod, his lips firmed. Then, obviously accepting she wasn't about to speak, Caye dropped his hand and walked out.

Mareka stumbled over to the bed and sank down onto it. She was going to be a mother—most likely, a single mother. Because, even this early on, she knew there was no way she could continue with this clinical marriage with Cayetano when the three years were up. Hell, he might want his freedom long before that.

She released a shaky breath and this time, when her hand stole over her belly, she allowed it to rest, allowed the feeling to settle and sink deep. Then she made solemn, silent promises to her unborn child—promises to protect, love, nurture and defend it, no matter what.

Awed and purpose-filled, Mareka was composed and waiting when the doctor arrived two hours later. She couldn't dwell on the fact that she missed Cayetano's presence with an acuteness that was terrifying and shocking. She would wean this rabid need. *She had to.*

Alone again, she spent another afternoon on her laptop, working with a few breaks until a shadow fell over her. She looked up to find Cayetano standing next to the lounger. 'You're back.'

His face shuttered. 'You don't need to sound so disappointed.'

'I'm…not. I'm just surprised…' She looked around. The

sun was just starting to go down. 'I thought you'd be late, that's all.'

'I'm told you've been out here all day.' There was light censure in his tone.

She bristled, then hated how that made her feel *alive*. How his masculine scent washing over her made her want to take huge, gulping breaths. 'Your spy network is on point, I see.'

His sculpted features grew stonier. 'You wish to fight, *guapa*, despite the specifically heated way our skirmishes end?' he asked in a dangerously silken voice.

And, as she was floundering in blazing recollection, he hitched up his trousers and settled down on the lounger next to hers. Feeling her bikini-clad body's Pavlovian reaction, she pulled up her knees and wrapped her arms around them. 'What do you want?' she muttered.

The flash of ire mingled with something that looked like…hurt disappointment. 'To see how the appointment with the doctor went. And to invite you to lunch tomorrow.'

Paradoxically, the giddiness of her reaction to his invitation made her glad to be able to say, 'I can't. I'm busy tomorrow. One of the women who runs the international STEM foundation for young girls is in town. I'm meeting with her.'

'Already?'

'You doubt my efficiency?'

'If I did, *guapa*, you wouldn't have been working for me.'

She cursed the blush that heated her face, just as she cursed the sardonic amusement that twitched in his. 'Should I say thanks or is this another interrogation to see if I'm going to be overdoing things?'

Amusement vanished, a hard glint entering his eyes. 'Hate me if you must, but there will be a level of oversight into your activities over the next nine months. But, in this case, I was merely pointing out that it's time for another public appearance.'

Another wave of heat came, this one of pure embarrassment, washed away her foolish giddiness. Of course he was doing it only for appearances' sake. 'Oh. Well, I'm sorry to disappoint you, but I can't cancel. I'm lucky to have caught her.'

The tightness didn't lessen, but again a curious look filmed his eyes. Surprise? Admiration? Sure she was imagining it, she pulled her glance away, just as he murmured, 'Perhaps she's lucky to have caught *you*.'

Her gaze jerked back to him, that warmth she hoped she'd caged for good blooming wild and unfettered inside her.

For the longest beat, they stared at one another, their breaths growing increasingly loud in the silence. When his gaze dropped down her face, lingered on her mouth and fell lower to her chest, Mareka's heart pumped. And within that cocoon of swirling emotions she began to wonder if, perhaps even accept that, the fascination she held for this man might never be contained. That, despite all her efforts, the crush she'd hoped to snuff out had against her will blossomed into something *more*, something highly detrimental to her emotional wellbeing.

'Mareka?' Her name was filled with a thousand questions and a million warnings, as if he *knew*.

It'll be a mistake to develop feelings for me...

She jerked her head away again, tightening her own features so she didn't give herself away. 'Like I said, I can't make it tomorrow.'

She knew him well enough to sense his displeasure and, for some reason, it didn't irritate her. Instead, she was delighted. Was she really that desperate for any crumb of attention that she would rejoice even when she couldn't take advantage of it?

'How many meetings have you planned?'

'One more this week, then another two next week.'

His jaw clenched. Silence stretched her nerves to the breaking point, a punch of pride stopping her from offering another date. Then she blinked away confused tears when she sensed him rise, his stare drilling into her.

'We will have to make the best of the time we have together, then,' he drawled. 'At the very least, breakfasts and dinners together. Without fail.' Edict delivered, he walked away, his heavy footsteps echoing her heartbeat.

That set the tone for the two next months.

They ate their first and last meals together, whether they were in Buenos Aires or, as Mareka chose after a brief discussion, at the Cordoba ranch when she didn't have face-to-face meetings. At each meal, Cayetano quizzed her about her health, the depth of his attention almost giving the illusion that he cared.

Almost. Because, on their unavoidable social engagements, he was courteous and cordial, drawing her into conversations long enough to satisfy the avid watchers that they were very much a united front. But the second the spotlight dimmed he retreated, his arm dropping, his face tautening.

The day the morning sickness arrived with cyclone force, she wasn't at all stunned when he made an appearance an hour after breakfast. She'd long suspected Cayetano's staff was reporting her every move to him.

'What are you doing here?' she croaked, drained with throwing up and chagrined that he had to see her like this when he looked so vitally healthy. *So damn magnificently male!*

He set a tray holding tea and dry crackers on her lap, sending a hard look at her laptop before pouring her a cup.

'You continue to doubt that I intend to be an equal partner in this?'

'I continue to feel like the glass case holding crown jewels—useful but not ultimately important.' The reply was drenched in bitterness she couldn't hold back.

He stiffened. 'What do you mean?'

Harsh laughter seared her throat. 'You know very well what I mean. You play the caring husband in public because you don't want your father or anyone to challenge your right to your company. You're here now because you think you need to safeguard this pregnancy.'

'I do not—'

'Yes, you do. "Are you well?" "Are you resting enough?" "Has the doctor prescribed something for the morning sickness?"' she snapped. 'Remind me when you last asked me anything to do with me instead of this baby?'

He stiffened harder, but she shook her head before he could supply a response that would no doubt confirm her position as a disposable cog in his life. 'Believe it or not, this baby is as important to me as it to you. Maybe even more.'

Tense silence came, then, 'What's that supposed to mean?'

'It means you didn't want children with me, or even want them at all. They were just an abstract possibility in your future. But, now you don't have a choice but to face fatherhood, you're treating me like a delicate flower you need to watch carefully in case I fail. I was quite capable of taking care of myself before you came along and I intend to take even better care of this baby. So you can carry on with your essential empire-building and leave me be.'

An even longer stretch of charged silence ensued, during which she squeezed her eyes shut and clutched her tea cup.

'The child you're carrying is now part of my so-called empire building,' he stated with frigid tones. 'A vital component, in fact. So, no, *tesoro*, I will not take a back seat. I will see you tonight at dinner if you wish to fight again.'

She stayed in her room for dinner that night, mostly because it turned out morning sickness wasn't just restricted to mornings, and also because part of her wanted to see his reaction to her defiance.

Because in the past it had turned up the heat in ways that set her heart racing in recollection...

Dressing for her appointment with the head of an international women's charity the next morning, Mareka refused to accommodate that whispered opinion. She had young women to help empower, lives she hoped to make better with a fraction of the support she'd had a decade ago.

And she most definitely wasn't going to think about the emails she'd sent her parents two weeks ago with her pregnancy news that were still unanswered. She'd felt a mixture of anxiety and joy when she'd sent them, hoping for a crumb of regard to bolster her. Had she been tech-savvy she would've recalled them. But maybe it was a good thing. Maybe it was time to finally accept that, as Cayetano had warned about feelings for him, there was no point harbouring deep emotions for her parents. She was in this alone. And she would endeavour to thrive, despite everything.

She selected a bold orange sheath dress, taking advantage of form fitting clothes while she still could. Blow-drying her hair, she left it loose and, on a wild whim, went with a bold red lipstick. Confidence boosted, she snatched up the clutch bag that matched her heels.

Forty minutes later, her third deal on starting a foundation for young women in business in London and Tahiti was agreed. Mareka had just finished signing on the dotted line when a hush came over the Michelin-starred restaurant in which she was dining. Glancing round, her nape started to tingle wildly with awareness, her heartbeat accelerating.

Even before he came into view, she knew the reason for her body's wild reaction. Sure enough, Cayetano strode into the restaurant, making a beeline for her with purpose brimming his face and body. When he reached her, he lowered his head and took her mouth in a brazen kiss that drew several gasps.

He nodded to the CEO, whose eyes were lingering much too appreciatively on Cayetano, before turning to Mareka's. 'Don't let me disturb you, *guapa*,' he said in a deep, seductive drawl that had her thighs clenching.

She smothered a snort. As if *anyone* in the world could ignore him. With another brush of his lips at her temple, she watched, eyes wide and most likely displaying many more feelings than she wished to, as he parked himself at the next table, murmuring to the waiter who'd hurried over to him, without breaking his focus on her.

Composure became a struggle as she finished her meeting. The moment it ended and the older woman left, Cayetano rose and sauntered over, every set of eyes in the restaurant following his powerful, breath-taking form.

'What are you doing here?' she whispered fiercely under her breath when he leaned over to brush a leisurely hand over her heated cheek.

'Surprising my wife in a lovely restaurant to celebrate her impressive new business deal. What else?'

'But we didn't…this isn't a scheduled engagement.'

'What can I say? I missed you. Enough for me to cancel my appointments to come see you.'

The words were delivered with enough acerbity for her to know he didn't mean them. And yet her heart leapt before she could stop herself. 'You mean you're here because I missed dinner last night and breakfast this morning?' she murmured, conscious of their audience.

His eyes glittered. 'Wasn't that what you were hoping for? For me to dance to your tune?' he drawled.

'You've never danced to anyone's tune in your life.'

His shrug was far too sexy and distracting. And she'd missed it, including the arrogance and curious heaviness it came with. 'Life has a way of surprising us.'

Her breath strangled in her lungs, foolish hope unfurling deep within. 'What does that mean?'

He seemed to debate his answer, a perplexed expression crossing his face before he shrugged. 'Don't overthink it, *tesoro*. Ah, here's the waiter with the wine now.'

The alcohol-free sparkling wine he poured and passed to her, coupled with his words of congratulations, fizzed its way through her, making a mockery of the undeniable fact that all this was a performance for him—that their audience was lapping it up and the tabloids would undoubtedly write reams about Cayetano lavishing his new wife with champagne and attention.

For the next half hour, while he repeatedly trailed his hand over her arm, toyed with a lock of her hair and tortured her with his devastating smile and intoxicating scent, she smiled as several prominent people dropped by, eager to be seen with the great Cayetano Figueroa.

Eventually, her starched smile threatening to split her face, she grabbed her clutch bag. 'If we're quite done with National Paw Your Wife Day, can we leave, please?'

His sexy smile remained in place but the hard glint in his eyes reflected his true feelings. 'More like Show the World You Can't Keep Your Hands Off Your Sexy Wife Day. And I think that mission is thoroughly accomplished, don't you?'

Her face was on fire and she knew she was still the focus of every pair of eyes. 'Whatever you do, please do not run your hand over my belly when we get outside. I think that would be one cliché too far and I can do without the rabid tabloid speculation.'

For a long moment, she thought he would do it just to spite her. 'I recall a time when you screamed yourself hoarse for my touch.'

'Well, I think we both agree that was a brief moment of madness.'

A muscle ticked in his jaw and his eyes turned so dark and volatile, her heart caught. A moment later he regained his control. 'I'll grant your wish only because you beg so beautifully,' he said, dry mockery abrading her skin. 'And because I won't be around to shield you from the gutter rats.'

Her breath caught and her heart dropped in alarming dismay. 'You're leaving?'

He gave a brisk nod, his face still a mask of tempered fury. 'I'm due in China for a two-week set of deal closings.'

'Two weeks?' She hated the squeak in her voice.

Serious green eyes trailed her face before his lips twisted. 'Yes. So, I guess you'll have the freedom you've been craving. You won't need to be worried about your husband laying his unwanted hands on you.'

His caustic reply made her flinch, but Mareka was more interested in why she stupidly yearned to ask why he wasn't inviting her to come with him, despite the charged atmosphere between them. Despite being a wife who accompanied him on his business trips not being part of their deal.

'You have no response to that?' he demanded, the acid throb in his voice intensifying.

Yes, she wanted to yell. *Take me with you. Because, despite everything that has happened, I'll miss you terribly.*

Thankfully, she managed to trap the words inside and maintain her composure even as yearning swelled and threatened to suffocate her.

'Will you be back for the ultrasound?' she blurted as he

led her outside, where their respective drivers stood next to their cars.

Cayetano froze, his eyes darting to her belly before returning to her face. A wild, visceral flash crossed his face. 'You want me there?' There was a thread she couldn't fathom in the question. And, because she didn't want to hang foolish, heart-bruising speculation on it, she pushed it away.

'Can I stop you?'

The last vestiges of cordiality vanished, leaving him a proud, stiff pillar of censure. 'No. In this too, you cannot.'

Some part of her knew she only had herself to blame for this streak of niggling she couldn't seem to stop. The other part of her welcomed it. Maybe this separation would be what she needed to apply the brakes on this emotional runaway train before it was too late.

If it wasn't already…

CHAPTER ELEVEN

HIS WIFE HATED the sight of him.

It was a truth that shouldn't have mattered one iota and yet it interrupted Cayetano's sleep and his waking moments. It kept him off-kilter in a way that both infuriated and shockingly bewildered him.

He was especially resentful that it threatened every deal he'd sought to finalise for the next two months, long after he'd returned from China. His board members and staff had been terrorised and he knew they were glad to see the back of him when he joined Mareka in Cordoba. His inability to focus in itself made him a nightmare to be around.

It didn't help that every conversation with Mareka was like drawing blood from stone. It would've helped if he could have stayed away from her, but the little witch had cast a spell on him. So here he was in Cordoba, waiting for her to return from another meeting in Buenos Aires while he battled with this unfathomable ache in his chest.

He poured himself a drink, then activated the app which showed him the security cameras at his Buenos Aires home. Scrolling through that morning's feed, he paused repeatedly on images of Mareka. She'd developed a deeper tan in the last few weeks. Her hair had grown longer too, the gold tints bleached lighter, making her glow even more breath-taking.

He paused on a video of her by the pool, her voluptuous

body sporting the sexiest bikini he'd ever seen. It was almost scandalous, the way the white fabric clung to her skin. And were her breasts larger?

Cayetano swallowed, his hand drifting down to his swelling shaft before he hissed in annoyed frustration and killed the motion. *Dios mio*, he wasn't a hormonal teenager, slobbering over a scantily dressed woman, even if that woman was his gorgeous, disagreeable wife!

A wife who'd proved to be a formidable champion of young women in the very short time since she'd got her charity up and running. The Mareka Figueroa Women's Empowerment Charity—and, yes, he'd experienced a punch of pride that she'd used his name—had already made impressive strides in education, sports and small business funding in a handful of deprived countries.

Far from being the gold-digger his father had labelled her, she'd directed every cent of the million dollars he'd given her into her charity. And she was fast turning into a media darling. He'd watched his wife handle tough journalists with aplomb but, even as he'd been awed by her, he'd felt the hollow ache within him intensify. She was giving him exactly what he'd asked for—an emotionless union meant to fool the world—yet Cayetano hated it.

Closing the app with a tight, self-deprecating curse, he started the call he'd been placing daily—not to his wife this time, but to his housekeeper. Relief swelled through him once the report had been delivered.

Yes, the *señora* was well.

Yes, she'd spent a few hours by the pool, then had attended her meeting.

Yes, she'd thrown up only once and her appetite was returning.

No, she hadn't asked about the *señor*.

He clenched his jaw at that last one, blaming himself for

giving in to the urge to ask. Hadn't he learned his lesson from the way his own parents treated him? But...was he being disingenuous? Hadn't Mareka given him a glimpse of what being cared about looked like and hadn't he shut it down?

With a rough growl, he tossed the phone aside, shrugging out of his suit. About to undo his shirt, he leapt for the phone again when it rang. But it wasn't who he'd hoped it would be. Another, louder growl left his throat when he saw Octavia's name on the screen. He wasn't ready to deal with her drama and he took petty pleasure in declining the call. Her nose had been wrenched severely out of joint when he'd suggested she make use of the many weeks of accrued vacation time, and maybe even take an extended break.

Just now, the only person he wanted to deal with was his wife. Against all his lofty assertions about being above emotion, he'd developed an obsession for the wife he'd hired to secure his birthright, and for the baby she carried.

As he stood beneath the umpteenth cold shower he'd taken in the last several weeks, he couldn't help but accept that it was a state of affairs that he'd never seen coming and that he was at a complete loss as to how to combat it effectively.

'Thank you, everyone. I promise I'll visit soon.'

Mareka ended the video-conference to a chorus of cheers, with a tremulous smile and tears in her eyes. The crown jewel in her ambitions—the education foundation in Papeete, Tahiti—had officially been opened. The moment she logged off, her hand dropped to her stomach, the need to connect with her baby a powerful draw. But, as had been happening shockingly frequently, a deep ache immediately replaced her joy. While she was ecstatic about fulfilling her dreams, the more she achieved, the more acutely she felt the loss in her own life.

Despite travelling along the road to empowering others' lives, the love she lacked in hers glared as bright as the neon lights she'd ignored before.

Specifically, the love of her husband.

The husband who'd warned her against developing feelings for him. The husband she now knew she loved with every fibre of her being. Perhaps if Cayetano had maintained the distance she'd riled against, she could've salvaged something from the pieces of her heart that had recklessly delivered themselves into his undesiring hands.

Instead, with his presence at most mealtimes, every gruff enquiry about her health and about their baby, with every compliment he made about her charity work that announced that he was keeping tabs on that, sparks of hope and joy fired within her, defying every attempt to suppress it.

Lately, with her baby growing stronger and bigger each day, Mareka had started to wonder if things needed to stay the way they'd agreed. Whether she could make another dream come true…

Maybe it was the reserves of strength and self-worth she'd discovered within herself recently. Whatever it was, the ultrasound was scheduled for tomorrow. Cayetano had stayed true to being present for every step of this pregnancy.

Maybe this was her chance…

Her thoughts were disrupted when Ariana—the housekeeper whom she'd discovered was married to the butler—appeared with a wide smile, a tray of Mareka's favourite punch and a selection of *tucumanas* and *pastafrolas*. The older woman had cheekily admitted she was under orders from Cayetano to keep a close eye on her. It meant Mareka was cheerfully chivvied into eating and resting at strictly regular intervals.

Ariana's clear delight at her task had warmed Mareka, as

had the priceless advice about pregnancy the housekeeper, with her ten grandchildren, had passed on.

'I'm going to become as big as a house if I keep this up,' Mareka complained, reaching for her second *tucumana*. The empanadas were heavenly, and deceptively bite-sized, and she devoured four before she put on the brakes.

'The *señor* will be pleased, *si*?' Ariana said, her gaze sharpening on Mareka's face.

'Yes… *Si*…' she echoed distractedly, her heart banging against her ribs, her mind racing at the idea which grew as Ariana bustled about for another minute before leaving her alone. The feeling that this was a pivotal moment in her relationship with Cayetno wouldn't leave her. And, despite the potentially painful outcome, she took extra care in dressing up before meeting Cayetano in the living room, where he awaited the doctor's arrival.

Her pulse was racing when she stepped into the room ten minutes later dressed in an emerald-green jersey dress with capped sleeves that loosely moulded her body. Yes, it turned out her favourite colour in her new wardrobe was still green.

He looked up when she entered, then rose and crossed the room to her. 'Are you well?'

Her heart dipped but she breathed through the trepidation because Mareka wanted to believe it meant something. That, if nothing else, she'd over-exaggerated the depths of his detachment.

'Yes,' she answered in a husky, breathless tone she decided she wasn't going to be embarrassed about. Where had guarding her heart got her? It had ignored all her fight and deepened her crush into love.

Maybe it was time to be brave. Time to…to… She bit her lip, the last defences unwilling to be dislodged just yet. 'You?'

Faint, bleak spectres danced across his face before disappearing. Then one corner of his mouth quirked up, a shrug following it. 'A few skin-of-the-teeth challenges, but nothing that couldn't be handled in the end.'

She nodded, cleared her throat and dragged her gaze from his far too distracting face and body—a body she'd missed with every fibre of her being. 'That's…umm… great.'

Awkward silence floundered between them, then he gave a low, mocking laugh, his face slowly hardening until it was an emotionless mask. 'Is this really that difficult for you—looking your husband in the face and having a simple conversation?'

Her gaze darted up. 'W-what? That's not what I'm doing at all. I'm… I was…' Her words froze when Ariana knocked and entered. The older woman's gaze swung between them, a flash of concern crossing her face before she spoke to Cayetano in rapid-fire Spanish.

He murmured back, his gaze never leaving Mareka. 'The doctor is here,' he said after Ariana exited. 'At least in this we can be united, *si*?'

Feeling the ground crack and tilt beneath her, but equally at a loss as to how to stop it, she nodded. Cayetano started to step forward then, frowning, he turned, gesturing her towards the door. She sailed ahead of him, viciously aware of his gaze on her, aware of the subtle changes in her body. Her breasts had grown heavier, her hips fuller. Even her skin felt that little bit more vibrant. Did he notice?

She shook her head, impatient with herself for her desperate thoughts. But that bleakness in his eyes flashed through her mind again and, as she was readied for the first glimpse of the life she carried, Mareka couldn't stop herself from glancing at Caye, from searching for further insights into how he truly felt. The look he returned was inscrutable, devastatingly characteristic of the ruthless, formidable magnate who conquered worlds before 9:00 a.m. each morning.

There was no give at all...until the sound of their baby's heartbeat echoed through the quiet room. She felt a shudder ripple through his body braced close to hers on the portable examination bed. Then his jaw sagged, his chest rising and falling rapidly as his avid gaze flew to the 3D screen.

An awed gasp left Mareka as she watched the tiny expressions chase across her baby's face, tiny fingers starfishing as it moved.

'Dios mio,' Cayetano rasped, a thick exhale moving through him. 'She...he...is...'

Relieved and moved by his emotion, that this pillar of self-control was lost for words, Mareka placed her hand on top of his. He startled, then his awed gaze found hers. 'I know.'

He swallowed, his gaze sweeping her face as the doctor smiled indulgently, clicked on a few buttons and nodded. 'Everything seems to be in order. You can carry on as normal, Señora Figueroa.'

Another wave of relief swept through her and, when Caye's fingers meshed with hers, she couldn't help but tighten her grip and allow a sliver of hope to filter through her defences.

Maybe something positive could come out of this. They remained caught up in the tight cocoon of emotion as the doctor finished up, handed them images of their baby and quietly left. One of Cayetano's hands remained tightly on hers while the other brushed back the hair from her temple, then drifted down her cheek to caress her jaw. After staring into her eyes for an age, his hand drifted down to hover over her belly.

Another swallow moved his Adam's apple. 'I want... I

need to touch you.' His voice was thick, stuffed full of emotions he'd claimed he didn't feel.

Her heart leapt, then she nodded before she could think better of it, before she could safeguard her heart. And, when his hand slid almost reverently over where their child nestled, she couldn't stop the soft gasp that shivered up from her throat at the reverence in the eyes that flew to meet hers. With mingled fear and hope rushing through her bloodstream, Mareka, blurted, 'Caye, I think we need to talk.'

He stiffened immediately, his jaw clenched as he abruptly removed his hand. She wanted to wail, to beg him to put it back. But she really was done begging for scraps, for love. She deserved more—unconditionally.

'Is this where you start to lay down ultimatums?' he ground out.

Her heart squeezed. She fought through it, rising from the bed so she didn't feel at such a disadvantage. 'Is that what you really think of me?' she challenged, her chin rising despite the despair swelling in her chest.

He withdrew further, aggressively shoving his hands into his pockets as if he despised himself for the need he'd just displayed. 'I've shown you how much I want my heir. You would be a fool not to recognise how much power that grants you.'

Pain slashed at the remnants of hope. 'That's what you would do in my shoes, is it?'

His face darkened at her taunt, then he shrugged. 'I can't help but remember that we got here in the first place because we were both getting something from each other.' He paused for a second, his gaze raking her face. 'Isn't that what you want to talk about? Something else you need from me?'

Yes, for you to love me!

But he'd effectively and cleverly cornered her. How could she ask for what she wanted now?

Are you going to give up that easily?

She wanted to hate that inner voice, but she couldn't deny that it had guided her heart's compass and ultimately been her companion for as long as she could remember. Perhaps now wasn't the time to reject it.

Sucking in another sustaining breath, she smoothed damp palms over her dress, unable to help her gaze from flicking to the bed. 'That moment just now, it wasn't some gateway for me to get leverage over you.'

Scepticism glinted in his eyes. 'Wasn't it?'

'Look, I know you hated showing your emotion like that…maybe because of your parents?'

When he stiffened further, she ploughed ahead. 'If you must know, I… I hate feeling like a spare part. Unless and until we can both deal with that, things will always feel… unbalanced. But I…'

He cursed something indecipherable under his breath, stopping her words. 'You're not a spare part.'

Years of residual bitterness swelled through her even as warmth filtered through at his response. But she'd been here far too often to let it linger. 'Tell that to my parents who didn't want me in academia because, if I failed, I'd be an embarrassment—and, if I succeeded, would've been competition. But anything else outside their field was considered a failure anyway.'

Fury flashed across his face. 'They told you that?'

'Not in so many words. But I discovered my mother's diary from her honeymoon when she realised she was pregnant with me. And…it was…it wasn't fairy-tale reading for a nine-year-old, I'll tell you that much. I was an obligation, a useless extension of themselves they had to endure then, and that never changed. Tell me how any child is supposed to navigate that,' she said in a strained voice, then shook her head. 'I've never told that to anyone.'

If she'd been expecting sympathy, she was to be disappointed. His face remained clenched. 'And you feel you're not able to stop history repeating itself?' he demanded tightly.

Determination charged through her, and she shook her head definitively. 'Not if I can help it. I know what it feels not to be wanted. I intend to make sure my child never feels that way. I want this baby more than anything. I can only hope that my own experiences help remind me of what not to do.'

He looked startled for a moment, then his expression grew even darker. 'Do I hear judgement in there somewhere, *guapa*?'

'You accused me of putting words in your mouth once. I'm only speaking for myself. I know I'm not perfect, that my childhood has probably damaged me—'

Another expletive interrupted her. 'Stop saying that about yourself. In fact, I think it's done the opposite.'

'It's hard not to when I told them I was having a baby weeks ago and they haven't bothered to respond. Or that my last phone call went to voicemail.'

He shrugged. 'That's their problem. You're the polar opposite of those...coldly detached people who attended our wedding.'

Then why don't you want me?

Luckily, the words remained trapped deep inside her. Realising after a minute that he was waiting for her to continue, Mareka cleared her throat. 'What I'm saying is, there's no need for this...strain between us. I...um...re-read the agreement. It said that, if we both agree that we can't make it work, then we can go our separate ways or we can re...'

His cynical laugh stopped her. 'Despite your protests, you're proving me right after all.'

'Would you let me finish, please?'

He lunged forward, his movements almost frantic, his body blotting out the light as he stopped an arm's length away. 'Why, when I know what you're going to say? You're either going to threaten to leave me, or demand custody, or you're going to renegotiate better financial terms. The answer to all of it is no. You would've found out by now that charity doesn't come cheap. I doubt the last thing you'll want is to let down all the people you've pledged to help. That alone should keep you where you are—as my wife—until our agreement is honoured.'

Her heart squeezed tighter. 'Cayetano, don't—'

His hand flew out of his pocket to silence her with a halting gesture. 'It doesn't have to be all bad right now. As of this morning, I've instructed my lawyers to match what you've spent on your foundation so far. But keep threatening to renege on our deal in any way, and I'll stop it. Is that clear?'

'It really is all about gaining the upper hand with you, isn't it?'

His gaze dropped to her belly and heavy emotion moved through his eyes. 'No, *pequeña*. It's also now about claiming what's mine. Like you, my parents have taught me a lesson—that I can't rely on anyone but myself. So this is ensuring that nothing is ever given or taken away from me that I can't control.'

'You do realise that I can walk away at any time, don't you? Even if it's just to prove to you that I don't want your precious money—that it's clear that you can't give me what I want.'

Green eyes turned black. 'You shouldn't test me like this, *guapa*,' he warned silkily. Then, reaching into his pocket, he drew out his phone. The instruction to his driver, despite being spoken in Spanish, was clear enough.

'You're leaving?'

'It's clear my presence here isn't good for either of us—or the baby. I think it's best to carry on with that empire-building you accused me of. *Hasta luego, tesoro.*'

The coolly drawled goodbye finally broke her. 'You can't just walk out!'

A mocking glance over his shoulder seared her as he sauntered towards the door. 'Can't I? How are you going to stop me?'

'God, you…you bastard!'

He stiffened for a moment, but he didn't turn round, nor did he stop.

Five minutes later, she stood at the window, shock, pain and terror spiking through her as she watched Cayetano drive off.

The handful of times she and Cayetano met over the next six weeks were painful in a way Mareka had hoped never to experience again. It was also clear she'd only experienced a less devastating version of rejection from her parents.

But, conversely, in those six weeks she learned a great deal about herself. She knew that what she'd said to him that last day was right—she wanted her baby fiercely. She was willing to and *could* do anything in her power to create a loving and happy home, one her parents had never bothered to give her. And, when she tried one last time to contact her parents and only received a lukewarm, 'We wish you the best with it,' she decided to save herself further heartache and shelve what was clearly an unsalvageable relationship. Whatever happened in the future with them, for now she needed to make herself and her baby her priority.

But, more and more, the voice at the back of her mind

urged her that there was one relationship she owed it to herself and her baby to try to salvage one more time.

'It's lunch time!'

Mareka looked up as Luna, her new assistant, bustled into her office and set down a tray front of her. The chicken salad looked delicious, but the nerves churning through her stopped her reaching for the food.

'Something wrong?' Luna asked, the layer of anxiety that seemed to cloak the younger girl, thickening.

When Mareka had accepted she couldn't efficiently take on her foundation's responsibilities all by herself, she'd been adamant about surrounding herself with women who needed the help her charity would provide. Luna's background of escaping domestic abuse and her determination to find self-worth beyond that had made it a no-brainer for Mareka to hire her. But Luna occasionally regressed, letting anxiety overwhelm her—something with which Mareka empathised.

'Not with the food, no,' she responded, then smiled at Luna's palpable relief. 'But I need your help with something.'

'*Si*...anything,' Luna responded enthusiastically.

Mareka bit the inside of her lip, wondering whether she had it in her to take the course she was contemplating.

Yes. This was too important to prevaricate about.

Sucking in a deep breath, she let it out slowly. Then she said, 'My husband is on a business trip. I'd like you to book me a plane ticket to join him.'

Luna's eyes widened, as most people's did when Cayetano's name was mentioned. With a little excited squeak that would've amused Mareka if she hadn't been shrivelling inside with nerves, her assistant all but flew out of the room to do her bidding.

CHAPTER TWELVE

SHE LANDED IN New York City sixteen hours later, and the car service Luna had organised for her whisked her away from JFK to Manhattan just before sundown. She'd taken pains to ensure her visit remained a secret. Or at the very least as last-minute as possible.

Was it because she'd been terrified Cayetano would stop her? Or, even worse, detail exactly *why* he didn't want her anywhere near him?

Yes to both!

Even now, two hours after arriving at the hotel she'd requested because it was one block from Cayetano's luxury penthouse, she couldn't stem the apprehensive tremors rippling through her body as she dressed.

The soft cream jersey midi-dress gently draped her body and showed off her rounded belly. A rich cashmere coat of the same length and colour completed the classy look, the combo bolstering her confidence.

She had a crucial hour's window in Cayetano's breakneck appointment schedule and, as much as she wanted to give up, she knew she couldn't return to Buenos Aires without taking this chance.

Securing diamond studs in her ears after several shaky tries, she added a platinum-and-diamond bracelet she'd only spotted recently in her jewellery collection but which had quickly become her favourite. The chain was delicate, the gem modest enough for Mareka to wear on a daily basis without feeling grossly ostentatious.

Slipping her feet into simple pumps, she snatched up her matching coffee-coloured clutch bag. As she descended in the lift, every sinew in her body pleaded with her to change her mind, to opt out of impending heartache. But then she caught sight of her reflection in the polished silver interior of the lift and saw the proof of her determination.

This was why: she owed it to her baby to try.

Did she want to do this on her own if she didn't have to? *What about your heart? The protection of not living in perpetual heartache?*

The walk ended quicker than she wished, the courteous doorman at the iconic New York skyscraper holding the glass door open for her, giving her no other choice but to step through.

The shiny chrome, polished glass and Modernist decor was a world removed from the deep comfort and elegance of Cayetano's homes in Argentina but it was no less jaw-dropping. Before she chickened out and changed her mind, she hurried to the lift and pressed the button for the penthouse. Before she could catch her breath, the lift ascended with smooth efficiency and spat her out half a minute later into a private foyer.

To be greeted with the towering, thin-lipped, heartrendingly beautiful form of her husband, arms folded.

'This is unexpected.' The statement was weighted with censure…and something puzzling. It was grim and probing, yet almost fatalistic. But she couldn't concentrate enough to decipher it because…*dear God*…despite his near-constant presence, she was starved of him. His hair was a little dishevelled, his five o'clock shadow making him positively sinfully attractive. Every cell in her body strained for this man she loved with terrifying ferocity.

'Mareka. Are you going to tell me why you've flown thousands of miles when I was due to fly back tomorrow?' Again, the mockery didn't quite pack much punch, as if his focus was pulled elsewhere.

His gaze did a lengthy survey of her body, pausing longest on her belly, then on the bracelet, the occasional enigmatic expression darting over his face. She yearned to ask him what he was thinking but, frankly, she was terrified.

Which left her with one option—to state her case so the chips could fall fast enough before she completely lost her nerve. 'We have a conversation to finish. And this time you're going to hear me out.' The words emerged more forcefully than she'd intended.

His eyes narrowed. 'I see you're emotional about something.'

'Yes, I'm emotional. I'm not a robot like you, Caye!'

For a blind moment, his eyes lit up with ice-cold fury. Then, fascinatingly, it disappeared layer by layer until there was nothing left. Nothing but the lines around his mouth deepening as his firm lips thinned. 'You're proving my point. You see why I can't permit myself to remain a slave to this…madness?'

'Why not?' she challenged. Maybe this was the perfect place to start—this madness that gripped them both.

He barked out a laugh, then shook his head. 'You want me to embrace something that has the potential to destroy me?'

'Not necessarily. Not if you look at it through another lens. If emotion brings you happiness, isn't that a good thing? You chase the high of impossible business deals every day. That's a different kind of love.'

'But business deals don't turn on me,' he insisted in a tone made of chilled steel. 'They don't manipulate, hold back or disappoint.'

She gasped. 'What's that supposed to mean? When have

I done that to you? Or are you talking about someone else—your parents?'

His lips twisted then, turning on his heel, he went through double doors that led into a breath-taking living room. The views alone were to die for, but she was busy experiencing a different death.

'My parents no longer have that kind of power over me. But, with everyone else, it's always only a matter of time,' he said bitterly.

'And you can see into the future, can you?'

'No. But common sense follows that, based on a shocking number of failed relationships, that's where we're headed. Especially if the thing holding it together is purely physical.'

'Physical…' she echoed dismally. 'That's all you think we have?'

He shrugged. 'Perhaps a mutual responsibility for our child.' His dismissive hand slashed through his own response. 'Why are you here, Mareka?'

'I came to see if there was anything between us worth salvaging. But I've barely walked through the door and I have my answer.'

That bleakness shadowed his face again, then he exhaled. 'You should've called. I would've saved you a trip.'

And, just like that, the rug was pulled from under her every hope. 'God. You really are something, aren't you?'

His nostrils flared and she fully expected him to cut her down. But, after a moment, he just shrugged again as if she wasn't even worth the effort. The last of her hope drained away.

'You said I wasn't a spare part but you can't wait to throw me away, can you? You know what you are? You're a coward.'

His whole body jerked, then he froze into an impregnable pillar. 'Watch it, *tesoro*.'

'Why, what have I got to lose? And don't you dare call me a treasure when you're treating me like dirt.'

'It's better this way.'

Her harsh laugh seared her throat and she feared the pain and bitterness coursing through her. But then she remembered that she'd been through this before. Certainly not as soul-destroying as this, but maybe, with the help of the love she intended to shower her baby with, she might not be completely annihilated. 'It's really not. And I feel sorry for you, because you'll only realise that when it's too late.'

He seemed poleaxed for a moment but of course, being Cayetano Figueroa, he eviscerated that weakness immediately. Watching her with a mocking smile, he folded his arms. 'Are you done?'

She glared at him. 'Why? Are you going to toss something conceited at me, like I need to calm down so I don't harm the baby?'

A charged look entered his eyes as his gaze dropped down to her body. 'I wouldn't dream of it. I have first-hand experience of how vibrant your passion can be. I only hope our son or daughter inherits it.'

She stared at him, nonplussed for a moment, before her heart reminded her of the risk she'd taken and how spectacularly she'd lost. She couldn't stay here. Fingers tightening around her clutch bag, she whirled and headed for the door.

'Where are you going?'

'Are you serious? What does it look like? I'm leaving.'

He arrived in front of her, not exactly barring her way, but not making it easy for her to go around him when his very presence was making her feel light-headed. Then she made the colossal mistake of swaying, her hand flying out to grab hold of something—anything. Unfortunately, the only solid thing was her husband.

With a thick curse, Cayetano caught and swept her into

his arms, striding with purpose in the opposite direction of where she wanted to go.

'What are doing? Put me down!'

'Tranquilo, guapa.'

'No! I will not be *tranquilo*.'

He didn't listen to her, of course.

He entered a bedroom decked out in pale gold and silver furnishings, probably meant to soothe and comfort hard-working billionaires who didn't love their pregnant wives. He laid her down with precise gentleness, his breathing hardly affected, then stepped back swiftly, definitively.

'I have a meeting with my lawyers. It won't take long. I'll be back in two hours.' Those eyes seemed to search hers when he added, 'Then we can go home and address a few things.'

She swallowed the lump that charged into her throat, squashing the foolish, deadly hope that threatened to rise. Home was simply a place he laid his head. A place where he guarded his unborn child.

Home would never mean her.

For a long moment, his lashes veiled his expression and, when he raised them, she thought she spotted flashes of bleakness steeped with desperate determination. But hadn't she been reading things from the very beginning that had only proved to be a mistake?

'You'll agree this limbo has gone on long enough, *si*?' he pressed.

Sorrow and pain rushed into the hollow spaces left by eviscerated hope. It was so debilitating, so all-encompass-ing, Mareka couldn't move. It was time to end this. Time to accept that they would never be. So she allowed him to believe her silence was acquiescence. Allowed him to fetch his phone and instruct the private kitchen to deliver far too much food. Allowed him to examine her critically as if he

wanted to say much, much more. Then, when he decided
she wasn't worth it, she allowed him to turn his back on
her and walk away.

She tried so hard to catch the sobs that rumbled up from
her soul the moment she was alone. When she failed, she
succumbed to it, hoping to find rock bottom soon so she
could reverse direction in time to save herself.

But rock bottom didn't come. Not in the next ten minutes or the half-hour that followed it. But the tears did run
dry once she accepted it was over.

And *that* finally propelled her out of bed: shoes; bag;
coat… A quick swipe of the vestiges of tears without the aid
of a mirror because she couldn't face herself—not yet, not
so soon. With a gulped in breath, and praying she wouldn't
encounter anyone to witness the soulless, heartbroken shell
of a person she'd become, Mareka stumbled out the back
entrance of Cayetano's apartment building.

Back at her hotel, her case took minutes to pack, since
she'd barely unpacked. Ten minutes later, she had checked
out and was heading for the airport.

As with everything that had happened since she'd walked
into the diamond emporium all those months ago, Mareka
was stunned by how quickly events had unfolded. She'd
left that place with a ring meant for another woman on her
finger. She'd stepped into a role with all the naivety of a
woman who believed she knew true suffering.

How wrong she'd been.

She stared down at the ring as her cab whisked her
through the night back towards JFK. Maybe it was cursed.
She half-snorted, half-sobbed, attracting the wary gaze of
the driver. Partially hiding her face behind a tissue, she
mopped up silent tears until the driver pulled up at the airport, relieved to be free of his emotionally addled passenger.

Inside, the ticket attendant's eyes widened when Mareka

presented her passport. 'Oh, Mrs Figueroa, your return ticket to Buenos Aires isn't for another three days. If you want, I can—'

'No.' The decision was visceral. 'I'm not returning to Argentina. Can I change the destination?'

'Of course. Please give me a few minutes.'

She knew she was being accommodated because of who she was but Mareka didn't balk at it. Very soon, she would be back to being anonymous Mareka Dixon.

The sharp pain that lanced her heart made her gasp. And made the attendant's fingers dance that little bit faster over her keyboard.

Mareka booked herself a business class seat to London, because she couldn't risk the breakdown she sensed bubbling beneath her skin being aired on social media by an avid public equipped with smart phones if she sat in economy. On top of that, the last thing she needed was for rife speculation about why Cayetano's wife was travelling in economy and not on his private jet.

She grimaced at the eye-watering price and, with a silent promise to make up for it, she took her seat, thankful when, after a few attempts to discreetly engage her failed, the attendants left her alone.

Halfway across the Atlantic, lifting her hand to swipe away yet another tear, her wedding and engagement rings caught her eye and her heart snagged. Cayetano had gifted her the ring. But Mareka hadn't expected their agreement to end this soon.

They were so beautiful, she couldn't bear it. She *didn't* want to. Fishing in her bag, she felt her pulse race as she prayed she'd kept the embossed black card. When her fingers snagged on it, her breath shuddered in relief, then she bit her lip. The woman she'd met had been almost as formidable as Cayetano. Would she even be allowed inside the hallowed rooms of the diamond jeweller?

She could only try.

The anonymous donations amounting to five million dollars that had arrived in her charity's account over the last several weeks notwithstanding, she'd become shockingly aware of how much funding was needed to make a true difference. And, as much as she loved these rings, it was a much too painful and constant reminder of how she'd had the love of her life in her arms for one brief night before her heart had shattered into a million pieces.

She dialled the number, ignoring the text alerts and missed phone calls as another taxi drove her from Heathrow airport. Mareka considered going home to her old flat but she feared she'd only crawl beneath the covers and mope until her baby was ready to be born. So, clutching her phone and her suitcase, she sat on a park bench across from the jeweller's outwardly nondescript entrance in Knightsbridge and waited.

The ping arrived two hours later. Ms Smythe would see her at noon.

'Mrs Figueroa, this is…unusual,' the talented, mysterious jeweller said when Mareka stepped out of the lift at the designated time. There was no inflexion in her voice or expression in her eyes as to whether she was pleased or displeased about Mareka's request.

She was just as formidable a woman today as she'd been a few short, life-changing months ago. And it was those very life changes that powered up Mareka's chin when before she would've cowered. That made her smile and nod…

'You're not a spare part.'

She hated the clarity of Cayetano's voice in her head, the vivid recollection of those words to her. He'd helped her realise and own her self-worth. Then he'd shattered her.

Deep breath in, she slid the rings off her finger. 'Yes, and I'm sorry to just drop in like this.'

Ms Smythe's inscrutable eyes stayed on her. 'I said "unusual". If I didn't wish you to be admitted, you wouldn't be here.'

'Well, thank you.' Mareka cleared her throat and held out her hand. 'I'd like to return these. I'll take a reasonable below-market price for the inconvenience.'

'This isn't a back-street pawn shop, Mrs Figueroa.' Her tone was chilled but painfully cultured. 'You won't find some burly individual with false gold teeth trying to strong-arm you out of what your property is truly worth within these walls.'

Her gaze dropped to the rings and then to Mareka's swollen belly. Something soft but heavy shifted in her eyes and the barest quiver fluttered her nostrils before she glanced back at the rings. 'Are you sure? Once I take possession of them, you won't get them back.'

Mareka pulled her longing gaze from the rings. They'd meant nothing but a means to an end for Cayetano. She couldn't let them mean anything to her.

'Yes, I'm sure.'

Ms Smythe nodded. 'Give me a moment to value them.' As she started to step away, her eyes dropped to Mareka's bracelet. 'That looks good on you.'

Surprise pulsed through her. 'This is one of yours?'

Perhaps she imagined the flash of pride in the other woman's eyes, and the ghost of a smile that fluttered over her lips, but the brisk nod was real. 'One of the pieces in my most recent commissioned collection. I wondered about...' She paused, seeming to catch herself.

Mareka jerked forward. 'What did you wonder about?'

Ms Smythe shook her head. 'That was uncalled-for speculation on my part. You must forgive...'

'Please.' She despised the needy quiver in her voice but she couldn't help it. 'I need to know.'

The way the woman's gaze brutally sized her up made Mareka pity anyone who was foolish enough to get in her way. And Mareka was just about ready to beg when the jeweller glanced down at the bracelet. 'I wondered about the inscription.'

Mareka frowned. 'What inscription?'

'*Esperanza eterna*: "hope eternal".'

The answer didn't come from Ms Smythe but from the deep, grave tones of the man she'd left in New York. In fact, by the time Mareka whirled to face Cayetano, the talented jeweller was already melting away, her movements as ephemeral as the muslin curtains that fluttered behind her when she disappeared.

Leaving Mareka alone with Cayetano, caught in the power of his seismic aura.

'What are you doing here?' One day in the future, she would stop sounding so breathless when she addressed him.

Green eyes rushed over her before latching onto her face. 'You left before I returned,' he said,

'And you followed me here? To do what—stop me because you're not quite done hurting me?'

His eyes darkened, a dramatic change that shocked her anew. 'Because your accusation was correct,' he delivered, his accent thickening. 'It was cowardly of me to leave things as they've been left.'

Mareka gasped, stung by guilt despite her shattered heart. 'No. What I said in New York wasn't…'

He exhaled and he seemed to cave in a little on himself, which was another shocking thing to witness. Enough to leave her speechless, even as he corrected that tiny error, his shoulders rearing back as he strode forward, a conqueror intent on stamping his will where he pleased. 'You were right—about all of it. I have been avoiding. And, if you hadn't come to see me, I would've kept on running.'

'Then shouldn't you be heading in the opposite direction?' she demanded, discovering she had reserves of bitterness within the sea of her heartache.

'No. Because while you were out of sight, but very much in mind, I hoped that you would remain with me, even held by the tenuous link of our agreement. But now...' He stopped his dark, bleak gaze dropping to the rings she'd dropped onto the square silk cushion. The rings the mysterious jeweller had curiously left behind... 'Now I know. You're leaving me, aren't you?'

A sob shuddered its way up her soul. Thankfully, it stopped short before it totally humiliated her. 'I have to. I have no choice.'

He seemed to cave in once more, deeper this time, a haggard look shrouding his face. 'I blamed my grandfather for putting me in this position. I raged at his unreasonableness. But, underneath it all, the true reason I resisted was because of this very thing. This desperate hell of failing the one thing I suspected I would come to crave with every fibre of my being.'

The tremors weren't quite done with her, it seemed. 'W-what are you talking about?'

He took long, precise steps, as if caught on a string—one connected to her. 'You captivated me. You challenged me. You turned me on harder than any other woman. You terrified me with your passion. You took my seed into your body and you embraced the daunting possibility of parenthood while I ran scared. You overcame my every attempt for you not to become my first thought when I wake and the last before I sleep.'

'Cayetano...'

The shudder that seized her ricocheted through him, because apparently they were connected... 'You have no idea how I've longed to hear my name fall from your lips one more time, like that.'

'I still don't know what this means.'

'It means you've been asking me to prove myself one way or the other. Coming back to the penthouse and finding you gone... I can't keep running. It's killing me. So here I am, surrendering.'

The joy that had been creeping up on her stalled, then rushed away. 'I don't want your surrender if it means you'll resent me for it down the line.'

He laughed, and when he spoke his voice was hoarse with untamed emotion. 'Give me the barest glimpse that you want me around and I'll never leave your side.'

She gasped. 'Cayetano. I don't... I...'

He surged another step closer. 'Tell me why you came to New York, *tesoro*.'

Because I want you to love me. The words screamed inside her, even now too terrified to emerge, in case this was all a fever dream.

'Please, Mareka. Tell me—was it to tell me you were leaving?'

This she could answer. 'No. It wasn't to leave you.'

But he wasn't satisfied because he was who he was: larger than life and unflinching about demonstrating it. 'But you're here now.' His gaze flicked to the rings. 'You're returning your rings. I've driven you away. Because you can never love me as much as I love you.'

Her jaw dropped, joy breaking the dam of her terror. 'You *love* me? But—'

'I had a deplorable way of showing it? I'm aware of that. I made false assertions at every opportunity. I neglected you and barely listened to you because I knew I wasn't worthy. I feared you would come to your senses one day and call my bluff on all of it.'

'So you're saying my gamble paid off? That coming to New York actually worked?' she dared to tease.

His nostrils flared. 'Watching you step out of that lift was both heaven and hell. I'd missed you, but I was terrified you were there to tell me that would be the last time I saw you.' His hand dropped to her belly, reverentially caressing it. 'That I would be a father from afar when it was the last thing I wanted.'

Her eyes brimmed with happy tears. 'You love me, Caye? Truly?'

Firm hands cradled her jaw, his eyes gleaming with the depth of feeling. 'So much. I was so desperate, I dumped donations anonymously into your charity in the hope that it would keep you too busy to leave me.'

Her eyes flare wide. 'That was you?'

'I'm not quite ready to divulge all my sins, but know that I've been watching, and am extremely proud of every achievement. And I will continue to support you any way you'll let me.'

'I love you. I love you so much, Cayetano. I was desperate I was losing you too. I'm so happy I'm not.'

She lunged forward and he caught her in his arms, his eager lips finding hers in relief, in love, in desperate reunion.

Mareka wasn't sure how long they stay locked together until a throat cleared delicately.

Ms Smythe watched them from across the room. 'Will I still be valuing the rings?' she asked.

'Only if it's so she can choose another one,' Caye responded before she could speak, because apparently this arrogant love of her life couldn't be cowed for long.

Suppressing a smile, Mareka reached for the rings. 'No, I want to keep them. They'll remind me what I've fought for. That it's been worth it.'

Cayetano sucked in a breath, his eyes darkening. 'Say that again.'

'It's been worth it, to know, to feel, that you love me.'

He took the rings and slid them one by one onto her finger. 'I vow this to you, *agapita*—you will never have cause to question my love ever again.'

'And I promise that, wherever you are, my heart will be the home you can come to for ever. Now, take me home. Let's start our lives properly.'

He swung her into his arms, his breath-taking smile lighting every corner of her world. 'What are you doing?'

'This was how it started. It is right that this is how it should continue. Besides, you have the rest of your collection to try on.'

'My collection?'

He nodded. 'The one that goes with the bracelet I had Ariana slip into your things two weeks ago.'

'Oh, my God, no wonder I didn't recognise it.'

'I needed my hope to reside next to your skin. I was thrilled when she told me how much you love it.'

He kissed her again as they stepped into the room that held her new, personal collection. The room where Mareka had sat all those months ago and picked the diamond that had led her into love. And, as she sat down, the lightest fluttering in her belly made her gasp.

Cayetano stilled. 'What is it?'

'I think our little one agrees. I just felt the tiniest, sweetest movement.'

Eyes filled with wonder and love, he lowered his head and kissed her. 'I love you. And I love our little one. With everything I am.'

'And we love you back. A million times over.'

EPILOGUE

Ten months later

'WILL THIS COLLECTION ever be complete?' Mareka tried for exasperation, but her heart was too full, the soft sleeping bundle in her arms making her joy overflow.

The enigmatic Ms Smythe had disappeared once more, as she always did after laying out her magnificent creations, leaving the Figueroa family alone.

'I can't help it when every piece looks so exquisite on the mother of my child.'

'Just the mother of your child?' she teased.

Cayetano's eyes flared with love and devotion so pure, she gasped. And, when he reached out and caressed their son Javier's cheek, her heart tumbled over.

'Choose your diamonds, my love. Then allow me to take you home so I can have the honour of showing you just how much I love and treasure you.'

* * * * *

THE TYCOON'S DIAMOND DEMAND

JOSS WOOD

MILLS & BOON

This book is dedicated to my sprint-writing partner
and good friend Katherine Garbera.

Lovely people make great writers and she's both!

I'm lucky to have you in my life, Kathy.

PROLOGUE

No *DAMN* WAY. Jens Nilsen stared at the email's subject line on his screen, and the black letters on the white page danced in front of his eyes. Håkon Hagen…*dead*? The day before he was due to hear that Jens's hostile takeover of his company was a done deal.

What?

How?

Jens scanned the email from his in-house lawyer, trying to make sense of the devastating news. Håkon had been rushed to hospital with a suspected heart attack. He was dead on arrival. Jens didn't wonder how his lawyer acquired the confidential information so quickly but knew it was accurate. He paid the man a king's ransom to know everything about his oldest enemy and he expected nothing less than up-to-date information.

In his home office in Bergen, Jens leaned back in his office chair and placed his feet on the edge of his desk, his eyes on the screen but his focus elsewhere. He'd put in years of work, twelve to be precise, and billions of dollars, to acquire Hagen International with the sole purpose of watching Håkon squirm when he told him he now owned the company that had been in Hagen hands for generations. How dared he take the easy way out by dying, and denying Jens his revenge?

The bastard.

Twelve years...twelve years *wasted*. Jens's feet hit the floor and he stood up, pacing the area in front of his Peder Moos desk. When he'd first met Håkon, he'd been a young fishing captain, overseeing his aunt's three-vessel trawler fleet, juggling fish quotas and the wild Arctic seas. He'd had a job he loved, a girl he was mad about, a good life... ambitious but not burning with it.

Then Håkon's daughter had left him.

He would've put Maja jilting him and the break-up video she sent him behind him, or tried to, but Håkon had made that impossible to do. Maja's father's decision to punish him for having the temerity to have an affair with his daughter/princess had ignited their more-than-a-decade-old feud.

Håkon added hardship to heartbreak, and his campaign of harassment had fired up not only Jens's anger but his ambition, and he'd waded into the fight. And he hadn't stopped swinging until he had as much power, financially, politically and economically, had as much money—he was a billionaire several times over—and as much influence as Håkon Hagen. All he'd needed, the jewel in his crown of revenge, was to watch Håkon's face when he informed him he'd acquired his company too.

But that wasn't going to happen now. And that was wholly unacceptable.

If Jens could exchange his empire based on shipping, gas and commercial fishing, his billions, just to see Håkon's reaction to knowing Jens owned Hagen International, he would. If he could drag him back from the dead to have that final confrontation, he wouldn't hesitate. Everything he'd done for years had been building up to that moment. He'd wanted to see the blood drain from

Håkon's face, to know he held his future in his hands—just as Håkon had once held his.

What was he supposed to do now? Revenge was the fuel that fired him, vengeance was all that mattered. Hagen International was just a company, it had no feelings and didn't care who owned or controlled it. The only link left to the company, to the famous Norwegian family, was Maja...

Maja. The girl who'd stomped on his heart and bolted from Bergen, just a few hours before they were due to say 'I do'. The person he once would've moved mountains and parted seas for. She'd promised she'd be at the court-house, had been prepared, she'd assured him, to endure her father's wrath to be with him. For the first time in his life, he'd felt wholly loved and valued, excited about his future, ready to trust, ready to love. Stupidly believing he wouldn't, this time, be abandoned.

What had he been thinking trusting her, anyone, with his heart and his dreams in the first place? From a young age he knew that if people could screw you over, they would.

And the need for revenge didn't die with death, it didn't fade away because Håkon was beyond his reach. He'd come this far, and he wouldn't be denied. Maja was out there, somewhere, and a still handy target for retribution.

Håkon might've waged the war, but she'd been the catalyst.

And, with Håkon gone, she was now a viable alternative target. The *only* target. Jens stopped pacing and squinted at the Hans Fredrik Gude landscape he'd purchased at auction last year. He'd outbid Håkon for the oil painting, and the auctioneers had achieved a record price for the artist in the process.

Håkon was gone, but Maja was…*somewhere*.

Jens leaned across his desk, picked up his phone and punched in a number. When his lawyer answered he issued a terse instruction. 'Find Maja Hagen. I don't know where she is, or what she's doing, but I want her found. *Today*.'

CHAPTER ONE

MAJA HAGEN'S FIRST major exhibition, and her first visit back to Norway in twelve years was going quite well…if she ignored the irritating issue of her father dying.

It was so typical of her father to cast a shadow over her first professional accomplishment. And if her thoughts were harsh, then that was because Håkon Hagen had been a harsh man. He was—*had been*—controlling, dominating and more than a little narcissistic. She'd even go as far as to say he'd been tyrannical, with a deep-seated need to keep all his soldiers, especially her, in a regimented, never-out-of-step line.

Was she sorry he was dead? She wished she could say she was, but she'd lost her father a long time ago. If she'd ever really had one. She'd had a man who provided her with a house to live in, fancy clothes and toys, and his instantly recognisable name. Love, affection and unconditional support, everything she'd needed the most, hadn't been part of Håkon's emotional landscape.

Maybe if she'd been his much-longed-for son, she might've experienced some affection from him. But she was just a reminder of her long-dead mum's inability to give him the male child to carry on the Hagen name. After her mum's death, and for the majority of her childhood, she lived with a cold, hard man who thought her presence in his life was a hassle.

Now he was dead, and she felt…nothing.

She'd seen, online, the photographs of her stepmother—Håkon had married his long-term mistress after Maja left Norway—outside the church yesterday, ready for his funeral. The funeral service had been strictly invitation only but, despite Håkon Hagen having few close friends—dictators and despots rarely did—many people had come to say goodbye to one of Europe's most influential businessmen. Despite his lawyer having her contact details in case of emergency, and him having informed her of her dad's death, she hadn't received an invitation to attend the service.

They'd had no contact for over a decade; she'd said everything she'd needed to say to her father twelve years ago and was happy to avoid the press hanging around outside the church and the cemetery. Håkon, pompous and patronising, always polarising, had made headlines one last time.

Right now, she should concentrate on her opening night. She wanted to hear the comments of the carefully curated guests, clock their reactions, and get their honest, unfiltered opinions because M J Slater never gave interviews or attended opening nights. It was just another quirk of the elusive, reclusive photographer.

Maja, dressed in a server's uniform of a white T-shirt, severe black trousers and service boots, picked up a tray of champagne glasses and slipped into the gallery of the premier arts centre situated on Rasmus Meyers allé. She moved to the side of the room and watched for reactions to her massive images hanging on the high walls of the light-filled space. This section of the famous Bergen art centre was dedicated to up-and-coming artists, a space to showcase the work of rising talents. Maja swallowed and rocked on her heels. After years of struggling, shooting portraits and weddings, she was starting to gain recognition as an 'interesting' and 'provocative' photographer. Best of all, her art was hers, wholly unconnected to her past and family name. No one knew M J Slater was, in fact, Maja Hagen, the only daughter of Norway's most powerful and influential businessman.

What would these people think if they knew she was Håkon's daughter? Would they like her work more, or judge it more harshly? If they knew she was Maja Hagen, they would either fawn over or despise it, and it would be viewed through a Håkon Hagen lens. She'd either fail dismally or be over-complimented, neither of which she wanted. M J Slater was an unknown artist, with no family baggage. Between her father and Jens Nilson, Maja Hagen had trunkloads of the stuff.

No, she wasn't going to think about Jens. Not now. Not today. Definitely not while she was in Bergen, in Norway. Coming back was hard enough without having to deal with the memories.

Maja deliberately shifted her focus back to her father. She wondered who would inherit Hagen International, the empire her great-grandfather started in the nineteen-twenties. Who would inherit his houses, his art, his billions? Her stepmother? It wouldn't be Maja herself. When she'd stormed out of Håkon's life, she'd given up her name, her country and any access to family money.

She didn't regret her decision. She was succeeding or failing by her own merits, removed from her father's criticism and the influence of his name. She'd freed herself of his control, and she now lived life on her own terms.

Maja watched a young man, dressed head to toe in

designer clothing, stop in front of her biggest image, an eight-by-six-foot monochrome photograph. He tipped his head to the side, and frowned, obviously unsettled by the provocative image of a ragged, dirty street child bending to pick up a discarded, but incredibly big and expensive, bouquet of roses and lilies. The juxtaposition was, she admitted, jarring.

Some people loved her work, others walked around the gallery frowning. She photographed the misunderstood and the isolated, the marginalised, people who stood on the outside looking in, and individuals who didn't quite fit in. Some hated their lives, others revelled in the freedom of not being accepted. Most just tried to get on with life, accepting the hand it dealt them, playing their cards as best they could, whether it was a ghetto in Mumbai or a luxury mansion in Dubai.

You could, as Maja knew, be as unhappy rich as you were poor. Did she put distance between herself and her subjects because she liked the concept of standing apart, because she refused to engage with people beyond a certain level of intimacy? Maybe. Probably.

Another perfectly groomed young man stepped up to look at the huge image. 'Who's this artist again?'

'M J Slater,' came the reply. 'I've never heard of him before, but Daveed Dyson told me he's someone to look out for.'

Daveed Dyson, the celebrated art critic, was talking about her? *Wow.* But why did everyone always assume M J Slater was a man? Not that she cared: as long as her identity remained a secret, they could assume she was a purple and pink spotted lizard.

'Where's he based?'

'No idea. There's no information on him.'

Scotland was her home now, Edinburgh her city. She was a UK citizen through her mum. Norway held too many bad memories, too much intense regret, guilt and pain, for her to stay.

The last time she'd been here, she'd been so young. So naïve. Initially so convinced love would triumph, that it stood a chance against financial power and influence. It didn't. Love withered when faced with wealth and power built up over generations, when it came up against someone as heartless, ruthless and controlling as her father.

Someone touched her shoulder and Maja turned to look at her frustrated business manager, Halston. She handed him a glass of champagne and ignored his scowl. He'd far prefer her to be dressed in a little black number, schmoozing and talking about her art with the very rich guests. He wasn't a fan of her need to remain incognito.

Maja looked away from Halston, pretending he was another guest. 'Did they like them? Hate them?' She didn't know...she never did. For most of her life, her father had made her feel she wasn't enough, and she still needed to feel validated and reassured. Would she ever outgrow that trait? She hoped so.

'That's why I came to find you,' Halston told her, making it look as though he were issuing an instruction to a server. 'It's a huge success, with one anonymous buyer buying your four biggest pieces earlier tonight at an exclusive preview.'

She placed a hand on her heart, relieved. 'Great. But we'll only be able to claim a hit exhibition when the art critics have posted their reviews in a week.'

'The curator is going to announce the identity of the buyer of the four images. Apparently, he's a big deal. I came to warn you not to react if you want to stay hidden,'

Halston told her before moving off. Finding a tall table, she placed her tray on it and slid behind a huge flower arrangement. Nobody would notice her here...

The atmosphere in the room changed and then the crowd in front of her parted, as it would for a king or queen. And Maja tensed, electricity skittering up her spine as every neuron in her body caught fire. Someone tapped a microphone and called for the room's attention. But Maja had eyes only for the man standing next to the gallery curator, looking as remote as Bouvet Island thousands of miles away. Her body immediately reacted to his presence, turning hot, then cold.

Jens was here...

Memories, so many of them, whipped through her. His hands in her hair as he moved her head to take their kiss deeper, his big hands on her hips as she stood between him and the wheel of his fishing trawler, his chin resting on her head as they returned from the fishing grounds north of Lofoten. Sneaking him past the groundsman and the housekeeper working at her father's holiday home on the outskirts of Svolvær and up to her bedroom, where he initiated her into the delicious art of sex. She'd had a few lovers since, but none who had made her feel the way Jens had.

There were a few remnants of the young man she'd known and loved in the face of the man standing across the room. His face, ridiculously handsome with rugged features, olive skin and navy blue, almost black eyes, looked a little leaner. His hair, the deep brown of a sable's coat, was as thick as before, cut shorter to keep the waves under control. He'd been big before, always muscled—working on a fishing boat was not for the weak or puny—but he seemed taller, more powerful.

But the biggest change was in his attitude, in his posture, in the sardonic tilt of his chin.

Her eyes flew across his face, and she could find nothing of the young man who loved to make her laugh, whose eyes lightened with affection, whose mobile mouth twitched with amusement. This was a harder, tougher, icier version of the Jens she'd known...

As devastatingly attractive, a thousand times more dangerous.

She placed her hand on her heart. Had her fertile imagination conjured up his presence? She squeezed her eyes tight, then lifted her lids and blinked. Nope, Jens Nilsen hadn't disappeared, he wasn't a mirage. She took in his designer dark grey suit, the pale green shirt, his perfectly knotted tie, and the pocket handkerchief peeking out from his breast pocket. Black-framed glasses gave him an added layer of intimidation, something he didn't need.

'Ladies and gentlemen, let us welcome one of our institution's patrons, Jens Nilsen, the esteemed and pre-eminent collector of Scandinavian, particularly Norwegian, art. At a private viewing this afternoon Mr Nilsen made a bid for, and acquired, M J Slater's *Decay and Decoration* series, four images in total, for an undisclosed amount.'

Maja couldn't pull her eyes off Jens. He was a force field she couldn't resist. She drank him in, clocking his changes, noticing what remained the same. His presence was a magnet, and she couldn't disconnect...

Her art, the fact that she'd sold her work to him, that this was a successful exhibition...it all faded away. Jens, and his presence, took up all her mental space.

Maja watched, fascinated, as he tensed. Someone who didn't know him well wouldn't notice his fractionally tighter shoulders, or the slight lift of his chin. His eyes narrowed, and he reminded her of a super-predator who'd caught the scent of his prey on the wind. Maja held her breath as his eyes scanned the gallery, his dark eyes skimming the faces in the crowd. He passed over her. As she'd told Halston earlier, nobody noticed the servers…

But why did he ask for a private viewing earlier? Did he connect M J Slater with her? Was that why he'd bought her work? No, that didn't make any sense…if he knew the artist was the woman who'd jilted him via a blasé video, he'd be more likely to burn her work than buy it.

Jens had no idea why she acted the way she did, that all of her actions—*most* of her actions—had been done out of a desperate need to protect him from her father, to keep Jens off Håkon's radar. Maja had never wanted Jens to be collateral damage in the war between her and her father. Yet here he was, and the floor under her feet rocked and rolled.

Then, suddenly, Jens's head whipped back at speed, his eyes slammed into hers and Maja took a step back, the heat of his gaze pinning her feet to the floor. Of course, he'd find her; Jens's sixth sense for danger, for out-of-the-ordinary situations, had served him well when he'd pitted himself against the stormy Norwegian and Barents seas. He listened to his instincts, and as his eyes raked over her, seared through her, she knew, without a shadow of a doubt, Jens knew exactly who she was.

Fight or flight…she'd never faced this decision before. Flight won out and Maja fled.

She'd known it wouldn't be long before he found her in the small, tucked-away reception area on the second floor of the gallery. Maja turned away from the window when she heard the soft click of the door opening. The air in the room rushed out and she felt light-headed and spacy.

Maja released a low curse, unable to make sense of her now upside-down world. She'd never expected to see him again, he was part of her past. She'd spent more than a decade trying to get over him, to forget. Yet here he stood, six feet three inches of brutal intelligence, physical brawn and restrained rage. How could his effect on her still be so strong, so potent?

'Jens…' She swallowed, internally wincing at her high-pitched voice. 'What are you doing here? How did you find me?'

'Admittedly, you're a hard woman to track down, Maja,' Jens said, closing the door behind him. He crossed his arms, pushed one big shoulder into the wall next to the door and crossed his left foot over his right ankle. He reminded her of a big cat about to pounce. And she was his prey.

'I didn't *know* you were looking for me,' Maja replied, ignoring her spluttering heart. There was no air in this room, she was finding it difficult to breathe. Maja felt her pulse inch upward and dots appear before her eyes.

No, she wasn't going to let emotion, and the past, the impact of Jens, override her common sense. She needed to pull herself together and start thinking instead of reacting. She doubted she would be able to control this situation, but she could stop acting as if she were a flapping fish he'd hooked. 'What do you want?'

His expression turned sardonic. 'Maybe just to say hello to the woman I once thought would become my wife.'

So many questions bubbled on her tongue. Did he know she was M J Slater? Why had he bought her *Decay and Decoration* series? Would he ask her why she was working as a server at this event?

His expression moved from saturnine to thoughtful. He walked across the room and picked up from the coffee table a brochure advertising her exhibition. He flicked his thumb against the edge as he looked down at the brochure. Maja, a knot in her stomach, walked over to him. She inhaled a hit of his cologne, something woody and citrusy. He smelled gorgeous but a part of her wished he still smelled of soap and the sea.

'After I heard of Håkon's death, I instructed my lawyer to track you down,' he said. 'He had no luck finding you.'

Frankly, luck was running short all around. 'I keep a low profile,' Maja hedged. 'And you just happened to be at this exhibition?'

'I've been collecting art for a few years now. Curators often reach out to me.' He smiled, but Maja shivered. Something was off and she still felt the urge to bolt out of the door.

'I was offered, but declined, an invitation to a private viewing of M J Slater's work earlier this week. But, annoyed by the lack of progress in finding you, and in need of a distraction, I thought I'd take a look. I came in earlier, about an hour before the gallery opened tonight.'

Right. It didn't sound as though he'd connected her with the artist, thank God. Maybe this really was a coincidence, maybe he'd followed her out of the gallery simply to reconnect. But that wasn't Jens's style. He didn't do simple, and the tension in his body suggested this was more than just a *Hey, you're back!* chat. What did he want? What could he be up to? Why did he still make her heart bang against her chest? And why was panic, the mental equivalent of a herd of spooked wild horses, galloping through her?

Jens flipped over the brochure, and Maja looked down at the printed picture of one of her few framed images.

She didn't like frames. She wasn't crazy about her photographs being harnessed by a border. Jens jabbed his finger at the image on the brochure and it took her some time to realise he was pointing to her tiny, but flamboyant, signature in pencil on the white matte board within the frame.

'You sign your m's with a distinctive flourish.'

Reaching into his jacket, he pulled out a slim leather wallet and flipped it open. Maja watched, rooted to the spot, as he pulled out a faded Post-It note and gently opened the small square. He held the corner between his thumb and forefinger so that she could see the writing.

Jens, I love you. I can't wait to marry you. M

And there was her distinctive 'M', the same one she used when she signed her work. One was a carbon copy of the other, and a three-year-old could tell they were written by the same hand.

No!

No!

She'd wanted to think otherwise but he *knew*. He'd linked her with M J Slater. Jens was now the only person other than Halston who knew that connection between the ex-heiress and the rising-star photographer. Maja bit down on her lip, her eyes flying from the note to the brochure. Dammit. It was such a little slip-up, but one with huge consequences.

'I never expected you to keep that note, you're not the sentimental type.' If he'd tossed it, they wouldn't be here.

Jens's cold, furious eyes slammed into hers and she shivered at the intensity of his gaze. 'I keep it as a reminder of what a naïve fool I was.'

Maja bit down on the inside of her cheek, tasting blood. Panic, hot and uncontrollable, bubbled in her throat and made her skin prickle. This small room now felt smaller, darker.

Hello, anxiety, my old friend.

Coming back to Norway had been a bad idea.

After growing up with a father who hated her, who tried to control everything about her, she'd wanted to break free. Of his control, of his influence and the associations attached to the Hagen name. She'd vowed she'd make her way in the art world, away from the sphere of her father's influence, and for the past twelve years she'd worked hard to achieve that goal.

She'd come back to Bergen only because this exhibition was an opportunity she couldn't miss, a launching pad into the big leagues, a way to get her name out to collectors and connoisseurs. She'd kept up her strategy of lying low, partly because she didn't want anyone digging into her past, partly because her elusiveness was her unique selling point. She avoided the media and refused all one-on-one interviews, wanting her photographs to speak for themselves.

As M J Slater she was shielded from the negative, and positive, connotations of being Håkon's daughter. She was, finally, being recognised, and maintaining her anonymity was beyond important. She'd made so many sacrifices and if she was 'outed' now, everything she'd worked so hard for would be lost. She had to persuade Jens to keep her identity a secret. But how?

'What do you want?' she asked, wincing at the anxiety in her voice.

'If it's an explanation of why I left you hanging at the courthouse, and why I sent you that video, why I ghosted you, I can do that, I owe you that,' she continued, hoping to move him off the subject of her art, the exhibition and her using a different name.

And after she apologised for leaving him and explained why, asked him to keep her secret, she could move on, and put him—and his breath-stealingly attractive face and body—in the past where he belonged.

Then she'd go back to her hotel room, call room service and order the biggest cocktail known to man.

Jens tipped his head to the side, narrowed his eyes and his smile held no warmth. Oh, God, she was in a world of trouble here.

'I'm not interested in explanations or apologies, Maja.'

She frowned, puzzled. 'Then what do you want?'

'Quite a bit actually,' he told her, his deep voice rumbling over her skin. 'Especially from you.'

CHAPTER TWO

JACKPOT!

Judging by the panic and fury in Maja's expressive eyes—a mixture of gold, green and smoky brown—Maja didn't want him, or anyone, knowing she was M J Slater. And that gave him the leverage he needed. It was the opening he'd needed, his path to revenge.

Jens raked his hand through his hair. Maja was the last Hagen standing, the only person he could target, but, for the first time in years, he didn't know exactly how he was going to get what he needed from her. Payback. Since discovering who she was just a few hours ago, and by sheer coincidence, he'd been on the back foot, not a position he felt comfortable with, not any more. He called the shots, laid out the terms, and operated from a position of strength. He'd forgotten how it felt to be indecisive, out of control.

Jens turned to look out of the small window, needing a moment to get his wayward thoughts, and jumping heart, under control. He'd told her the truth when he'd said that he'd come to this gallery as a distraction, but he'd immediately felt a connection to her work, and, even before he'd known who she was, had made an excellent offer for her four biggest, and best, images.

He'd done the deal and had been on his way out when he'd noticed her signature on the matte board of one of her few framed images. He'd stared at her signature for some time, unable to believe what his mind insisted was true, that M J Slater was Maja.

His expensive lawyers, and their investigative team, hadn't been able to trace her, and he now knew why. Had she changed her name legally or was M J Slater just a pseudonym she used for her work?

He could ask, but Maja was no longer the sweet, biddable girl he remembered.

She still wore her blonde hair the same way, long and loosely curled, and had the same leggy, slim figure.

Back then, like tonight, she wore no make-up, but then she'd never needed any. Her skin was clear, her dark eyelashes and eyebrows highlighting her fantastic green and gold eyes. Years ago, she dressed in bold colours and wore her frequently unbrushed hair in messy buns. Her fingers and clothes were always splattered with oil paint. He remembered names like Indian Orange, Viridian and Prussian Blue, and he'd laughed when she couldn't explain how it came to be on her butt cheek or on the side of her breast.

She was older now, and ten shades bolder than the girl with whom he'd spent that long-ago summer, a woman in every sense of the word. Powerful, compelling, and twice as dangerous.

Loving her had caused him untold grief and Jens knew, because he was a man who paid attention, she'd acquired polish and confidence, a smidgeon of power, in the years they'd spent apart. He was about to step into a field planted with landmines and he needed to watch his step.

Possibly every twitch, maybe even every breath he took.

After years of dealing with Håkon, he'd assumed Maja would be an easier proposition. How wrong he'd been.

Memories snapped at him, and images popped into his

mind. Standing next to Aunt Jane as he watched his mum walk away with a wave and a smile, never to, in any way that mattered, return. Watching her, albeit from a distance, conquer the West End and then Broadway, hoping that after this play, that musical, another award, things would change. That in her next email—infrequent and sporadic—she'd tell him she was prepared to acknowledge him, the son she'd left behind and kept secret. He'd craved her acknowledgement and approval, and dreamed of a life where Flora would be a real mother.

Maja leaving him, wholly unexpected and completely devasting, had tossed him back into a place he'd never wanted to revisit. She'd caused long-buried emotions to slap and swipe him, scratch and claw. He'd hated her for sending him back there.

After she'd left, he'd used every bit of self-control he could muster, and gathered every last drop of his anger and fear, vowing to use them to fuel his ambition. He'd stopped believing in relationships and emotional connections and decided he didn't need anyone's approval but his own. He'd never again allow himself to feel rejected and abandoned. He'd left his childish need to be loved and validated behind.

He preferred action to wallowing in unproductive sentiment. Revenge to reconciliation.

It was simple… He couldn't make Flora acknowledge him, Håkon was dead but Maja would regret messing with him. And if she had to pay for her father's decisions, then so be it.

Sins of the fathers and all that.

Jens pushed his shoulders back, picking up and discarding possibilities on how to use Maja's secret identity to extract retribution. He knew something no one else did, that M J Slater was Maja Hagen, the daughter of Norway's most famous, now dead billionaire and that she desperately wanted to retain her anonymity. How could he use that information?

'Why haven't you been recognised?'

She lifted one slim shoulder and let it drop. 'Nobody expects a server to be Håkon's daughter or the artist. And Håkon rarely released photographs of me to the media, so I was never a household face or easily recognisable.'

She'd told him she and Håkon had a strained relationship but, judging by the bitterness in her voice, it had been a lot more troubled than he realised. Interesting.

'Why are you keeping your identity a secret?'

'Why do you think you have the right to ask me that?' she swiftly retorted. 'What I do, and how I live my life, has nothing to do with you!'

'So if I went out there and announced to the world that you are Håkon's daughter, you'd be fine with it?'

Panic, then fear, flashed in her expressive eyes, and he noticed her full body tremble. 'Don't you dare!' she whisper-shouted. 'I swear... Jens...' The little colour in her face leeched away. 'You *can't* do that.'

'Oh, you have no idea what I can and can't do, Maja,' he assured her. Because he preferred to keep his adversaries off balance, he switched subjects.

'I'm sorry about your father,' Jens stated.

Maja released a disbelieving snort. 'No, you are *not*. I've read about your feud with my father, Jensen. You probably raised a glass when you heard about his death.'

'Okay, I'm not,' he admitted.

What he did feel was cheated. By dying before Jens had time to inform him the hostile takeover of Hagen International was successful, Håkon had robbed him of his revenge. Håkon's dying had ended their feud before he knew Jens was the winner. Jens might've been ahead of the game, and might've had Håkon on the back foot, but it meant little since Håkon had left the world thinking he still retained control of his company.

And the world assumed they were still equals. He needed everyone to know he'd bested Håkon, that the promises he'd made to himself as a scared, hurt twenty-four-year-old were fulfilled.

'So, is stating inane trivialities something you do now?' Maja asked, her voice dripping with disdain.

'If I have to.'

If it served his purpose. He'd do whatever he could, short of crossing the line into doing something that could land him in jail, to obtain the revenge he needed, the payback his pride demanded.

Maja made a show of looking at her watch. God, she was beautiful. Lovely and sexy, she sent blood coursing south and stopped the airflow to his lungs. He cocked his head, surprised at how much he desired her.

It was such a pity he was going to have to destroy her. But he'd made a vow, to himself and to his aunt, the woman who took him in because his mum couldn't be bothered to take him with her to Broadway, or anywhere, that he'd take Hagen down. Any way he could. Håkon was now beyond his reach, but Maja wasn't.

And, by God, he was going to make her pay. *Someone* had to.

He leaned his shoulder into the wall and wished he felt as relaxed as he looked. Memories of them rolling around in bed bombarded him—tangled limbs, streaking hands, gasps and groans—and he needed to banish them. Immediately. He could not afford to be distracted by the memory of great sex.

'So how was the funeral? Did you cry? How are you going to spend the many billions he left you?'

Her eyes turned a deeper gold, and Jens knew he was wading into dangerous waters. She made him feel raw and off balance, tumultuous and out of control. Like that stupid, in love, trusting kid he'd been, the one with dreams and hope. He'd been hot-headed and temperamental, but he wasn't like that any more. He sucked in a deep breath. Then another, relieved when his heart rate slowed down. He needed to be cool and collected. Precise and deliberate. *Focused.*

'I won't discuss my father with a man I haven't seen in twelve years,' Maja quietly stated.

She'd acquired polish in the intervening years. Strength and dignity.

'I won't say it was nice seeing you again, Jensen. A complete surprise, yes,' Maja said, her voice as cool as the wind that blew off the Svartisen glaciers. 'I'd appreciate it if you kept my identity as M J Slater a secret.'

She was worried he wouldn't, he could see it in her eyes. But she wouldn't beg and he respected her for that. Maja rocked on her heels, then lifted her chin. 'Goodbye, Jensen.'

It had been a long time since someone turned their back on him, even longer since anyone walked away before he was done. He was one of the most powerful men—if not the most powerful man—in the country, on the continent, with a vast multibillion fortune at his disposal. He dated A-list celebrities, prima ballet dancers, supermodels and sports stars. Although his relationships were brief, he called the shots. Conversations, dates, and sexual encounters happened on his schedule, not someone else's.

He no longer allowed people, events or situations to unbalance him or upset him, nor did he permit people to dig under his skin. He refused to feel vulnerable or exposed. Vulnerability, mentally and emotionally, equalled weakness. Inadequacy, ineffectiveness and helplessness were not part of his emotional landscape.

Emotions ate away at his control. He didn't understand, or tolerate, them, so he never indulged in them, ever. Anger was always tempered by reason, affection by an innate inclination to distrust people and the things they said. Sex was a biological impulse, and he didn't have time to make convivial connections. The emptiness he sporadically experienced was a throwback to him once believing he needed his mum to acknowledge that he was hers, that she was proud to claim him, to feel whole. He was happy in his own company, content to be alone and he didn't need anyone to validate his existence. He knew better than to expect, or want, that.

He was overthinking this, giving it too much energy. *None* of that mattered. He had what he craved, revenge, in his sights.

If Maja thought she was walking out on him again, she was wrong. That wasn't something he'd allow. It was time for him to take control of this situation.

'We're not done, Maja,' Jens said, his tone icily calm.

She stopped, and slowly turned around, frustration pulling her eyebrows together. 'There's nothing more to say, Jens.'

'You promised me an explanation about the past,' he reminded her. Not that it would change anything…he'd set his course and there would be no deviations.

Maja's mouth moved and he knew a silent curse had passed over her lips. She'd clearly hoped he'd forgotten her earlier promise. He never forgot, and he didn't forgive. They said the best revenge was to move on, to be happy, to flourish and to find inner peace.

Rubbish. Jens wanted none of that.

He looked at his watch 'But that will have to be another time. I need to get back, my absence will be noticed.'

'Don't let me stop you,' Maja muttered.

Feisty. Again, it was unexpected. 'I expect to see you at my home, the Bentzen estate, tomorrow night. Be there at six.'

Her eyes widened in shock. Was she annoyed he'd made her sound as if she were a parcel, to be directed around at his whim? Or was she surprised that he lived in the mansion once owned by her maternal grandparents?

'You own the Bentzen mansion?' she demanded.

'I do.' The estate had come on the market a few years ago and, on hearing that Håkon planned to add the estate to his property portfolio, he'd swooped in, made an excellent offer and yanked it away. Håkon had been, it was reported, incandescently furious.

He'd never planned on living there but, having recalled Maja's telling him how much she loved the sprawling nine-bedroomed house in the exclusive suburb, he'd thought he should, at the very least, inspect the property he'd purchased purely to annoy Håkon.

The tour hadn't gone as expected, and he'd fallen in love with the house, its amazing views and extensive grounds. He now spent as much time as he could in Bergen and was in the process of moving his headquarters from Oslo to this pretty city so he could live in the house full-time.

'When did you buy—?' She shook her head and pursed

her lips, and Jens knew she was trying to ignore her curiosity. 'That's not important. I have no intention of seeing you again.'

'Be there or I'll walk downstairs and tell everyone you are M J Slater. It won't take the press long to join the dots. Your anonymity, which I suspect is very important to you, will instantly disappear.'

Fear and frustration tightened her mouth, and he knew he had her. He wasn't sure why flying under the radar was so essential to her and it didn't matter.

She sucked in a deep breath, shook her head and then her eyes narrowed. 'You wouldn't do that to me.'

That was where she was wrong. There was little he wouldn't do to exact his revenge. Sacrificing her identity? He'd do it if he had to and not think twice about it. But not today.

Right now, just the threat was enough.

'Be at the mansion at six,' Jens repeated, keeping his expression impassive. He knew she was looking for an argument she could use, a way to wiggle out of this situation, but she was out of options. He held all the power, and she knew it.

'Please don't tell them who I am, Jens.'

He heard the tremor in her voice and steeled himself against it. Payback was all that mattered.

'Then you know what you must do.'

Maja knew she had no choice but to meet Jens tonight. She'd spent the day trying to work out how to extricate herself, but he'd pushed her into a corner. Her only option was to make the six o'clock appointment and that was why she sat in a rental car a few yards away from that oh-so-familiar front door. She looked over the extensive gardens and sighed.

This charming brick mansion, built on three levels, was once owned by her maternal grandparents and the only place she and her mum could truly relax. They'd left Oslo on any pretext to visit Bergen and her *mormor* and *morfar*. She'd ridden her tricycle in the spacious hall, snuggled up to her grandparents on couches in the main living area and the den, and learned to swim in its incredible heated pool.

She remembered amazing views, many bedrooms, the four-car garage, and that her grandmother loved the huge solarium. The housekeeper had lived in the apartment above the garage, and Maja had spent many hours exploring the large garden. Bentzen House had been a refuge until her grandmother and mum had died in a car accident shortly before her tenth birthday. Her heartbroken grandfather had followed a few months later and the executors of the estate, of which she had been the heir, had sold Bentzen House. She still wished they hadn't.

Maja's life changed after their deaths, it became bleaker and darker as she slowly realised her uninterested father neither loved nor liked her. It didn't take her long to discover that Håkon didn't find her smart enough, pretty enough, charming enough…

In a nutshell, she wasn't the son he so desperately wanted.

While she'd had a million regrets about *how* she'd left Jens—dumping him by video had been a cowardly act but one Håkon had forced her into—she didn't have a single regret about leaving Norway, striking out on her own, and leaving the Hagen legacy behind. She'd walked away from unimaginable family wealth and knew she'd make the same decision again. She was still Maja, but she wasn't a Hagen, not in any way it counted. She liked not being linked to her famous father and she'd protect her anonymity, her work and her pseudonym with everything she had.

She'd worked so hard to get to this point in her life, all her career success was hers alone, and she wasn't prepared to jeopardise her independence, artistic and emotional. Besides, she wasn't done with Bergen, she wanted to reacquaint herself with the city she'd known as a child. She wanted to spend time at the harbour, photographing the cheerful and charming houses or wandering down the narrow streets, ducking in and out of tiny, interesting independent shops.

She wanted to see more of Norway too. She wanted to get out onto the water, and was considering a cruise to Svolvær, to experience the Arctic beauty in all its rugged splendour. Maybe when she was done with Jens, she'd do that. It would be an excellent way to recharge her depleted emotional batteries. She couldn't do that if the world knew who she was. And to stop that from happening, she needed to meet with her ex.

Maja leaned back in her seat and rubbed her damp hands on her thighs, trying to gather her courage.

She'd pulled on a lightweight thigh-length cotton jersey, and wore skinny dark jeans and high-top trainers. She'd arranged her hair into a messy bun, anchored with a few pins she'd jammed into her hair. She didn't wear any lipstick, nor did she check whether she had mascara flecks under her eyes or on her cheeks. She'd made no effort for Jens Nilsen. She would not give him the satisfaction of thinking she wanted to impress him. She didn't want him to think she cared about his opinion. She didn't. Not one little bit.

Their years apart had changed him, of that Maja had no doubt. The fine lines fanning from the corners of his eyes were deeper and his eyes were now more black than blue, hard and uncompromising. It was obvious his mouth had forgotten how to smile. Yesterday she'd sensed his every muscle was on constant high alert, ready to spring into action, to jump into a fight.

Jens was tense from the top of his expertly cut hair to his size thirteen feet. He was a champagne cork about to be released, a pressure valve about to blow. But, worst of all, he'd morphed into a man just like her father. Someone she'd always feared and frequently loathed. Hard-headed and ruthless, unyielding and relentless.

Even back then, there was a part of her that had been a little relieved to be given an excuse to walk away from Jens. His intensity and self-confidence had intimidated her. Despite being so young, she'd known she would've been low on his list of priorities, and that she'd resent his single-minded focus on his career. It wasn't that she hadn't believed he loved her—he had, as much as he could. Twelve years ago, he'd been so like her father in too many ways that counted, and the realisation had terrified her.

And a part of her had known marrying him would be jumping from the frying pan into the fire.

But she did regret how she'd ended their relationship. She'd hurt him, embarrassed him, broken her promises to him and done it all in a callous manner. And Jens wasn't someone who'd let that slide. He wanted payback. But at what cost?

She had to meet with him and find out what he wanted. And whether she could give it to him. If she didn't, M J Slater would be outed, and the world would know she was the privileged and supposedly pampered daughter of one of the world's wealthiest men.

The career she'd worked so hard to build would be, to all intents and purposes, over.

She sighed. The over-large wooden front door opened, and Jens leaned against the doorframe, his eyes connecting with hers through the windscreen. He wore navy chinos, and an untucked grey button-down, sleeves rolled up to reveal muscular forearms and a very expensive, vintage Rolex. He looked fabulous, and she briefly wished she'd taken a little more care with her appearance.

Do try to remember that you are not trying to impress Jens Nilsen!

She watched, warily, as he walked over to her and yanked open her door. He gestured for her to get out but Maja, who could be stubborn, gripped her steering wheel and glared at him.

'You're wasting my time, Maja,' he curtly told her.

And who appointed him king of the world? 'I haven't decided whether I am coming inside or not.'

His blue gaze was uncompromising. 'You're coming inside, Maja.'

She lifted her chin. 'What makes you so sure of that?' she demanded.

'One, you don't want to run the risk of me telling the world who you are. Two, you're curious as to how far I'll go to get what I want. Three, you want to see what I've done to your grandparents' house, whether I've changed anything.'

Seriously? Could he be more arrogant if he tried? And damn him for being right. Before she could find her words, and fire them off, he stepped back and pointed to the front door. 'I'll be waiting for you inside.' He glanced at his watch. 'Don't be long, I don't have time to waste. I still have work to do tonight.'

Maja stared at his tall frame as he walked away from her. How dared he issue commands and expect her to curtsy and then obey? She didn't need to be here…she didn't want to be here. And she was done letting Jens Nilsen call the shots.

She'd start the car, go back to her hotel and take a hot shower. After a good night's sleep—or, more realistically, a night tossing and turning—she'd reassess the situation in the morning and work out a way to talk to, and deal with, her ex-lover.

Or…

Or should she go inside and get this over with? The sooner she dealt with him, the sooner she could move on. Maja bent down, picked up her bag and left the car, slamming the door shut. She stomped up to the open front door and walked into the familiar hall. It was empty of her grandmother's ornaments and her grandfather's collection of walking sticks, but the wide staircase was the same, as was the gleaming parquet flooring. Huge, modern, expensive paintings hung on its high walls.

Jens sat on the third step of the staircase, his forearms resting on his knees. 'How long has it been since you were last here?' he asked from his unconventional seat.

She rubbed the back of her neck. 'I was nine, nearly ten, when I last visited the house. Eighteen when I was last in Norway.'

His eyebrows rose, and Maja saw the doubt in his eyes. 'I didn't only walk away from you, Jens, I walked away from my father, and from being a Hagen. I reinvented myself. I went to university, got a degree, and started work. I have been supporting myself ever since.'

He looked sceptical and she couldn't blame him. Daughters of billionaires seldom walked away from a lifetime of wealth and ease, but she had. It hadn't been easy, but she hadn't taken a penny from Håkon since she left Norway.

When she'd turned twenty-five, she'd inherited the proceeds from the sale of this house, and her grandparents' investments, but those first few years alone had been tough.

Maybe if she underscored how estranged she was from Håkon, Jens would leave her be. 'During my last argument with my father, I told him I didn't want anything more to do with him. Håkon didn't believe me, and his lawyer delivered an ultimatum on his behalf. I either apologised and resumed my place as a Hagen, or I had to give up all claims on him and Hagen International.'

'Håkon, always so kind and cuddly,' Jens snidely commented.

'My point is, I chose the latter, I've had no contact with Håkon for twelve years and don't consider myself a Hagen.' She worked hard, tried to be a good person, paid her taxes, and flossed her teeth. What had she done to deserve to be slapped in the face with her past?

'But it's what *I* think that matters, Maja,' Jens softly informed her, his voice both seductive and sinister. 'It's what *I* want that's important.'

She threw up her hands and turned to face him, frustration and fury bubbling up from her stomach into her throat. 'Then tell me! Stop toying with me.'

Jens stood up and came to stand in front of her, his expression implacable and his eyes unreadable. 'Years ago, you promised to marry me, Maja, and that's exactly what you are going to do.'

CHAPTER THREE

MAJA BLINKED AS his words sank in, and then she released a small laugh. Jens had always had an offbeat and dark sense of humour that often made an appearance at wholly inappropriate times. Then she noticed his unchanged expression, his bleak and cold stare, and realised he wasn't joking. She crossed her arms across her chest and bit down on her tongue to stop herself from demanding to know why he wanted to marry her, what game he was playing, and what he'd get from it.

His motivations didn't matter because there was no way she was going to do it.

'In your dreams,' she scoffed. 'That's not going to happen. Not today, not tomorrow or any time in the future.' Maja threw up her hands, distressed. 'You can't *make* me marry you! You're not a Viking raider and I most definitely am not a prize to be claimed.'

His dark eyes remained steady on her face. His expression didn't change, and Maja swallowed. Oh, she recognised the light in his eyes, the sheer determination. She was his entire focus. He meant every word he said and when Jens said he was going to do something, in that tone of voice, with that light in his eyes, he was an unstoppable force. Marrying her was now top of his priority list. But *why*? They hadn't seen each other for over a decade.

'I don't understand why you want to do this,' she told him, agitation causing her to speak an octave higher, her words tumbling over each other.

'You don't need to understand my motives, Maja. You just need to fall in line, which you will, because if you don't I will dismantle the life you spent the last twelve years building,' Jens told her, sounding completely assured. 'Follow me,' he said, before he turned and walked into the bigger of the three reception rooms.

Maja watched him walk away, moving silently despite being so broad and tall. In a daze, she dropped her bag onto the chair next to the hall table but her feet were glued to the floor.

Marriage? *Seriously?*

It was, genuinely, the last thing she'd expected him to say, or suggest. How could he want to marry her, the girl who'd dumped him via a blithe video twelve years ago, the daughter of his biggest rival? What was he thinking? *Was* he thinking?

Maja jammed her hands into the back pockets of her jeans and rocked on her heels. Of course he'd thought this through, Jens wasn't someone who made irrational and impulsive decisions. She didn't know his reasons for his out-there suggestion but she knew he had a plan…

He *always* had a plan.

Once, a long time ago, she'd thought marrying Jens was the be-all and end-all. It was all she'd wanted, being his wife was all she'd desired. He had been, was still, magnetic and charismatic, dizzyingly attractive. And any woman with strong instincts recognised he was the alpha male of the pack, and being his mate came with significant advantages.

But even back then, when she was alone, doubts would

creep in. Away from him, she'd remember their conversations, and she'd realise that there were often times her initial plans for the day—to paint or to read or to visit with her friends—had changed because Jens wanted to do something else. And if she tried to get her way, he'd either boss her into doing what he wanted or give her the silent treatment until she changed her mind. She'd resented his inability to compromise or to see situations from her point of view.

And once she'd seen it, she couldn't stop. She'd started looking for similarities between him and her father and initially only found two—his ambition and incredible work ethic. As she'd looked, she'd found more—impatience, streaks of intolerance, and overriding self-confidence. By the time they were to marry, there had already been a part of her that craved an out.

Then Håkon had given her one. He'd given her an ultimatum. Break it off and have nothing else to do with Jens or he'd systematically and with great precision dismantle the fishing operation Jens managed for his aunt and would one day inherit. Håkon had threatened to have their fishing quotas yanked, buy out the mortgage loans and get them evicted, and poach their staff. Jens would have had to start from scratch.

Either she walked away and he'd leave Jens untouched, or stayed to watch Håkon dismantle everything Jens and his aunt had worked for.

Maja had chosen to run...

If she'd married him, then Jens would have been fighting a battle he couldn't win and she would have become a faded version of herself. Just as her mother had done; she'd withered away under Håkon's heavy hand. If she'd married Jens back then, she'd have risked her independence, her creativity, and her hard-fought battle to find herself.

If they married now, the same would happen. She could see the signs. How could she get out of this? What could she do to change his mind?

What if she just called his bluff, and walked out? What if she told him to do his worst? Well, his worst would be him revealing that she was M J Slater, and she'd lose her anonymity. Art connoisseurs and critics would look at her through a different lens, her art would be compromised. She didn't want her career to be influenced, in any way, by her connection to her father and the Hagen dynasty. She'd worked too hard to allow that to happen.

Maja paced the hall, feeling alone, scared, and cornered. Would it help if she explained why she'd dumped Jens in such a cowardly fashion? Would it help for him to know she had been trying to protect him from her father? Or would that simply anger him further? Would he believe her? Would he even care?

Maja walked into the exquisitely decorated room to join him. Because, really, she had no other option.

Jens walked over to the hidden drinks cupboard in the corner and hit a button. The door slid back, revealing ten different whiskies and every type of spirit available. The fridge under the shelves held all the mixers. It was a hell of a hidden bar. He reached for his favourite twelve-year-old whisky, tossed a bigger than normal measure into a crystal tumbler and threw it back, enjoying the warmth, then the burn.

He had a new goal, a fresh mountain to climb, a new challenge to conquer. Maja was going to marry him—just as she'd promised twelve years ago. And as she walked down the aisle in an expensive wedding gown, he'd show the world he'd bested Håkon, that he was the winner. That he had everything of his. It was the only way to get revenge and, hopefully, Håkon would flip over in his grave.

Maja in a wedding dress would complete the circle. It made sense. His wanting to be with Maja had kicked off his feud with Håkon and his declaration to marry her would be the ultimate 'up yours'. They'd become engaged and he'd insist on them marrying soon.

And then, in front of a packed church, he'd leave her at the altar, just as she'd left him all those years ago.

An eye for an eye, a tooth for a tooth…

But between now and then, he'd have to ride out a few storms.

Blackmailing Maja into marrying him and then jilting her at the altar was his only shot at getting retribution. Last night, he hadn't known how to use her secret identity as leverage, but it hadn't taken him long to figure it out.

And in six weeks, two months at the most, he'd be done with the Hagens for good. They'd be nothing more than a speck in his rear-view mirror.

Jens didn't ask Maja what she wanted to drink, he just lifted the bottle of Macallan and dumped two fingers into crystal tumblers. He carried the glasses over to where Maja stood and pushed one into her hand.

'Butler's night off?' Maja sarcastically asked.

He shrugged, not bothering to explain that there was no butler and that he only had a housekeeper come in a few times a week to clean. He sent his laundry out and had ready-made meals delivered for nights he didn't feel like cooking for himself.

As a child of privilege, she wouldn't understand he still wasn't used to his incredible wealth. That he allowed himself no time to enjoy it. He still subscribed to his aunt's ethos of purchasing only what he needed, not what he wanted. He owned this mansion because he'd bought it out of revenge, and the impressive Oslo flat because he needed to live somewhere close to his company's headquarters. He'd built a luxurious cabin on a private island to the east of Svolvær on land he'd inherited from his aunt for those times when he felt he couldn't breathe, for when it felt as if the city were closing in on him. He had a small boat for when he needed to get out onto the ocean, one car—the Range Rover outside—and a Ducati superbike for when he wanted to get somewhere fast. Or when he needed the wind in his hair and couldn't get out to his boat.

He wasn't into 'stuff', didn't have multiple houses around the world, and when he needed a private jet, or helicopter, he rented one. His only indulgence was art… paintings and sculptures, with a specific emphasis on Scandinavian art. He'd spent many hours listening to Maja about the techniques of her artistic heroes, her favourite paintings, had loved watching her paint and draw. It was the only thing that had stuck after she'd abandoned him.

Jens placed his empty glass on a side table and walked over to the huge doors, reaching up to move the bolt. The doors slid into the walls with a whisper, and he stepped out onto the terrace, immediately heading for the balustrade stopping his guests from falling into the huge heated pool below. He loved to swim—it was his favourite way, apart from sex, to relax.

Sadly, swimming was the only option on the cards tonight.

He turned his head to look back. Maja still stood in the doorway, her eyes on him. She was both puzzled and furious, and she looked exhausted. He had that effect on people. 'What exactly do you want from me, Jens? What are you planning?'

Okay, he'd tell her. Again. Maybe his message would, eventually, sink in. 'We're going to get engaged, plan a huge wedding and you're going to walk down the church aisle in a white dress.'

'So you said,' Maja retorted. 'But, for the sake of moving this conversation along, why would I do that? Why do *you* want to do that?'

'Explanations aren't going to change the outcome, Maja, so we'll skip them.'

'You're expecting me to marry you without an explanation, without some sort of rationale for your ridiculous demands?'

Basically. Jens looked away from her and into the still, fresh night. This situation was complicated and if he had any sense he'd walk away from it, close the door on the past and move on. But that wasn't an option and walking away from his chance to do to her what she did to him was too good to pass up.

He glanced at the huge hot tub at the end of the decking, wishing he could sink into the super-hot water and let the jets massage away his tension.

'I want revenge, Maja, it's that simple.' Jens turned his back to the railing. She wasn't going to let this go without an explanation, so he'd give her the edited, slightly embellished version. 'I presume you know that your father and I locked horns over the years.'

Her expression turned impatient. 'You two were engaged in a decade-long feud, Jens. I read about it, decided you were both fools and refused to read Norwegian business news again.'

She made them sound as if they were children when their fight had been deadly serious with billions of dollars at stake. 'Before Håkon died, I staged a hostile takeover of Hagen International.'

She frowned at him, wrinkling her nose. 'What does that mean? That you were going to buy it without his consent?'

'It's more complicated than that,' he explained. 'Your father was the majority shareholder of the organisation, but he wasn't the only shareholder. The company revenues were sinking, shareholders' dividends also dropped over the past few years. I bypassed your father and approached the shareholders directly and made an offer to buy them out.'

'And they were prepared to sell to you?'

'Yes, I acquired enough shares to make me the principal shareholder. It cost me a bloody fortune, but I was in a position to force your father to dance to my tune.'

'And that was something you wanted to happen, right?'

'Absolutely,' he replied, his voice rising. He cleared his throat, cursing his lack of control.

Keep it tidy, Nilsen. Cool and calm.

She narrowed her eyes, folded her arms and tapped her foot. 'How did the feud start? Did something happen between you and Håkon after I left?'

And wasn't that the understatement of the year?

Her father had wanted to put him in his place for having the temerity to think he could marry Maja in the first place, and he had done his best to destroy him and his business. He'd threatened Jens's and his aunt's livelihoods because Jens had had the cheek to sleep with his daughter, because Jens hadn't known his blue-collared place. He wasn't going to waste the energy explaining that to Maja because, surely, she already knew how their feud had started. She had been the cause of it.

'Your father is dead, and you're here,' he stated, being deliberately cryptic.

'If I could just explain about—'

'I don't need explanations, Maja! There's no excuse for what you did, for the way you did it, so save your breath.'

Maja pushed both hands into her hair and held her head. 'Jens—'

The heat under his temper increased and he felt a bubble of frustration pop, annoyance burn. That he wanted to fight with her, to yell and shout, was a surprise. That wasn't the way he operated any more. She made him feel raw and off balance, tumultuous and out of control.

He didn't like it. At all.

Anger, disappointment and hurt swirled, begging for his heart to let them in. If he opened that door, they'd walk in and take over. Not happening. He needed to focus his attention on revenge. It was easier to handle, clear and sharp.

He gulped at the cool night air, letting it wash over him. He needed to get this done. He'd tell her what he expected to happen, what would happen. She needed to be very clear about what he expected from her.

'Some time soon, I will have to confirm I initiated a hostile takeover of Hagen's and that my takeover bid was successful. I'm going to take flak in the press. I will face accusations of pushing him too hard, that our feud led to his heart attack. That it got out of control.'

'Did it?'

He shrugged. Håkon had enjoyed their feud, far more than Jens did. If he was ruthless, then Håkon was amoral. There wasn't a line he wouldn't cross, and Jens had figured that if he was keeping the old man occupied, then some poor sucker out there was saved the ignominy of dealing with Maja's father.

'News of our engagement will negate any bad press.' Not that he cared what people thought about him and his actions. 'We'll tell everyone that, through you, Håkon and I reconciled, and that he approved of our relationship.'

'And you think people will believe that?' she demanded, radiating scepticism. 'I haven't been seen in my father's company for more than a decade, Jens.'

'When asked where you were or why you were never seen together, he always said you were determined to live your life out of the limelight, and that you wanted to keep your relationship private. And people will believe what I tell them to.'

Maja snorted. 'God, you're arrogant!' She wasn't wrong. 'And trust my father to find a smooth way to explain away my absence from his life.'

'It was a surprisingly effective strategy. Nobody, not even me, suspected you were estranged.' She'd covered her tracks well, and Jens knew Håkon's fierce pride wouldn't have let anyone suspect he and Maja had had irreconcilable differences.

'But now you're back and you're going to stay here, and plan our huge, glamorous wedding.'

She looked at him blankly for a few seconds. When his words settled, she shook her head so hard a thick hank of hair fell from her bun. 'Oh, I am so not doing any of that!' Maja sat down on the edge of a chair and then immediately sprang to her feet, vexatious energy radiating from her. 'This is ludicrous, Jens! Marry? You? I have three words…no, damn, and way.'

He'd planned for this reaction and knew how to counter her resistance. He knew her weak spot.

'That's your choice. But if you do not agree to marry me, move in here and plan the wedding, I will draft a press release and send it to every entertainment editor of every newspaper, print and online, out there. In it, I will detail our relationship, how you broke up with me, and how you left Norway and your father behind. That you were estranged for years.'

He watched as the colour left her face and wondered why he felt a little seasick. It wasn't as if she were innocent. She was the spark that had ignited the war. She had left him. She had *jilted* him. This was payback. He was entitled to it...

He pushed back his shoulders and injected steel into his spine. He needed to find some control. 'I will tell everyone M J Slater is Maja Hagen, and insinuate you used your contacts as Håkon's daughter to snag the exhibition at the gallery. I will also express regret at having purchased your images, that I believe I overpaid and that, on closer examination, your work is derivative and puerile.'

He was a respected collector and had a reputation for spotting new talent and new trends. His word was respected in art circles. A dismissive comment from him could ruin careers bigger and brighter than hers.

She was bone-white now and Jens watched as she swayed, her eyes brilliant in her marble-like face. She cared less about her past as Maja Hagen than she did about being outed as M J Slater. She wanted to protect her artistic identity and her work. Interesting.

'If you say that, about my art, I'll never sell another image again.'

He would never do that to an artist, any artist—even Maja—but she didn't need to know that. He couldn't tell her she was the best photographer he'd seen in a while, and that, on seeing her work, he'd felt the hair on the back of his neck lift. Before he'd even known who she was, he'd known she was a once-in-a-generation talent.

But she didn't need to know that. She just needed to

agree to what he wanted, and what he wanted was for her to become his bride. And because he knew she'd do anything she could to protect her name and her reputation, he knew his 'yes' wasn't far off.

She held up a hand, and he noticed her trembling fingers. 'So, I either marry you or lose my career and my reputation?' she shouted, her words dancing on the wind. She put her hand to her head to hold back her messy hair and bit down hard on her bottom lip. When she released her grip, he saw teeth marks on her lower lip. Desire speared through him and he fought the urge to rush over to her and kiss those marks away.

He wanted to take her in his arms, to turn the anger in her eyes to desire, to feel her sink against him, her slim body pushing into his. The heat they'd generate would cause the paint on the walls to blister, would make the water in the pool boil.

No. Sex wasn't important, payback was. He *needed* to do this. He needed to close the circle and move on.

'Don't do this, Jens. *Please.*'

'I want to announce our engagement in the next week or so. I'll leave it to my PR department to release the news when it's guaranteed to make the most impact. We'll marry, in a glitzy, huge ceremony in six to eight weeks,' he told her. 'Which you are going to organise because I have more important things to do.'

'And how long do I have to stay married to you, or is this a life sentence?' Maja demanded, her voice shaky.

He hadn't thought that far ahead, mostly because he knew they wouldn't be getting legally hitched, as he intended to walk out on her before she got to the altar. He thought fast. 'A year,' he stated. That sounded...reasonable, he supposed.

He saw the capitulation in her eyes, in the way her shoulders slumped. Instead of feeling triumphant, he felt a little sick, and cold. Inside and out. Where was the hit of adrenalin, the rush of success? The satisfaction? He shrugged off his questions and told himself that it would come, that he'd experience satisfaction when he jilted her at the altar.

'Glitzy weddings are not organised in six weeks, Nilsen. They take years of planning.' He lifted his eyebrows, wondering why she was arguing a minor point when they had other, bigger issues at stake.

'I just spent billions acquiring Hagen International, Maja,' he told her. 'Do you really think I couldn't get someone to plan a lavish wedding in that time if I threw money at it?'

Maja closed her eyes and clenched her fists. He'd put her in an untenable position. But she wasn't going to back down. Maja was a fighter and that was what he'd loved about her. 'I won't do it, Jens.'

'You *will* do it, Maja. You don't want the world to know who you are and if you walk out of here without agreeing to do this, I will tell them.' He paused before continuing, letting his threats sink in.

'Take the rest of the weekend to come to terms with the idea, to wrap your head around marrying me,' he added, suddenly, and strangely, tired. 'I won't announce our engagement until Monday at the earliest.' He gestured to the still-full glass she held. 'Can I get you something else to drink?'

The glass whizzed past his head, and he heard it crash on the pool deck below. It was a good thing her aim hadn't improved in the intervening years. He hoped none of the glass shards had landed in the pool itself, they'd be a problem to find in the crystal-clear water. He wiped a splatter of whisky from his cheek and sighed. That whisky was too good to waste, and the glasses had been a matched set of twelve, rare and eye-wateringly expensive.

New blotches appeared on her neck and chest, and her cheekbones turned scarlet. 'You threaten me, blackmail me, demand that I marry you and then calmly ask me what else I'd like to drink? What *else*? Why don't you ask me to sleep with you while you are at it?'

Well, that would be a phenomenal bonus. But...*no*. He was arrogant but not an idiot. He knew that, despite need and lust rolling through him, tightening the fabric of his trousers and heating his blood, despite never wanting a woman more than he wanted Maja, he couldn't let that happen.

He knew that if he slept with her, if he held her close, stroked her amazing skin and tasted her again, he'd be lost. In her, and in the sexual heat they'd always managed to generate. In having her, his need for her would grow, and that would complicate things unnecessarily when the time came to walk away from her. He needed to be able to stay dispassionate, and emotion-free. He needed to be able to leave, and sleeping with her would make that difficult, if not impossible.

But, damn, he wanted her. Seeing her standing in front of him, close enough to smell her heated skin, he burned for her.

He caught Maja's smirk and knew she was waiting for him to lose his cool and his control. He wasn't the impetuous, hot-headed boy she'd known, the one who'd been stupidly, indescribably in love with her. The man who would've done anything and everything for her. He'd craved her back then, convinced that every moment they were alone and he wasn't inside her was a lost opportunity...

He'd put all his dreams for the family he'd never had, for the acknowledgement he'd never felt, the love he'd never known, onto her and had thought she was the answer to all his prayers. Now she was the means to exact his revenge.

That was where her usefulness started and ended.

If he wanted sex, physical relief, he could easily arrange dinner and a few hours in bed with one of a handful of female friends who understood that sex didn't come with strings. Besides, sex wasn't what he wanted from Maja. No, that was a lie, he still wanted her, as much as he ever did. He wanted to wrap her hair around his fist as he nibbled his way down her throat, to her nipple, down her stomach, lower...

But sex would only complicate what was already a convoluted situation. If he took one wrong turn, one misstep, he'd lose himself in her and that wasn't something he wanted, or was prepared, to do.

He forced himself to lift a lazy eyebrow. 'I'm not interested in sleeping with you, Maja.'

Internally, Jens braced himself, waiting for the out-of-the-blue lightning bolt to nail him for that massive lie. When nothing happened, he sent a disbelieving look at the clear sky and shook his head. Maja, and her presence, were turning him from a logical, clear-thinking and practical man into an idiot.

And that was before he touched her. If they connected physically, there was no doubt she'd melt his brain. And his scruples.

'You're not my type any more.'

He thought he saw hurt flicker across her face, but it was gone too soon for him to nail it down. But her deri-

sion and annoyance were easy to see. 'Why are you acting like this, Jens?'

Because she and her father had forced him to. Because
being robotic, and difficult, and emotionally detached were
far less risky than opening up and letting yourself be *seen*,
out of control and full of emotion. He couldn't let her get
under his skin.

'You don't like being treated the way you treated me,
do you?' he whipped back.

He stared at her, off balance. It had been a long time
since he'd been challenged or made to work hard for anything he wanted. What he wanted was, usually, immediately granted. Nobody argued with him or pushed back.

And if he was tired, then she had to be as well. 'Go back
to your hotel, Maja,' he told her, furious with himself for
not keeping better control of this conversation and situation. 'We'll talk later.'

She lifted her head, and her green-gold eyes nailed him
to the terrace.

He recognised the determination in her eyes and
watched as she pulled in a deep breath, then another.

'You've put me in a horrible, untenable situation, Jens,
and I'll never forgive you for this,' she told him, her voice
full of venom.

Forgiveness wasn't something he expected.

'I'll marry you in six weeks on one condition,' Maja
stated.

'You're not in a position to make—'

'Listen to me!' Maja's fierce interjection had him tipping his head to the side, surprised by her scalpel-sharp
tone. 'I wish I had the guts to call your bluff, to believe
that the man I knew would never do this to someone he
once professed to love, but I don't recognise you any more.

Or maybe I do. You've turned into my father, a ruthless, hard-hearted, selfish bastard. Merciless, iron-fisted and cold-blooded.'

They were only words, and he'd heard them before. But instead of rolling off his normally thick hide, they landed as red-hot acid drops on his skin.

'If I agree to marry you, I need your assurance that you will not tell anyone I am M J Slater,' she said, her voice croaking with fear. 'Do I have it?'

'I want the world to know you as Maja Hagen. I'm not interested in your pseudonym,' Jens told her.

'Do you,' she asked through gritted teeth, *'promise?'*

He nodded. And after a beat, Maja nodded back. So she trusted him to keep his word. Interesting. Did she know, or simply sense, that he wouldn't break his promise? He lied, and manipulated words and situations for his benefit, but he never broke a promise. His mother had made too many to him that she'd never kept, and breaking his own was a line he wouldn't cross.

The only time he would ever do that would be when he jilted Maja. He was promising to marry her, with no intention of showing up. This one, never-to-be-repeated time, his need for revenge outstripped his desire to keep his word. And he refused to analyse how he felt about that.

She slowly nodded. 'So, I'll be Maja Hagen for this sham engagement. We'll keep M J Slater out of this.'

That worked for him.

Maja cleared her throat and Jens knew there was more. 'Then I have only one more thing to ask…'

'What is it?'

'The reviews for my exhibition come out a week today. I'd like you to delay the announcement of our engagement until after then.'

Why? What difference did it make? He lifted one eyebrow, silently asking for an explanation.

Maja ran her fingertips across her forehead, her eyes on the floor. 'You're asking for a lot, for me to upend my world, but I'm just asking for a week.' She placed her hands on her hips and lifted her left foot and placed it behind her right calf. Her top teeth bit down into her bottom lip. 'The exhibition is a big one, and my first truly major one. I worked hard to land it. It's the culmination of years of hard work.'

He was aware of how difficult it was to break into the big leagues.

'The exhibition is due to run for another month, but the art-critic reviews will be published a week today. Once they are out, my reputation will be…well, if not cemented, then a great deal more solid than it was before. It might even be able to withstand a bombshell exposé stating that M J Slater is Maja Hagen.'

'I've already said that if you agree to marry me, your secret will be safe.'

She sent him a harsh, narrow-eyed glare. 'Forgive me if I find it difficult to trust you,' Maja shot back. 'I'd like the reviews out before we get engaged. Just as a little extra insurance.'

He couldn't blame her for not trusting him at his word. 'You aren't in the position to demand anything!'

'Yet I still try.'

She was fluent in sarcasm. 'You started this,' he said, his voice barely more than a deep growl.

She nodded. 'And you're ending it, Jensen. Congratulations, you're a bigger jerk than my father.' She met his eyes, fierce and furious. 'Do we have a deal?'

He nodded.

Maja sighed. 'Brilliant,' she muttered. 'Not that you care but…'

He knew what was coming and braced himself to hear the words.

'I hate you so much right now.'

Jens watched her walk away from him. In a few weeks, she'd walk down that aisle towards him, watched by the cream of Nordic and European society. He'd catch her eye and smile. Then he'd slip away and leave her standing there. Alone, gutted and utterly confused.

Just as she'd left him…

CHAPTER FOUR

A WEEK LATER Maja left the guest suite Jens had allocated her at Bentzen House and walked down the long hallway to the staircase. She lifted the long skirt of her designer strapless red dress off the floor so she didn't trip. It had been a while since she'd donned ice-pick heels and she watched every step as she made her way down the stairs, gripping the banister tightly. At the bottom of the steps, she shook out her skirt, released a thankful sigh and adjusted the low bodice. First hurdle down, a million to go.

In about twenty minutes, Bentzen House would welcome about a hundred carefully chosen guests for a last-minute summer soirée with a surprise announcement. A string quartet was set up on the terrace, waiters would serve glasses of vintage champagne and exquisite canapés. Huge vases of flowers were everywhere, and the mansion glistened and gleamed. Only the guests, and the host, were missing.

Maja hauled in a deep breath. This would be their first outing as a couple, and tomorrow the news of their engagement would appear online and in any publication that mattered. It had been a long, nerve-racking and exhausting day...week. She'd received the reviews of her show this morning, all of which were positive and, frankly, wonderful. She was, apparently, a 'prodigious talent', had a 'sharp eye for composition', and was a 'photographer on the rise'.

Her images were emotional, sensational and deeply moving, and her show was declared a triumph. M J Slater was a roaring success...

But Maja had no one to share her success with. Halston sent her a text message of congratulations, but didn't bother with a call. Her phone remained silent the rest of the day. It was at times like these when Maja realised how lonely she was, how her secret identity kept her separate from people and friendships. No one was excited for her, she had no one to help her celebrate. She was on her own... successful, but solitary. Triumphant but a little tearful too. Her reviews were wonderful, everything she wanted, yet she didn't feel as amazing as she'd thought she would.

The moment wasn't nearly as good as she'd thought it would be.

Maja swallowed, and bit down on the inside of her lip, cursing herself for feeling maudlin. She was a professional success, the rest of her works had sold, and she was financially flush...what else could she want? Not to be married, but there was nothing she could do about that. Not for the next year, at least.

Maja looked at her reflection in the antique mirror above the hall table, barely recognising the sophisticated woman staring back at her. Hair pulled back into a sleek knot, make-up subtle but impeccable. Diamond earrings glinted. She looked like a billionaire's daughter.

Maja the photographer was gone, and who knew when she would be back? She'd also run out of time, today was her last day of living anonymously, of being free to walk the streets unrecognised, to be herself. Tonight, she'd enter the elite, luxurious world she'd thought she'd left behind.

From now on, she would be hounded by the press, have cameras and phones shoved in her face, and have questions shouted at her.

Tomorrow, everything would be different. In the morning she'd meet with an event planner, hired to help organise her unwanted but over-the-top and off-the-cuff wedding. The wedding she wanted no part of.

She frowned and tapped her finger against the elegant table. Why should she get involved in any wedding preparations? Getting married wasn't what she wanted to do, so why did she have to choose the flowers and the cake and everything else? The wedding was Jens's circus, he was the ringmaster, and he could organise his own show.

Maybe she could quietly quit the wedding arrangements, doing as little as she could get away with. She had to be careful, a little sneaky, because she didn't want him to act on his threat.

She'd give as little input as possible without raising Jens's suspicions. It would be a difficult path to walk but there was no way she was going to *help* him blackmail her. Maja felt her throat close, and her breathing turn shallow… She just needed to stay married for a year. Then she could divorce Jens, slink back into obscurity, and go back to her very normal life. M J Slater wasn't an artist who did exhibition after exhibition so, after twelve or eighteen months, M J Slater could make a reappearance in carefully selected galleries.

Her career would be okay, and M J Slater, providing Jens kept his word, would remain anonymous. She'd be the shadow behind the artist for ever, basking in her alter-ego's reflected glory.

She'd been either controlled or ignored by her father for most of her life and was used to taking a back seat.

But M J Slater was a creature she'd fashioned and formed. If the world discovered the link between M J Slater and Maja Hagen, she'd lose control and the world's perception of Maja Hagen would taint and tarnish M J Slater. She couldn't let that happen. She could stand in the shadows, but she was damned if her art would.

But what would it be like to be able to claim her work? To openly receive the praise and the criticism, to stand next to her work and be proud? How would that feel? Amazing? Scary? Fulfilling? But what was the point of wondering? Publicly claiming her art was an impossible dream...

Maja heard footsteps on the stairs above her head and looked around to see Jens half jogging down the stairs, looking incredible in what she knew was a designer tuxedo. The suit emphasised his wide shoulders and long legs, and he looked *GQ*-perfect. He'd brushed his hair off his face, and his stubble was neatly trimmed. He looked sophisticated, debonair and heat-of-the-sun hot.

Jens saw her and he abruptly braked, his eyes widening. He swallowed and rubbed the back of his neck. He started to slowly walk down the staircase, his deep blue eyes not leaving her face.

At the bottom of the stairs, he pushed his cuff back to look at another expensive watch. 'You're early,' he brusquely stated.

She shrugged, and, when his eyes dropped to her chest, realised that the movement showed more of her cleavage than she'd intended. 'I was ready, so I came down.'

'You look amazing,' he told her, his voice gruff. His compliment was unexpected. 'Nice dress.'

'Your stylist came over ninety minutes ago, with six dresses, matching shoes and bags, a hairdryer, a straightener and a bag full of make-up and went to work.' Maja gestured to her dress. 'This is all her.'

Maja noticed the heat in his eyes and her cheeks reddened. Caught up in his admiration, she lifted her hand to straighten his tie and cursed herself.

Keep your hands off him, Maja!

But why did he always have to smell so amazingly good? Masculine but sexy, fresh and, yes, fantastic.

Keep your eye on the ball, dammit!

He was blackmailing her into doing what he wanted, but that didn't mean she had to make the process easy for him by falling into his arms. She'd be polite when she received congratulations on their engagement, but she sure as sugar had no intention of pretending she was over-the-moon happy. She was *not* going to make this situation easy for him.

The rather large fly in her wine glass was her still bubbling desire for the man. She might think he was a ruthless emotional guerrilla whose moral code was incredibly flexible, but he made her blood run hot and her stomach squirm. When he looked at her with fire in those navy eyes, when they accidentally touched, she morphed into a force field of magnetism and electricity, sparks flying from her. She wanted him…

More than she ever did before.

Jens lifted his thumb and brushed it over her jaw and Maja shivered. 'You are going to act the happy fiancée, aren't you, Maja?'

She lifted her chin. 'Is that what you expect me to do?'

'That's what I expect,' Jens replied, his voice soft but infused with determination.

'Just to be clear, tonight will also require some PDA.'

PDA? It took her a moment to work out the acronym.

Right. They were going to sell their engagement with public displays of affection. Heat pooled between her legs at the thought of Jens's hand on her bare shoulder, her spine, on her lower back. If he kissed her, even lightly, she might dissolve on the spot. If he did more, she would find herself in a load of trouble...

Bed trouble. Naked trouble. Make-her-scream trouble.

Maja dropped her eyes from his and swallowed a sigh. Young Jens, six years older than her, had had way more experience than her, and he'd been an amazing lover. But Maja suspected his bedroom skills were now as sharply honed as his boardroom skills. Under his hands, she'd melt and murmur, scream and squirm, and possibly even leave burn marks on the sheets. She so wanted his hands on her body, his mouth over hers, her naked breasts pushing into his hot chest...

She wanted him. Almost as much as she didn't want to want him.

Jens looked at the open front door, where a hired-for-the-night butler stood just outside, waiting for the first of the guests. 'The guests will be arriving soon,' Jens stated, pushing his hand into the inside pocket of his tuxedo jacket. 'You'll need this.'

He thrust a classic red ring box at her, with gold detailing, and Maja's eyes shot up when she saw the familiar logo on the outside of the box. She flipped open the box and saw a square-cut, deep blue stone. It was huge and set in a delicate platinum band.

'It's a fancy vivid blue diamond, just under ten carats,' Jens informed her. 'You'll be asked.'

'Would your guests really be that rude?'

Jens nodded. 'Yes. And no, you don't know how much it cost, you didn't ask.'

She knew blue diamonds were exceedingly rare and was pretty sure the ring must have cost seven figures, and she was terrified to wear it in case something happened to it. Unfortunately, she loved it far more than she should. 'It's stunning.'

'People expect a ring,' Jens gruffly stated. 'You didn't get one the last time around.'

She hadn't expected one, had told Jens to put the money into the business or save it for their honeymoon. She hadn't needed fancy back then…she needed it less now, but a big engagement ring made a statement.

Jens plucked the ring from the box, snapped it closed and tossed it into the drawer of the hall table. Picking up her left hand, he slowly slid the ring onto her finger, and she watched his tanned fingers as he moved the diamond ring up her finger. Was he thinking about the last time he'd proposed, how she'd laughed, then cried, how his eyes had looked a little moist? How they'd made delicious love for the rest of the night? How happy they'd been?

How had it all come to this? So complicated, so chaotic.

'By the way, your reviews are amazing, Maja. Congratulations.'

Her eyes flew up and she didn't pull her hand from his. 'You read them?' she asked, surprised.

'Yes,' Jens replied, looking surprised at her question. 'They raved about your sensitive portrayal of your subjects, said your portraits were jarring but not patronising, and everyone complimented your composition and used words like "visual games" and "carefully constructed". You are a talented photographer.'

She wanted to step closer and push her nose into his neck, to wind her arm around his neck and let him hold her tight. It had been so long since she'd been held, comforted, complimented. Jens's words made her stomach flip over, and she was transported back to those days of ease and sunshine, when she thought nothing could kill their love. How wrong she was.

She pulled back and yanked her hand from his grip. She dropped her eyes and blinked rapidly. She didn't want him to see the emotion in her eyes.

Jens cleared his throat. 'Is something wrong?'

She folded her arms and gripped her upper arms. 'What's wrong is that I'm being blackmailed into marrying you, and I'm being shoved back into a world I hated, that I ran from. It's wrong that I have to go back to being Maja Hagen, Håkon's daughter, your fiancée.'

Her heart screamed, and her soul sighed. She was caught between the devil and the deep blue sea, and she was drowning. She wanted to go back to Edinburgh, where no one knew who she was, where she could breathe. She knew who she was in Edinburgh, knew what she was doing, and where she was going. Now there was an impenetrable fog between her and her future. And, yet again, a powerful man was directing the weather, a fact that made her both furious and frightened.

Maja heard the rumbling of a powerful engine and knew the first guests had arrived. They were out of time, and maybe that was a good thing because she didn't want to fight with Jens, not right now. She needed all her strength to get through this evening, to pretend to be happy. To smile and lie through her teeth.

Jens threaded his fingers through hers and pulled her to his side. 'Let's take it one step at a time. Getting through this evening is the first step. Tomorrow can look after itself,' he murmured. 'You do look amazing, Maja.'

Appearances were deceptive. She wore a fantastic designer dress, sported a ring that could be seen from space, and was clutching the hand of Europe's most eligible bachelor.

But Maja would give anything and everything to be eighteen again, standing at the wheel of Jens's fishing boat, the wind in her hair and Jens's arms around her, his mouth on her neck, his laughter being carried away by the wind.

There was happiness in simplicity, peace in honesty and she'd give everything she had to go back to who they were before.

Jens stood at the back of the biggest of his reception rooms and looked over the crowded room and smoothed down his black tie. He pushed back his sleeve to look at his watch. It was close to midnight, and nearly time to announce his engagement to his enemy's daughter.

Jens looked for Maja and saw she was talking to a younger couple on the far side of the room. The huge wall behind her held all four of her *Decay and Decoration* images, and they made a powerful statement. They were amazing, she was exceptionally talented, and she deserved the kudos she'd received today. But she was celebrating, if she was celebrating at all, in private. She'd hit a massive milestone today and, because she hadn't left the house, he knew she hadn't done anything special or significant.

An achievement like hers deserved to be celebrated.

Yanking a bottle of champagne from one of the many ice buckets dotted around, he moved through the room, making his way to Maja's side. He had eyes only for the woman in the cherry-red dress.

She was stunning. And, despite having been away from this ultra-sophisticated world for a long time, she was holding her own, quietly charming, effortlessly nice. But, because he knew her better than most, he caught the strain on her face when she thought no one was looking, the sadness in her eyes when she looked at her work, saw her chest rise and fall when she released a deep sigh. He knew she found these cocktail parties hard work, that, despite having been born into an aristocratic family, she frequently felt out of place. He understood that. He'd felt out of his depth on more than one occasion—sometimes it felt as if everyone spoke in code, or played a game with constantly changing rules.

He was now wealthy enough, powerful enough, to ignore the players, to make up his own rules, but Maja had been raised to be polite, to be a credit to her father and the Hagen name. Between her pretending they were a couple in love, fending off questions about their relationship, and accepting condolences on her father's death, he knew she felt overwhelmed, and was hiding it well.

She wasn't happy, and he wanted her, just for a moment or two, to feel happy, triumphant, proud, because she was an amazing artist who deserved to be lauded and praised. He was an art connoisseur, someone who greatly appreciated how much work it took to reach her level of success...and he'd want any artist to have their moment. To roll around in their success, to lap it up. Few artists got the kudos they deserved and when they did, they had the right to celebrate their achievements.

That was his story, and he was sticking to it.

Jens ignored someone wanting his attention and walked towards Maja. His fiancée...

He was engaged to Maja. *Again.*

He forced himself to remember that she was his fiancée in name only, and their relationship—if they could call their snappy interactions a relationship—was very fake and very temporary. He was here to accomplish a goal, to close the circle, to get what he needed from her. Revenge. Retribution.

Payback.

Maja's head shot up and their eyes collided. Jens stepped up to her and placed his hand on the smooth skin of her lower back and lowered his head to kiss her bare shoulder. Silky skin, head-swimming scent. Tiny sparks erupted on his spine and danced over his skin. He hadn't had such a physical reaction to a woman since...since Maja.

Jens straightened, noticed the shock in her eyes and looked at the couple in front of them. 'I'm sorry to interrupt but can I steal Maja from you for a minute?' Jens asked his guests. Not giving them a chance to answer, he steered her away and onto the terrace. Taking her hand, he led her past the band and around the corner, slipping into his study through the door he'd unlocked earlier. Leaving the light off, he took the empty champagne glass from her hand and filled it with champagne from the bottle of Dom Perignon he held. He lifted the bottle in a toast.

'Here's to your fabulous, incredible, amazing art, M J Slater,' he softly stated.

Maja stared at him, not knowing how to take his statement. 'Uh...'

He ran his hand over her shoulder, down her arm and linked his fingers in hers. Great art deserved to be celebrated and that was all he was doing. Celebrating her success, her talent. 'Close your eyes, Maja.'

'Why?' she whispered.

'Just do it.'

Jens waited until her eyes closed, and her lashes lay on her cheeks. Pulling his phone from his inner jacket pocket, he pulled up the arts section of a reputable newspaper and started to read the best parts from her many reviews. His eyes bounced between the screen and her face, and a smile lifted the corner of her mouth.

'A force to be reckoned with,' Jens ended, slipping his phone back into his pocket, his eyes on her lovely face. 'Congratulations, Maja. That's a hell of an achievement.'

She sighed and kept her eyes closed as she sipped her champagne. 'Yeah, it is. I rock. I kicked art butt today.'

A laugh rolled up and out of him and Jens felt as surprised by it as Maja looked. She'd always had the ability to keep him off balance, to knock him off course. Back then, he could be mad as hell at something, and a quip from Maja would have him laughing. He would be knee-deep in accounts, feel her hand on his back and twenty seconds later he'd have her up against a wall, kissing her.

Her eyes opened, slammed into his and lust flared in her eyes. The pulse point in her neck fluttered, her heart rate was up. So was his, and his heart was trying to punch its way out of his chest.

Neither looked away for what felt like hours, possibly years, and Jens wondered if she was remembering the nights they spent in each other's arms, laughing, loving, burning up the sheets. The chemistry between them had always been instantaneous, a connection resulting in massive sparks and fireworks.

The urge to kiss her, to lay her across his desk and strip that gorgeous gown off her body, was irresistible. As he took a step to close the gap between them, she held up her left hand and flashed her ring.

'You said that you'd make the announcement at midnight. It has to be past that,' Maja informed her, her voice shaky.

Right. He straightened his tie and hauled in some much-needed air. To buy himself some time, he glanced at his watch and raked his hand through his hair. He reached for the doorknob and opened the door.

'Jens?'

He turned to look at her and lifted his eyebrows. She lifted her empty glass. 'Thanks for…that. For celebrating with me, just a little.'

He clocked the gratitude in her eyes and wished he could've done more. Flown her to Paris and arranged to have supper in the Louvre. Taken her on a private tour through the Metropolitan Museum of Art. Money, lots of money, could get you pretty much anything you wanted.

'Ready?' he asked.

Maja shook her head, tension sliding into her. 'No. But that doesn't matter, does it?' she said, her voice low but resigned. They were back to being adversaries. The moment had passed, and they were who they were before.

That was how it should be. Besides, revenge was so much easier to navigate than a relationship.

Jens took Maja's hand and asked the bandleader to quieten the crowd. When all eyes were on them, he placed his hand on Maja's hip and forced a smile onto his face. 'Ladies and gentlemen, thank you for being here tonight. I would like to announce that Maja Hagen has done me the great honour of agreeing to become my wife.'

He felt a shudder run through Maja and waited for the gasps of amazement and mutters of congratulations to settle down. 'We plan to be married very, very soon, so keep an eye out for your wedding invitation.' Jens picked up a glass of champagne, wished it were whisky, and turned to face Maja. He lifted the glass. 'To Maja.'

The crowd echoed his words, but Jens didn't take his

eyes off her incredibly lovely face. Attraction sparked, then burned and he lowered his head to kiss her.

In the dim light, she looked up at him, desire in her eyes. 'Don't, Jens,' Maja softly begged him, her words just loud enough for him to hear.

'It's expected,' he replied, his voice raspy with need, his thumb running over the ball of her bare shoulder. Her skin was so smooth, luscious… He knew he shouldn't touch her, understood he was flirting with fire, the possible destruction of all his plans. Right now, he didn't care. He needed to feel the lick of the flames she'd created.

'Tell me you want me to kiss you,' he growled against her lips, sounding desperate. He was.

He could demand she marry him, could blackmail her and bully her into walking down the aisle, but he wouldn't take anything she wouldn't give, he would never force himself on her.

Every muscle in his body clenched as he kept his eyes on hers, watching as she wrestled with the need to taste him again, to place her hands on him. He'd been around block, more times than he cared to admit, and knew their sexual attraction was as strong as before, possibly even more potent. He wanted her more than he did before. How was that possible? Was it because back then she'd been a girl, but now she was a woman, and more beautiful for being stronger and more experienced? She'd come into her power, and he wanted to experience it.

But, despite their audience, kissing him still had to be her choice. A part of him hoped she stepped away, that she had more sense than he possessed.

He waited. Then waited some more, refusing to drop his eyes, back down or step away. She matched him stare for stare, breath for torrid breath. He was scared she'd back away, scared she wouldn't. He lifted one eyebrow in a silent dare and watched the sparks in her eyes turn into flames. She narrowed her eyes, placed her hands on his chest and stood on her toes to reach his mouth…

Closer, closer…

And then her lips met his and he was lost. Or found. Unable to wait for another second to have his hands on her, he slid his hand over her lower back and pulled her into him, and he tasted her groan. He slid his tongue into her open mouth and when it touched hers, he felt her stiffen. It could go either way, she could either pull back or she could dive into the kiss. The odds were fairly even.

Her hands snaked up his arms, gripped his biceps and she twisted her tongue around his and all the blood in his system gushed from his head. The only thing he could do was to gather her close, as close as they could get, her hard nipples pushing into his chest, his thigh between hers, one hand in her hair, the other flat between her shoulder blades keeping her in place. Tongues tangled and duelled, slid, and Jens sighed, unable to believe he had his longest fantasy, his biggest wish, his favourite regret, back in his arms.

Kissing Maja was heaven and hell, the best of both, and everything in between. When they kissed, when they touched, everything between them—fathers and feuds—fell away and became irrelevant. All that mattered was the way they made each other feel…

Jens moved his hand so that both hands held her head, moving her so that he could deepen their kiss. Without warning she jerked back, putting space between them. 'I think we've given everyone enough of a show,' she said, keeping her voice low.

Then Jens realised everyone was watching them, some

laughing, some sniggering. On the plus side, their kiss would go a long way to show his colleagues and contemporaries he'd claimed Håkon's daughter, that he was the winner in their long-standing feud. But why didn't it feel as satisfying as he'd imagined? As good as he'd thought it would feel? He shrugged it off. He was just tired, sick of people, and he had a headache.

And as the crowd surged forward to offer their congratulations, he knew he'd feel better in the morning, be back to feeling like himself. He was in control.

Much later, Maja returned from the bathroom and slipped into the highly decorated room, heaving with the great and good of Norwegian society. Her nose itched from the competing perfumes and colognes, and her head felt as if it were about to split apart. Spots danced in front of her eyes, and she wished she could go home...

Back to Edinburgh, back to where everything made sense.

Maja moved along the back wall of the room towards the open doors and stepped outside, grateful for the crisp air. Moving down the balcony, she turned the corner and leaned her back against the wall and closed her eyes.

She'd been catapulted back into her father's A-lister world, had her cheeks kissed fifty times and thanked people for their murmurs of sympathy. She'd ducked questions about why she hadn't attended Håkon's funeral, telling them she'd had a migraine on that morning and said her private goodbyes later in the day, and explained that she'd been living a quiet life out of the media spotlight.

She'd thanked people for their congratulations on their engagement, repeating Jens's story that they'd met a few months back, and it was a whirlwind romance. Unified by their love for Maja, Jens and Håkon had agreed to a ceasefire, and they were gutted a heart attack took Håkon before he could walk Maja down the aisle.

He'd lied, she'd lied, they'd both ducked and weaved. And she was exhausted and sick to her soul. After growing up under the shadow of Håkon's narcissistic personality, she wanted to live in sunshine, in honesty. But Jens, their past and his feud with Håkon had yanked her back into the murkiness that always accompanied the need for control and power.

Maja gripped the railing and dropped her head, staring at the immaculate garden below. She was a pawn on Jens's chessboard, just as she'd been on Håkon's. She was here because Jens decreed it. After all, he had power and wealth and possessed a secret he could brandish like a sword.

And she'd kissed him. Worse, she'd liked—no, *loved* it! She'd loved every second of being in Jens's arms again, adored the contrast of her soft body against his hard muscles, how his gliding hands and clever mouth made her forget that he was using her, that he was blackmailing her into marriage.

If it weren't for the career she'd worked so hard at, the name she'd made for herself, she'd tell him what to do with himself and where to go. But she had too much to lose...

So what could she do? There *had* to be something.

Maja bit down on her lip, forcing her aching head to think.

She could...well, she could make this situation as hard as possible for him. She could ramp up her level of uninterest. After tonight, she would make life very difficult for Jens. He might want a bride, but he'd have to drag her up the aisle by her hair.

She would not lift a finger to help him and refused to

make the process easy for him. She'd keep her distance, mentally and emotionally, especially physically as she was so very attracted to him. He'd soon realise he'd bitten off more than he could chew.

She'd planned on slow-walking through her wedding preparations, but she was upping that to outright passive resistance. She wouldn't engage, talk to him or offer her opinion. On any subject, at any time. Jens, a man of action, someone who preferred arguments to silence, would hate every minute of her passive, robotic stance. And she was counting on him cracking before she did.

CHAPTER FIVE

'I WOULDN'T NORMALLY bother you with this, Mr Nilsen, but I'm not making any progress with Ms Hagen.'

In his penthouse office in Oslo, Jens glanced at his computer screen, annoyed at being interrupted by the video call. Especially by the wedding planner. He had a multi-billion-dollar empire to run, he didn't have the time, or interest, to talk about flowers and food.

Jens sat up straight and gave his full attention to his caller. 'What do you mean you're not making any progress?'

'I've had a few meetings with Ms Hagen, but I cannot get her to make a decision about anything,' Hilda told him. 'You might be paying me exceptionally well to organise a wedding in just a few weeks, but I'm not a miracle worker and I can't get anything done without input. I was wondering if *you* could give me directions on the flowers, the cake, and the type of music you want. We're running out of time.'

No, he damn well couldn't! 'Is Maja meeting with you?' He snapped out the question.

'Yes, but she can't make up her mind. She often says she needs to talk to you before she gives me an answer. She promises to email but never does. We are no further along than I was when you first retained my services.'

Which he'd secured with a high six-figure deposit.

What was going on? Two weeks had passed since their engagement party, but it sounded as though his very expensive wedding planner was working with a ghost. Or a zombie. He told Hilda he'd get back to her and swung his feet up onto the corner of the desk, his irritation rising. He didn't discount Hilda's words because whenever he raised the issue of their wedding with Maja, she handed him a blank stare and shut down. He asked for her opinion and got no reply, he mentioned the list of tasks they needed to accomplish, and she shrugged, uninterested.

Being ignored, dismissed and not having his orders followed was an unusual situation for Jens. He was used to people doing what he demanded. A man in his position never had to ask twice—what he wanted was what happened.

Yet the wedding planner was stymied because Maja was being, at best, uncooperative. At worst, she was quietly sabotaging his plans. The part of him that wasn't furious admired her for her courage. There weren't many people who had the guts to defy him.

Jens rolled his fountain pen between his fingers, aggravated. He understood that being blackmailed into getting married wasn't the best way to inspire someone to plan a wedding, but when he'd stumbled on his path to exact revenge, he hadn't factored in Maja's unwillingness to take part in the preparations.

He should've. He usually considered all the angles and imagined all possible outcomes. Annoyingly, Maja falling back into his life had short-circuited some of his synapses. He was trying to run his company, was deciding what to do with Hagen International. There was a possibility the company could be immensely profitable with some restructuring. But he'd lie awake at night reliving their limb-melting, searing, devastating-to-his-control kiss.

Her lips had been so soft, her body so yielding, it fitted perfectly into his…

The strident beep of his phone pulled him out of his favourite fantasy and Jens killed the reminder for his about-to-start meeting.

Standing up, he reached for his jacket and walked out of his office, briefly stopping at his assistant's desk. He issued a series of orders to cancel all meetings, hold his calls, order a helicopter to fly him to Bergen. Two hours later he was parking the SUV he left at a local airport in the garage of his mansion in Bergen.

He and Maja needed to have a conversation, *immediately.*

Jamming his phone into the pocket of his suit trousers, he shrugged out of his jacket and left it on the passenger seat. He didn't bother going into the house. He had a good idea where Maja was. Tucked away into the bottom corner of the estate, surrounded by tall trees, was an art studio built by Maja's grandfather for her grandmother. The previous owner had left it as it was, and the last time he'd checked, it had been filled with easels and paints, as if Maja's grandmother had just walked out, planning to return. Maja, as she'd told him years ago, had spent many hours in the light-filled room, drawing, painting and sculpting. It was where her love of art was born and nurtured.

He'd bet his fortune he'd find her there.

He was right. She sat curled up in the corner of the couch, flicking through one of the many art books lying around. Jens noticed an unfinished canvas on the easel and the smell of turpentine hung in the air. And Maja's fingers were streaked with paint of the same colours as those on the canvas. So she'd started painting again. Interesting.

She didn't look surprised to see him and gestured to the canvas. 'Pretty awful, right?'

He could see that she was out of practice, but she still retained some level of skill. It was far better than he could do, ever. But he wasn't here to talk about her art.

'Maybe you should be giving your attention to our wedding, not to your rusty painting skills,' he coldly suggested.

'Ah.' She pursed her lips. 'I was wondering when Hilda would call you.'

He slid his hands into the pockets of his trousers, wishing she didn't look so fresh, so effortlessly sexy. This would be so much easier if he weren't so attracted to her. 'What's going on, Maja? Why can't she get a straight answer from you?'

'I can't make up my mind,' Maja told him, her eyes on the pages of the book resting in her lap. Yes, she looked amazing in her skinny jeans and patterned top, but she'd lost a little weight, and her cheeks looked a little thinner than they were a few weeks back. Her skin was pale, and she'd started biting her lower lip.

She was under mental strain. So, he very reluctantly admitted, was he. This was far more difficult than he'd expected it to be.

Every night he went to bed thinking that, in the morning, he'd be strong enough to let go of the past, to move on and that he'd release her from their engagement—his blackmail attempt—and he'd let her go on her way. But every morning, after spending the night tossing and turning and wishing she were next to him, under him—naked and moaning his name—he woke up and realised that he couldn't let her, or his need for revenge, go.

He wasn't ready to move on, not yet. Not until he'd left

her at the altar, turned his back on her, and walked away. Not until he got retribution.

He needed to *win*. But winning was costing them more than he'd bargained for. She was obviously deeply unhappy. Strangely, so was he. He couldn't work out why. This was what he *wanted*.

He needed to get out of his head and focus on the problem. 'I am paying Hilda a king's ransom to organise a huge, glamorous society wedding at short notice, Maja!'

She sent him an 'I so don't care' look before flipping a page in the book. 'I know, and, because everything is so expensive, I don't want to make the wrong choice.'

Jens walked over to her, picked the book up and tossed it onto the cushion next to her. 'That's nonsense! You know exactly what you want! You are a creative person, money isn't an object, so this shouldn't be a problem for you.'

Maja looked past his shoulder, and he sighed. He didn't have time for this. 'I'm going to call Hilda, get her over here and we can thrash this out,' Jens told her.

'Have your meeting without me,' Maja said in a flat voice. 'You're the one who wants to get married, you can have what you want.'

'You're not making this easy, Maja!'

What a ridiculous statement! He was blackmailing her, why should he make it easy for her? But then why should she want to organise the society wedding he so badly wanted? If the shoe were on the other foot, he wouldn't help her to tie the noose around his neck either.

He gripped the bridge of his nose and sighed. They had five hundred people saving the date, the pre-wedding invitations had been sent and RSVPs were rolling in, but nowhere to stage the wedding, nothing to feed their guests and no cake to cut.

Not that he was going to be around to see all that. By
the time any guests arrived at the wedding reception he
would be heading for the South of France. Or the Amalfi
coast. Or somewhere…

'I need you to drop this, Jens.'

That wasn't going to happen. He wasn't done with her
yet, hadn't got what he needed from her. This was his one
chance to come out on top. To get what *he* wanted. He'd
tried to get Flora to acknowledge him as her son, he'd been
at war with Maja's father for over a decade, Maja had already left him once. This was his chance to triumph over
the Hagens. And he would. He would not be the one left
to pick up the pieces. Failure was not an option.

'You've taken away my stable, normal life and my career. You've upended my life, and I don't know what the
future holds. Have you any idea how that feels?' she cried.
'I feel completely disorientated.'

Of course, he knew how she felt, it was exactly how he
had when she'd left. Alone, bewildered, slapped by the
events, and not knowing where to turn or what to do. But
he'd also been heartbroken, and unable to speak to anyone, not his co-workers and friends, because Maja made
him promise to keep their affair a secret. They had been
friends in public, lovers only when they'd been alone. No
one knew that she'd once held his heart in her hands.

He'd been forced to nurse his confusion and pain in
silence, just as he had when his mother left and never
looked back. With the added frustration of dealing with
her father, who'd decided to punish him for the temerity
to have an affair with his daughter. He'd lost crew members he'd thought were loyal when Håkon offered to pay
them triple and every time he'd tried to employ a new
deckhand, the person in question suddenly got a better

offer from Hagen International. Suppliers stopped ordering from him, his fishing quotas had been revoked, reinstated, rinse and repeat.

After his aunt's death a year after Maja left, the gloves had come off and his vague threat to take Håkon down became a vow and a promise. He'd sworn he'd show Håkon, Maja and the world that he was a force to be reckoned with, that he couldn't be pushed around. He'd refused to stand in the shadows any longer, and when he'd stepped out, he'd come out swinging.

He'd started by remortgaging the trawlers and taken a gamble by investing in an innovative, mostly automated fish processing plant, and the returns on that venture had been more than he'd imagined. He'd rolled that money into more lucrative ventures, bought more trawlers, and then tossed some money at a start-up gas-exploration company with new tech. They'd sold that company for a ridiculous sum, and he'd directed all his energies into becoming big enough to take Håkon down.

And he'd succeeded. Only the world would never know. Because Håkon had taken that from him too.

Tired, annoyed and irritable because his plans were skidding off the runway, Jens sat down on the high stool next to the door and rested his feet on the crossbar and studied his reluctant fiancée. Maja was a shadow of the girl he'd laughed and loved with and held little resemblance to the vibrant woman he'd met in the gallery ten days ago. It seemed as if the idea of marrying him had sucked every ounce of vitality from her and she was simply going through the motions, doing the bare minimum of what she had to do.

Jens looked down, his eyes on the intricate patterns of the old carpet below his feet.

He hadn't given a moment's thought to what would occur between Point A—her agreeing to marry him—and Point B—walking away from her when the priest asked him whether he took her as his wife. In all his planning, he'd never considered Maja's lack of cooperation, or how frustrating her lack of interest would be. That he'd have to deal with a woman who barely listened to him, and rarely responded.

And honestly, looking at her now, he was also a little worried about her. He didn't think she was eating, and, judging by the dark circles under her eyes, she definitely wasn't sleeping. But most perturbing of all, she'd stopped fighting, engaging or interacting with him. But he was too far down the road to turn around and retrace his steps. He could only go forward. Stick to the plan and see it out. He had to show the world he was good enough to do battle with the revered Hagen family. He wanted the world, and his mother, to know that he was successful and acceptable enough for Maja's name to be linked with his.

Their gazes met and in her eyes, he saw her plea to be released. She looked dejected and frustrated.

It was an accurate summation of their stalemate. But he wasn't prepared to spend the next few weeks like that. He was already frustrated enough. He wanted Maja and not being able to have her was messing with his head. He lay awake at night and turned and burned. It was a minor miracle that he'd yet to set this house on fire. If he laid his hands on Maja, he gave his house ten minutes before it went up in flames.

The heat they'd generate would be impossible to control. And that was why he'd kept his distance, moved back to Oslo…he didn't trust himself whenever he came within five feet of her. Even just sitting here in this dusty room, her lovely, light scent rolling over him, he found it hard to control his impulse to take her in his arms, kiss her madly and take her to bed.

That won't solve anything. In fact, it will make matters much worse.

He hadn't accumulated his wealth and power by being clueless, and when he faced an obstacle he couldn't climb over, he found another way around it. He needed to pivot, to find another way to achieve his goal. But what? And how?

He was a smart guy and he needed to figure it out.

Maja lifted her feet onto the old couch and wrapped her arms around her knees, tipping her head back to look at Jens. He'd been in Oslo the past few days and she hadn't expected him back in Bergen for a few more. She'd been enjoying exploring the Bentzen estate on her own, remembering her mum and grandparents. This house was a link to them and her past, but it wasn't hers. She just got to enjoy it for a short time, the only perk of this crazy arrangement between her and Jens.

A very annoyed and unhappy Jens. She'd realised that Hilda was running out of patience, but she hadn't thought she would go running to Jens for at least another week. Damn.

'How do we move forward, Maja?'

She turned her head to look at him and caught the too-brief flash of emotion in his eyes. Was Jens having some regrets or was that her imagination? 'It isn't my job to make the process easy for you, Jens.' She pointed a finger at him, then at herself. 'You blackmailer, me victim.'

Another flash of regret, this time tinged with frustration and, maybe, sympathy. Maja focused her attention on his non-verbal cues. Was he wavering? If he was, how could she exploit his momentary hesitation? She knew his indecision wouldn't last long.

Jens wasn't one to back down from a fight and arguing with him would put his back up. Maybe, instead of being bolshy, if she told him how she was feeling, she could find the empathetic, sometimes even sensitive, frequently thoughtful man she fell in love with. She could only try.

'This situation is hard for me, Jens,' she told him, allowing him to hear the emotion in her voice. 'Not only am I living in the house that has a thousand memories of the people I loved most, the people whose death rearranged my world and my psyche, but I also have to plan a wedding I never wanted. I know we planned to get married in court, but you promised we'd have a proper wedding later. I wanted small, lovely, romantic...*easy*. This wedding is the exact opposite.'

'We could've had that wedding if you didn't bail on me, Maja.'

Maja's fingertips massaged her forehead. 'I *know*, Jens! Please don't think I'm oblivious to what I sacrificed. I understand what I gave up. I think about it every day.' She'd walked away from love, from the only man she'd ever loved, before and since. She'd done it for the best reasons, but it still hurt.

Maja hadn't planned on saying that much and expected him to blast her, but his expression turned thoughtful. He nodded. Was he agreeing with her? Was that a nod to say he'd experienced the same emotions? Why couldn't he give her more? He was the most elusive, aloof and reticent man she'd ever met. Would it kill him to engage with her a little more?

Would it help to tell him why she'd left, that she'd been

trying, as best she could, to protect him from her father's narcissistic wrath? It couldn't hurt. She twisted her left wrist in her right hand, trying to find the words to explain. Maybe if she did, he'd shift off his marriage-for-revenge idea.

It was worth a try. 'Can we talk about—?'

'Unless you are going to tell me that you're going to work with Hilda, I'm not interested!' he snapped, his words bullet-fast and equally painful. His eyes iced over, and his expression hardened. There was no reaching him now.

'This is your last warning, Maja. Either get with the programme, or I'll issue a press release stating that the engagement is off and I'll reveal you are M J Slater.'

Maja pushed the balls of her hands into her eye sockets, pushing back her tears. He wasn't budging, had no intention of letting this go. Like her father, once he decided on a course of action, no matter how destructive it was, he couldn't be shifted. She was trapped with no way out.

Maja couldn't give up her anonymity, so she had no choice but to organise the wedding and marry him. A year…it was just a year. Twelve months, three hundred and sixty-five days. It would go by in the blink of an eye…

You can do this. You have no choice, Maja.

Maja forced herself to look at Jens, annoyed by him scrolling through his phone. As if sensing her eyes on him, he looked up. 'We need to get back to the house immediately.'

Arrogant much? 'Why, what's the rush?' Maja asked, not moving from her seat. Jens held out a hand for her to take, but she ignored it and stood up.

He gestured to the door and stood back to let her leave the studio first. 'Hilda copied me in on an email she sent to you. She wants you to meet her at a hotel that might, for the right price, consider hosting our wedding a month from now. She's sending a car to collect you in an hour.'

Maja shook her head. 'You go—' She saw his frown and sighed. She had to be cooperative if she wanted to have any hope of going back to the life that she'd created for herself. Part of her considered calling Jens's bluff and sending out that press release herself.

But she wouldn't, because M J Slater was her creation, something completely apart from her identify as a Hagen, untouched by preconceived perceptions. Her art was judged completely on its merits. She liked it that way. Didn't she? Sure, she'd thought about how nice it would be to be publicly acknowledged, to claim her work, but she wasn't ready for M J Slater to be burdened by Maja Hagen's baggage.

Jens shortened his stride as they walked back to the house. They passed the pool and climbed the stairs to reach the terrace. At the French doors leading into the main reception room, he stopped.

'Fighting with you is exhausting, Maja.'

'I'm tired too,' Maja admitted, feeling deflated. She wasn't eating properly and hadn't had a full night's sleep since she'd met Jens. She felt as if she were living on fresh air and emotion.

'I wish we could go back to being Jens and Maja, sailor and painter,' she said, her words soft. She wanted to recapture, if they could, those halcyon days they'd spent twelve summers ago before the furnace of life had remodelled them.

'But we can't. What's done is done, and our choices have brought us here.'

'We can change our minds, Jens, we can make different choices,' she insisted.

He looked tempted, just for a minute, but then determination firmed his mouth and cooled his eyes. 'I've got to do this, Maja.'

He stepped away, and Maja wanted to grab him and shake him and tell him he didn't, that things could be different. But nothing she'd said or done so far had shifted his perceptions. Or not enough to persuade him to alter his plans.

She wasn't getting anywhere…and worse, she was running out of options.

Jens stopped and turned back to look at her. He held her eyes as the temperature in the room rose and the air became thinner. Her eyes darted to his mouth, and she pulled her bottom lip between her teeth, biting down. She wanted him to kiss that slight sting away.

When she met his eyes again, he looked unembarrassed at the display of his desire, and she knew he wanted her as much as she did him. In every way a man wanted a woman. In every position possible.

Maja wasn't sure who broke their hot stare, her or him, but she knew that if it had lasted one second longer, there was no telling what could have happened.

CHAPTER SIX

IT HAD BEEN years since he'd visited Ålesund, and this was Jens's first visit to the Hotel Daniel-Jean, situated a little outside the picturesque town that was the gateway to the famous Geirangerfjord and Hjørundfjord. This hotel was only a few years old, originally a luxurious mansion owned by the matriarch of the historic, and wealthy Solberg dynasty. An extensive renovation, the addition of two wings and the conversion of the outdoor buildings and stables into luxurious suites and a spa earned the hotel excellent ratings and a fierce reputation for high standards and uncompromising luxury. From the passenger seat of the helicopter, Jens noticed lush lawns running down to the rocky beach of the fjord. A large jetty ended with a pretty gazebo, perfect for wedding ceremonies.

With the Sunnmøre mountain range looming over the crystal-blue waters of the fjord and the hotel able to handle a large reception for discerning guests, he was already impressed.

Fifteen minutes later, Jens sat at the hotel bar, with a good view of anyone entering the hotel lobby, a beer in front of him. He looked at his watch. He'd had his assistant check with Hilda's and was informed Maja and the wedding planner caught the two o'clock flight from Bergen to Ålesund. Travelling by helicopter was quicker and he'd bypassed Ålesund airport by landing on the hotel's helipad. He reckoned his fiancée and his wedding planner would arrive in half an hour, maybe a little less.

He was still surprised at his impulsive decision to join them. In Bergen, he'd watched Maja unenthusiastically greeting Hilda from his study window. She'd reluctantly tossed her overnight bag into the boot of the wedding planner's car, before slipping into the passenger seat of the huge Mercedes. And as they'd driven away, he'd wished he were going with her.

Then he'd realised he could, and should, and would. And as he'd packed an overnight bag and sent instructions to his helicopter pilot to file a flight plan to Ålesund, he'd assured himself he was following her to Ålesund, checking on the hotel to make sure that his orders were being followed, his demands being met.

He was gatecrashing their hotel inspection because he wanted to get this wedding business done and dusted— he hated loose ends. It wasn't because Maja was Maja and wherever she was he wanted to be. He wasn't a pining, driven-by-hormones teenager, for the love of God!

No, he wasn't twenty-four any more, and naïve, and his happiness didn't, and never would again, depend on a woman. Maja had crawled under his skin twelve years ago but now he had an impenetrable exoskeleton. He'd been burned once, he'd never become emotionally entangled with anyone, much less Maja Hagen, again.

When he left Maja standing at the altar, he'd close the book on this part of his life and start a new chapter. He'd never think about his mum again, forget that Maja left him with a breezy, vague explanation, and that her father stomped all over his life.

It would all be *over*...done.

Jens took a big sip of his beer and remembered her attempt to explain, yet again, why she did what she did. He'd closed her down, not wanting to hear what she had to say. Was that because he was afraid she had a vaguely good reason for her actions and because he might be tempted to forgive her? And if he forgave her, would he lose his reason for revenge?

No, he'd shut her down because an explanation now couldn't, wouldn't change a damn thing, including his mind. Maja was the only one left who could give him what he needed, what he deserved.

Some might say he was taking things too far. He didn't see it that way. He saw it as evening the score.

'I always thought that Ålesund was the perfect setting for a fairy tale, and the hotel is stunning. From what I've seen so far, and if it can handle the volume of guests, I'm sure your fiancé would agree it's a suitable venue for the wedding.'

Jens looked around to see Maja and Hilda walking into the wood-panelled bar. Maja wore a soft white T-shirt tucked into steel-grey wide-legged trousers. Her hair was pulled back into a loose bun at the back of her head.

'We'll see,' Maja coolly replied, her left hand holding the strap of her tote bag. Blue fire flashed from the diamond he'd placed on her finger. It looked good on her. He desperately wanted an opportunity to see her when his ring was *all* she wore.

He shifted in his seat, uncomfortable in his suddenly tighter trousers.

'We have a meeting with the hotel manager in half an hour,' stated Hilda—small, elegant, a little fierce. 'I think it's the perfect venue, elegant and upmarket, frankly magnificent. I love its grey slate roof, bright white walls and blue trim. It's a very romantic setting.'

Maja, who still hadn't noticed him, looked out of the huge, round bay window, taking in the amazing view of the mountains looming over the fjord. 'Man, that view grabs me by the heart and won't let go,' she murmured, pulling out a chair at one of the round tables close to the window. 'Do we have time for a coffee... *Jens?*'

He half smiled at the shock on her face. He lifted his beer in a mock toast, slid off his seat and walked over to them. Ignoring Hilda, he dropped a kiss on her temple, and left his lips there, enjoying her scent and smooth skin. When he eventually pulled back, he clocked the confusion in her eyes at his public display of affection.

'My schedule opened up and I decided to join you,' he explained, keeping his tone bland.

She narrowed her eyes at him, instantly suspicious. Smart girl. Jens sent her an enigmatic smile and turned to greet Hilda. He explained his arrival and expressed his approval of the hotel. 'I'd like to see more before we say yes,' he told Hilda. 'But it looks promising.'

'It's a long way from Bergen,' Maja said, reluctant, as always, to give an inch. 'Can we expect people to go so far out of their way to attend a last-minute wedding?'

'Dear girl, the guests at your wedding are wealthy beyond meaning, and if they don't own a plane, they will charter one to get here. Come now, you're a Hagen, you should know this.'

Jens didn't have a problem crossing swords with Maja, but he was damned if he'd let anyone patronise her. He placed his hand on Maja's back, handing Hilda his most intimidating glare. She, like many before her, instantly deflated. 'Why don't you meet with the hotel manager while my fiancée and I explore the hotel?' he suggested.

It wasn't a request and Hilda was smart enough to understand that. She nodded and with a small, apologetic smile, bustled off.

Jens pulled the chair out for Maja. 'Do you still want coffee, or would you prefer something stronger? A glass of wine? A cocktail?' He glanced at Hilda, glad to see the back of her. 'A bat to whack her with?'

Maja flashed a quick smile and his stomach flipped over. 'She's hard work. Can you see why I don't like spending much time with her?'

He knew she was angling for a way to get out of the wedding preparations, but he wasn't going to give her one. 'You're her client, don't let her speak to you that way. What do you want to drink?'

She ordered an Irish coffee and placed her elbow on the table, her chin in her hand, her eyes on the stunning vista outside.

'When last were you in Ålesund?' Jens asked, taking the seat opposite her and stretching out his long legs. He had a gorgeous view in front of him, and an even lovelier woman next to him. His phone was off, and he was, currently, unreachable. He felt the tension in his shoulder muscles ease, and his jaw loosen as he relaxed.

The world wouldn't stop if he did nothing for a minute or two.

Maja looked at him, the butterflies in her stomach on high alert. With his broad shoulders, aviator sunglasses hooked into his shirt and wind-tousled hair, he looked like an advert for a very expensive men's cologne. She'd been surprised to see him here, then not surprised at all. Jens was too much of a control freak to let something as important to him as their wedding be in someone else's control. When it was important, Jens liked to get his hands dirty.

She saw the tilt of his head and remembered his question about Ålesund. 'Oh, I was a kid. We came up here on a school trip,' Maja answered him, thinking about the fairy-tale town she'd passed through earlier. Ålesund, a picturesque, art deco town captured the essence of Norway. The buildings' facades ranged from pastel shades to vibrant jewel colours and perfectly complemented the deep green of the valleys, the Prussian blue fjords and the snow-capped mountains.

It was so very beautiful, a beauty that slapped you in the face and grabbed you by the heart.

And Ålesund, with the majestic Sunnmøre in the background and the dazzling waters of the fjords slapping the shore, was the prettiest stone in nature's jewellery box. 'I'll never forget the view from Aksla mountain,' Maja mused. 'Have you been?'

'I have,' Jens replied.

Maja half turned to face him. 'Sea, islands, mountains, all stretching as far as the eye can see. The day I went, it was glorious, a sunny clear day and I swear we could see for ever.'

Jens half smiled and her stomach flipped over. He was dressed in dark jeans, expensive trainers and a black loose, linen jacket over a white T-shirt. He looked fantastic, as a hot billionaire on holiday should.

With him her emotions were on a constant, unending roller-coaster ride, veering from resentment to attraction, dislike to desire. It was exhausting. Maja stared straight ahead, not wanting him to see the tumult in her eyes.

Feeling movement behind her, she watched the server place the cream-topped, whisky-flavoured coffee in front of her and thanked him. She lifted the glass and took a healthy sip, enjoying the rich combination of flavours and the hit of alcohol.

She looked over at Jens and saw his wince. 'Are you going to tell me that it's no way to drink good whisky?' she asked, lifting her eyebrows.

The smallest of smiles tugged the corners of his mouth. 'Would you listen to me if I did?' he asked.

Was he teasing her? Her answer would be the same either way. 'Of course not.'

Jens didn't intimidate her. He annoyed, frustrated and made her furious, but she wasn't intimidated.

His mouth definitely twitched. After finishing the last inch of his beer, he rested his big hands against his flat stomach. 'So, where are you staying tonight?'

Maja released a little sigh of pure pleasure. 'The hotel manager has arranged for me to spend the night in the honeymoon suite. Hilda is staying in Ålesund.' Maja took another sip of her Irish coffee and looked at him over the rim of her glass. 'And you?'

His smile was slow, amused and sensual. 'Where else would I, as your fiancé, stay but with you, Maja?'

Cool and competent, Jens steered the SUV, a courtesy car loaned to him by the hotel's manager, towards Ålesund's harbour. Maja was quite certain he could ask for the moon, and it would be hauled down from the heavens. When you were a wildly rich man prepared to drop many millions on a wedding at the resort, what you asked for, you got.

She wished she could've refused his offer of a dinner cruise up the Geirangerfjord. She'd only agreed because her other option was to join him for dinner at the wonderfully romantic, stunningly intimate restaurant at

Hotel Daniel-Jean. The cruise was the lesser of two romantic evils.

She was looking forward to the hustle of being on a busy, touristy boat. There was nothing romantic about being surrounded by camera-clicking people and it was exactly what she needed.

Maja sighed. The hotel was a dream destination for any bride, elegant and romantic. The exquisite ballroom could accommodate many guests, the extensive gardens were luxurious and incredible, and the wine list and food choices top drawer. The honeymoon suite was…*spectacular.*

How could she spend the night there with Jens? It was sublime, with an outside bath overlooking the fjord, a private deck, a massive bed to roll around in, Dom Perignon in ice buckets and expensive chocolates on pillows. Massive arrangements of white roses in silver vases scented the air. The suite screamed romance and great sex…

And she had to keep away from it for as long as possible because, in that romantic room, she might give into temptation and ask Jens to take her to bed.

If she did that, she'd be taking stupidity to new heights. He was blackmailing her, manipulating her into doing what he wanted. He intended to marry her, but she still didn't know why. Oh, he said he wanted revenge, but how would their marrying satisfy his need for payback? No, he had something else up his sleeve and until she knew what that was, she couldn't let her guard down.

And that meant no intimate dinners and only going back to the room when they had to…

Jens turned the SUV into a parking space and walked around the bonnet to open Maja's door. She sucked in crisp, clear, glacier-fresh air. The harbour was as busy as she expected it to be in the height of summer, with two sightseeing boats docked at the pier. Maja watched as people hurried up the gangplank, chattering excitedly.

Excellent. There were lots and lots, and lots, of people to dilute any wisps of romance.

Jens lifted her precious camera bag from the passenger-seat floor. 'Are you happy for me to carry it?'

She held out her hand to take it and Jens handed it over. The weight of the bag felt familiar and reassuring. When she met Jens's eyes she shrugged. 'My camera bag is like my security blanket,' she told him. 'When I'm not carrying it, I feel naked.'

'I get it,' Jens replied. He placed a hand on her back and guided her to the harbour. 'What do you want to do first? Go cruising or take a walk through Ålesund?'

Maja looked at the sightseeing boats. Judging by the excited tourists standing at the railings, and the almost empty gangway, the boats looked ready to leave. They would be the last on board, there was no time for a walk. But Jens didn't pick up his pace and didn't seem to be in any hurry to embark. Her dad had been the same...people, planes, trains, cars and ships departed on his schedule. Was it a billionaire thing?

The gangplanks on both ships started to rise, and Maja darted an anxious look at Jens. 'Jens, we'd better hurry up.'

'Why?' he asked, puzzled. 'And you didn't answer my question—do you want to take a look around Ålesund, or do you want to get on the water?'

Maja pointed to the sightseeing boats. 'I want to get on the water, but our boat is about to leave.'

Jens looked confused. 'That's not our transport. I couldn't think of anything worse than being cooped up with hundreds of people on a packed tourist ship, even for a few hours.'

It wouldn't be her first choice either, but she needed to be on a big boat to put some space and distance between her and Jens. Maja noticed a smaller boat in the inner harbour; it looked as if it would take about fifty guests. Not as many people, but it would do. Maybe that was their boat.

Jens placed a hand on her shoulder and steered her in that direction. They passed a few catamarans, a restored trawler and Jens slowed down when they approached an exquisite superyacht moored next to the smaller cruise vessel. Maja's heart kicked up at its sleek lines. It looked brand new. If it wasn't, then it hadn't been in operation for long.

'Forty-three metres long, five staterooms, hot tub, jet skis and a crew of seven,' Jens told her. 'Shall I tell you about the engine capacity and specifications?'

Back then, he'd enjoyed her love of the sea but had been confounded by her uninterest in the mechanics of the vessels that sailed it.

'I'm good,' Maja told him. Sure, the yacht was lovely, but they needed to get onto the boat moored next door. Like the others, it was ready to depart, and they needed to hurry up. The guests already on board stood at the railing or were claiming seats on the deck, settling in.

Maja started to walk towards the small ship. Jens's hand tugging her shirt stopped her fast walk to the boat. 'Where are you going?' he asked, lifting his eyebrows.

She gestured to the ship. 'I thought we were going on a fjord cruise, but if you don't hurry up, we're going to miss it.'

Jens jerked his thumb at the superyacht. 'We are, but on the *Daydreamer*. We'll be the only guests on board, so we'll get to decide where we are going, and for how long.'

A yacht? All to themselves? She sent a longing look to the vessel next door as her heart dropped to her toes. 'Oh.'

If they were lovers, and happy about being together, it would be wonderful to walk onto the sleek yacht hand in hand, looking forward to each other's company and to being alone as they took in the stunning scenery all around them.

But they weren't. Jens held her career in his hands, and she couldn't, mustn't forget that they were sliding into a marriage neither of them wanted all because Jens couldn't forgive and forget.

You could stop it, right now. If you just admitted that Maja Hagen is M J Slater, this would all go away. The reviews are in, you've established your credentials, and you have a major exhibition under your belt. Nobody could accuse you of trading on your father's famous name.

Maja bit the inside of her lip. She couldn't. Not yet. Maybe not ever. It was the one thing untainted or touched by a past that haunted her. She wasn't ready to give that up.

Maja held the strap of her camera bag, her fingers itching to capture the sleek lines of the boat, the white paintwork a dazzling contrast to the cerulean-blue sea.

'It looks amazing, Jens,' she reluctantly admitted.

'You haven't been on board yet,' he replied, sounding amused.

'No, but I did a photo shoot on a similar yacht a few years back and I know what to expect. Thank you for hiring her—'

A strange look crossed his face and Maja frowned. Wait...

'You did *hire* her, right?'

Jens tried to guide her to the yacht, but she planted her feet and waited for him to turn his attention back to her. 'Jens...what did you do?' she asked, lifting her eyebrows. She thought she knew but she wanted him to say it.

He scratched the side of his neck. 'My assistant couldn't find a private charter at such late notice and I'm not in the mood to be pleasant to strangers, so...' His words trailed off.

'You *bought* it?'

His powerful shoulders rose and fell. 'It's berthed here but the owner rarely used it. But she doesn't like to hire it out. I asked, she said no. So I offered to buy it and she said yes.'

Maja lifted her boot and ran it down the back of her calf as she took in his words. He made it sound so simple, but this yacht had to be worth more than ten million pounds, and he'd started negotiations no more than an hour ago. The man didn't let the grass grow under his feet...

Or whatever the seafaring equivalent of that saying was.

He sent a quizzical look at the boat. 'So, I now own a yacht.' He looked a bit puzzled at the thought and Maja's heart tumbled around her chest.

He placed a hand on her arm and squeezed. 'And she's a beauty. Shall we go and see what I bought, Maja?'

The *Daydreamer* was as luxurious as Maja expected but a great deal more spacious. The living-room area was impressive, panelled in expensive wood and dotted with cream-coloured seating, looking like a lounge out of a glamorous show house. The yacht also boasted a smaller den with a large screen to watch movies and a spectacular kitchen with all the mod cons. She followed the yacht's captain down to the master cabin and sighed at the huge king-sized bed covered with sparkling white linen. The en suite bathroom held his-and-hers sinks, a bath, a power shower and a separate toilet.

She very much approved. How could she not?

Jens and the captain left to explore the engine room and she looked around, thoroughly impressed. There was a hot tub on board, but she hadn't brought a swimming costume with her. Maybe she could quickly pop into Ålesund and buy one; she wanted to sit in the warm bubbles of the hot tub while drinking a glass of wine and watching the light bounce off the mountains and the fjord.

She wanted to sit in it with Jens, to admire his broad chest, what she knew was a ridged stomach, and his wide, muscled shoulders. Spirals of heat warmed her belly. Why was she still so attracted to him? Maja pulled open the nearest cupboard door and blinked at the array of dresses hanging in the space, tags still attached. These had to belong to the previous owner, left here so she didn't need to worry about packing. Her father had been the same—he'd kept duplicate items of clothing at his Olso and Bergen apartments, at their house in Svolvær, and in storage at various hotels around the world. Maja rolled her eyes. It wasn't hard to pack a bag or to get your staff to pack one for you.

Curious, she opened another cupboard and saw a couple of shirts. There were also dresses, capri pants, stylish, colourful clothing and all with their tags intact. Maja squinted at a tag, and noticed the clothes were designer and that they'd yet to be worn. Pulling open a drawer, she saw a pile of panties and bras, in various shades of the rainbow and styles. In another drawer, she found swimming costumes, including a black and white one-piece with high-cut legs and brightly patterned bikinis. She winced at the price. Wow. How could something with so little fabric cost so much?

She heard footsteps on the steps. Jens stopped halfway

down the stairs, looked at the scarlet bikini in her hand, and raised one eyebrow. 'I approve. It's a great colour.'

'It's not mine. The wardrobe is stocked with clothes.' Maja placed the bikini back in the cupboard drawer and closed the door. 'So, are you happy with your purchase?'

'I am. I'm going to come back at some point and do a proper inspection.'

He was the CEO of a multibillion-dollar empire, and she knew time was a commodity in short supply. 'Do you still have your captain's licence?'

Maja wasn't surprised when he nodded. The sea was in his blood.

Jens walked down the last few steps and stepped into the cabin, a map in his hand. He looked around and nodded his approval. 'This is a nice master suite. Much bigger than the other four cabins.'

Before leaving the hotel he'd changed into cotton shorts and a loose, light blue button-down shirt. Her gaze slid over and down him, taking in the tanned v between the lapels of his shirt, the hint of the fine chest chair she'd loved to rub her nose in, and the bulge under the zip of his trousers. He wore no shoes. Like her, he'd kicked them off when they stepped onto the yacht, and Maja reacquainted herself with his very nice feet. Big, sure, but still elegant.

She could easily imagine him walking into the bedroom from the bathroom, with just a towel around his lean hips. The towel falling and him looming over her as she lay naked in bed, watching him with hungry eyes. Rolling over to straddle him, the early morning light streaming in from the windows, watching the stars out of that same window as she lay on his chest after making love…

He belonged in this room, with her. The thought rolled over her and she had to drop her eyes from his face, scared he'd read her mind. She was afraid he'd do something about relieving the sexual tension building between them, and even more scared he wouldn't.

But she couldn't keep her eyes off him for more than a minute and she saw his Adam's apple bob, and he rubbed the back of his neck. Yeah, he was also thinking about the best way to put this big bed to use.

One of them had to be sensible. They shouldn't rock the boat. Because if they started stripping off and sending clothes flying, they might never come up for air.

'What have you got there?' Maja asked, nodding at the map in his hand, happy her voice sounded normal.

He looked down, and it took him a few seconds to respond. She liked that she could throw this supposedly cool, always thinking, unemotional man off balance. Maybe if she kept doing that she'd be able to find the boy she'd loved beneath the layers Jens had built up over the last decade.

There was always the risk of him doing the same thing to her. Could she allow him to peek under the cover, past the barriers of protection she'd constructed? She didn't know how far they'd get, because the elephant in the corner—Jens blackmailing her into marriage—was always present.

Time would tell.

Jens spread the map on the bed and Maja walked over to him and looked down at the topographic map. Jens jabbed a spot with his short-nailed finger. 'We're here,' he said.

'I can think of worse places to be,' Maja assured him. 'So, what's the plan?'

'Well, food first, I'm starving.'

So was she. She'd snagged a chocolate-covered strawberry from a bowl in the honeymoon suite at the Hotel

Daniel-Jean, but she'd eaten nothing substantial since leaving Bergen.

'I asked the chef to prepare a meal. Scallops for a starter, lobster for the main course, and sorbet, I can't remember the flavour, for dessert.'

He didn't ask her if she was happy with his selection, but he didn't need to. It was his boat, his staff and he could order what he wanted for dinner.

Honestly, she would've been satisfied with bangers and mash, but freshly caught seafood sounded amazing. Was it a coincidence that he'd remembered that scallops and lobster were her two favourite foods?

'That sounds perfect,' she told him.

They were in a stunning cabin, on an amazing yacht and were about to take a cruise, the only two people on board. She'd been worried about the romance of the hotel, and the honeymoon suite, but being alone on a luxurious yacht upped the sexy factor by a thousand per cent.

Oh, she was in a heap of trouble here. But, to be fair, she hadn't anticipated Jens buying a yacht! Who did that? Billionaires, apparently.

'So what would you like to do?' Jens asked. He looked down at the map, moved closer to her and Maja found her shoulder pressing into the top of his biceps. She didn't pull away and neither did he. Not smart…oh, well. 'We can either hug the coast, or I can ask the captain to head into Geirangerfjord and we can look at the Seven Sisters waterfall cascading down the cliffs.'

'That sounds good.'

He traced a route on the map. 'I wish we could carry on, head on up to Trondheim, Rorvik, and then into the Arctic Circle, Bodo and east to the Lofoten chain of islands.'

She did too. But that wasn't a trip they could take when

there was so much distrust and residual damage between them. That was a trip for lovers, not for two people engaged in a battle of wills and emotional warfare, struggling to keep their hands off each other.

But this moment felt like a rare truce and she didn't want to go back to sniping at each other, not just yet.

She waved at the map. 'If you had a choice to go further, stay on this boat longer, where else would you go?' she asked him, aware she was leaning into him as she used to do. She didn't move away when his arm crossed her back and his hand loosely held her hip. They shouldn't touch like this, it was dangerous, but she wasn't going to make a big deal about it. Besides, she liked his hands on her. She always had.

'Svolvær,' he answered her, and her breath hitched. Svolvær was where they'd met and fallen in love. 'Well, east of Svolvær. I own a small island. I inherited it from my aunt.'

She'd love to go back to Svolvær, the place where it all started, the beginning of their story. She wondered if Håkon had still owned the Hagen holiday home in the small city when he'd died. The house she'd sneaked Jens into, the place where he'd initiated her into the wonderful world of sex. Well, it had started there...her education had continued on his boat and in his tiny apartment.

Hot now, Maja stepped away from him, jamming her hands into the back pockets of her pants to keep from reaching for him. She cleared her throat. 'Maybe you should tell the captain we're ready to leave,' she told him, her voice sounding a little ragged.

'That's a really good idea. We should go up.'

They should. Immediately. But neither of them moved. Jens watched her for a few seconds, his blue eyes pinning her to the spot. Maja held her breath as he lifted his hands and rested his thumbs on either side of her chin and he gently, so gently swept them up her jaw, pinpricks of delight following in their wake. He looked, just for a moment, a little disbelieving, as if he couldn't understand why she was here, how he came to be touching her. One thumb skated over her bottom lip while his other hand cradled her face, causing havoc to course through her body.

Don't kiss him...don't kiss him...don't...

Her feet rose to her toes, and her mouth aimed for his, and when their lips connected, Maja felt Jens tense. Would he turn away, would he kiss her back? Was this the worst idea in the world?

They hovered there, not moving, for just a second, and Maja felt Jens shudder and his hands, still holding her face, tightened, just a fraction. His sigh hit her lips and she waited to see what he would do. And then she waited some more, suspended. After what seemed like a minute, a month, a year, Jens's lips softened and he fed her a simple, sweet kiss and gently pulled away.

'We should go up,' Jens said, his words jagged, 'before we do something we regret.'

She should back down, step away, but she couldn't, not just yet. Maja fought the urge to apologise, to explain, to tell him she'd missed him, that he was always at the back of her mind, and that nobody affected her as he did.

Nobody raised her heartbeat and caused a firestorm in her belly, between her legs, nobody infuriated her and confused her as he did, nobody came close. He was an anomaly, a one-off, a constant source of confusion and the well of her want.

He walked into any room she was in, and the air disappeared, and the walls retracted, and her only thoughts were how long it would be before she found herself in his arms. How could she want, hate and crave him?

And why was she on this boat? Why had she put herself back in this position of wanting what she shouldn't, pretending that he hadn't upended her life, praying that she'd find the good, decent man she loved so much under the steel-hard revenge-seeker?

He doesn't want to hear your explanations, remember? He told you so.

Maja dropped back down to her feet and stepped back from his hold on her. She pushed her hair back and tried, and failed, to smile. 'Great. I could murder a glass of wine,' she said, trying to be brisk.

She walked away from him, heading for the stairs leading to the lounge area of the boat. From there she could walk out onto the deck and up to the top deck of the yacht. Maybe up there she'd find enough air to fill her lungs and get her brain working again.

And maybe it was time to accept that she was weak for him, that he was impossible to resist and that she and Jens would soon find themselves naked, together. And sooner rather than later.

CHAPTER SEVEN

THEY ANCHORED IN a secluded cove and, after a spectacular dinner of lobster and scallops on wild greens, followed by a light peach sorbet mousse, Jens refilled his and Maja's wine glasses from the bottle resting in the cooler. Then he sat next to her on the huge lounger on the wooden aft deck. He adjusted the cushions behind his back and sighed his appreciation. The deck ended two feet from the edge of the built-in lounger. The rest of the yacht was behind them, and in front of him was the fjord edged by steep cliffs. It was just past eleven at night and the falling sun was occupying itself by painting pink and purple streaks on the sky. It was absurdly quiet, and soul-stealingly beautiful.

Jens felt his shoulders drop and the cords in his neck relax, his stomach muscles loosen. He never realised how stressed or tense he was until he was out on the water. Only in these moments of quiet contemplation did he realise that his fourteen-to-sixteen-hour workdays, the endless meetings, being responsible for a workforce of more than fifteen thousand, took a mental and physical toll on him.

He always said he should take more time and visit his *hytte*—his wooden cabin on his island east of Svolvær—more often. He loved the outdoors, as most Norwegians did, but *friluftsliv*—the outdoors lifestyle Norwegians lived for—wasn't a priority.

He had to get back to it, to hike, to fish, to breathe fresh air and marvel at nature. He should schedule time to sit on the water drinking wine with a pretty girl.

He glanced at Maja's profile, taking in her glazed-over eyes, her slightly open mouth. She'd forgotten about the wine, him, and where they were. The artist in her was assimilating the colours, trying to work out how to recreate them, either on a canvas or on her computer using a complicated filter.

'Where's your camera?' he asked, surprised it wasn't in her hands.

'Right here.' She used her wine glass to gesture at the space next to her.

'You don't want to capture the sunset?'

She tipped her head, considering his question. He'd expected an immediate 'yes' and was surprised when she shook her head. 'Not this time.'

'Why wouldn't you want to?' he asked, curious.

She didn't pull her eyes off the sky. 'Because, later, the colours won't match up to my memory and I'll be disappointed. Sometimes we can't capture perfection and we dilute it if we do.'

Jens lifted his wine glass to his mouth, enjoying the slide of the cool liquid over his tongue. She was a mixture of philosophy and practicality, thoughtfulness, and pride. Sensitivity and seriousness. She was more than she was before, a deeper version of the girl he knew. And he wanted her with a need that bordered on insanity.

He still didn't know how he'd managed to stop himself from lowering her to the bed earlier, how he'd resisted. It was his greatest act of self-restraint, bar none. He'd wanted nothing more than to undo the buttons of her shirt, push her trousers down her legs, and help her with her shoes.

Slide her bra strap down her shoulder, feasting on every inch of skin revealed to him.

He'd managed to stop himself from stepping over the line, but he didn't know how much longer he could resist her. He knew he should. Making love to her was never part of the plan and would complicate the situation far more than was necessary.

This was the woman—fascinating or not, gorgeous or not—that he was blackmailing into marrying him, the woman he was going to leave at the altar. If he slept with her, he'd be opening himself—them—up to piling sexual attraction upon long-ago hurts. It would be the equivalent of the *Daydreamer* ploughing into an iceberg.

He was staging this wedding to exact revenge, on her, her father, and to put his past behind him.

He heard the camera shutter whirr and looked right and into the lens of her camera. Why was she taking a photograph of him? He lifted his eyebrow. 'Really?'

A mischievous smile appeared on her lips, one he remembered her wearing a lot more often when they were younger. 'It would be a great stock photo, maybe its title could be "a billionaire on his boat".'

He smiled, reluctantly amused. 'You might earn enough royalties off it to buy a soda.'

'You're selling yourself short. I'd earn enough to buy a meal,' she teased. He'd missed this, missed Maja's sly and subtle humour. Twelve years ago, she'd tempered his ambition, reminded him to smell the roses, to slow down, relax. If they were together, properly, in a real relationship, he could easily imagine her mocking his wealth, reminding him not to take life so seriously, to slow down and enjoy the fruits of his hard work.

If she hadn't left…if Håkon…

Just give it a rest, Nilsen.

It was late, the sun was finally dipping behind the mountains, bringing an end to the long summer's day. The purple in the sky was now violet and the pinks were fading fast. It wasn't the time to discuss the past…there was nothing to *discuss.*

Jens downed the rest of his wine and put his glass on the deck next to him. He bent his knees and rested his wrists on them. He looked relaxed but he wasn't. As he knew Maja was, he was conscious of the sexual tension buzzing between them, the need and the want. Like him, she was fighting temptation. He didn't know if she was winning or losing, all he knew was that it was getting harder, by the second, to sit here and not touch her.

Maja placed her camera back in her bag, snapped it closed and placed it on the table behind her. When she looked back at him, her eyes locked on his. Would she make the first move? Would he? Who would cave first? Because someone would…

Jens rolled off the lounger and stood up, walking to the railing and gripping it, his knuckles immediately turning white.

If you sleep with her, you can't jilt her. You can't make love to her and then leave her at the altar. That isn't fair…

None of this was fair. It wasn't fair that his mum had abandoned him, that Maja had dumped him, Håkon had tried to ruin him. Life wasn't fair, he knew and lived that truth. He'd done some things he wasn't proud of, made some tough business calls that might've been legal but not, necessarily, honourable and he always regretted them after the deal was done. If he slept with Maja, knowing he intended to jilt her, he'd feel the same way.

He was a cold, unemotional bastard and blackmailing

her into marriage was bad enough. But sleeping with her knowing that he would leave her at the altar later was a line he didn't think he could cross.

Jens didn't look back at her when he spoke. 'I'll tell the captain to take us back to port.'

Maja didn't answer him and when he turned around to look at her, he caught the soft smile on her face. 'Why don't we stay on the boat tonight, and take the day tomorrow, maybe even stay tomorrow night too? It's lovely out here, and so quiet. I think you need some quiet, Jens. I know I do.'

He did. He hesitated, weighing up the pros and cons. Con: being alone with her was a temptation, he didn't know if he could resist her. Pros: the serenity and, as she said, the quiet.

Then Maja wrinkled her nose. 'But the hotel manager did give me the honeymoon suite for free. I feel bad for not taking him up on his offer.'

If he could buy a bloody yacht, he could pay for a hotel suite they didn't use. He looked around and knew he wasn't ready to return to Ålesund. 'I'll make it worth his while,' he told her. 'And if we tell him we'll have the wedding there, he'll be more than happy.'

Maja stiffened and Jens winced. The talk of their marriage always managed to kill the mood. He sighed. 'Shall we stay on the water, or shall we go back in, Maja?'

She hesitated, but when she looked at their amazing surroundings, he knew her answer. 'Stay.'

He swallowed his sigh of relief. 'You can have the cabin we looked at earlier, help yourself to clothes,' he briskly told her. He wasn't going to make love to her. *He couldn't.* He'd reined in his imagination and was thinking clearly again. But in case he slipped again, he thought it better to put his cards on the table so there couldn't be any misconceptions or misunderstandings.

'No matter what happens between us, Maja, we're still getting married.' And he'd still jilt her. He gestured to the boat, then the view. 'This is lovely, but it changes nothing.'

'Message received.' Maja nodded, her expression unreadable. Instead of speaking, she lifted her wine glass. 'Could you get me some more wine? I plan on spending a few more hours here, inhaling the view and enjoying the quiet. Would you like to be quiet with me, Jens?'

He could do that. Just for a few hours.

Jens hadn't expected to get much sleep—he never did—so he was surprised he slept a solid six hours on the wide lounger on the aft deck, covered by a light blanket. After a breakfast of *vafler*, Norwegian waffles topped with cloudberries, he needed to exercise, and was desperate to stretch his muscles. He told the deckhand, Lars, to unload the yacht's jet skis while he swam to the shore and back, an easy mile.

When he returned, Lars was attempting to teach a bemused Maja how to ride the jet ski. She looked completely befuddled by the powerful machine and Jens left Lars to it. The younger man had more patience than he did, so he climbed onto the most powerful of the two machines and took off, loving the wind in his hair and the power between his legs. He skimmed across the water, indulging his inner speed freak. After an hour of doing tricks and turns, hauling out some old skills, his body felt loose and his muscles warm, and he headed back to the *Daydreamer*. He stopped a fair way from the yacht and turned his back to the handlebars to watch Maja on the jet ski. She was barely going faster than he could swim, but she looked as though she was having fun.

Her curls were tighter, damp from sea spray, and her life jacket didn't quite manage to hide her curves. She wore the scarlet bikini she'd found in the cabin, and he thoroughly approved.

Jens yawned and tipped his head up to the sun. When last did he take a day off? Ages ago. He'd last been on a jet ski ten years back. He grinned as Maja let out a screech as she took a turn too fast, smiling at her huge grin of delight when she managed to steady the jet ski without flipping it over.

It was nice to sit here, not thinking about his business, about the wedding. Oh, both hovered on the edges of his mind, but he refused to give them space. He was allowed, wasn't he, to take a day off from the pressures of both?

Aunt Jane wouldn't approve, she always felt deeply uncomfortable doing nothing. He smiled at the memory of his irascible aunt, seventeen years older than his mum, forced to take him on when she'd chosen to remain a spinster and childless. She'd been forthright and unaffectionate, but she'd loved him in her own way. As much as she could.

He'd felt safe with her. And that was the biggest compliment he could pay anyone. She was still the only person who always did what she said and who'd never let him down. He couldn't imagine her on this vessel, in his house in Bergen. She'd be bemused by his wealth, definitely unimpressed.

Jens flipped his sunglasses onto his face as he watched Maja chugging over to him, the jet ski idling just enough to keep her moving forward. Man, she drove like a granny, and it made him smile.

She slowly braked and eventually, about three years later, drifted over to him, her eyes sparkling as she faced him.

'That was so much fun! Exhilarating!'

He grinned at her and folded his arms to keep from curling his hand around her neck and pulling her in for a kiss. 'You didn't go fast enough to hit exhilarating. I doubt you went faster than a geriatric on sleeping tablets.'

She wrinkled her nose at him, and he grinned, feeling light-hearted and relaxed. If he pulled her onto his jet ski and draped her legs over his, they could make love right here, right now. The thought hit him out of nowhere.

You're not going to make love to Maja, remember? That would complicate everything.

His brain got it, but the rest of his body wasn't interested in being sensible.

'I was being cautious,' Maja responded, pulling him back to reality. 'It's my first time on a jet ski. I didn't want to fall off!'

Because he liked the spark in her green and gold eyes, he flicked the toggle of her life jacket. 'That's what life jackets are for.'

'The water, in case you didn't notice, is freezing! Not all of us have ice in our veins, Nilsen!'

Jens frowned. Was that what she thought? That he had ice in his veins? He considered her words and reluctantly admitted she wasn't far off the mark. For more than a decade, he'd operated in a state of suspended animation, not allowing his blood to heat, finding little amusement in anyone or anything.

He was ruthless, cold and hard, but he got the job done.

Maja laid a hand on his forearms and squeezed. Her eyes, when he looked into them, flashed with remorse.

'That came out wrong, Jens, I didn't mean to criticise you. I was only referring to your insane tendency to swim in cold water.'

She looked sincere and that might be true, but there was no escaping the reality of who he was. Circumstances and choices, his and others, had forced him to eschew emotion and shut down. It worked for him, he'd built a mammoth business and had power and influence.

But Maja dropping back into his life had him second-guessing himself.

It was a beautiful morning. The hot sun bounced off the blue water and a white-tailed eagle flew in lazy circles high above his head. This was a very rare day off and he didn't want to spoil it by arguing with Maja. He simply wanted to be a guy on a jet ski in the company of a pretty woman, taking in the outstanding scenery. Their issues could wait and, for as long as he was on the yacht, he would shove all thoughts of revenge to the back of his mind. He was allowed to step away for a few hours, maybe even a day, wasn't he?

Before he could talk himself out of his decision, he lifted his finger to his lips and released a piercing whistle. The deckhand immediately responded by walking to the railing.

'Sir?' he called.

'Maja and I are going for a spin up the coast. Do you feel like a swim, Lars? If not, we'll pootle over to you,' he said. 'We might get there next year but we'll get there.'

'It'll be quicker if I swim over,' Lars replied, grinning.

'Oh, ha-ha!' Maja muttered, rolling her eyes.

Lars whipped off his shirt, dived into the water and Jens noticed Maja's shudder. The kid was a fish, he noticed, impressed by his strong stroke. As Lars swam over to them,

Jens helped Maja onto his jet ski, telling his lower body to behave when her thighs gripped the outside of his thighs. Her arms encircled his waist, and she rested her chin on his shoulder. 'Not too fast, Jens,' she warned him.

That would be a problem as he had only two speeds: fast and very fast.

'I won't flip this beast over,' he told her as Lars reached her jet ski and hauled himself up. Jens gunned the accelerator and pulled away. Maja chose that exact moment to let go of her grip on his waist, and she flew off the jet ski and plopped into the water.

She bobbed on the surface, her hair hanging in rats' tails down her face. He slowed down as he did a wide turn and puttered over to her, cutting the engine when he came close. Maja glared at him and launched an impressive stream of water at his face. 'You said I wouldn't fall off!'

In fairness, he'd said he wouldn't flip the jet ski, not that she wouldn't fall off. But Jens, because he was too smart to say that to a blue-lipped Maja, reached down, grabbed her by the wrist and easily hauled her onto the jet ski. 'I suppose you want to go back and jump into a warm shower?' he asked, disappointed in advance. The sun was hot, and she'd dry off in no time, but he knew Maja wasn't a fan of being cold.

Instead of agreeing with him, she manoeuvred her leg over the side of the jet ski, snuggled in behind him and wrapped her arms around her waist, her grip anaconda tight. 'Now you can go. I'd tell you to go slow but that's not in your nature but, word of warning, if I go off again, you're coming too.'

He grinned. Was he having fun? Maybe. It had been so long he'd forgotten what that felt like.

* * *

Maja swirled the cognac around in her balloon glass, bury-
ing her nose in the glass and inhaling its base notes of
maple, molasses and nuts. After another spectacular dinner, perfectly cooked Wagyu steaks and *frites*, Jens dismissed his staff, and they made their way to the aft deck
to enjoy the royal-blue and bright pink sunset. Maja sank
down onto the wide cushions, stretching out her legs. She
was happy, tired and very relaxed. By silent agreement,
she and Jens ignored their upcoming wedding, their shared
past, and any other contentious subjects. They'd laughed a
little, smiled a lot, simply enjoying the stunning day, the
six-star service by the yacht crew and the amazing scenery.

Tomorrow they'd be hurtled back into the reality of their
situation. But would Jens allow them to have tonight? She
hoped so. Something about being on this yacht and away
from her real life, Bergen and their situation made her
feel brave. Or maybe she would be voicing what they both
wanted. She knew he desired her as much as she did him.
The heat between them wasn't going anywhere. Maybe if
they got it out of their systems, they could move past it.
They could set each other on fire—just looking at each
other made sparks fly and wildfires start. Despite the issues between them, and their complicated pasts, they'd
been building up to this since they'd reunited weeks ago.
How they'd lasted this long, Maja didn't know.

She watched as he sat next to her, relaxing on the reclin-
ing cushions, his long fingers wrapped around the bowl
of his glass. With his messy hair and stubbled cheeks, and
slightly sunburned nose, he looked younger tonight than
he normally did, and not nearly as remote.

He looked like the young man she'd been so in love with.

'I want to make love with you.'

Maja was shocked that the words slipped out so easily, and nearly slapped her hand against her mouth.

Jens stared at her with burning eyes, but he didn't move a muscle and Maja knew that if she wanted him naked, she would have to make the move. She put her glass down and scooted closer to him and lowered her head to skim her lips across his mouth. How could something so wrong feel so very right?

Should she stop this now, while she could? Sensible Maja said yes, but she wasn't interested in anything *she* had to say. She wanted Jens, she craved him. She needed him, needed tonight. Maja knew she was playing with a firestorm and that it had the potential to consume her. But she didn't care. With him, it didn't matter she was dancing with fire. She was prepared for the lick of flame, the searing of her skin and her soul.

'This isn't a good idea, Maja.'

'I know, but so what?' She lifted her shoulders in a careless shrug. 'I'm so tired of doing what I should, Jens, what's sensible and safe. I want you to make love to me. I need you inside me, completing me, making me feel the way only you can.'

'How do I make you feel, Maja?' he asked, his thumb rubbing the length of her collarbone.

She lifted her hand to hold his face, her fingers skating over the short stubble on his jaw. 'You make me feel like me,' she replied. And it was true: naked in his arms, everything superfluous melted away and she became the essence of who she was, unimpeded by her birth name. She liked being Jens's lover, she always had.

She turned her head, found his lips with hers and knew this was where she wanted to be, right now, possibly for ever. His mouth covered hers and then his tongue was inside her mouth, seeking, taking, exploring. He made her feel as if she were surfing the edges of a tornado, flying over the edge of a snowy cliff, surfing a monster wave.

He tasted of the cognac they'd been drinking, tinged with the colours of the sunset they'd watched sink between the mountains and behind the sea. He tasted of deep purples, and violet indigos, of masculine intensity and raunchy sex. He tasted wild and free, and she wanted more.

She wanted everything he could give her.

Jens pulled his mouth off hers to look down at her and, in the romantic lighting in this area of the yacht, she saw the sexy combination of need and longing in his eyes.

He groaned. 'You're killing me, Maja.'

'You'll kill me if you don't take me inside and make love to me, Jensen,' Maja informed him, pushing her nose into his neck and inhaling the scent of sea and soap. She wouldn't ask again. Jens would either take her up on her offer or this was as far as they would go…

Maja waited for him to make up his mind, conscious of his fingers on her butt pushing into her flesh. She knew he was running scenarios, weighing up the pros and cons, but she thought that with every few passing seconds he lost a little tension, and became a little more relaxed.

Maybe, just maybe she'd get lucky. Maybe he'd kiss her neck again, run his lips over her jaw, down her neck, lick the top of her breast…

Maja was midway through her fantasy when he yanked her shirt up her body and cold air hit her skin. Her eyes slammed into his and within those dark depths she saw frustration—with himself or with her?—and pent-up desire. Despite it being chilly, she remained on her knees, her nipples pebbling against the lace of her bra. She swallowed when she saw Jens looking at her as though she was everything he'd been waiting for, all he'd ever wanted.

He cupped her breast, testing its weight, and his thumb rolled across her nipple, and pleasure skittered through her, into her womb and between her legs. He did it again, and she arched her back and released a small gasp.

'Do you like that?' he growled.

'You know I do,' Maja replied, her voice sexy and scratchy. 'Do it again.'

He teased her other nipple before lowering his head to pull it, fabric and all, into his mouth. The night air rattled over her body, but she didn't care. The appreciation she saw in his eyes and the need on his face created a warm buzz within her. Nothing mattered but Jens loving her...

Jens yanked her towards him, and her legs wrapped around his hips. He rose to his feet, easily holding her weight. After dragging his mouth across hers, he walked her into the lounge and steered left to walk down the narrow hallway leading to the master suite. The lounge and galley were deserted, and the running lights tossed shadows onto Jens's face.

He walked down the stairs, deposited her on the bed and leaned over her. He brushed her hair off her face and lightly gripped her chin. 'I didn't bring protection, did you?'

Maja had to think. No, she had a box in Edinburgh, but sex hadn't been on her mind when she'd packed for Norway. She shook her head. 'But I'm on one of those fancy IUDs,' she told him, forcing herself to think. 'And it's been a while so I'm clean.'

He nodded. 'I always use condoms, so I am too,' he told her. He ran his hand down her chest, creating a band of fire before stopping at the button of her jeans. 'Are you sure, Maja?'

She stroked her fingers through his hair. It was as soft as she remembered. 'Yes. I *need* you. I need this.'

Jens, with his hands on either side of her head, fed her a long kiss, and Maja locked her arms around his neck, welcoming his weight, his chest flattening her breasts. His tongue invaded her mouth and tangled with hers, pushing her for more, testing to see the depths of her passion.

Hers matched his, and Maja knew there was a good possibility of them setting this room on fire, possibly even the boat. She pushed her hand up and under Jens's shirt, needing her hands on his bare skin. His back was a series of dips and hollows, smooth skin over hard muscle.

Jens pulled back to grab a fistful of material behind his neck. He yanked the fabric and his shirt slid over his head. Instead of returning to the bed to kiss her, he stood up and Maja leaned back on her elbows, her eyes sweeping over his broad chest, taking in his toned abs and lean hips. A trail of dark hair snaked into his trousers and the moisture in her mouth disappeared when he pushed his trousers and underwear down. He was better than a fantasy, real and hot and *here*. Jens sent her a crooked smile.

'Like what you see?' he asked, his tone low and harsh.

She did. 'Very much so,' she assured him. 'I like the older version of you as much as I did the younger.'

He reached for the band of her trousers and his hot fingers slid between the material and the bare skin of her stomach and Maja gasped. So *good*. Impatient, she batted his hands away and flipped open the clasp and pushed her trousers down her hips, sighing when Jens pulled the fabric down her thighs with a sharp jerk. He took in her tiny panties and dragged his finger down her stomach and over her lace-covered mound. He pulled aside the fabric to look at her, his expression pure appreciation. 'You are so very beautiful, Maja, every inch of you.'

Jens dropped to his knees on the floor between her legs and Maja sucked in a deep breath. He couldn't be, no, he wasn't going to…but then he did, and his hot mouth was on her, seeking, probing, lifting her…higher, higher.

This was such an intimate expression of desire and Maja never allowed her other lovers the intimacy of this act. Only Jens knew how to kiss her, to love her this way, and it was a memory of him she never wanted to be tainted. Maja pushed her fingers into his hair, her breath coming in short, rapid fits and starts. She loved this, loved the combination of his fingers and mouth, his slick tongue and clever lips, but, for their first time after so long, she wanted more.

She needed him inside her, filling all those places where he fitted best, rocking her up and over. She needed to hear his ragged breath and him calling her name as he came.

Sitting up, she gripped his shoulders and when he looked up at her, she stroked the tip of her finger over his forehead. 'I want you inside me, Jens. This first time after so long…'

He didn't need any further explanation, he simply rolled to his feet in a fluid motion and placed his hands on either side of her head, lowering his body to connect with hers. Maja's knees opened and he settled himself between her legs, hot and hard and masculine. He gripped her thigh and pulled it up and over his hip, as his erection probed her slick entrance. The sound of their breathing, hers rapid and his harsh, filled the cabin, and the air around them heated. Maja, bombarded with sensation, closed her eyes.

'No, look at me as I take you,' Jens commanded her, and her eyes flew open. He looked like the man he was, demanding and rugged, less smooth than he normally was. She liked him wild and untamed. A little unhinged. She loved that she could make him feel that way.

He balanced himself on one hand, his other still on her thigh as he slowly, too slowly, slid inside her. This… *him*…was what she needed, what she'd been missing. Jens pushed inside her and rocked his hips and a million torches ignited deep inside her, spreading heat and light into her. Maja lifted her hips, rocked against him and felt a ripple of tension course through him. He was barely holding on and she liked—loved!—that she could make this hard man burn for her.

Jens moved his hand from her hip under her butt and lifted her into him, and Maja tilted her hips, gasping when his shaft rubbed against a spot deep inside her, causing her to shudder. She rocketed up, unable to stop the tide of light and colour and sensation.

She shivered with anticipation and then she fell, tumbling and twisting in a maelstrom of light. She heard Jens calling her name, urging her on, but his words came from far away and she vaguely felt him tense, before releasing deep inside her.

As she floated down, Maja drifted her hand down his back, not able to breathe but deciding it didn't matter. She'd missed his weight on top of her, his strong body covering hers, his deep voice urging her to take more, telling her how much he craved her, how sexy she was.

He was the best lover she'd ever had, the only one she'd ever lost control with. The only one she wanted.

Making love, and giving each other pleasure, were something they truly excelled at, and when they conversed without words there were never any misunderstandings.

But their mouths, their pride and their past got them into trouble.

But for now, in the warm cabin, listening to the slap of water against the hull, his body heavy on hers...this felt good. More frightening, it felt right. As if he was the only man who was supposed to be in her bed. And in her life.

This wasn't how she should feel about a man who was blackmailing him into marrying her.

CHAPTER EIGHT

THEY MADE IT back to the honeymoon suite at the Hotel Daniel-Jean late the next day, sleep deprived and buzzy from making love. They both needed rest and when Jens requested the room for another night, the hotel manager quickly agreed. After some heady kissing and heavy petting in the shower, they stumbled to the bed around six and instantly fell asleep, with Maja's head on Jens's shoulder, and half her body lying on his.

When she woke, Maja decided it was the best sleep she'd had in a decade. She was also ravenous. Maja gently lifted Jens's watch, saw that it was nearly eleven and considered closing her eyes again. She was about to when Jens rolled her onto her back and positioned himself between her thighs. After a long, deep kiss her thighs dropped open and Jens entered her, as slow and as soft as a lazy spring morning. He brushed her hair back from her face and watched her as he moved his hips, his fjord-blue eyes clocking her every gasp, sigh, and smile.

Once or twice he seemed to be on the verge of releasing an endearment or allowing soft words to fall onto her skin, but at the last moment, he hauled them back. But his body spoke to hers in sexy and sinful ways. Then Jens slid his hand between their bodies and found her hot button, causing her to shudder, then shake and she forgot everything else. She crested, and he followed moments later with a harsh groan.

After they cleaned up and pulled on the soft cotton robes the hotel provided, Maja walked onto the private balcony and sat down on the comfortable wooden bench swing, tucking her feet up under her bottom. Inside, she heard Jens talking to the waiter delivering their late supper and a bottle of wine.

Ten minutes later, Jens walked onto the deck and handed her a glass of wine and sat the bottle on the pretty wrought-iron table.

'There's a steak ceviche, lobster tails and a green salad inside. I also ordered *tilslørte bondepiker*.'

The dessert—whipped cream, apple sauce, and breadcrumbs roasted in sugar—was one of her favourite treats.

He sat down next to her and, using one foot, rocked the bench. After tucking a pillow behind his head, he released a satisfied sigh. She wondered if he'd bring up the subject of the wedding and this venue and was glad when he didn't. She wasn't ready to confront reality. She'd liked the bubble they'd been occupying the last thirty-six hours and didn't want it to be popped...not just yet.

On the table, Jens's phone buzzed, and he used voice activation to answer it. He pulled Maja's thigh over his and curled his hand around her knee. He spoke in Norwegian, and when she heard a gravelly voice return his greeting, she instantly recognised the voice of the captain of the *Daydreamer*.

'Captain Sig, I'm not sure if I'm going to do a proper inspection of the yacht in the morning,' Jens told him.

The captain spoke rapidly and because Maja's Norwegian was very rusty, she wasn't sure she understood everything they said. When Jens ended the call, she half turned to face him. 'What was that about a fishing boat?'

'A fishing trawler caught fire about fifty miles north of Svolvær. He told me because he knew I sailed out of the same harbour as the owner of the boat in distress.'

Maja knew how dangerous a fire on a sea vessel could be. 'Did the crew get off?' she asked, immediately worried.

Jens nodded. 'Thankfully. They were rescued by a trawler who heard their mayday call. No injuries, but the boat is leaking oil and is still on fire.'

'Do you know the owner of the boat? From…before?'

Jens closed his eyes and his fingers dug into her skin. 'Yes, it was owned by Gunnar Solberg.'

Solberg… Maja recognised the name. 'Didn't Gunnar Solberg work for you and your aunt?' Maja asked.

'Mmm. After you left, he borrowed money from your father, bought a couple of trawlers and went into competition with us. Gunnar poached some of our crew and tried to grab our quotas. But, like so many other small operators, Gunnar is barely holding on. The boat that's on fire is his only vessel, and his crew won't have work now.'

She felt sorry for Gunnar, but she was stuck on why her father had meddled in the Svolvær fishing scene after she left Norway. It was small fry to him, and it went against his selfish nature for him to loan money to a small-time fisherman. That wasn't his style. Unless there was something in it for him. She started to ask Jens what he knew, but he held up his hand and instructed his phone to call Captain Sig again.

Maja concentrated hard to understand their rapid conversation. 'Is a vessel en route to tow Gunnar's trawler into the nearest harbour?' Jens asked the captain.

'There is, but it's a few days away. Even with the insurance money, assuming Gunnar kept up with the payments, rumour has it that he won't be able to afford to tow the boat in, repair it and get back to sea.'

Jens told the captain to hang on, took a sip of his coffee and gripped the bridge of his nose and closed his eyes. He did that when he was thinking through a problem. After a minute, he lifted his head and tossed a series of commands into the phone.

When he cut the call, she raised her eyebrows. 'You're paying to have his boat towed and repaired? The salaries of his crew while they are out of work? Why? It doesn't sound like he was loyal to you.'

Jens shrugged. 'Most of his crew are older men, some of whom are close to retirement, and they'll struggle to find work if he doesn't provide it. Gunnar also has a sick wife and an autistic son. He doesn't need this hassle on top of everything else he has to deal with.'

Maja remembered how proud the fishermen were, how much they hated to be pitied. 'I'm surprised Gunnar would accept your help,' she mused. And she was shocked that he still had his finger on the pulse of Svolvær's fishing scene.

'He won't. That's why I'll run the expenses through the foundation I set up to help fishermen and their dependants. No one knows I run and fund it. Well, Sig does now, but I've asked him to keep my involvement quiet.'

Clever. Maja was impressed by his easy offer. And surprised. In so many ways he was exactly like her dad, then in others, the complete opposite. Håkon would never have stepped in to help a 'simple' fisherman repair his boat, or have it towed, especially if it cost him time or money. Jens didn't hesitate. He was such a conundrum…one Maja couldn't work out. He could be unbelievably harsh, a clone of her ruthless father. Then he did something kind and thoughtful, and she didn't know which side of him dominated. Apart from being the man who made her body sing, who was he?

Jens reached for the newspaper he'd placed on the table and flipped it open, his eyes running over the headlines. She placed her feet beneath her bottom, her eyes dancing over the unfamiliar letters. She'd let her Norwegian slide. There was only one picture on the front page, that of a dark-haired woman, and she instantly recognised the face of the famous musical theatre star.

'What's Flora been up to now?' she idly asked. 'A new show, another hit or an even younger lover?'

Jens stiffened and when his eyes met hers, she pulled back, blasted by the ice in them. 'I can't tell you how little I care about some egotistical Broadway star.'

Whoa! His voice was colder than his eyes. It had just been an offhand comment, and she couldn't understand his sharp reply. He tossed the newspaper onto the table and stood up and stomped into the bedroom. When he returned, he wore navy shorts and a white button-down shirt. And a remote expression on his face.

Maja reached for the newspaper and squinted down at the article, forcing her brain to translate the words. She got the gist: Flora was being nominated for an award, something about her being a credit to Norway. She turned her attention to Jens, who stood a few yards from her, his arms folded and his expression belligerent. What was it about this entertainer that set his teeth on edge?

'Do you know Flora? Have you met her?' she probed, needing to understand his reaction.

Jens snorted. 'You could say that.'

Right, he was back to being emotionally remote and inaccessible. *Fabulous*. But, because she was curious, she pushed for more. 'How do you know her, Jens?'

His smile was shark-like and held no humour. 'Oh, in the most biblical way of all.'

He'd *slept* with her? Right, that was more information than she needed.

Jens's eyes bored through her. 'I wasn't one of her many lovers, Maja.' He sighed. 'Although she would deny it with her dying breath, Flora is my mother.'

That was the last thing she'd expected to hear. And the pain bubbling under what was supposed to be a toss-away statement had her cocking her head, intrigued. Then again, everything about him fascinated her. 'Tell me more, Jens.'

Jens wasn't surprised by her question. He'd opened the door by mentioning his relationship to Flora and he'd silently invited Maja to indulge her curiosity about his past. Within the space of a day, they'd come to a point where she felt comfortable enough to pry into his life. Did she think they were on their way back to being friends and lovers?

They weren't. He couldn't let them be.

Jens walked back into the suite, carrying his wine glass. He was already wrestling with how he was going to carry out his plans for revenge now that he'd made love to her. He'd known, dammit, that making love to her would complicate everything, but he'd been unable to resist her...

Still couldn't.

How would he get the outcome he wanted if he didn't follow through with this course of action? How would he get his revenge now? Every time he thought about their fake wedding and his plan to leave her at the altar, he felt fidgety. He didn't know if he could do it, whether he should.

Maybe if he told her about Flora, maybe if she realised how dysfunctional and messed up he was, she'd slam on brakes, and he wouldn't have to. It was a coward's way out, he knew that. But if she knew that his mother's casual cruelty and lack of interest caused him to be cold-hearted and hard-boiled, then she'd pull back and they'd be back on the same footing they were in Bergen. Maybe he'd be able to put some distance between them again. It was worth a shot. But he'd only give her the bare minimum, just enough information to make her understand he was irredeemable.

He took a seat at the wrought-iron table and tapped the newspaper with his index finger.

Stay cold, Nilsen. Unemotional. Inaccessible. Do not let her see how much your mother leaving affected you.

'Flora is the woman who birthed me. She's currently starring in a production in the West End. She'll be in Oslo next week to accept an award for her contribution to Norwegian art and culture.'

He forced himself to look at her and Maja's eyebrows, as he expected them to, flew up and shock jumped into her eyes.

'Can't you see the resemblance between us?' he asked. It was one of the reasons his mother gave him a wide berth if they happened to be at the same A-list function. Anyone seeing them together would immediately know they were related. They had the same eyes, the same nose and mouth.

'I can, actually,' Maja admitted, glancing at the paper. 'You look like a masculine version of her. She must've had you when she was very young.'

'She was eighteen when I was born, she's in her mid-fifties now,' he answered, sounding as if he couldn't get enough air. He always got uptight when he thought about his mother. And since he'd never spoken about her to anyone, it was no wonder his heart wanted to jump out of his chest. He needed to take it down a notch. Or ten.

'She looks good.'

'Yeah, it's amazing what surgeons, a strict diet, plastic surgery and collagen injections can do.' Now he sounded bitter and resentful. Well, he *was* bitter and resentful.

'How did you come to live with Jane?' Maja asked.

Should he continue this conversation or cut it off? He had an internal debate and decided that as she was his fiancée—manoeuvred into the position or not—he could give her a little more information than most. 'We lived in Oslo,' he said, his words scalpel sharp. 'Flora was a dancer at a club.'

He didn't want to explain Flora had been an exotic daughter. 'Was it a…' she hesitated '…gentlemen's club?'

He nodded, just once. Maja, thankfully, didn't ask whether Flora provided services other than dancing. It was a question he'd never asked and didn't want to know the answer to.

'How did she go from working there to being a West End star?'

Jens drew patterns on the newspaper with his finger. 'One of the entertainers, a singer, didn't arrive for work one night and she filled in. Fortuitously, it was the very night a musical theatre producer from Broadway was in the room. He shipped her off to New York and she sent me to her sister.'

'And your dad?'

He was a blank space on his birth certificate. 'No idea.' He doubted Flora knew who his father was either.

Maja didn't react to his sharp statement. 'Why didn't your mum take you to London with her?'

Ah, the million-dollar question. The one he'd asked himself a million times as a kid. According to Jane, he couldn't go because Flora moved into a communal house-share. There wasn't space for him, and it wasn't a good 'environment'. Then, as her star rose, the excuses not to have him with her just got bigger and bolder. It was better for him to stay in Svolvær, to be raised as a Norwegian—between rehearsals and shows, she didn't have time to spend with him. But there was no way he'd let Maja hear him whine.

'Simply, she couldn't be bothered to be a mother.'

He felt uncomfortable with the sympathy he saw in her eyes and looked away. He didn't need it from her, or from anyone. Why had he opened this door, let her stroll on through?

'How often do you speak to her, see her?'

This was harder to answer, tougher to admit. 'I haven't seen my mother since she dropped me off with Aunt Jane a few days after my fifth birthday. For the first few years, I received the odd phone call, a letter now and again. When I was eighteen—'

He stopped abruptly, not wanting to revisit that memory. He hated that, even after so long, he still wanted his mum to acknowledge him, introduce him to her world as her son. Why was that still so difficult for her to do? He was now successful, wildly so, rich, and educated. While he couldn't claim to be charming, he knew how to conduct himself in public.

Flora shouldn't be ashamed of him. Or maybe she was? Ashamed of the son who reminded her of the way she'd lived before achieving her own success.

Why was he dwelling on her? She wasn't worth his time or energy, and she shouldn't form part of his emotional landscape. He didn't need her. He didn't need *anyone*.

'What happened when you were eighteen, Jens?'

Nobody, not even Jane, knew about his abortive trip to London, how he stood outside the stage door for hours in the rain begging the security guard to let him see Flora.

Jens rolled his empty glass between the palms of his hands. 'Long story short, I stood outside her theatre for six hours one day, eight the next, trying to get to see her. I finally got a note to her through a security guard.' Jens had written three bullet points on that note: Jane, Svolvær and that he was either going to see her or he'd find a journalist interested in his story. 'She wasn't thrilled to see me.'

Maja let him talk, she didn't push him, and he appreciated that.

'When I got to her dressing room, she was in a temper. She demanded to know what I wanted, what the hell I was doing there.'

'You just wanted to see her, you were hoping to reconnect,' Maja stated as she lifted her feet onto the bench and wrapped her arms around her knees.

Exactly. 'She didn't want to.'

That was a mild description of their conversation. Flora had brutally told him she wasn't interested in him and never had been. He'd asked whether she'd ever admit he was her son, she'd made it clear she never would. He was an embarrassment and didn't fit into her world. Then she'd offered him money to go away and told him that whatever the papers offered him for his story, now or in the future, she'd double it to keep her from being associated with him.

'How did you leave things with her?' Maja asked, anger turning her eyes gold.

Jens gripped the bridge of his nose before answering her. 'She spoke, I listened, and then I walked out without saying another word.'

He sometimes wondered if Flora had ever done an Internet search on him, whether she ever saw the newspaper articles detailing his business successes. She had to know about his successful career—he'd been interviewed often and photographed on many red carpets and at celebrity events. But she never reached out and her silence was an ongoing reminder that she'd simply acted as an incubator for a child she'd never wanted. He was a long-ago stain on her youth, something to be ignored and dismissed.

He was in his mid-thirties and she'd yet to acknowledge him. If he was honest with himself, he knew she never would.

Jens pushed back his shoulders. He was done with this conversation, over feeling sorry for himself. He didn't whine or wail, he was someone who preferred action to introspection, doing to thinking. Why he'd even told Maja this much, he had no idea. They'd had sex, great sex, sure, but good sex wasn't a reason to spill his secrets. If it was, then he would've blabbed to several women who'd shared his bed over the years.

Jens felt irritated with himself. He stood up, injecting steel into his spine as he did so. 'I'm going for a run,' he coldly informed Maja, irked by the empathetic expression on her admittedly lovely face. He didn't need it. He didn't need *anything* from her.

She surprised him by nodding. 'I think that's a good idea. You need space and I probably could do with some too.'

He started to ask her why she needed space from him, then remembered that he was trying to put some emotional distance between them. And he'd succeeded. So why did he suddenly feel as if he wanted to reel her back in, stop her from going anywhere?

'Have something to eat, don't wait for me,' he said. 'If you want anything else, just call Reception. Then get some sleep. We'll be heading back to Bergen first thing in the morning.'

He hated the way he sounded. So cold. But better that than whining to the woman he was blackmailing into marrying him, about his mummy issues. He'd known that sleeping with her would be a bad idea, that it would add a layer of confusion to an already chaotic situation. He'd steamed ahead regardless.

He should've stayed sensible, resisted temptation and kept his trousers zipped.

Maja heard Jens move into the bedroom of the spectacular suite and her soft curses danced on the scented night air. She was horrified by his mother's actions, and a little hurt that he'd never told her any of this when they were together.

Maja pushed her self-pity away. This wasn't about her. She dropped her legs, let her bare toes touch the slate tiles and gripped the edge of the swing with both hands. His mother, and her refusal to let him be part of her life, hurt Jens badly. She now understood, on a deeper level than before, why he'd loathed their secret relationship. He would've thought she was embarrassed to be seen with him when she'd only been trying to protect him from her father.

But, in hindsight and with this new information, her insistence on secrecy would've been salt in his emotional wounds, her words a reminder of his mother and her rejection of him. Maja bit down hard on her lip and scrunched her eyes. Regret, hot and acid, swept through her. Had she known...

She couldn't change how she'd acted, but she could tell

him the real reasons why she'd left, the part Håkon had played in her leaving. She had no idea whether anything she said would change his mind about her and the past, but he needed to know. She was sick of half-truths, lies and misunderstandings. How could they go forward if their foundation was built on shifting sands? But was she sure she wanted to go forward? With him?

Could she start again with Jens, meet him on level ground, see if they could resurrect a relationship from the scorched ruins of the past?

His hard exterior was a shell, and his sharp tone and cutting words were his way to keep the world at a distance. That wasn't who he was…she could see that now. Under his armour was the grown-up version of the man she once loved. A man who wanted to be acknowledged, loved, but was afraid of being rejected. Just as his mother had rejected him, just as Maja herself had. Or was she kidding herself? Did she want to believe he was better than he was because she was besotted by his body, entranced by the way he made her feel?

Jens appeared in the doorway to the suite, his face a thundercloud. 'I didn't bring any running shoes.'

She clocked his glittering eyes, the frustration on his face. He always used physical exercise to relax and to calm his washing-machine mind. He reminded her of a caged cat, a panther or a cougar about to jump out of its skin.

Maja lifted her thumb to her mouth, flicking her nail against her front tooth. She wanted to talk to him, explain why she left him and why she never returned. But when his eyes slammed into hers, she knew he wasn't ready to listen, wasn't in the right state of mind to hear anything she had to say.

He was frustrated, tense and probably regretting telling

her about his mum. He wasn't a guy who wore his heart on his sleeve... Even twelve years ago, he'd kept his emotions under wraps. She'd known he'd loved her, but expressing his emotions wasn't something he'd known how to do.

Judging by the frustration pouring off him, he still hadn't fully learned that skill. For Jens, it had been, and was still, excruciatingly hard. And that was why he was left with a cauldron of bubbling emotions and nowhere to put them.

And if she pushed him to talk, he'd close down and retreat behind his thick wall of icy control. She knew that he'd get annoyed and he'd respond with cool indifference, all his arrogance on display, and they'd retreat to their lonely corners snapping and snarling. She didn't want to do that...

They could fight when they went back to Bergen. That wasn't what either of them needed now...

And if talking was out, then there was only one way to reach him, to help him. So Maja reached for the knot on her gown and pulled it apart, allowing the gown to drop from her shoulders onto the slate floor behind her. She'd pulled on matching underwear earlier, midnight-black panties and a matching low-cut bra. She pulled the band from her hair and her hair tumbled down her back.

She watched Jens swallow, his eyes travelling up her naked body, painting streaks of heat over her skin.

'Is sex your way of patting me on the head to make me feel better?' he growled.

She held his eyes. 'If you're going to be a jerk, then I'm going to go inside and go to bed. Alone,' she added, her voice pointed. He looked away and rubbed the back of his neck, a little flustered.

When he lifted his head, she saw lust in his eyes, but

couldn't help but notice the determined set to his jaw, the tension in his mouth. He hated being on the back foot, not being in complete control.

He stalked over to her and gripped her jaw, his expression tough but his fingers gentle. 'This is just sex, Maja. Nothing more.'

He needed to think that. It made him feel as if he had a handle on the situation. Maja didn't know what was happening to them, where they were going or how they were going to get there, but she knew, with absolute certainty, that this was more than sex, more than two bodies bumping.

He'd get there...hopefully.

'When we get back to Bergen, things will be different,' he insisted.

Was he telling her or himself? Maja wondered.

Those dark blue eyes narrowed, and he looked like the predator he was. The back of his hand skimmed over her breast and the corner of his mouth hitched when her nipple pebbled against the lace of her bra. Her skin flushed pink. He lightly pinched her nipple and lust skittered through her, a bolt of dark energy.

'But I will take what you are offering, Maja.'

CHAPTER NINE

WITH THOSE LOW, heat-soaked words, Jens, carrying the wine bottle and two glasses, led Maja over to the far side of the wooden deck, where the magical half-light bounced off the bubbles of the hot tub sitting on the edge of the deck, suspended over the water-covered rocks below them.

Maja kept her eyes on his face as his hand drifted over her hip and around her back to find the clasp of her bra. It fell to the floor, draped over her bare feet. She tipped her head to the side as she watched him. His openly appreciative gaze heated, and she welcomed the familiar throb between her legs, the ache in her breasts. She wanted him to touch her but knew he'd ignore any demands to hurry things along. Jens wasn't in the mood to take orders...

Then again, he never was. And never did.

Jens half filled their glasses and left them sitting on the edge of the hot tub. His finger skated over her shoulder, across her collarbone, down to the swell of her left breast. He touched her as if this were the first time, as if he were learning her shape and textures all over again.

Maja gasped as Jens's finger brushed over her nipple. It tightened under his light touch. It was only one finger on one nipple and she was climbing, burning. And yearning for more. Would anyone ever make her feel like this again? Was it fair to expect anyone to? Would she ever be able to be with anyone but Jens again? She didn't think so.

She had the horrible feeling that after their time together was done—however long that might be and despite his stupid blackmail attempt—Jens would always have her heart. She'd given it to him twelve years ago...

He was intense, sharp, abrasive, he could be brutal. But she craved him...

Jens's breath skimmed over her cheek and his words landed lightly on her skin. 'Stop thinking,' he murmured. 'You don't need to do anything but feel what I do to you. Just be in the moment, open your senses. Feel my finger on your breast, taste my breath, and hear the sound of the water.'

Jens ran his finger down each bump of her spine, sliding it under the band of her panties, from her back to her front. He hadn't even kissed her yet and she was already wet, throbbing, desperate for him to touch her intimately, to fill her. This was supposed to be about him, but she was the one in need of more.

'Kiss me, Jens. Kiss me and then take me,' Maja said against his cheekbone.

'I'm too hard already and I'll only last three seconds if I do that.' To prove his point, Jens took her hand and placed it on his erection and Maja sucked in her breath. Her fingers drifted down the long, rock-hard length of him. He was so strong, so masculine.

Jens grabbed her wrist and gently, reluctantly, pulled her hand away and lifted his hand to tip her chin. She fell into the deep blue furnace in his eyes, her body on fire.

Maja moved closer to him, her breasts flirting with the cotton of his shirt. Jens encircled her hips with one arm and yanked her into him. Her stomach slammed into his hard erection and his tongue swept into her mouth. He tangled and teased her, his hand on the back of her head changing the angle of their kiss to discover another part of her mouth. His other hand slid beneath her black silk panties, and covered most of her butt. He went lower, then hoisted up the edges of her panties so he could stroke the tender skin of her inner thighs, allowing his fingertips to dance over her feminine folds.

He had too many clothes on, and she craved her hands on his bare skin. Maja shuddered as she found and undid his shirt buttons, breaking off the last one because she needed to have his broad chest and his hard, ribbed stomach under her fingers.

'Jens... Jensen...this...you...' she said, unable to form a complete sentence. Instead of talking, she stood on the tips of her toes to run her tongue along the underside of his jaw, to nibble on the cords of his strong neck.

Frustrated, needing him, she looked up to find his eyes on her face. All the air rushed from her lungs, and she desperately wanted to ask him what he was thinking. How much did he love this? What did he feel for her? Did he need her as she needed him? Was there more between them than a blackmail attempt, heartbreak and desire? She started to ask, then chickened out, knowing that words would only get in the way.

She would let their bodies talk and, at this point, they had a lot to say. She had just one, rather salient point, in her opinion, to verbalise. 'Jens, if you don't touch me soon, I'm going to scream from frustration. With volume.'

Jens looked down at her, a dark-haired Viking in complete control of himself and his surroundings. 'Go for it. Nobody is going to hear you.'

His thumb caressed her nipple, just briefly, before he pulled away. Maja groaned, as loudly as she could.

'You're killing me here, Nilsen,' she told him.

Jens turned away from her and stepped closer to the hot tub, bending to drag his hand through the water. Maja knew this image of Jens, bare-chested, his dark shorts hanging off his hips, looking at her with lust in his eyes, would be one she'd never forget. 'Take off your panties, Maja,' he told her.

He'd always taken charge in the bedroom but today there was an extra note of command in his voice. Whether it was an affront to her independence or not, Maja didn't know and didn't care. His bossiness in bed turned her on, so she slipped her thumbs under the band of her silk panties and pushed them down her hips. She kicked them away and waited for his next order.

He was a man with a plan, and she couldn't wait for it to unfold. It was deliciously intoxicating to hand over complete control. Her heart couldn't pump any faster, her lungs were unable to pull in more air.

Jens nodded to the hot tub. 'Hop in and sit on the edge of the hot tub.'

Maja took his hand and stepped into the hot, sweet-smelling water, immediately ducking her head under. She popped out, smoothing her wet hair back from her face.

'You look like a sexy mermaid,' Jens told her, but didn't make a move to join her in the tub. But, judging by the action in his trousers, he was paying attention. A *lot* of attention.

'One minute,' Jens told her. He left her sitting on the edge of the tub and walked into the suite. She tipped her face to the fading sun, enjoying the silky air and the still-light night. She heard his footsteps and her eyes widened

when she noticed the navy and black cotton scarf he held
in his hand. It was one of hers. She'd worn it on her trip
to Bergen a couple of days ago. He held it up. 'Do you
trust me, Maja?'

She nodded. Yes, she absolutely did. Jens walked over
to where she sat and kissed her shoulder.

Could a person die from being so turned on? Jens tied
the scarf around her head, blocking the bright sunlight.
'Being deprived of your vision heightens all your other
senses. Have a sip of wine and tell me if it tastes better
with your eyes closed.'

When the glass touched her bottom lip, she placed her
hands over his and took a sip, letting the liquid rest on her
tongue before swallowing. 'It's deeper, mellower.'

'Does the water splashing the rocks sound louder? Is
the night softer?'

Maja tipped her head to the side and nodded. The water
swished over a rock and released a slight hiss as it pulled
back. Then she heard the rustle of clothes hitting the floor.

Maja didn't know where Jens was until she felt his wet
hands on the tops of her thighs, gently widening her legs.
He was in the hot tub in front of her and Maja blushed.
'No, don't close your legs, Maja.' His voice caressed her
bare skin, igniting baby fireworks on every inch. 'You are
so very pretty, everywhere.'

Maja gripped the edge of the tub, her head tipped back,
feeling uninhibited and free, as wild and untameable as
the wild land surrounding them. Time ticked by, as slug-
gish as the blood moving through her system, as warm
and thick as hot molasses. Seconds and minutes held no
meaning, all that mattered was Jens's hands on her legs,
what he was about to do to her and then, later, with her.

She could stay here for ever…

Maja jerked as his mouth, a little rough, a lot hot, wildly experienced, covered her sex and she arched her hips.

Maja whipped her head back and forth and Jens pleasured her, first with his lips, and then with his tongue. Then his fingers joined in, and he slid one finger into her, then two. Her orgasm built, a star about to explode, but just as she was about to let go he pulled back, and she thumped his shoulder with her fist.

'I asked you to trust me, Maja. I promise you I'm going to give you everything, all that you need. And more.'

He repeated the sweet torture, keeping her on the edge of pain-tinged pleasure but then he reached up and ripped the scarf off before his eyes slammed into hers. With his fingers still inside her, and his thumb on her clitoris, he leaned forward and whispered his order against her lips. 'Let go for me. Now.'

Maja screamed and dug her fingernails into his shoulders, now a shooting star streaking through the Milky Way. Despite the force of her orgasm, she needed more, she still felt incomplete. Slipping off the edge, she moved into the tub, causing warm water to slosh over the side and sending Jens's wine glass crashing to the deck. Neither of them cared. All that was important was to have him inside her, to ride another star again.

Maja wrapped her legs around his hips and Jens banded his arm around her waist, his mouth seeking hers in a kiss that was one part desperation, three parts fully turned-on male as she rode him.

Watching him, she saw his eyelids fall a little, the muscle in his jaw tense and his mouth flatten. He was holding himself in check, but she wanted him wild and out of control. Maja pushed her hand between them to take him in her hand, her thumb caressing his tip. He groaned and rested his forehead against her collarbone, every muscle in his body rigid.

'I can't tell you how much I want you, Maja.'

His voice was barely a whisper, the words dragged up from the depths of his soul. Maja felt powerful, a goddess, ruler of all she saw. This man, and her power over him, made her feel invincible.

Jens pushed into her, just a little. 'You feel amazing.' He lifted his hand and combed his fingers through the strands of her wet hair.

He surged into her, filling her up, as deep as he could go. 'So, so good,' he muttered.

He felt better, wonderful…amazing. She gasped when he lunged up and into her, hitting a spot she didn't know existed, one that sent tremors through her body.

She needed to hold off, just for a few seconds. Just long enough to lean back and wait for him to look at her, for those dark eyes to burn into hers. She touched his jaw with the tips of her fingers and brushed her thumb over his sexy bottom lip. 'Jens?'

'Mmm?'

'Let go. Do it…now.'

And, with a roar that was as primordial as their surroundings, Jens did as she ordered.

When she was sure Jens was asleep, Maja slipped out of bed and reached for his white shirt and slipped it over her head. It fell to mid-thigh and the sleeves dangled past her wrists. Turning the cuffs back, she tiptoed out of the bedroom, navigated the furniture in the sitting room and walked onto the secluded patio. On the swinging bench seat, she pulled her heels onto the cushion and wrapped her arms around her bent legs, her eyes on the mountains and the fjord.

She wished she could sit here and soak up the view in the magical light of a Norwegian summer night, but she needed to think, to work through the events of the past few days. Tomorrow they'd be leaving for Bergen and their truce, or whatever these past two days had been, would be over.

She had no idea what would happen when they returned to the Bentzen estate…would Jens cancel the wedding and agree to let her go? Would he still insist on them marrying? Had anything they'd said or done lately made any impression on him?

Jens was so impassive, utterly unreadable, and extracting any information from him was like trying to pull blood from a stone. He took being the strong and silent type to ridiculous lengths. She was still surprised he'd told her about his mum, given her that much information. Did he realise that she now knew his biggest secret? That she could use the information about his mum to blackmail her way out of being blackmailed?

She could demand that he cancel the wedding, and if he didn't, she could tell the tabloids Flora was his mum. But that would require proof and she had none. And, besides, there was no way she'd do that to Jens.

Maja sighed. Despite his few words on the subject, she'd heard the pain in his voice, and knew his mum's desertion was a deep and unhealed wound.

Up until today she'd never understood how their clandestine relationship had impacted him. Being a secret would've burned him every day, in every way, and would've deepened the emotional cuts inflicted by his mother.

If she'd had the smallest inkling of what his mother did, if she'd known about her refusal to acknowledge him, if she'd even suspected he had deep-seated issues about being thought of as a secret, she would've found another way, done things differently.

Maja clenched her fists and raised them to her temples. What would she have done differently? What other options had been available to her? Would she have had the courage to go up against her father? To put Jens, and his aunt, in financial danger? Would she have stayed, taken the chance? She had to be completely honest, she owed that to herself...probably not.

Because a part of her had been relieved to get that ultimatum from Håkon, a small slice of her soul had been looking for a reason to leave Jens and her father had handed it to her.

She'd loved Jens but she'd hated feeling like the lesser partner in their relationship. She'd adored him but had found herself frequently echoing his opinions, or going along with what he'd wanted, because she hadn't wanted to fight to be heard. She'd been besotted with him but had often felt overwhelmed by the force of his personality. She hadn't wanted to admit it, but he was an A-type personality, dynamic and strong-willed, so like her father.

Too much like her father.

But she was older now, stronger, and she wasn't the pushover she was when she was younger. She wasn't someone who just accepted what happened to her any more, she made her own luck, charted her own course. But she wasn't without her own arrogance; she'd thought she could sleep with Jens this time around and keep it surface-based... How wrong she was. From their first kiss she'd felt herself falling, sliding back into affection, maybe even love.

Whatever she was feeling, she was in too deep. Her feelings for Jens—despite his stupid blackmail attempt—went far deeper than they should.

She could, maybe, possibly, be on the precipice of falling in love with him again.

But her feelings were her responsibility. She couldn't force Jens to feel more than he did. He loved her body, relished the sex, but that didn't mean he felt more for her than lust and desire. And that was…well, not okay, but she was old enough to know she couldn't force him to love her. Besides, there were still too many misunderstandings between them.

The one thing they could be was honest.

Jens's need for revenge was based on erroneous information. He only had part of the story of what had happened twelve years ago. She needed to tell him why she'd really left, shed light on her final days in Norway. If he knew the pressure she'd been under from Håkon, and if he knew her father had threatened to destroy Jens if they'd continued to see each other, maybe he would understand why she'd run. She'd been young, insecure, scared…he'd take that into account, surely.

Jens wouldn't keep blaming her for Håkon's actions after she left him. He wasn't an irrational man. If they could have an honest, open conversation they could sort this out, work through it. But twisting a steel rod was easier than getting Jens to talk.

But they were out of options and talking was something they needed to do before they found themselves in another situation, a marriage that would result in pain and misery.

The helicopter took off from the helipad at the Hotel Daniel-Jean and Jens looked back at Maja sitting behind the pilot. She wore a halter-neck navy-blue-and-white polka-dot dress, her bare shoulders more tanned than before. She'd pulled her hair into a ponytail and oversized sunglasses covered half her face. She looked fantastic, but then she always did.

He'd woken up this morning, found her side of the bed empty and went looking for her. He'd found her on the bench seat, her eyes on the mountain, deep in thought.

He'd recognised her expression, she'd been working something through, and he'd quietly retraced his steps, giving her space. In the shower he'd decided that, after an intense two days, backing away, creating some space, was an intelligent thing to do. And, if he had to judge by her muted response to his attempts at conversation over breakfast, she needed breathing space as much as he did.

Their 'time out' was done and he now had to plot a way forward and reassess their situation.

The flight to Bergen would take about an hour, so he had sixty minutes to decide which way to jump. Needing quiet, he pulled off his headset, making it impossible for the pilot or Maja to talk to him.

The question was simple...should they go back to how they were before, or did they need to find a new path forward? He'd told himself he wouldn't sleep with Maja, but that resolution went out the window when she asked him to take her to bed. He should've said no, but he was a man, not a monk, and no woman had ever turned him on quicker than Maja did.

But...*damn*. Making love to her was not just about a clash of body parts, a means to a blissful end. He couldn't forget he'd handed her his heart and she'd stomped on it. He was in danger of repeating old, very stupid mistakes.

He had a choice to back down, let her go or to continue with his plans for revenge. Could he cancel the wedding and watch her walk away and carry on with his life? Wouldn't that be an admission—silent or otherwise—that what she, and Håkon, did was okay? That leaving him with blithe, vague explanation via a breezy video was acceptable behaviour? His pride and self-respect wouldn't let that happen.

The second option was to cancel the wedding, ask her to stick around, to see whether they could have a relationship. What an absurd idea!

After she'd left, he'd stopped believing in relationships and emotional bonds, and he no longer required anyone's validation except his own. He was utterly self-sufficient, and he liked being that way. A second chance with Maja meant upending everything he believed in.

The easiest, most sensible and the safest option was to stick to his plan. The wedding invitations had been dispatched and their union was being touted as the wedding of the season. Cancelling it now would cause an uproar and media scrutiny would be intense. No, it was better for the wedding to go ahead...

But would he...could he still jilt her?

Jens looked down, barely noticing the lakes and fjords and the small villages far below them. He *had* to jilt her because, despite sleeping with her, he still favoured taking action over indulging in unproductive sentiment. He felt more comfortable with revenge than reconciliation.

As the pilot put more distance between them and Ålesund, as he flew him away from the romance of the fjords and the mountains, Jens's heart hardened. They'd shared two days, and they'd had great sex. She was still the reason Håkon had put a target on his back, and she was the one who had snapped his heart in two.

Nothing, really, had changed. Or that was what he was choosing to believe.

CHAPTER TEN

'I'LL SEE YOU in my office in fifteen minutes.'

Maja took the overnight bag Jens held out to her, caught
off guard by his curt, cold tone. Before she could answer,
he walked across the hall and disappeared into his home
office, shutting the door behind him.

That one sentence was all he'd said to her since leaving
Ålesund. They were back at the Bentzen Estate and Jens
had reverted to being the impossible, remote, slightly supercilious man she'd met in the gallery a few weeks back.

Marvellous.

Maja looked down at the two overnight bags she held
and frowned. Firstly, she wasn't Jens's butler, so she had
no idea why he expected her to carry his bag to his room.
And secondly, she wasn't quite sure where she was supposed to sleep now. In the guest room she'd occupied before she'd left for Ålesund, or in Jens's master suite? And
if she was welcome in his private space, did she want to
share it with him?

Maja placed his bag by his office door and carried her
bag up the stairs. In the guest bedroom, she unpacked
her clothes and freshened up. Through the open windows
she heard the sound of a car on the driveway below. She
pulled back the curtain and looked down onto the driveway, frowning when she saw Hilda's Mercedes. Why was

the wedding planner here? Had Jens called her? What was going on?

Maja left the bedroom and walked down the stairs. Jens was pulling the tall front door open.

'What's going on?' she asked him.

Jens didn't even bother to look at her, but greeted Hilda and ushered her into his study, brusquely ordering Maja to join them.

He gestured Hilda to a chair and walked around to sit in his expensive ergonomic chair behind his expansive desk. 'Forgive me for not offering you coffee, Hilda, but I'm way behind schedule.'

Hilda pulled her tablet out of her bag and nodded. She pulled the e-pen from its holder, poised to take notes. 'Please, go ahead, I'm listening.'

Jens tapped his index finger on the closed lid of his laptop. 'The wedding will be at the Hotel Daniel-Jean, two weeks on Saturday. I will pay the deposit as soon as we are done here.'

Hilda smiled, her budgie-like head nodding. 'Perfect. I think that will work—'

'What other information do you need?' Jens cut her off. He was back to being the cold, impersonal, bolshy billionaire and Maja didn't like this version of him. And before they went any further, before they made any more decisions, she needed to talk to him, to tell him why she'd left, and what role her father had played in their break-up.

Until he had all the facts, they couldn't make any more life-changing decisions. And getting married was a damn big deal.

'Jens, can I talk to you?'

His navy eyes connected with hers for a fraction of a second before he transferred his attention back to Hilda.

'Maja will take you into the smaller of the two sitting rooms and she will spend as much time as she needs to make the process of organising the wedding as easy as possible.'

Maja's eyes widened in shock. *What?* Why was he acting as if she were a wind-up doll? 'Hold on a second—'

'Maja, I need to work, and Hilda needs direction for a wedding that will take place in a fortnight. Decisions need to be made. *Today.*' Jens didn't give her a chance to respond but turned back to Hilda. 'Can you spend the rest of the day with Maja?'

'It would be my pleasure.' Hilda nodded, her expression enthusiastic.

Maja would rather poke hot sticks into her eyes. But she recognised Jens's determination, and knew that once Hilda got hold of her, there would be no escape. She'd had enough conversations with the wedding planner to know what questions she'd ask so she decided to condense hours of boredom and annoyance into a few sentences. Then Hilda could go, and she could tackle Jens.

'Shades of cream and white for the flowers, roses, and peonies. Soft and luscious arrangements. A string quartet playing before and directly after the ceremony, a live band for the reception. A blueberry buttermilk cake with a blueberry jam filling for the wedding cake, lemon for the groom's cake. What else?'

'The colour scheme?'

'I told you,' Maja replied, a little impatiently. 'Soft whites and cream, maybe with hints of a fresh green. Romantic and elegant.'

Hilda nodded, writing furiously. 'I can have mood boards done within—'

Maja waved her words away. 'Jens is paying you a fortune to get this done. I trust your taste.'

'What about your wedding dress, your attendants' dresses?' Hilda asked.

Maja closed her eyes and counted. She was *this* close to screaming. 'I'll sort that out.' She wasn't having brides-maids. If she had her way, and she intended to, there would be no wedding. She was only answering Hilda's questions to get her out of the room so she could talk to Jens.

'Do you have enough to work on for now?' Maja asked her, praying she said yes.

Hilda stared at her tablet and finally nodded. 'I might have questions—'

'You have my phone number,' Maja assured her. To make sure that Hilda got the hint, she walked over to where she sat and picked up her bag. Hilda looked at Jens, and when he didn't say anything, she stood up and took her bag from Maja.

She slid her bag over her shoulder and told them she would be in touch. When Maja heard the front door close, she sat down in the seat Hilda had vacated and fixed her eyes on her fiancé's hard face. 'You and I need to talk.'

Jens gestured to his still closed computer. 'I have work to do, Maja.'

She tipped her head to the side. 'I think you misunder-stood me, Jens. That wasn't a request.'

Some events and conversations were turning points in a person's life and Maja knew that whatever happened next would impact the rest of her life.

This was it, a come-to-the-light conversation with huge consequences. The urge to run was strong. She and Jens had to navigate the future and find a way to deal with each other going forward.

Maja shifted in her chair, crossed her legs and noticed her shaking hands. How would their conversation go?

Would they fight? Be reasonable? Would they be able to find a way forward that didn't involve blackmail and marriage?

And would she know, at the end of the conversation, how much of the young man she loved remained, whether he was truly like her father and who Jens really was?

She'd seen flashes of the old Jens on the yacht and in Ålesund, had caught glimpses of the young man she'd known and loved. Jens could be funny and lovely, thoughtful and relaxed, the antithesis of the hard man in front of her. Bergen Jens was too like her father, hard, tough, abrasive and demanding. Those elements of his personality had scared her as a young girl, and she hadn't known how to handle them. Or him.

But she was an adult now, and better able to handle his domineering streak. She wasn't a wilting flower who'd crumble at a harsh word. She could stand up for herself, fight her corner, and wouldn't let herself be pushed around. She could handle Jens Nilsen.

Maybe.

Jens rested his forearms on his desk and his intense, irritated blue eyes met hers. 'Say what's on your mind so that I can get back to work, Maja.'

He didn't dance around the subject, and she was grateful.

Maja scooted to the edge of the seat and cupped her knee with her linked hands. After a minute of discarding one opening sentence for another, she settled on: 'You need to know why I left twelve years ago.'

His expression hardened. 'You said everything you needed to in that video, Maja. I don't see the point of raking through old history.'

He couldn't sound more uninterested if he tried. But behind the boredom, his 'couldn't care less' expression, she saw a spark of curiosity in his eyes and decided to push on. 'I left because it was the only way I could protect you.'

'What are you talking about? Protect me from whom?' Jens demanded.

'From Håkon,' Maja replied. 'The reason I didn't tell him about us, tell anyone, is that I didn't want him finding out about you until we were married. I needed Håkon in a position where he was forced to accept you, where he had to welcome you into his world. But he found out about you, and us, the week before, and I had no choice but to leave.'

'Hold on! Are saying Håkon forced you to leave me?' Jens demanded. Was that shock in his voice? It was hard to tell.

'Yes, he's why I left.'

'Explain, Maja.'

Maja decided not to call him on his bossiness. There were too many misunderstandings between them, and they needed to clear the air. They didn't need to fight about his high-handed attitude as well.

But she couldn't help her 'don't test me' glare. 'Håkon insisted I stop all contact with you.'

'Why? Because you were his princess?'

Maja snorted. 'I wasn't. What Håkon wanted was a son.' Was that really her voice? It held all the weariness of an old, out-of-tune piano. 'My mum nearly died when she had me and the doctors said it was dangerous for her to have more. Håkon pushed, determined to have his son. She resisted for a decade then, worn out by his persistent nagging, she fell pregnant again. She lost that baby, another girl.'

'You never told me that.'

They'd both kept parts of themselves hidden. 'I became

a symbol of his failure, the unwanted girl child,' she added. 'Håkon disliked me but he needed control over me and what I did. I was, after all, a Hagen.'

He didn't speak so she carried on with her explanation. 'Anyway, after he found out about us, he told me that if I didn't cut off all contact with you, he'd sink your business, and make sure you never worked in the industry again. I didn't want that happening to you, so I ran.'

He stared at her. 'Maja, he did that anyway.'

What? She frowned. 'What do you mean?'

'Why do you think we've been feuding for the past twelve years?' Jens half shouted. 'He made it his mission to destroy me. Did you think our feud came out of nowhere?'

Her mind was a tumbleweed racing across a desert. 'He started it?' Of course, he did, it was vintage Håkon. Maja stood up, walked around to stand behind her chair and gripped its back. 'He said that if I went back to you, he'd buy out the leases on your boats, your fishing quotas, buy the building Jane lived in and evict her. But he did that anyway, didn't he?'

'He tried, but we came through it okay.'

She looked at him, thinking that he'd done better than okay. He'd become the only man who could match Håkon dollar for dollar, ruthlessness for ruthlessness.

'Why didn't you come to me?' Jens asked.

'I couldn't. He insisted on the video and watched as I sent it to you. I didn't feel like I had any other option than to do what he wanted.' Maja linked her fingers together and squeezed. 'I knew how powerful he was, Jens, and I wanted to protect you.'

Did he understand that? Was she getting her point across?

'Protecting me wasn't your job,' he snapped. He stood

up and leaned his shoulder against the wall and looked out onto the landscape gardens beyond his window. It was such a stunning day and they were inside, arguing.

Then Jens, very deliberately, started to clap. Maja stared at him, and spread her hands, confused.

'Oh, kudos to Håkon,' Jens stated, his eyes now a bitter blue. He dropped his hands and shook his head. 'He outplayed, out-manipulated and outmanoeuvred me, the cantankerous bastard. I wasted twelve years because he wanted to play God. Well played, the son of a bitch.'

Jens had thought he knew what anger was, but the rage swirling through his system was more powerful than anything he'd experienced before. He fought the urge to plough his hand into the wall, to overturn his desk. He wouldn't, he was still in control. Just. But he did take a few moments to indulge in imagining how good it would feel to lose his temper, how satisfying it would be to throw his art deco lamp into the far wall, to launch his chair through the window.

But instead of losing his temper, he bunched his fists, his short fingernails digging into the skin on his palms. His jaw was tense enough to crack teeth and white-hot rage threatened to blister his skin.

Twelve years, wasted. He'd spent so much energy, and lost sleep cursing her. He was furious with Håkon, with Maja, with himself...

He also felt like an idiot, and that added another layer of rage.

It was so much to take in, too much to work through. A part of Jens wished Maja had kept this to herself, the rest of him struggled to make sense of the fact that Maja never, really, betrayed him. She'd left him, misguided as it was, to protect him. And in telling him that, she upended his world and turned it inside out.

This was the emotional equivalent of standing under a shower of boiling water, each droplet stripping a few millimetres of skin.

Jens couldn't look at her, not yet. He needed time to make sense of what she'd said, the past. Out of the corner of his eyes he saw Maja rock on her heels, looking unsure as to what came next. He was too, although he'd never admit that. He'd learned that when he felt off balance and weakened, it was best to say nothing.

He heard Maja murmur, 'Jens, please talk to me.'

He couldn't, not yet. If he did, he would make this situation worse. And it was horrible enough already.

He turned to look at her straight on, and inwardly winced. She'd never been able, fully, to hide what she felt for him. All her emotions passed through her eyes. Under the layers of confusion, he saw affection, desire and the need to understand, and be understood. The need for connection. It was obvious that she wanted more from him, far more than he could give. He saw her hope that they could get through this, her desire for a reset, or a completely new start. Jens didn't know if she loved him, but he recognised the emotion jumping in and out of her eyes and across her face. She was in too deep...

Was he?

Maybe. But it didn't matter whether he was or not, he couldn't go there. Too much emotion caused complications, rewired the brain, and turned simple situations into chaos. She'd just stripped away the foundation for his revenge and he didn't know how to process the fact that she hadn't abandoned him all those years ago. He hated this churning feeling, his lurching stomach, the hitch in his breath. Feeling foolish and feeble, and insecure. He felt as he had when he was a child and that was wholly unacceptable. He hadn't worked every hour of the day for twelve years, built up a massive empire, commanded respect, to allow Maja, and his past, to destroy his sense of self-worth.

When faced with a fight, he didn't buckle or bend, he came out swinging. He never went down, and if and when he did, it wouldn't be without a fight.

He knew how to handle anger...so he embraced it, let it fuel him. His spine straightened and he lifted his chin and narrowed his eyes. If she wanted a conversation, she would get it. But he knew she wouldn't like it.

Game, he decided, on.

Maja had genuinely thought that having the truth of their break-up out there would allow them to move on, allow Jens to disregard his need for revenge. Her explanation had initially rocked him, but then his emotional shutters had dropped and she was on the outside trying to find a way in. He looked hard, emotionless, expressionless.

And why did she sense he was about to drop another conversational hand grenade? Something still didn't make sense between them, and she knew whatever it was was going to rock her world.

She didn't want to hear it, she wanted to go forward, blissfully ignorant.

'Can we just draw a line under everything, Jens?' she asked, sounding a little desperate. 'Can't we just give each other a blanket forgiveness for everything we did in the past?'

Jens's eyes slammed into hers and she knew he wouldn't allow her to duck out now. Whatever he needed to confess clearly burned inside him. He couldn't *wait* to tell her. She narrowed her eyes. *Why?*

'I never explained my reasoning for wanting to marry you, Maja.'

She frowned. 'You wanted revenge by making me fulfil my promise to marry you.'

Jens didn't drop his hard blue eyes from hers. 'You're half right. I also wanted to marry you so that I could leave you at the altar, just like you left me.'

His words dropped but it took Maja a minute to make sense of them. No! Nobody would go to such lengths, put themselves to so much trouble and expense, to get payback. Would they?

'You are not being serious, right?' She felt dizzy and spacy, as if her world were spinning far too fast.

Jens placed his hands flat against the surface of his desk. 'I blackmailed you into marriage so that I could leave you at the altar. I believed, *believe*, in an eye-for-an-eye type of revenge.'

But their circumstances were very different this time around. Twelve years ago nobody had known their plans to marry, and their break-up had been completely private. This time around, Jens had hired a wedding planner to throw a huge wedding in front of five hundred high-profile guests and planned on leaving her standing at the altar, alone. She would've been the laughing stock of Norway, of Europe, the lead headline in every publication around the world. Maja Hagen dumped by billionaire.

She'd known his intentions were, at best, suspect, but to take her on this ride simply to embarrass her publicly? Why would he do that? What would he gain from hurting her that way?

Revenge—against her, against her father—was more important than her feelings. That was the simple answer.

Her father would've done the same, he'd been a master of finding the punishment, or humiliation, to fit the crime. Jens had followed his example.

All her old doubts came roaring back, as hard and hot as before. She'd wanted a reset, to try and have a grown-up relationship with Jens, but how could she trust him? How could she give everything of herself to him, knowing he had the same ruthless streak her father possessed running inside him? What if she—or their kids, if they had any together—some time in the future, made the wrong move, upset him in some way, and he reverted to this vengeful petty behaviour? How could she go forward knowing that, with Jens, she felt as if she stood on shifting sands? That his love for her would depend on whether she pleased him or not?

She could never take that chance, not again. She'd lost her father because she'd silently questioned his every action and had never been sure of his motives. Håkon had never respected her needs or safeguarded her emotional well-being. He'd never put her first.

Maja gripped the back of her chair and dropped her head, the memories of her father flooding her system. The school reports she brought home that were never opened, the father-daughter dances he never attended, him leaving her alone, night after night in their huge mansion, with only the TV or her laptop to keep her company.

From the age of ten she'd raised herself, believing herself to be a disappointment, unwanted and unneeded. Håkon had betrayed her over and over again… Jens would probably do the same. Even if she got over him wanting to marry her for revenge, how could she put her heart in the hands of a man who was so like her father? Would she ever feel truly safe with him? Or would she have to be helpful and perfect, constantly walking on eggshells to receive Jens's attention and love?

'What else is on your mind, Maja?'

She hated that he could read her so well. Should she tell him that she saw her father in him, that they were, occasionally and in certain situations, two peas in a pod? He wouldn't welcome being compared to her dad.

And if it hurt him, if it stung…well, then maybe he'd also feel as if he'd been slammed into an electric fence. She wanted to hurt him too.

She hesitated. 'They say that girls either fall in love with men who are exactly like their fathers, or they are the complete opposite. You and Håkon are so very much alike.'

Shock skittered across his face. 'I am not *anything* like your father!'

She'd thought he'd say that. 'You're smart, driven, passionate about your business and very ambitious. You don't suffer fools gladly and you have a vengeful streak a mile long,' Maja pointed out, her tone bitter. 'You have to come out on top, every time.'

He didn't look away. 'You're right, I do. I wouldn't have feuded with your father for twelve years if I wasn't determined to win.'

She couldn't do this any more. His need for control, his need to control her, would always be greater than his need to be happy. She'd left Norway because she didn't want to be controlled by Håkon, and she'd spent the last decade living by her own rules. Was keeping M J Slater's identity secret so important that she was prepared to let a man tell her what to do, to chart the course of her life? What had she been thinking? Had she been thinking at all?

Maja felt embarrassed and furious, with Jens but mostly with herself. He couldn't have played this game without her participation.

Maja raised her hands, her palms facing forward. 'I'm done, Jens.'

Shock briefly skittered across his face. 'Meaning what, Maja?'

This was the most honest, most hurtful conversation they'd had, ever would have, but Maja knew it was better to be hurt by the truth than fooled by a lie.

'I love you, I always have, probably always will, but it's not enough. I can't be controlled, I *won't* be coerced or controlled. I wouldn't stand it from Håkon, and I certainly won't tolerate feeling like that with you.' Knowing she was on the edge of breaking down, Maja turned and walked away.

From the man she loved more than life itself. But this time, crucially, it was her choice to walk away. Hers. She was the captain of her own ship, the creator of her life.

She'd never give anyone, not even Jens, that power again.

CHAPTER ELEVEN

JENS STRODE INTO the lobby of The Thief, one of the coolest hotels in Oslo. The hotel, right on the water's edge, surrounded by cafes, amazing art galleries and fantastic restaurants, was one of his favourites places to meet colleagues and clients. He loved the modern artwork on its walls and its stylish décor.

But he didn't notice any of that today. Since Maja had left him over a week ago, he couldn't shake off his irritability and anger. He'd failed in his quest to get revenge, to close the circle. He'd handled Maja badly, and it was galling to admit he'd lost control. He wasn't someone who tolerated failure, in others or in himself. He was jumpy and jittery, off balance and out of sorts.

He was resolved to call off the wedding—his bride and his need for revenge were both gone—he just needed to instruct his PR person to draft the press release. But he had this need to understand *everything*, or as much as he could, before he made any irreversible decisions.

Because, in all honesty, his ability to make rational, sensible decisions seemed to have deserted him. And he was swamped by the need to go back to where it all started. His *issues* didn't start with Maja or Håkon. No, they went back further than that. If he was going to move forward, and he wanted to, he needed to understand his dysfunctional relationship, if thirty years of neglect could be called that, with his mother. It was time to put as many of his demons as he could to rest. He'd based his need for revenge on flawed reasoning, and he'd hurt Maja in the process. Before he could pick up the pieces of his life, he needed to make sure he had *all* the pieces of the puzzle. That meant going back to the start, to Flora, to see what he was missing.

It was fortuitous Flora was in Oslo to receive an award and it was common knowledge she was staying at The Thief. According to the hotel manager, a man Jens knew well, Flora was in her room, but she wasn't taking visitors. Jens asked him to dial her room number again, took the receiver from the manager. He introduced himself, told Flora he wasn't going away and that they could either speak in her room or he could wait for her in the lobby. Within a minute, he was in a lift heading for her floor. Flora, dressed in a silk trouser suit, opened the door to her suite. She didn't look pleased to see him. *Shocker.*

'What do you want?'

'You're back in Norway, for the first time in over thirty years,' Jens smoothly replied, although his heart was beating as fast as a hummingbird's wing. 'I thought we should chat.'

Flora motioned him into the suite and Jens took in the fine wrinkles make-up no longer covered, her hard blue eyes, and her tight mouth. She looked remote, ice cold and fully uninterested. Did people see the same dissatisfaction when they looked at him? Someone perpetually discontented by life, talented but emotionally empty?

'If you are here to beg me to acknowledge you, I won't,' Flora defiantly told him.

He started to respond then stopped, shocked as a missing puzzle piece dropped into its empty spot. He didn't need her to. Not any more. He no longer needed to be accepted by this miserable, empty-hearted woman. She'd had little to no input into his life, she hadn't given him anything but his looks and an inability to trust, his issues of abandonment. He didn't want to be like her, in any way. It was time to let her go. But if this was the last time he'd see her, he needed to make sure those demons would never rear their ugly heads again. He looked at the small, elegant woman and when his words left his mouth, he was surprised at how gentle he sounded. 'Why did you give me up?' he softly asked.

She sighed, her hand fiddling with her thick gold necklace. Flora walked over to the couch and sank into the plump cushions. Sitting down, she looked older, as if the world had chewed her up and spat her out. Was that how he would look when he was sixty, discontented and miserable?

Flora lifted a too thin shoulder. 'Jane wasn't particularly maternal,' she finally answered him, 'but I was far worse.'

Jens lifted his eyebrows, staying silent in the hope she'd continue. 'When I got the offer to go to New York, I knew I didn't love you enough to take you with me. In fairness, I didn't love anyone enough. I'm not capable of putting other people first, not really capable of loving anyone either.'

He was astounded by her honesty. But instead of her words hurting, he felt cleansed by them. It helped to know she would've dumped anyone she perceived to be a handbrake. Her leaving was all about her, not him. She was self-absorbed, probably narcissistic, deeply, comprehensively selfish. He got it. Flora was the problem, not him.

'Leaving you with Jane was the best thing I did for you, my one unselfish act,' Flora quietly stated, sounding old and weary. 'I couldn't be a good mother, any type of mother. I didn't have it in me. Jane did.'

Jens pondered her statement. She was right, handing him to Jane—straightforward but stable—had been the right thing to do. Flora had hurt him but she'd done what she'd thought was right for him. Maja had also acted in his best interests when she'd left him twelve years ago. Both situations had been painful but both women had done what they'd thought was right. How was it possible to feel hot, and cold, at the same time? Miserable but unburdened? Grateful that they both loved him, in diametrically opposite ways and situations. That they had put him first, no matter what it had cost them? He felt foolish, full of regret, but more like himself than ever before.

Flora tossed her deep brown curls. 'So are you going to go to the press or not?'

No, he didn't need to. Who would care and how would it change his life? Flora giving him to his aunt would be news for about five minutes and then everybody would move on, and the world would keep turning. And he'd already wasted too much energy on her. Sorting out his relationship with Maja would be a far better use of his time.

Jens sighed. For a hotshot businessman, a super-effective deal-maker, he'd made a series of miscalculations and errors in judgement. He might be able to swim through the shark-infested waters of international business, but he was unable to look at relationships clearly.

Was it any wonder, since he'd had so little practice? Because he'd been raised to be like his aunt, unemotional, he shied away from talking about his feelings. Maja was the only woman who'd managed to slide under his electric fence guarding his heart, then and now.

And yes, he was as much in love with her as he'd ever

been. But, because he'd been consumed by revenge and the need to get even, to be acknowledged, to be seen to be the winner, he'd lost her before they'd even started. Jens felt a rush of emotion, of regret, and, instead of talking himself out of it, running from it, he squared his shoulders and faced his past.

Flora was Flora, uninterested in him, and he no longer cared. Maja, coerced by Håkon, had left her home, her country and broken ties with her father, all gutsy moves for a teenager and she'd done it to protect him. Maybe she could've chosen another route, acted differently, but she'd been eighteen, a kid.

It was also time for him to stop feuding, even if it was only in his own mind, with Håkon. The man was dead, for the love of God! He'd been pretty awful in life, hard and selfish, full of revenge and selfish to the core. Emotionally cold and uninterested. Inflexible, self-indulgent, controlling, spoiled, resentful, arrogant...

He fully understood why Maja thought he and Håkon were so alike. For all the reasons that Maja had said. Everything he'd hated about Håkon were the things he most disliked about himself. Jens wanted to look away, to move his thoughts on to something more pleasant, but he had to face himself. Everyone did at some point in their lives. He had a choice to make...

He could imitate Flora, be selfish and eschew relationships, and live his life in the semi-darkness of loneliness. Or he could fight for the light.

Most of that light was Maja. She brought joy and happiness into his life. He might have all the money he could need, enough for several lifetimes, have power and influence, and be praised and pandered to, but life without Maja meant nothing. And his obsession with revenge had cost him the only thing that had ever meant anything to him.

He needed another chance, a second chance, to be happy…to live and love and laugh. How could he convince her that he wanted her in his life, that she was all that was necessary for him to be happy?

He put his powers of critical thinking to amass his fortune, and to strike complicated deals. It was time to use those skills to get Maja to agree to marry him, to be his.

For as long as they both might live…

'Jens?'

Jens jerked his head up, remembering where he was and who he was with. Flora. *Right.* He walked over to her and placed a brief kiss on her cheek. It was the first time he'd touched her in over thirty years. And it would be the last. It was a brief hello, and a final goodbye. 'Congratulations on your award, Flora. Have a good life.'

Tension and discontentment drained from his system as he left his birth mother, and his past, in that stylish hotel room and walked towards his future.

Back in Edinburgh, after many sleepless nights, Maja stepped out onto the tiny balcony leading off her bedroom. Usually, her view of Edinburgh Castle always held her attention but lately her attention span was all over the place. She'd left the Bentzen estate after her confrontation with Jens and caught the next flight back home. She'd been back a week and was still trying to gather her shattered and battered heart together.

Maja rested her hip on the railing. While she loved Scotland, she couldn't help but acknowledge that she adored Norway. The country had seeped back into her pores, invaded her soul. There was still so much of it she wanted to rediscover, more of its natural wonders to admire. She loved the cobalt blues of the fjords, the verdant greens of the valleys, the purple and white mountains, and skies so endlessly clear it hurt her eyes. But how could she go back to Bergen? How could she live in a city that would for ever be filled with memories of Jens?

Maja yawned and took another sip of her strong black coffee. She should get back to learning her new photo-editing software, but she was getting nowhere. As best she could, she pushed any thoughts of Jens away, but, since she often found tears running down her face, she knew she needed to deal with finding him, loving him, and losing him again. Some things couldn't be avoided, and this was one of them.

But where to start? Maybe the answer was not to 'start' anywhere but to allow her thoughts free rein. Her thoughts tumbled over and over, and she watched them float by, concentrating on those that felt right, the ones that came through strongest.

That she was tired of secrets and sick of shadows was her first revelation. She had to come out from hiding behind her M J Slater pseudonym. She wouldn't have got into this mess with Jens in the first place if she hadn't been so hell-bent on protecting her pseudonym, if she hadn't been so against the world linking her art with her being Håkon's estranged daughter.

But she *was* his daughter, she *was* a Hagen. She couldn't run away from it any more. And she didn't want to. She might be Maja Hagen, but she was a separate entity from her father. If a couple of critics said she was trading off her last name, what did it matter? She had great reviews and a successful exhibition as M J Slater to counter those accusations. She knew the truth, she knew how hard she'd worked to get where she was. She always said she wanted her art to speak for itself and it did, it always would. It would speak no matter who signed her images. And she wanted to sign them as Maja Hagen...

Because Maja Hagen was the woman who'd left Norway, who'd made mistakes and struggled to find herself. What had started as a way to protect herself had become a limitation and she was done with limits. She'd used her art as a shield, and she hid behind it. And as long as she kept her identity a secret, she couldn't fully engage with anyone. Not with lovers, friends, or clients. It was a barrier, a way to keep her safe.

Maja Hagen was done with being safe, so she sent a text message to Halston.

Can you prepare a press release explaining that M J Slater is Maja Hagen?

Halston immediately replied.

Seriously?

Yes. Keep it simple and send it through to me for approval when it's done.

Now it was time to deal with her six-foot-something problem of loving Jensen Nilsen. What was she going to do about him? And even if he wanted a relationship with her—his silence said he didn't—could she ever trust him? If they got together and they hit a bump in the road, would their relationship survive the crash? They had the ability to hurt each other, in every way possible. Could he love her the way she needed him to?

She didn't think so. He'd planned to leave her at the altar, so caught up in his need for revenge that he was prepared to humiliate her on an industrial scale.

Jens had massive trust issues, ones she didn't think would ever go away. His mum had never acknowledged him. Maja had promised to marry him but had run out on him instead. Håkon had tried to destroy him. Why would he trust anyone?

Maja loved him, she always would. But love without trust was a car without an engine, a river with no water. Without trust, there was no reason to continue.

Maja placed her coffee cup on the table, her diamond ring flashing blue fire in the sunlight. She held the stone with her index finger and thumb, admiring the deep blue colour. It reminded her of Jens's eyes and the deep blue of the fjords. She'd have to give him the ring back. There was no way she could keep it. But that meant seeing him. She couldn't let a third party handle the transfer of such an expensive ring.

They'd have to meet at some point. She had clothes at his house, toiletries, and she wanted to know if she could have the art books in her grandmother's studio. They needed to end this chapter in a civil, sensible way. She couldn't run away again...

Maja heard someone trying to attract her attention and looked down to see a blonde bike courier on the pavement, a package in her hands. The courier looked up at her, squinting in the sun.

'Maja Hagen?' When Maja nodded, the biker told her she had a delivery.

Maja walked downstairs. She took the plastic envelope and ripped it open. Inside was a plain white, square envelope, with her name written across it in a bold black fountain pen. She recognised Jens's handwriting...

Her heart rate picked up. 'Do you need me to sign for it?' Maja asked, looking for a reason to delay opening the envelope. Jens was a direct guy, someone who didn't shy away from confrontation, and his sending her a paper and pen message couldn't be good.

The courier shook her head, walked away and Maja turned the envelope over, then over again. Back in her flat, she paced, putting the envelope down, and then picking it up. Finally, irritated by her actions, she ripped the envelope open and pulled out the thick, expensive invitation.

Jens Nilsen and Maja Hagen
invite you to join them
to celebrate their wedding
at the Hotel Daniel-Jean...

Maja frowned. Why would he send her a copy of their wedding invitation? Why hadn't he cancelled the wedding? What was he trying to say?

She flipped the card over. Jens had scrawled a sentence. It took her a while for the words to make sense.

I'm going to be there. Are you?

CHAPTER TWELVE

THIS WAS THEIR wedding day and she was in the back of a taxi. Maja had flown into Ålesund hours ago and dressed in a bland hotel room and wondered if she was making the biggest mistake of her life. The taxi pulled up to the entrance of the Hotel Daniel-Jean and Maja laid her hand over her heart, telling it to calm down.

She was about to walk through the lobby, clutching a bouquet of white and cream roses, dressed in a simple but deliciously gorgeous wedding dress of French-lace-covered satin, her make-up and hair as good as she could get it…

And she didn't know if Jens would be waiting for her in the gazebo at the end of the pier. He could be playing with her, this could all be one huge set-up, his way to exact payback… Was this a mistake? Was she setting herself up for failure?

Maja looked over the shoulder of the driver to the clock on the dashboard. She was on time. She turned her head to the side and watched an elegant couple slip into the hotel, hurrying to be there before the bride. She resisted the urge to roll down the window and ask them to check whether a suited and booted groom was waiting for her.

Maja pushed her fist into her sternum and wondered, not for the first or five thousandth time, what she was doing. There was a chance she was walking into more heartbreak, a press firestorm, a PR disaster. She'd just claimed her name back, and the art world was excited to discover the real identity of M J Slater. She was courting trouble with this stunt.

If Jens failed to appear, or walked away before they said 'I do', she'd be a headline tomorrow. She would be laughed at and commented on over morning coffee and marmalade on toast. She would be Norway's, maybe even Europe's, morning entertainment.

But, if Jens was there wanting to marry her, they would be extraordinarily happy, and her life would be complete. When she thought about it like that, there wasn't a chance she wouldn't take, a move she wouldn't make, to be with him. She loved him and, because she did, she'd do anything, risk anything, to have Jens in her life...

That didn't stop the butterflies in her stomach from whirring and buzzing. But she couldn't sit in this taxi, biting her lip. She needed to move, to face whatever lay beyond those impressive hotel doors.

Maja thanked the driver, opened the door and stepped out onto the driveway, shaking out the folds of her dress. She'd opted out of wearing a veil, deciding instead to thread a few luscious cream roses, touched at the edges with blush pink, into her twisted-back hair.

You can do this, Maja. You have to know.

She'd had the mantra on repeat but, now that she was facing a long, lonely walk to the gazebo where the ceremony was to take place, her knees felt a little soft. She would not stumble at this last hurdle. She would not run away. She had to see this through, she had to *know*...

There was such power in making decisions for herself, in having the freedom to chart her own course. She was taking a chance on Jens, risking her heart again. It felt wonderful, and terrifying. This could backfire horribly, but she knew if she didn't, she'd regret not being brave for the rest of her life. Jens deserved her bravery, and she owed it to herself.

Maja walked through the lobby onto the wide veranda of the hotel and looked down. Hilda's team had set up flower-decorated chairs, placing them in regimented rows on the lush lawn. The rows were bisected by a white carpet leading up to the stairs of the pier. Big screens on either side of the pier were there to transmit the ceremony to the guests. Maja stared into the shadows of the gazebo, conscious of her knocking knees and a pool of sweat gathering at the base of her spine.

She looked into the rose-festooned gazebo and her heart settled when she saw Jens standing by the simple altar, his hands clasped and his head down. He was there, waiting for her. He'd been prepared to take the risk of her not showing up, was willing to be vulnerable, and he'd put himself in a position to be humiliated...for her.

Maja understood, on a deep fundamental level, how much courage it took for him to do that, especially since he had no idea whether she'd arrive or not. This was Jens putting his heart on a plate. And what a gift it was. Maja placed her free hand on her heart and allowed her pretty bouquet to rest against her thigh.

As if sensing she'd arrived, Jens lifted his head, and across the swathe of lawn their eyes connected. His shoulders dropped and a small smile touched his mouth. None of their guests suspected how monumental this moment was, what they'd gone through to be here.

Maja lifted her bouquet and used her free hand to lift the hem of the dress off the floor to walk down the steps to the lawn, and onto the white carpet that would take her to the altar, and Jens.

He was everything, and the only thing, she needed.

'Maja...'

Maja stepped into the gazebo, and Jens was convinced his heart was about to fly out of his chest. She was here. *Finally.*

She used her bouquet to gesture to his clothes. 'I like your outfit, Nilsen.'

Getting ready for his wedding was a blur and, unable to remember how he looked, he stared down at his stone-coloured trousers, the matching waistcoat, blue tie and cream shirt. He'd rolled the sleeves up to his elbows. A perfect cream rose, just about to bloom, was pinned to his waistcoat.

'I prefer yours,' he told her, his voice hoarse. Maja wore a Boho-inspired dress with a deep V-neckline. Her make-up was minimal, her hair was in a casual twist, decorated with baby roses. She looked breath-stealingly beautiful.

'I wasn't sure whether you'd be here,' Maja admitted.

He'd been hanging around the gazebo for hours, hoping to see her arrive, his heart in his throat. 'Funny, I wasn't sure you'd—'

Jens heard the officiant clearing his throat and turned to look at him. He nodded to the guests and Jens remembered they had an audience. Their every word and gesture was being transmitted to the big screens outside.

Jens turned to the officiant. 'We need a few minutes,' he told him. He found the camera mounted amongst the roses on the roof of the gazebo and slashed his throat. He waited for the light on the camera to go from green to red. When it did and the priest left the gazebo, he knew they were alone. Jens placed his back to the guests, his big frame hiding Maja from them, and looked down at his fiancée, the woman he desperately wanted to be his wife.

'I told you I would be here,' Jens said.

He took her hand and placed it on his heart, which was beating far too fast, wondering if she understood what it took for him to wait for her, the risk he'd taken, how scared he was.

She thought he was tough, unemotional, but this past week had been hell. He'd had no idea if she'd show up or not or hand him another dose of rejection. He'd thought about reaching out to ask her but had known he couldn't. He needed to show her that he was prepared to risk his heart, risk feeling humiliated for her. Despite feeling uncomfortable and vulnerable, he would walk through the fires of hell to make her understand how much he loved her.

Did she realise she was all that mattered?

She gestured to his clothing and then tipped her head back to nod at the full church. 'So, are we doing this?' she asked, trying to sound brave.

He knew, instinctively, that his being here wasn't enough, that she needed more from him than to simply rock up. She needed words, big and bold.

He could only think of a few. 'I love you, *min kjære.*'

Her big smile, the one he wanted to see every day for the next sixty years, was brighter than the sun. 'I know.'

He tipped his head to the side. 'How?'

'Jens, I'm old enough to know that love isn't only smooth words and over-the-top gestures.' She took his hand and rubbed her thumb over his knuckles. 'Love can also be standing up in front of five hundred guests, making a silent but powerful statement that I am who you want. You wouldn't risk being jilted unless you loved me.'

She squeezed his hand. 'But you could've told me before and saved us both a lot of angst.'

He rocked on his feet. 'I know but I needed—'

'To do this? To make the big gesture? I get it.'

She did. She got him. Jens lifted his hand to grip her neck. He rested his forehead against hers. 'I'm so in love with you, Maja. And I'm so tired of being without you.' He hauled in a breath. 'I'm done living my life like this. I'm done with feeling empty. I'm done with making work my priority and treating sex and women as temporary pleasures, here today and gone tomorrow.

'I saw Flora,' he admitted.

She pulled back, shocked. 'You did?' *Wow.* 'Is she going to acknowledge you?'

He shook his head and Maja grimaced in sympathy. She thought he was disappointed, but he wasn't. 'We can talk more about this later, but I no longer need her to acknowledge me.'

Before she could comment on that bombshell, he spoke again. 'Maja, I need you to know that I don't want to marry you because you are Håkon's daughter. I'm done with revenge. You, and any children we have, will be my *only* priority,' Jens added. 'I will be a good husband and a good father, Maja.'

'I know you will, Jens.'

He had Maja exactly where he wanted her, in a white dress, standing at the altar, telling him she loved him, but it wasn't enough. He needed to give her more, to give her everything. And that meant putting their future in her hands. 'Are you sure that this, being here, is what you want to do, *min kjære*?'

* * *

Maja laughed as she gripped the material of Jens's shirt and twisted her fingers, pulling the fabric tight against his chest and him a little closer to her. 'Jensen Nilsen, are you determined to give me a heart attack?' she asked, a wide smile on her face.

Jens placed a kiss on her temple before pulling back, his hands on her bare shoulders, his expression sincere but determined. 'Don't get me wrong, I'm not going anywhere. You told me you love me so you're not getting rid of me now.'

Too right she wasn't!

Jens spoke before she could, his hand coming up to cradle her face, his thumb on her lower lip. 'I just don't want you to feel pressured into marrying me. I know the last two months have been crazy and maybe you need some time to make sense of everything. We don't *have* to get married.'

What rubbish! She knew exactly what she wanted, and she'd tell him if he'd just give her a chance to speak.

'I'm happy to go out there and tell everyone the wedding is off. We can go home, or to my *hytte*, anywhere you like, and talk it through,' Jens suggested. 'We can take as long as you need.'

She knew a way for them to be together, and it was pretty damn simple. 'Or we can get married, right here and right now,' she suggested, looking up at him.

Excitement and relief fought for dominance in his lively blue eyes. 'Are you sure?' he asked her, moving his hands to her hips. Maja was glad he held her as she wasn't sure she could stand upright on her own.

'I'm *positive*, Jens. I want you in my life. I've *always* wanted you in my life. From the moment I saw you, twelve years ago and in the gallery a few weeks ago, I knew you were the one.'

Jens untangled her fingers from his shirt to lay her palm flat on his chest, above his heart. Through the thin fabric, she picked up its rapid beat. 'I felt the same. My heart knew it, but my mind, and my pride, needed some time to catch up.'

She lifted an eyebrow. 'Some time?'

He half winced, half smiled. She met his eyes and, within those gorgeous navy-blue depths, saw her future. She wasn't alone any more. Jens was going to be with her every step of the way. He'd run the risk of being jilted and put himself in a vulnerable position for her. Then, after telling her he loved her, he loved her enough to step back, to give her time to think. He'd relinquished control, and that was such a big deal for Jens. That, more than anything else, reassured her.

'Uh…folks…?'

They both whipped around at the interruption. The priest stood at the entrance of the gazebo, his hands clasped behind him and his expression worried. Maja felt Jens's arm around her waist, and she leaned into him, happy to soak up his strength.

'Do we have a problem?' the priest asked gently. 'Because I have a congregation who needs to know whether to stay or to go.'

'Just a minute more,' Jens told him.

Jens opened his mouth to speak but Maja put her finger on his lips. 'My turn, darling.' She smiled, happiness rolling over her in warm waves. 'I love you.' She stroked his jaw with her thumb and shuddered with love-tinged desire. 'Will you marry me, right here and right now, Jensen?'

Jens covered her hand with his. 'It will be my absolute pleasure.'

He ducked his head to kiss her, then pulled back at the last moment, choosing to lay a long, open-mouthed kiss on the side of her mouth. 'No, the next time I kiss you, you'll be my wife.'

Jens loved her, they were going to get married, and they were each other's future. Right, what now? Should she stay here, or walk down the aisle again?

Luckily, her clear-minded, but equally happy-looking, fiancé took charge. He motioned to the priest to take his place, picked up the bouquet she hadn't realised she'd dropped, before straightening a rose behind her ear. 'Ready?' he gently asked her, his mouth quirking in that sexy smile.

Maja nodded. 'For you? For this? Absolutely.' She shook out her dress and stroked her hand down the bodice. 'Shall I walk down the aisle again?'

Jens smiled and shook his head. He took the hand he held and pulled it under his muscled arm. 'No, just stay with me, side by side.'

Side by side…

For ever together. Starting right now.

EPILOGUE

MAJA LOOKED AT the huge image on the gallery wall in Soho and wrinkled her nose. She'd captured Ben, their two-year-old son, jumping in a rain puddle, his grin, so like his father's, as wide as the sun. The photograph, the only one of Ben she'd allow to be exhibited and definitely not for sale, was the inspiration for her current collection, called *Sunshine and Joy*.

It was the opening night of her first major exhibition since Bergen and she was as nervous as a shocked cat. She was convinced the critics would hate her photographs and nobody would buy anything. Maja was pretty sure she was going to be a one-hit wonder.

She turned to look at Jens, who stood by her side, his big hand rubbing her lower back. 'What was I thinking?' she demanded, keeping her voice low. 'Giving up my pseud- onym, thinking I could exhibit again?'

'Relax, darling.'

Easy for him to say! Every one of her images, rang- ing from the photograph of two homeless people roaring with laughter, to an exceptionally old lady talking to her equally old dog, were ripe with emotion. The thread run- ning through all the photographs was joy, something Maja had experienced a lot of over the past three years.

And because she was so happy, she was drawn to finding moments of happiness in her work. But happiness wasn't a good subject for an exhibition. Critics and curators preferred angst and despair, they made for better subjects.

'I should never have agreed to this,' Maja muttered, frowning. 'I told you it was a bad idea.'

Jens turned her to face him and lifted his hands to hold her face. He dropped a kiss on her mouth and she, as always, tasted his desire. It didn't matter that she was seven months pregnant with their second child, their sexual buzz never went away. He pushed a curl off her forehead, and she fell into the blue of his eyes. He loved her, so much.

She, and their children, one at the hotel with his beloved nanny, one on the way, were the reason his world turned. He kept a tight rein on his businesses, but often worked from home, taking frequent breaks to spend time with her or Ben, and to give her time in her darkroom or studio. When he did go into the office, he made sure he was home in time to bath Ben and put him to bed.

He was an amazing entrepreneur but an even better husband and father.

'*Min kjære*, the world has enough images of destruction and darkness. It needs images like yours.' He placed his hands on her shoulders and told her to look around the room. 'Look at the smiles, the way people look at your images and then look at them again. They want to fall into the world you've captured.'

He dropped a kiss on her temple and Maja's breath caught at the love she saw on his face. 'I'm the lucky guy who gets to live in your world, Maja. I am so grateful for that.'

She touched his jaw with her fingertips. 'It's our world, Jens.'

He shook his head. 'These photographs, they're all you.

Our wonderful lives, our children, also all you. I can't imagine what my life would look like without you in it.'

She thought about their already rumbunctious son, loud and oh-so-busy, and knew that their second son, who'd make his appearance in a couple of months, would be as energetic. She placed a hand on her bump and grinned. 'It would be quieter, that's for sure,' she told him, laughing.

'I'll take noisy and busy and ridiculously happy over quiet and empty any day of the week,' Jens assured her. He looked over her shoulder and squeezed her hand. 'Esteemed art critic coming in.'

She nodded, pasted a smile on her face and squared her shoulders. This was what she'd wanted when she'd shed her M J Slater skin: to stand by her work. She could cope with someone criticising her work to her face. Maybe.

'Maja Hagen! Let's talk about your art...'

Before stepping back, Jens squeezed her hand and sent her a reassuring smile. 'You've got this,' he quietly told her.

Maja nodded. Yes, she had. As long as she had him, she had *everything*...

* * * * *

MILLS & BOON MODERN IS
HAVING A MAKEOVER!

The same great stories you love,
a stylish new look!

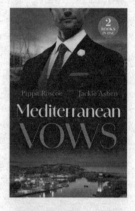

Look out for our brand new look
COMING JUNE 2024

MILLS & BOON

COMING SOON!

We really hope you enjoyed reading this book.
If you're looking for more romance
be sure to head to the shops when
new books are available on

Thursday 9th May

MILLS & BOON

MILLS & BOON®

Coming next month

TWINS TO TAME HIM
Tara Pammi

Sebastian rubbed a hand over his face. Any momentary hesitation he'd felt about having two little boys to care for, to nurture and protect, dissipated, leaving behind a crystal-clear clarity he had never known in his life.

Whatever instinct had propelled him to demand Laila marry him…it carried the weight of his deepest, most secret desire within it.

For his sons to be happy and well-adjusted and thriving, they needed their mother and he needed them. Ergo, his primary goal now was to do anything to keep Laila in his life.

And while he'd never have admitted it openly to his brute of a father, Sebastian had always known he could be just as ruthless as his twin.

He was keeping his sons and he was keeping their mother in his life, even if it meant he had to seduce every inch of logic and rationale out of Dr. Jaafri. And he would make sure she not only enjoyed the seduction but that she had everything she'd ever wanted. He would make all her wishes and dreams come true. It was only a matter of getting her to admit them.

Continue reading
TWINS TO TAME HIM
Tara Pammi

Available next month
millsandboon.co.uk

OUT NOW!

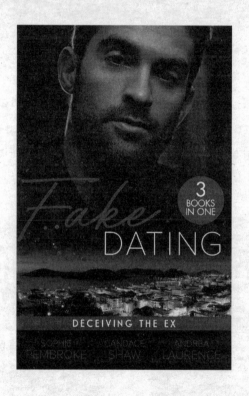

Available at
millsandboon.co.uk

MILLS & BOON

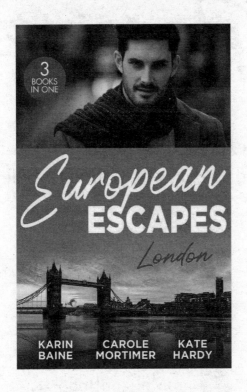

LET'S TALK
Romance

For exclusive extracts, competitions and special offers, find us online:

- **f** MillsandBoon
- **X** @MillsandBoon
- **○** @MillsandBoonUK
- **♪** @MillsandBoonUK

Get in touch on 01413 063 232

MILLS & BOON

THE HEART OF ROMANCE

A ROMANCE FOR EVERY READER

MODERN
Prepare to be swept off your feet by sophisticated, sexy and seductive heroes, in some of the world's most glamourous and romantic locations, where power and passion collide.

HISTORICAL
Escape with historical heroes from time gone by. Whether your passion is for wicked Regency Rakes, muscled Vikings or rugged Highlanders, awaken the romance of the past.

MEDICAL
Set your pulse racing with dedicated, delectable doctors in the high-pressure world of medicine, where emotions run high and passion, comfort and love are the best medicine.

True Love
Celebrate true love with tender stories of heartfelt romance, from the rush of falling in love to the joy a new baby can bring, and a focus on the emotional heart of a relationship.

HEROES
The excitement of a gripping thriller, with intense romance at its heart. Resourceful, true-to-life women and strong, fearless men face danger and desire - a killer combination!

 **afterglow BOOKS**
From showing up to glowing up, these characters are on the path to leading their best lives and finding romance along the way – with plenty of sizzling spice!

To see which titles are coming soon, please visit

millsandboon.co.uk/nextmonth